# Flare of Unrest

C A Lewis

ISBN: 979-8-9863413-4-7 (Paperback)

ISBN: 979-8-9863413-5-4 (Ebook)

Cover Design by Rachel Ruhl

Map created with Inkarnate

Typeset created with Atticus

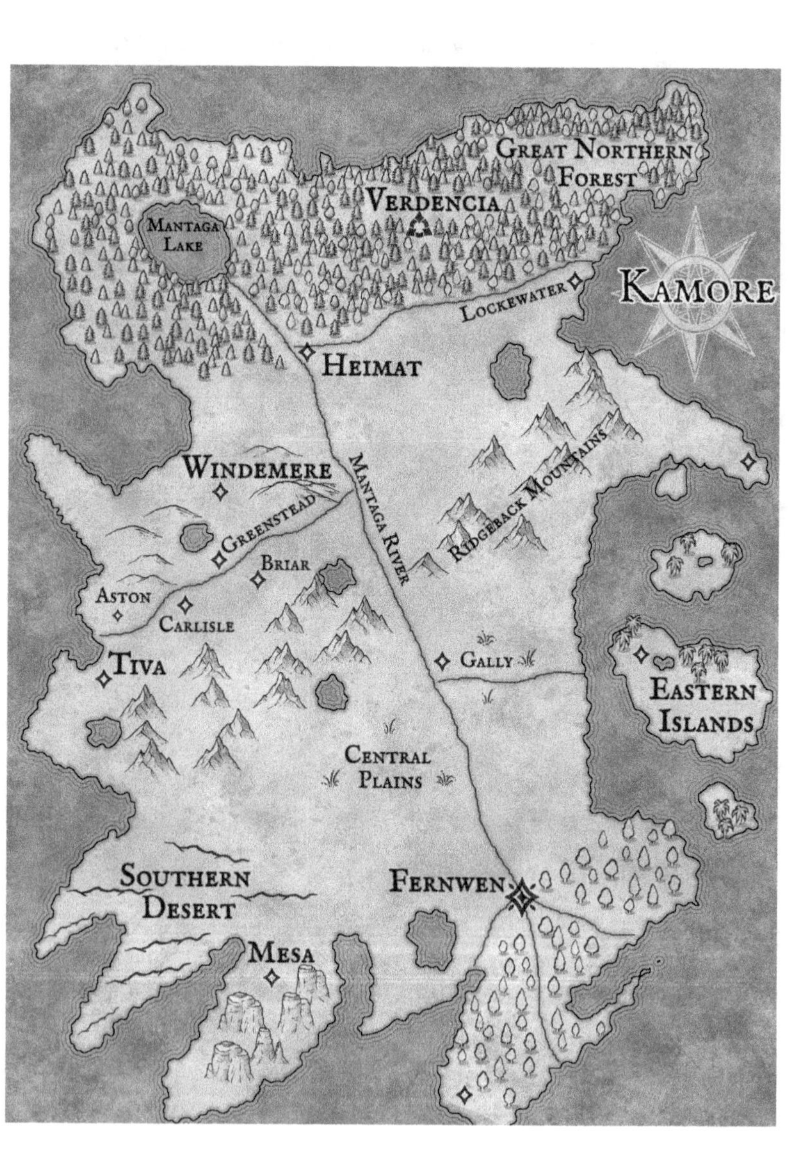

KAMORE
GREAT NORTHERN FOREST
VERDENCIA
MANTAGA LAKE
LOCKEWATER
HEIMAT
WINDEMERE
GREENSTEAD
BRIAR
ASTON
CARLISLE
TIVA
RIDGEBACK MOUNTAINS
MANTAGA RIVER
GALLY
EASTERN ISLANDS
CENTRAL PLAINS
SOUTHERN DESERT
FERNWEN
MESA

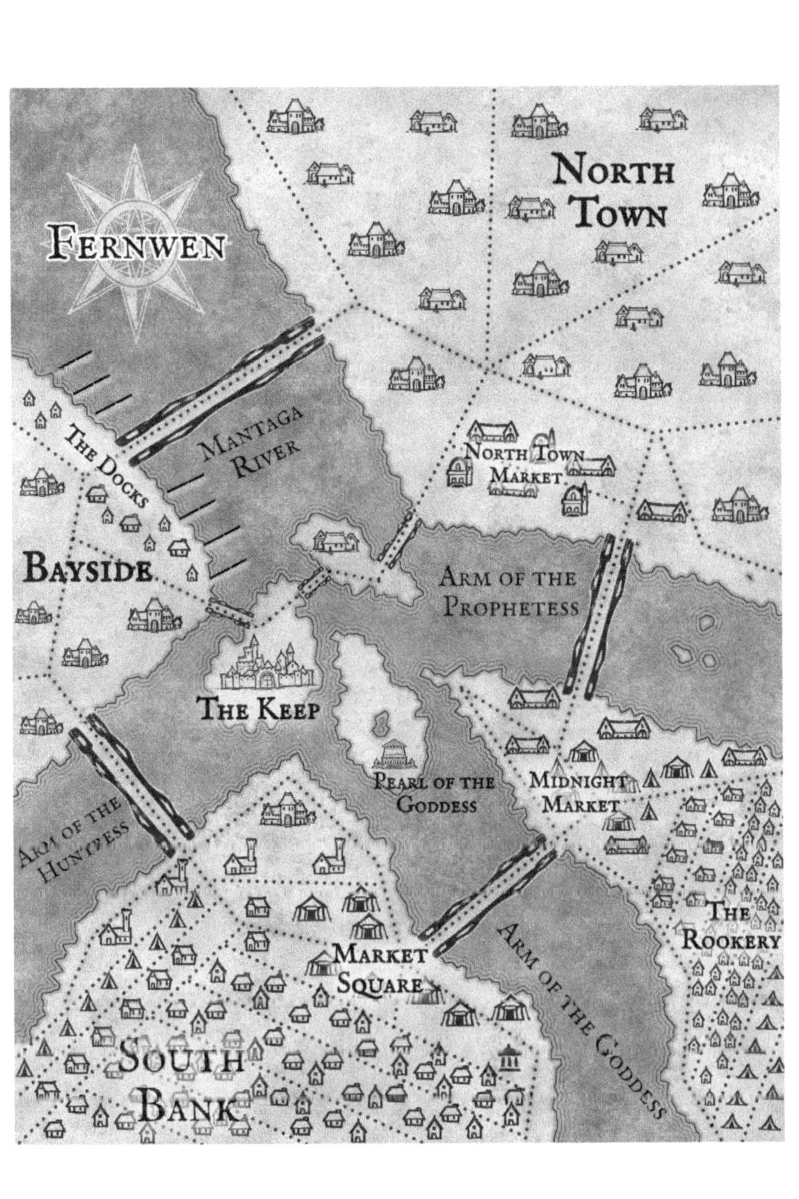

FERNWEN
NORTH TOWN
MANTAGA RIVER
THE DOCKS
BAYSIDE
NORTH TOWN MARKET
ARM OF THE PROPHETESS
THE KEEP
PEARL OF THE GODDESS
MIDNIGHT MARKET
ARM OF THE HUNTRESS
THE ROOKERY
MARKET SQUARE
ARM OF THE GODDESS
SOUTH BANK

# Chapter One

R ae woke with a start, bolting upright in her cot. The tension left her shoulders as she recognized the inside of her tent. A shiver made its way up her spine and she rubbed her now bare shoulders. The sudden jolt of wakefulness had jostled her blankets, so they pooled at her waist. The flash of cold reminded her of their whereabouts. And the events that led them to this place.

Rae clenched the blanket and wrapped it around her, holding it close. Her eyes strayed to the corner of her tent, where Tyee's dark coat hung from one of the wood supports. Keeping a tight hold on the blanket, she rose from her cot and grabbed the smooth material from its perch.

She shuffled back to the warmth of her cot, bringing the coat with her. Rae held it in her lap and stroked it absentmindedly as she thought about the man it belonged to and the goodbye they shared.

*The members of the Circus had gathered to the east of the Elven city of Verdencia. It was time for them to leave the city and head to Mantaga Lake. Duncan had negotiated with the Elven and the Shifters of the Forest to secure a place for them.*

*"Here. Take this to keep you from getting cold." Tyee shrugged off his coat and held it out to her.*

*Rae lifted one eyebrow. "I think you'll need it more than I will." With a snap of her fingers, a flame danced above her finger. Her eyes glittered as they met Tyee's stolid gaze.*

*Her face fell a little when she took in his solemn expression.*

*"You're staying, I take it."*

*Tyee sighed as he maneuvered Koko closer to Arwen, Rae's golden mare. "Would you just take the blasted coat?" He shoved it at her once more.*

*"Alright, alright. Keep your shorts on." Rae huffed as she accepted the coat and draped it over her shoulders. She lifted her chin to meet Tyee's gaze and found his face next to hers. She met his dark eyes with her golden ones and felt her heart race. Rae gave him a searching look but said nothing, waiting for him to answer her.*

*Tyee placed a hand on her cheek and gave a slow nod. He whispered, "I have to. I need to find answers about what this means. But as soon as I have them, I'll come find you." He dropped the hand from her cheek to cradle hers, still bandaged from where he forced his life energy into her through her blood. "You have my word."*

*Rae swallowed the lump in her throat and leaned forward, pressing her lips to his. Tyee responded as if it was his first drink of water after a year-long drought. Heat flooded her insides as Tyee's leg bumped against hers, trapped between their two horses.*

*Arwen grew impatient and moved to create space between herself and the brutish stallion. Rae felt the icy chill of the air as she and Tyee were ripped apart. The shock of cold air and separation took her breath away. Her eyes jumped to Tyee's, and all she saw was determination. He kept his eyes on hers, urging Koko forward. He held out an arm to her and his eyes held the question he couldn't ask.*

*Without hesitation, Rae swung her leg around and used her acrobatic grace to throw it over Koko's back, landing so they faced each other. Tyee's muscular arms steadied and shifted her to a more comfortable position as he made room for the woman. Arwen shook her head, enjoying her freedom but staying close to monitor the Crafter she was bonded to. Koko remained steady as the weight he carried increased; it was a testament to his training that he didn't stumble or balk at the addition of another rider.*

*As soon as Rae was settled, Tyee pulled her into another kiss, tangling one hand in her hair and using the other to hold her close. The heat returned as Rae felt every part of her body press against Tyee's lithe frame. Fire pooled in her belly as the horseman deepened the kiss. Her palm pulsed as she brought her arms up to circle Tyee's neck, holding him close as the kiss turned from raw passion to something deeper. She felt them both slow and infuse the emotions they couldn't voice into the intimacy they shared.*

*It was absolutely terrifying.*

*But Rae was tired of denying what she felt for the aloof horseman. With every inch of her on fire, she opened the connection between them; the one that had solidified into something more after they shared blood on the battlefield. Rae sent a lick of flame across the bond and smiled when she felt Tyee shudder against her.*

*Closing her eyes, she broke the kiss and rested her forehead on his. Both of them struggled to take halting breaths as the fire raged inside.*

*"I'm going to hold you to that, Drifter." Rae's eyelids fluttered before she forced them open, giving him a window into the emotions swirling inside. "Don't try dying to get out of it now."*

*Rae felt Tyee's chest rumble as his eyes softened. "Don't worry, Birdie, I've got plans for the next time I see you. The last thing I want is to get out of anything." His voice turned husky, invoking thoughts of the night they shared.*

*A blush dusted Rae's neck, but she kept her gaze steady as she forced out the words she needed to say. "You told me once I could hurt you."*

*Tyee's eyes widened before narrowing, a questioning look transforming his expression.*

*"Looks like I was wrong to think you were the only one that felt that way." Unable to bear a response to her admission, Rae buried her head in Tyee's chest and pulled him close. "Do what you need to, but ride swift once it's done. You could break me easier than you think."*

*Before Tyee could respond, Rae pulled away and whistled to Arwen. She graced his lips with one more soft kiss and bounded to her horse. She squared her shoulders and didn't dare look back, afraid she wouldn't be able to leave if she did.*

*But she pulled the coat tighter around herself, knowing Tyee would be watching.*

Holding the coat to her face, she took in a deep breath and caught a whiff of leather and horseflesh. Shaking her head, she willed the memory to the recesses of her mind. Dwelling on what could have been would only drive her to frustration. Tyee had made his decision and would do what he needed to learn about the heritage denied to him for so long. And she had a duty to her people.

A wistful look took over her expression as she shrugged on the coat and prepared for a new day. The thought of staying with Tyee crossed her mind briefly when she'd proposed it to him. But she'd dismissed the thought as quickly as it came. As much as she hated being separated from the horseman, there were bigger things at stake. Her happiness would only come after her people were free. She needed to trust distance wouldn't break them and that they could make it through this next chapter.

Rae swept her hair into a braid with little more than a thought, donned a fur hat and matching gloves, and strode out of her tent, heading to the makeshift paddocks housing the horses. A ride in the cold would help clear her head and prepare for the fight bound to ensue between her and Duncan.

The time to attack was upon them, whether Duncan was ready or not. It would be up to her to rally their people and prepare them for the fight for freedom.

It was time for the Resistance to show what they were made of.

The feeling of the wind beneath his wings would never get old.

Bane soared just above the tree line as he flew north and to the coast, where the rest of their people were. It felt good to be back in the form he'd spent so much time in. For so long, it felt like a punishment to be stuck as a falcon, unable to communicate with the rest of the Circus.

But now, all he tasted was freedom.

He let out a piercing cry and dove beneath the trees. Bane sped through the maze of trunks, zipping up and down to avoid branches and leaves. Several times, he did a barrel roll in midair to avoid an unseen obstacle.

The small heart in his breast pounded in unison with the Gift pumping through his veins. It was dangerous to travel so fast within the trees, but Bane couldn't deny his desire to chase the adrenaline that came with it. His eyes searched the forest as fast as he could fly, looking for where the rest of their group hid.

As his search proved futile, Bane found his mind wandering to silver eyes and the acrobat they belonged to. Zeke was strong, loyal to a fault, and funny as hell. He wasn't afraid to defend the ones he loved or share his emotions.

*I should be more like him.* The silver eyes in his head glinted with disappointment at his self-deprecating thought. Zeke would tell him to knock it off and go on to list all the qualities he admired in Bane.

*What a difference a few weeks can make.* Bane thought to himself. The two men had yet to define what they were to each other, but they'd spent every moment they could together since recovering from their injuries.

Bane's heart fluttered at the memory of seeing Zeke on the ground in the middle of the battlefield. Even then, he couldn't imagine a world without the fair-featured man.

And now... Bane wouldn't think about that. No need to give power to the fear in his heart.

Bane focused on his surroundings and gave a start. He'd overshot the clearing he'd been aiming for. He used his wings to bank up towards the sky before turning back to the opening in the trees.

Bane landed on a branch in the familiar part of the forest to get his bearings once more.

Time was of the essence as he searched for clues that would lead him to Reg and the rest of the people from Heimat. While he remained still, Bane felt the chill of winter enter his bones. The last leaves clung to some of the branches, unwilling to accept their demise. The snow had yet to fall in force, only small spatters of light flakes, but Bane knew it was only a matter of time.

He needed to find their people before winter made it impossible to travel. The rest of the Circus was busy creating a settlement next to Mantaga Lake, on the western end of the great Northern Forest. Bane's task was to locate the others and call on one of the creatures of the forest to lead them to the lake. Then he would continue to Heimat to check on Rich and the others.

His keen eyes caught the game trail they had left Reg and the others on. Taking to the wing once more, Bane set his sights on arriving as quickly as possible. He let out another cry and rose as high into the trees as he could. There were more branches to contend with at this height, but the Shifter knew what he was doing. Tucking his wings in, he angled to the ground and let gravity accelerate his descent. At the last possible minute, he spread his wings wide and glided as far as he could.

Bane continued in this manner for what seemed like hours. The Shifter couldn't deny the ecstasy he felt every time he let gravity pull him faster. After a while, the air shifted. It became cooler as the trees thinned out, and Bane could taste the tang of salt in the back of his throat.

*I must be getting close.* He thought to himself, craning his neck to look for signs of an encampment. Thoughts of the redheaded girl he cared for filled his mind. A sinking feeling in his gut indicated the anxiety he felt about not knowing where she was. Gemma was a special girl, and he didn't know what he'd do if something happened to her.

He pumped his wings faster, determined not to let any more minutes slip by. *She'll be okay. She's stronger than she looks.*

Bane broke through the trees and took to the skies. He rode the updrafts as high as he could, taking in the northern ocean in all its frigid glory. The dark water churned beneath him before crashing into the rocky shore. The roar of the ocean was deafening to his heightened hearing, and the winds buffeted Bane from all sides as he hung in the air. He felt a shiver run through his small body as the cold stole what little heat he had.

Bane looked in both directions, searching for signs that their people had been there. The group was composed of mostly young and old, with only a few fighters like Reg for protection. That meant they would do their best to stay out of the wind. As much as Bane appreciated the power of the wind and the waves, the ones he was looking for wouldn't be here.

The Shifter made his way back to the tree line, landing on a branch that overlooked the game trail he had followed to the coast. He used the falcon's unbelievable eyesight to look for clues. It had been a little over two weeks since the battle, but it was the first time Bane had felt up to the journey and could prove his health to his Da. Gar hadn't wanted to let his son out of his sight, but Bane's insistence whittled the old man's resolve. His heart warmed at the thought of his Da, rough on the outside but warm and inviting once you earned his loyalty.

Bane's childhood had been a hard one; losing his Ma had changed everything. His Da had always been stoic, expressing little emotion, but once his Ma was gone, the man retreated even further into himself. He couldn't help but think how different life would've been had she lived.

Bane remembered joining the Circus in fragments. He'd been a teenager, but spent a lot of his time in one of his raptor forms. His Da always insisted he take an avian form when they were in towns or cities. Spending long periods of time in his animal form always messed with Bane's memory. The falcon he took the form of had a different way of processing the world compared to that of a human. Bane struggled to remember things beyond the environment he found himself in.

His Da told him he had heard about the Circus from a fellow traveler in Galley, but Bane never remembered seeing his Da talk to anybody. He recalled the warmth of the sun, the scratching of mice in the underbrush, and the feel of the wind in his feathers, but not his Da talking to someone. Nonetheless, the pair had found themselves in Windemere, sitting amongst the rows of Mortals and watching the performance.

Gar insisted they stay until curtain call so they could talk with the Ringmaster despite Bane's incessant chattering from his shoulder. Bane wasn't willing to risk Gar's safety should something go wrong, despite being able to recognize the presence of Magicae in all forms using his Sight.

Ever since his Ma's passing, Bane found trust to be the hardest thing to give to strangers. She died trying to protect him and he wouldn't let his Da do the same. But Gar was just as, if not more, stubborn than his son. They waited for the Ringmaster, Bane, hoping that he would reject their acts and they would not be accepted into the impressive collection of Magicae.

But Duncan welcomed them with open arms, as was his nature they came to realize. Bane regretted a lot of things from their time on the road, but joining the Circus hadn't been one of them. He would never admit it to his Da, but the Shifter had been wrong the night they joined the Circus. Taking that leap was the best thing they could have done.

It was his duty to give that sense of belonging to the rest of the people from Heimat.

Bane ruffled his feathers and gathered his thoughts. *Come on, Bane. Get your shit together. Red is counting on you.*

He had let his eyes wander as his mind did likewise, but now, the Shifter did his best to look for details hidden within the surrounding nature. On a second look to his right, Bane noticed where a patch of grass was flattened. He took off from his perch and landed on a lower branch to the right of the game trail he'd been following.

Sure enough, there seemed to be signs of life and a trail for him to follow. Bane let out a cry and traveled the almost imperceptible path he hoped would lead to the others and the little girl he was determined to find.

*I'm coming, Red. Just hold on a little longer.*

Bane flew as fast as he dared while keeping the faint trail in his sights. The ocean raged like the emotions boiling inside. The Shifter knew this was only the beginning of the long road ahead.

The time for the Magicae to fight was here. The only question was, could they win back their place in a world that feared them?

# Chapter Two

"You're getting better there, son," Myra said with a rare grin. "But you'll have to wake up earlier than that if you want to beat me."

Myra offered a hand to the boy she considered a son. Mallick had lost his footing and attempted a new spin move to catch his mother unaware. Myra had easily deflected the blow, sending the young man to the dirt. The first rule Myra had drilled into the young soldier was the fight wasn't over until someone had a kill shot. Studying his mother's posture, the young man gripped her forearm and pulled her down in one smooth motion. Using her weight to counterbalance his own, Mallick pulled himself into a low standing position and raised his sword.

Myra sent him an admiring look and flashed him a feral grin. "That's my boy!"

Before Mallick could blink, Myra twisted to avoid his sword and scrambled to a standing position. The two circled each other in the courtyard of the castle that once housed Kamore royalty. This had been their routine since Mallick was a little boy. The two sparred once in the morning and once in the afternoon to ensure the morning lessons were put into practice before the next day.

Nobody could deny Myra's skill with a sword. She'd grown up in the streets of Fernwen like so many others, but had spent every day watching the guards train from a spot on the courtyard wall. She spent her nights practicing what she learned, and when she was old enough, she joined the guard's pool of new recruits. Her discipline and desire to win caught the attention of her commanding officers, leading to her impressive rise through the ranks. She was the youngest commanding officer in the history of Kamore.

Not only did she possess physical prowess, but Myra had a shrewd mind perfect for developing battle strategy. In training exercises, her battalion consistently scored the highest in terms of positioning and strategy.

And it was her mind that made her so dangerous.

In Myra's world on the streets, there had been a hierarchy determined by age, social status, and blood. Specifically, if there was power running through your veins.

Myra was never at the head of the hierarchy for that reason alone, and she detested not being able to take control, even at a young age. She saw the orphaned and poor Magicae parade around in the gutter as if they were the Goddess Herself. From that moment on, she knew it was up to her to bring justice to those Mortals that lived without power inherently in their veins.

And thus, the thirst for power began.

Myra climbed the ranks, not because she wanted to leave the slums, but because she knew it was the quickest way to take the government seat she needed to eradicate their world of those vermin.

Once she controlled the military, it was a single step away from taking over the entire government.

Myra was extremely shrewd indeed.

As the pair circled each other, Myra noted her son's posture and watched for his tell. Mallick always bent his knees before striking. Right there—Myra lifted her sword instinctively and felt a jolt of adrenaline as the clash of steel on steel rang through the late autumn air. She let out a cackle before launching her own attack.

Myra's sword was like lightning as she used her physical prowess to push the boy back. She performed an array of uppercuts, lower cuts, and parries as she attacked. Her feet drove her movements just as she'd been taught.

Mallick was on the defensive, focusing on mirroring Myra's movements. His concentration remained unbroken despite the sweat beading on his brow.

Myra flashed a feral grin as the boy's right arm dropped slightly. Seeing her opening, she lunged forward and thrust her sword before making a circular motion. Mallick's sword was ripped from his grasp. In the second it took him to process what happened, Myra swiped one leg and dropped him to the ground.

With a boot on her son's chest, Myra boomed. "Yield, Son. You've been outmaneuvered once again." This time, she pointed the tip of her sword at the young man's neck, signaling there would be no room for tricks.

Mallick swallowed and ducked his head, holding his head upright. Once Myra moved her sword, he acquiesced. "I yield."

Myra gave a nod, removed her boot, and held out a hand to the young man. "You're getting better, Mallick. I was hoping you'd take a chance earlier and I couldn't be more proud of you for taking it. Half the battles I've won were because I caught my opponent unawares after they thought I was out for the count."

Mallick grunted, his loss still chafing as he let his mother help him up. "I thought I had you once I pulled you down."

Laughter rumbled deep in Myra's chest when she clasped her hand on Mallick's shoulder. "You almost did," she admitted. "But you still need to work on your footwork. Let your feet drive your attacks." She took a moment to demonstrate what she meant before gesturing for him to try.

Mallick watched her movements before copying them next to her. He ran through them, driving his thrusts with the movement of his feet. They continued working in that manner until a bell tolled in the distance.

"Time to go, Son. Good work." Myra wiped the sweat from her brow and sheathed her sword. She frowned when she noticed Mallick still running through the movements they'd been practicing. "Mallick." Myra's tone had an edge to it that hadn't been there previously. Not listening to directions tested her patience the most.

Hearing the edge in his mother's voice, Mallick stood at attention at once. He'd learned the consequences of not listening the first time at a young age. Not all the bumps and bruises he received were from the training yard.

"Sorry, Mother." Mallick hesitated, seeming to struggle with forming words for what he wanted to say next.

Myra raised one eyebrow and snapped, "Spit it out."

Mallick set his jaw and looked his mother in the eye. "You said once I could hold my own in the training yard, I could see combat." Myra narrowed her eyes but gestured for the boy to continue. Mallick gulped, but did as he was bid. "And when I could beat everyone in the training yard, you clarified I had to hold my own against you. Correct?" Mallick watched his mother carefully, anticipating it coming to blows between the two of them.

Myra pinched the bridge of her nose between two fingers and took a deep breath. When she met her son's gaze, an unknown emotion filled her eyes. "Son, you don't know what you ask of me. No mother wants to send her son to war."

"But so many do every day." Mallick clenched his fists as he struggled to control the tone of his voice, knowing Myra would not respond well to a response that lacked logic and reasoning. He cast a glance around them before lowering his voice. "You told me about the failure in Heimat. We need as many competent soldiers in the north as possible."

"Be that as it may, I will not send my only son into a battle he is not prepared for." Myra held up a hand when Mallick began to protest. "I will consider it. But do not ask me again." Her tone held no room for argument.

Mallick nodded briskly and waited to be dismissed.

"Dismissed, soldier." Myra watched as the young man walked away and thought to herself. *It'll be a cold day in hell before I let the only thing keeping Naomi in line just walk away. You'll stay right where I can see you.*

She frowned and followed him inside, escaping the frosty kiss of a dusting of light snow.

"Only if you can catch me." The spindly, ten-year-old with matted hair spat and took off running.

"Shit, not again." The giant fruit vendor growled through bared teeth. Rubbing his dirt-caked hands on his apron, he yelled after the orphaned street urchin. "I'm gonna lop those thieving fingers off if I lay eyes on you again, Naya. You hear me?! I mean it this time." He threw his hands up and walked back to his stall, cursing under his breath.

The young girl laughed with abandon, racing down alleys in her bare feet. Fernwen was cold and muggy, with winter knocking on its door. The smell of sweat and dirt permeated the thick air. Naya didn't stop running, even as she ducked into a doorway.

"I got the goods, kiddies!" At this point, her eagerness got the best of her. She tumbled over the stool sitting in the middle of the small room. "Dammit. Learn to pick up your bloody things." Naya shook her head.

Luckily, she caught herself before she spilled any of her prized contraband.

"Hawk, Aurora! Which one of you hood rats—"

"Naya, is that language really necessary?" A gruff voice sounded in the kitchen.

Naya gulped. It had been months since the old woman came to check on her investments. "Apologies, Mrs. Battaglia. I didn't know you'd be stopping in today." Naya prayed to whatever gods there were that the little ones hadn't been here when the old woman arrived. The weird tingling had started in her chest, the same one that always came when the gnarled battleax showed up unannounced. Her heart fluttered as she glanced around the dark and bare living room, trying to see if the little ones were home. Naya knew it was unlikely they'd stayed inside, but she still had a sinking feeling.

"What are you doing in the living room? Get in here. I do not have time for your antics." The callused woman was throwing open cabinets, looking for something.

Naya gently shrugged off her bag of stolen goods and silently kicked it under the threadbare couch. Whispering prayers and pleadings under her breath, she stepped into the poor excuse of a kitchen.

"Well girl, where is it?" Esther Battaglia reached towards the too-thin ten-year-old and started patting the girl's pockets.

Despite the assault on her person, Naya could've wept with relief. There was no trace of the twin orphans she'd acquired after moving into this hovel. The old woman was clawing at her now, but nothing mattered other than the twins staying undiscovered. If this demon woman found them, Naya would never forgive herself.

"Where's what?" Naya stopped herself from spitting at her so-called state-mandated guardian. Spitting only resulted in black eyes.

Battaglia gripped the front of Naya's shirt and shoved her against the wall. Her head cracked as it slammed into the decaying wood, the old woman moving too fast for Naya to brace herself. The little girl saw stars as the crone hissed, "My payment for looking after an ungrateful whelp like you. Where is the powder you promised me last time I was here?"

Naya cursed silently as she fought to clear her throbbing head. *Dammit, I'm an idiot.*

"Well, little tramp? Do you have it or not?" Battaglia shook her before slamming her into the wall again. This time, Naya was ready and avoided hitting her head, but still couldn't escape the wiry grasp of her assailant. "I'm sure any buyer in the warehouse district would pay a pretty penny to take you off my hands. Goddess knows there aren't enough young girls to satiate some of those monsters."

She dropped Naya in a heap and stalked toward the washbasin. She slammed open the last cupboard beneath it and crouched to get a better look.

Naya struggled to rise and keep her wits about her. She needed to think fast if she was going to get out of this one.

"It's in the other room. I'll go get it."

Battaglia whipped around and narrowed her eyes. "I already searched that room. There's nothing in there."

Naya gripped the wall and hobbled toward the other room. She could hear heavy steps behind her as the crone followed. "I was out getting it today."

Naya gritted her teeth and took halting steps on the dirt floor. She whispered desperate prayers to any being who would listen. Reaching the sorry excuse for furniture, Naya dropped to her knees and reached under for her satchel. Searching fingers found it and she slipped her hand into it, crunching up the crackers inside. She hoped with everything she had there'd be enough time to crunch them fine enough.

"Well, where is it, orphan?" The crone's bony hand gripped the back of the young girl's neck.

Naya's heart dropped to her stomach. She scrambled to keep crushing the crackers but screeched when her head wrenched back and her sack fell to the floor. Battaglia threw her charge to the ground and jumped on the old knapsack.

Naya collapsed when she hit the floor again. Her body throbbed, and she knew she was in trouble. Struggling to rise, she tried to drag herself out of reach.

"You little bitch." Battaglia screamed and marched toward the broken girl. "Do you think I'm stupid? How dare you think you could con me like this. You pitiful excuse for a ward." The short, wiry battleax threw the bag at Naya's head. The little girl saw stars when Battaglia yanked her shirt and flipped her over. "You're a waste of space. I should've drowned you when I had the chance."

She knelt down and closed her hands around the girl's neck, squeezing as she whispered, "This has been a long time coming, girl."

Naya started struggling as Battaglia kept an iron grip on her neck. She tried to use her legs to knock the crone off, but to no avail. She scrambled and clawed at the gnarled hands around her throat. The girl saw darkness at the edge of her vision as she ran out of air. Her last coherent thought was whether the kids would find the fruit she'd taken that morning.

"Augh!"

Without warning, Battaglia let her go. She felt the woman slump to one side before rolling off of her.

Naya laid there stunned and gasping for sweet, sweet air. After a few deep breaths, she rolled to her side and felt the place where withered hands had been moments before. Wincing with pain, she gathered the courage to look at her attacker.

Naya froze as her foggy brain struggled to comprehend what she saw before her. Battaglia lay prostrate on the floor, as still as the air in the city on a hot day. Limp arms reached towards her neck amid a pool of dark red liquid. Naya turned from the gruesome sight, still struggling to understand what had happened.

*Now what?*

# Chapter Three

Gemma was cold. It was always too cold by the sea, but by the sea gave her a better view of the surrounding landscape. The cold was worth catching sight of the bird Bane promised he'd send.

The redhead pulled her coat closer as the wind howled around her. She looked at the trees, taking comfort in the greenery sprawled there.

*At least I have the plants.* She thought to herself. *They grow for me and reveal their secrets when I ask nicely.* She furrowed her bushy eyebrows. *And they never tell me I have to stay back.*

Being left behind by Rae, Bane, and Zeke stung more than the little girl cared to admit.

She had been such a good girl, but it wasn't good enough. It was never good enough. Not for her Momma and not for her new friends. Gemma felt tears prickling at the corners of her eyes with thoughts of her Momma. All she wanted was to make her proud, and it seemed like nothing ever did.

Gemma looked at the ocean and watched the waves roll in. She rubbed at her eyes, trying to keep the tears at bay. The five-year-old spent as much time as she could away from the others in the group. The adults were nice enough, but the kids called her names when the adults weren't watching.

*"Aren't you the general's daughter?" One of the little boys asked.*

*"Yeah, she is!" Shouted a little girl.*

*"So you're the reason Mommy sent us away." Sounded another little boy, clutching a toy rabbit close.*

*Gemma closed her eyes tighter, hoping they would think she was still asleep. When they didn't go away, the redhead grabbed her coat and left for the solitude of the sea.*

*Before she could escape, one of the older girls said, "There she goes again. Running away instead of facing the truth. Wait until she realizes her parents didn't want her because she's one of us."*

Gemma could feel her anger and frustration surfacing again.

Those kids assumed they knew everything about her when they knew nothing. Gemma's parents were wealthy, but being wealthy wasn't the same as being free. Her life had been dictated by rules that were ever-changing as she grew older. She didn't understand why so many people talked about her Daddy and whispered as if they were afraid of him overhearing their conversations. Gemma couldn't comprehend why fear clung to the people surrounding him.

All she saw were strong arms that picked her up and spun her whenever she wanted, a smile that lit up the room, and eyes that danced with joy. Her Daddy yelled sometimes, but so did everyone else she knew. Even her Momma raised her voice when she got frustrated. Gemma refused to believe her Momma sent her away because her parents didn't want her anymore. She couldn't bear the thought of being abandoned by the two people she loved most in this world.

The Herbalist found her gaze wandering to the trees once more. Acquiescing the pull of her blood, Gemma moved closer to the forest. She held her hands out and watched the vines creep forward until they draped themselves over her hands and arms. She giggled as their leaves tickled her skin and watched with wide eyes as flowers began to bloom up and down the vines.

The loud cry of a falcon caused Gemma to look up at the sky with hope in her heart.

The little girl scrambled to disentangle herself from the plants before turning back to the sea. With her heart thumping frantically and the blood roaring in her ears, she sped towards the sound of the cry.

Soon enough she saw Bane's unmistakable falcon form beelining for her.

At least she hoped it was Bane.

"Bane!" Gemma flailed her arms, trying to make sure she got his attention. As he approached, she heard a chattering sound. Confused by Bane's behavior, the little girl cocked her head and peered at the bird. Gemma racked her brain, trying to think of what Bane was trying to say.

A memory flashed in her mind and Gemma instinctively held up one arm. The falcon let out a cry before swooping down to land lightly on the arm she offered. Bane walked up her arm until he perched on her shoulder and nuzzled her cheek. He chattered once more and held out one leg. A piece of cloth was tied to it and Gemma could just make out the letters R-E-G.

Gemma traced the letters, listing them as she did so, but not comprehending what they meant. She gave Bane a quizzical look. "I can't read." She hung her head, her mind whirring. When she looked up, she had a grin on her face. "Maybe Reg can help! Follow me!" Gemma's steps became filled with purpose as she strode into the forest, ignoring the way the plants reached for her and the connection she could provide.

Nan pulled her coat tighter and exited the wagon, dropping lightly onto the snow-covered ground. Her thick boots kept her toes from freezing and her wool underlayers kept her legs and torso warm as she left the heated wagon. Despite the icy wind, Nan trudged down to the water's edge to take in the sunrise over Mantaga Lake.

Her Abuela had always made it a point to watch the sunrise when she could.

The promise of a new day meant there was another chance to spread more love in the world. Her Abuela spread kindness wherever she went, insisting on helping everyone they encountered on their travels whether it was with a warm meal, a place by her fire, or the shirt off her back. She believed she didn't cross paths with anyone the Huntress didn't want her to and therefore; it was her duty to uncover why they were meeting.

Her Abuela had been the best person she'd ever known.

Nan felt warmth spread from her core outward as the sky took on a rosy glow. All around her was white. Even the lake had a fresh dusting of snow over the light blue sheen of ice across its surface. The crystals of frozen water glistened as they caught the early morning sun.

Nan sighed in contentment, still not believing the events that had led to this moment. She knew the winter would be long, but everything seemed easier with the promise of a new home.

Her eyes crinkled at their corners when she smiled, unable to contain the joy inside.

"It's too cold for you to be this happy." A teasing tone had her head swiveling to her right. Nan's smile only widened as she took in Duncan's matching grin.

Reaching out, she squeezed his side and said, "You're one to talk." Both of their smiles grew until they broke into chuckles.

They quieted, content to a companionable silence as they watched the rosiness on the horizon intensify in color, hinting at what was to come.

After a while, Duncan pulled her into a one-armed hug. "Best to take advantage of this peace while we have it. After our showing in Verdencia, Myra will be more determined than ever to find and destroy us." He gave a heavy sigh. "Rae asked me about battle plans last night. I didn't have the heart to argue and obliged her in discussing tactics and what needs to be done before we can leave." There was a hollowness to his voice that made Nan frown.

She tilted her head to get a better look at him. "But you'd rather focus on building than preparing for another battle," she guessed.

Duncan shook his head and took his arm from her shoulder. "No. Myra is coming for us, and we need to be prepared." He refused to meet her eyes, and Nan knew he wasn't telling her something.

*But what else would cause him such distress?*

"Yes, but that's not the only thing weighing on you. Burdens should be shared before they result in a collapse." Nan threw him a pointed look. *And he wonders where Rae gets her inability to ask for help from.*

Duncan gave another sigh and picked at his coat sleeves before meeting her encouraging gaze.

"She knows I'm alive. I'm the reason she won't stop looking for us." He looked away and said the words he was reluctant to say. "I should turn myself in and give the rest of you a chance. Maybe Myra could turn a blind eye if she had the person she was looking for."

Nan's stomach dropped and her insides became drenched with ice. She knew Duncan was self-sacrificing when it came to his people, but this was too much. She gripped his wrist and forced him to look her in the eye.

"We both know Myra can never be satisfied. You're a fool for even entertaining the idea. Our people need you alive and here, leading them to a better future. Even if that means more battles need to be waged." Nan's eyes were like steel as she willed the Ringmaster to understand.

A wind ruffled their hair and Nan recognized it as a lapse in the man's tight control of the winds in his core.

Duncan's expression was unreadable as he held the Herbalist's gaze. "But what if–"

"That sky sure is beautiful, isn't it?" A voice interrupted Duncan before he could finish his thought.

Nan kept the frustration from her face as she turned towards the speaker. She felt some of her tension loosen from where it coiled in her belly at Chiara's serene expression. Recognizing an ally when she had one, Nan welcomed the Head Herbalist into their conversation.

"That it is, dearie," the old woman grasped one of Chiara's hands in hers before continuing. "Come, join us. We could use that steady head on your shoulders to help us."

Chiara cocked one eyebrow and directed a pointed gaze at Duncan. "So early for conversation that needs a steady head. What were you discussing?"

"The difference between being self-sacrificing and being a fool." Nan answered before Duncan could respond.

Chiara glanced between them with a puzzled look on her face before settling on Duncan and lifting her eyebrow in expectation.

Duncan shook his head and walked away, striding towards the path around the lake.

Chiara turned to Nan. "Men. I swear, as soon as I think we've made a breakthrough, we take two steps back. I'll talk to him after he's had a while to walk it off."

Nan's eyes glittered. "The two of you have become quite close, haven't you?" Nan was fishing and didn't try to hide it.

Chiara rolled her eyes at the older woman. "We've always been close." Her expression gave nothing away.

Nan knew better than to pry more than she already had. She placed a hand on the Herbalist's arm. "Fine. Keep your secrets. But I do have something I need to discuss with you. It's regarding the magic in our veins. We've been around long enough to know the subsequent generations receive less and less power. We need to do more research on the decline of our Gifts and why Rae and Bane are so unique."

Chiara's eyes narrowed in focus and gave a nod. "I've been mulling that over since we left Verdencia. Damien confided that both Rae and Bane believe their power echoes that of the original Magicae from your story. But you scoured your books and found nothing, right?"

"I, I found nothing in the books I have, but that doesn't mean the information isn't out there." Nan put a hand to her temple as if it would help her remember. "Ever since my accident, I haven't been able to get my memories in order. I need to remember the end of that story, the one I started. I can't shake the feeling I'm missing something important." She closed her eyes and willed the memory of her Abuela and that night to the forefront of her mind.

Chiara's eyebrows knitted with concern. "Nan, don't push too hard. The last thing we need is for you to have another episode."

Nan waved her off and shook her head. "Believe you, me, the Huntress isn't ready for me yet." She sent Chiara a wink. "The afterlife will have one hell of a reckoning once I get there. And they thought my Abuela was a lot to handle."

She let a soft chuckle escape her lips. "Let me try the books again. This time I'll look for information on the original ancestors instead of focusing on the Gifts from the Goddess. It might be futile, but it beats sitting around doing nothing."

"One more look won't hurt. I'll come help," said Chiara.

"Nonsense. Enjoy the peacefulness of the morning while you have it. I would be obliged if you would stop by the wagon after lunch, though. Help me with a memory tonic if I still can't remember the end of that story." Nan patted Chiara's cheek with an affectionate glance.

"Of course, Abuela. I will do just that." Chiara gripped Nan's arm before making her way closer towards the lake.

"And don't let Duncan get away with not talking to you." She called after Damien's mother.

Chiara let out a chuckle. "He never does."

Nan couldn't wipe the smile from her face as she turned back to her cozy wagon. She had a mystery to solve.

George's breaths came in puffs of smoke as his feet pounded the cold, hard ground. Ever since the battle in Verdencia, the only thing that could settle him was some sort of physical exertion. Hence the running.

He pumped his arms harder in the midmorning air, relishing the burning in his lungs and muscles. He ran another mile through the woods before slowing to a stop.

Gasping for breath, he leaned over and placed his hands on his knees. After a few moments, he could breathe easy again and straightened to a standing position.

Thoughts crowded in as his adrenaline wore off and George moved to lean next to a tree. He was worried about his Ma, Tommy and the rest of his family, Rich and the rest of his friends, and the city as a whole. He was worried Duncan wouldn't take the necessary action when it came to it. George could only imagine what horrors Vincenzio was inflicting on the city he loved with all his heart.

And the worst part? There was nothing he could do about any of it.

He was safe, almost a hundred miles away, while his loved ones were going through hell or worse.

And he felt like shit about all of it.

*I never should have left.* He slammed his hand on the tree, his guilt and frustration bubbling up again.

"Someone woke up on the wrong side of the bed."

George looked to his right and groaned. "Not now, Tam."

"Why? Feeling sorry for yourself again?" The Forger lifted one eyebrow.

He couldn't suppress the growl in the back of his throat as he glared at the woman. "And what if I am?"

Tamara's eyes hardened. "If you are, snap out of it. You have people here counting on you whether or not you like it. Those innocent children and elderly are depending on you to get them through this. You need to figure your shit out."

"I know they're counting on me, Tam. I'm not an idiot. But my family is in Heimat."

"And they're *Mortal*. Vincenzio and his lackeys won't target them." Tamara's eyes blazed.

George felt his temper flare, and he took a step toward the glass Forger. "You think that man gives a *damn* whether you're Mortal if you're caught being sympathetic to Magicae? My family might not be in danger because of their blood, but Goddess knows they're in more danger because of who they stand for."

Tamara held her hands up in an act of surrender. "I'm sorry, George. You're right. Being associated with all of us puts them in more danger than anything else could. But worrying about them doesn't do you any good. It only puts you and the rest of us at risk. We need you at your best if we're going to get through this." She poked a finger into his chest to punctuate her point.

George looked at her finger and considered her words. Tamara was right. He was no use to his family if he wound up dead. They needed him to be strong. He met her dark eyes and felt something shift inside. He gave her a nod.

"I just miss them so much."

Tamara's eyes softened. "We'll be home before we know it."

George lifted an eyebrow. "This winter already feels long, and it's only beginning. We won't be home soon enough."

Tamara chuckled. "Especially when you start thinking about your Ma's cooking. What I wouldn't do for another bite of her beef stew."

"Ugh. Don't remind me. Everything she makes is like heaven. I would do anything to be back in that kitchen." George's tone turned desperate, and he didn't bother hiding it.

Tamara put an arm over his shoulder and squeezed. "We'll get through this together. We need to decide what has to happen before we can return to the ones we love. Step one, make sure our people have a safe settlement before we march."

"Step two, survive this place as the temperatures continue to drop." George shrugged her off.

Tamara shook her head. "Be serious, George. I also have loved ones I want to return to."

George felt his cheeks redden at how inconsiderate he was being. He mumbled an apology before saying louder, "The next step would be to gather as much information about our opponent as we can."

Tamara gave him an approving nod. "And I know someone who's a master at blending in with a crowd."

George sent her a smirk. "I should finish my run."

Without another word, he took off, pumping his legs and keeping his thoughts focused on what he could do to make sure he made it home to Heimat as soon as possible.

# Chapter Four

Verdencia was carpeted under a thick layer of snow. A snowstorm hit the city shortly after the Circus took their leave. The city in the trees looked picturesque, with smoke curling up from wooden treehouses and through the uppermost limbs into the gray winter dawn. Snow-lined branches provided a fluffy backdrop to the curious structures the Elven resided in. Most were simple wooden structures built in the towering trees, but some were made of the trunks themselves. The massive treehouses built amongst and within the branches of the giant oaks and tall pines were feats of engineering and magic. Bridges made of rope and wood and branches connected the structures to each other.

The only cottages on the forest floor were meant for the guards patrolling the outskirts of the rune-protected perimeter and any visitors to the long-forgotten city of Verdencia.

Few people visited them these days, but the Elven people insisted they be maintained in hopes of a future where they could welcome guests with open arms. Since the battle in the forest and the Circus's departure, the Elven people had grown restless, especially the younger generations.

Tyee was paying the price for some of that restlessness as he woke in one of those cottages, his head pounding and his mouth dry as a bone. Putting a hand to his temple, he let out a groan, cursing the Elven wine stronger than what he was used to.

*I'm going to kill Fritz.* Tyee thought to himself as he reached for the pitcher of water on the table beside him. Rolling onto his side, he fumbled for the glass next to it and knocked it onto the floor.

"Fuck," Tyee muttered as he forced himself to sit up. With his brain filled with fog, he didn't bother searching for the displaced cup and pulled the pitcher to his lips. He took several long gulps and savored the feeling of cool crisp water quenching the thirst alcohol never could. Once the pitcher was empty, Tyee rubbed his sleeve against his mouth and set it back on the table.

Reaching his arms to the sky, Tyee took a moment to stretch his muscles. The horseman sighed and stood to face the day. He was filled with immediate regret when spots colored his vision. He stood still and closed his eyes, willing the dizziness to go away. After giving it a few moments, Tyee opened his eyes and made his way to the chest holding his few belongings. He dressed as swiftly as he could and splashed his face with cold water to drive the pounding from his head.

A glance out the window had him cursing again. Tyee had spent the night drinking and partying with Fritz, one of the guards in charge of maintaining and checking the runes that protected the Elven perimeter, in the amphitheater. Tyee never bothered to ask after the reason behind the celebration, having assumed it was related to the victory against Vincenzio's soldiers or the Circus's departure. Whatever the reason, the Elven sure knew how to throw a party.

Tyee could only remember flashes of the night before but was sure he'd enjoyed the festivities. The state he was in now was the only confirmation he needed for that to be true.

But now he needed to go check on Koko.

He reached for his coat and frowned as he gripped unfamiliar fabric. For a moment, he forgot the reason it was missing and started searching for the beloved piece of clothing. It was the one thing he'd taken from the stable where he'd met Koko. It was filled with so many memories; he couldn't leave before finding it.

Tyee pulled apart his trunk until clothes and blankets littered the floor. Letting out a frustrated sigh, he slammed one hand against the wall. Tyee swore when he felt the telltale prick of a splinter in his palm. His arm recoiled immediately, and the horseman brought his hand close to investigate.

Tyee's blood ran ice cold when he saw three angry red lines, still healing from the battle two weeks prior. The longest line ran vertically down his hand, in line with his middle finger while the other two ran from opposite diagonals, crossing and stopping at the long line about a third of the way down. Tyee still didn't know exactly what the rune meant, but it had been enough to give Rae what she needed.

*Rae.* Memories flooded Tyee's head, reminding him of why his leather trench coat was missing. His stomach twisted into knots at the thought of the golden girl.

Their last kiss on Koko's back held a promise that neither of them could put into words.

*You could break me easier than you think.* Her admission repeated itself over and over inside his head, sobering him faster than any tonic could. The decision to stay hadn't been an easy one, especially after everything he endured at the hands of the Queen and her general.

But something had awoken deep inside him. Ever since the dream or vision of his mother singing that lullaby, Tyee knew he needed answers. This wasn't something he could avoid by running. This feeling deep inside would haunt him for the rest of his days unless he faced it head-on. Once Rae suggested it, staying was his only course of action; no matter how hard he wished it could be otherwise.

Tyee clenched both fists and lifted his chin, determination blazing in his eyes. The sooner he got started, the sooner he could follow the Circus and the acrobat he couldn't get out of his head. He reached for the door, intent on leaving the cottage a mess, when a knocking sounded, insistent and desperate at the same time.

"Tyee! Mate, we overslept. Old Tota will have our heads the way it is. Oy, ma—"

Tyee threw open the door, cutting Fritz off mid-sentence and shooting daggers at the large, red-haired guard. "And whose fault is that?" He spat the words out, warning the younger Elven he wasn't in the mood.

Unperturbed, Fritz rolled his eyes. "You know the way to my cottage. You could've just as easily found me, so simmer down Dødelig."

Tyee's eyes flashed. "Duda-what?"

"Deu-de-lee. It's our word for a Mortal." Fritz's tone tinged with impatience. "But we can discuss that later. Grab your horse and let's get going. Only Skaber can help us now." He watched Tyee's eyes fill with confusion and scowled. Reaching a hand the size of a dinner plate out, Fritz took Tyee's arm and pulled him through the open door. "I'll explain on the way. Tota's place is deeper in the forest and we're already late. Trust me on this. Please."

"All right. But I'll hold you to that." Tyee closed the cottage door behind him and strode to the paddock and his midnight stallion.

Tyee shivered despite the fur-lined cloak he now wore. It was warmer than his leather one but didn't offer the same sense of comfort. He pulled the unfamiliar fabric closer and focused on the forest in front of him. It was a winter wonderland in the Great Northern Forest. It hadn't seemed possible, but the snowstorm had hit this part of the forest harder than in Verdencia.

The snow and ice were as beautiful as they were deadly.

Koko's steps were jolting as he forced his way through the thick blanket of snow, puffs of smoke curling from his nostrils with every labored breath. It was clear the horse was still recovering from the battle and out of shape from the past two weeks of rest. The stallion never complained, simply persevering, happy to be away from the prison that was the paddock.

Tyee gave Koko's neck an encouraging pat as guilt flashed like lightning. The bond between them meant the stallion would do anything and everything he asked, or hurt himself trying.

*Just a little farther, old friend, and then you can rest.* Tyee made the horse a silent promise, knowing he would need to be more diligent about helping Koko regain his strength and endurance. *We'll get through this.* With another rub, Tyee looked up to where Fritz led the way on his scraggly forest pony.

"You still owe me some answers." He barked, raising his voice.

Fritz threw a bewildered glance over his shoulder before his body drooped with recognition. His laughter boomed as he slowed the pony beneath him. "Scared me there, mate. I forgot you were behind me for a minute." He put a hand to his temple. "It was the glogg last night. I told Cena she made it too strong again." The guard let out another loud laugh, his long red hair bouncing behind him. "Although I did wake up before midday this time, so that's an improvement."

Tyee gritted his teeth against the other man's rambling, frustration building at the circumstances he faced and the man riding next to him. "Aye, the brain fog is real, but that doesn't help me."

Fritz sobered when he read the expression on Tyee's face. "Relax. This is nothing to get your bloomers in a bunch over." His lips curled into a smirk as he assessed the reasons for Tyee's impatience. "Unless there's a woman." He gave the horseman a sideways look and tapped a finger to his chin. "Weren't you the one my Da saw with that gorgeous blonde? He said it was quite the kiss." Fritz shot him a wink. "No wonder you're itching to get out of here as fast as possible. I would be too with a gal like that waiting for me."

Tyee gave a dangerous chuckle. "You wouldn't be making those comments if you knew her."

Fritz shot him a grin. "So, it's true. And she's the Crafter, no? The one who can control more than one element?" When Tyee furrowed his brow, the guard continued, "We learned about the Magicae in the presentation they put on for us. And Cena treated her in the infirmary; she asked as many questions about her as she could." Fritz took a breath and let Tyee soak his words in. "She's one of the Vandrere isn't she?"

Tyee gave him a pointed look. "Fritz. Listen to me carefully. I have no *idea* what the bloody hell you're talking about." He drawled, keeping his voice low and talking slowly to emphasize his point.,, tucking the unknown word away for later

Fritz had the decency to look sheepish and held his palms up. "Mate, I'm sorry. I can't imagine how hard this has been for you. We made good time and are almost at Tota's place." He cast a glance through the trees to the sky. "Give or take an hour and we'll be there."

The talkative guard brightened a little as realization dawned on him. "By my estimations, we'll only be two hours late; talk about breaking a record. And with a hangover to boot? No one will believe it."

Tyee narrowed his eyes and gave a disbelieving frown. "Two hours late? And a new record? Does nobody respect time around here?" He let his questions hang in the air, waiting for Fritz to answer.

"Give me a sec to organize my thoughts. Clearly, we come from two different worlds." Fritz sighed, as if the explanation of his people was a chore he hoped to avoid.

Tyee tapped the pommel of his saddle, giving his nervous energy an outlet. His emotions were tangled between intense curiosity for the culture that was his birthright and instinctive disdain for the people that allowed Sylvie to hold a position of power. Thoughts of the cruel woman made his lips curl. He had avoided the general but knew it was only a matter of time before their paths crossed again. And when that day came, he would be ready. He would learn what he needed to from this Tota character and make sure none of the Elven could take him by surprise again.

Fritz's voice roused Tyee from his musings. "I think the easiest way to do this is for me to give a little background and then invite you to ask questions. To be completely honest, I've forgotten everything you've asked and figure this is as good a place to start as any. Forsta?" At Tyee's raised eyebrow, Fritz put his palm to his forehead, shaking his head. "Of course. You don't know any Elvish."

"Observant of you." Tyee quipped, continuing before Fritz could respond. "I'd rather we start with Tota. I have one hour to learn as much as I can before meeting her and not go in blindsided."

Fritz nodded. "Makes sense, I guess. Although Tota is the last place I would've started. She's the oldest Elven in all of Kamore, which is cool, but she mostly keeps to herself. Even the Queen knew better than to give her a direct order when she moved everyone to Verdencia. Hmm," the guard cocked his head as if he was thinking. "I don't even know if she's been to Verdencia. Huh, imagine that, one of the Elven that's never seen her city before." He glanced at Tyee and noticed the exasperation on the horseman's face. "Sorry! I'm on a tangent again. I get to talking and it's like my mouth has a mind of its own. But you wanted to know more about who she is, right?"

Tyee nodded, praying he would hear something useful in whatever remained of their last hour. "And why she's important. Unless being old is the only reason the Elven defer to her?"

The other man frowned. "Okay, so first tip, don't call Tota old. I mean she is, ancient actually, but the Elven don't make it a habit of reminding any elders of their age."

Tyee rolled his eyes. "I'm not that dense. Give me some credit. I'm trying to understand why Queen Ulla wouldn't even try to give this woman a direct order. It seems like whatever the queen says goes." Tyee caught the brief scowl that came unbidden to Fritz's face. "Unless I'm missing something?"

Fritz schooled his features to clear the emotion from his rounded face. "Queen Ulla has our best interests at heart." His reply was political, and Tyee could tell he was holding something back.

"Of course she does," Tyee replied diplomatically. He would prod the young Elven about his monarchy at a later date. When time wasn't of the essence. "But again, this Tota must be more than simply an old woman. In the Circus, we never would've left one of our elders to weather the unknown alone. Unless they gave us no choice. I have a feeling this Tota gave the Queen no choice in leaving her to her own devices."

Fritz laughed. "You got that right. Tota has a mind of her own and is as stubborn as old Moss here." He leaned forward and stroked the pony's mane. "Remind me to tell you the story about Moss and me after the yearly bonfire.

It's quite the story. Most people don't believe it's true after they've heard it." His eyes shone as he got lost in the memory.

"I'm sure it is, but back to Tota," Tyee interjected before Fritz could decide the story was worth telling after all.

Fritz shook his head, the memory fading from his eyes, and rubbed his pony's neck. "More persistent than a creeper vine, aren't you? Let me start from the beginning. Tota means grandmother, but most people, including me, have never known her by any other name. She is the oldest living Elven, and her memory reaches centuries into the past. There's a rumor that the forest itself sustains her.

"My people did not always live amongst the trees, but Tota always has. She is a living, breathing account of our history and the collective knowledge of our people. Queen Ulla was apprehensive about sending you to such a woman but her advisors, which include my Da, insisted it was the best way for you to get your answers and for our community to continue without incident." Fritz paused and met Tyee's gaze. His eyes softened, and he continued, "You fit in here more than you know. Cena and her sister both told me they liked you way more than they should have."

Fritz held Tyee's gaze while he paused. An unknown emotion swirled in his hazel eyes. "All of us know this is a stepping stone for you. And you'll find many of the Elven unwilling to invest in a relationship they know is going nowhere. But if you find yourself entertaining the idea of staying, our people would welcome you with open arms."

Tyee was the first to break eye contact. He stared into the trees covered in snow and mulled over the guard's cryptic words. *There's something he's not telling me. But what?*

Tyee kept his thoughts to himself for now. There was a shift in the air around them as they continued down the snow-covered trail. Tyee had a feeling in his gut they were nearing their destination. This would be his last opportunity to get more information about the ancient woman.

"Thanks, Fritz, that means a lot." Tyee's eyes were sincere as he looked back at the young Elven. He gestured to the surrounding forest. "We're getting closer, aren't we? The air got thicker."

Fritz studied him for a moment. "You're feeling the runes Tota placed around the edges of her territory. If we had come with ill intent, they would've—" Fritz paused as if looking for the right word. Finding it, he continued, "persuaded us to bypass this part of the forest. Our senses of direction would be muddled and we would be herded to exactly where Tota wants us to go. But we passed. Tota's runes are unique because she believes in their ability to sense the difference between friend and foe. The Queen's runes are designed to keep everyone out for the safety of Verdencia and the people she protects." He paused again and tapped a finger to his chin. "There's a reason the Queen doesn't trust the runes as implicitly as Tota, but it's quite a long story." Fritz cast a hopeful expression towards his companion.

Tyee let out a groan and gave the infuriating guard a hard look. "Another time, maybe," he gritted out. *Huntress, he'll be the death of me.*

Fritz gave a slight pout but picked up where he left off. "I should've known. Anyway, Tota has the most impressive mastery of the runes anyone has ever seen and many attribute her power to the faith and trust she puts in the marks she makes." He winced and gave Tyee a sideways glance. "She's not a gentle teacher, though. Tota believes in giving everyone a chance as long as they wish her no ill, but she has little patience for laziness and incompetence."

"You act as if you speak from experience," Tyee mused, warming to the infuriating man despite his frustration.

"Ya got me there, mate. My father sent me and each of my siblings to learn from her. He always said there was no point in learning from anyone other than the best. And no matter how we complained, we always had to go back every summer. She's a tough one, but her methods yield results. We were each at the top of our class for runes and magic. Arithmetic, on the other hand, not my strong suit."

Tyee soaked in Fritz's insights and gave a nod. "Thank you. That helps put her in perspective." He sent the Elven a smirk. "You didn't make it easy for me, but we got there eventually."

"I did my best to stay off-topic, but you were too persistent and a little ornery," Fritz replied with a matching grin.

"Touché. We'll blame that on the hangover." Tyee countered. "And I think you're the reason for that. So you have nobody to blame but yourself."

Fritz rolled his eyes but said nothing. The pair rode in silence, listening to the sounds of the birds and the crunch of the snow beneath the horses' hooves. Weak winter sunlight filtered through the trees, creating long shadows and patches of absolute darkness.

Tyee took a deep breath and let it out, creating a puff of smoke in front of him. The lack of sunlight made the early afternoon seem colder. He rolled his shoulders back and tried to warm himself up a bit. He had been so focused on Fritz and getting the information he needed, that he didn't realize the chill setting into his bones.

The call of a crow sent goosebumps across his skin.

"And this is where I leave you."

Tyee turned to Fritz in slight surprise. "You're not coming the rest of the way?"

Fritz shook his head. "No, mate. Tota's house is just over that hill. You can't miss it." He swallowed. "The Queen insisted you encounter the old woman alone." He picked at the straps on his saddle before meeting Tyee's questioning look. "I'm sorry, mate, but that's all I can say. Please give Tota my regards."

Tyee read the pain and regret in Fritz's gaze and didn't push. Instead, he reached a hand out. When the young Elven clasped his forearm, Tyee pulled him into a one-armed hug. "I will. And thank you for everything. Your acceptance means more than you know."

Fritz grinned, relieved at Tyee's silent way of accepting his words without pushing him. "Be sure to find me when you get back. We'll share a bottle of Cena's glogg and swap war stories." And with a wink, he turned his pony around and headed back the way they came.

Tyee watched him leave before squaring his shoulders and facing the path that would lead him to his future.

"Come on, Ko. Let's go see whether Tota lives up to the hype."

Koko snorted in response and crested the hill.

# Chapter Five

Duncan walked down the path by the lake, contemplating his options. Nan was convinced Myra wouldn't stop pursuing their people even if he turned himself over to her.

But he wanted to hold on to some sort of hope this could all end without the bloodshed he anticipated in every other scenario.

They'd both served during Andre's presidency. They never agreed on policy, but had always been cordial outside of governing meetings. And Myra's honor had to be hidden somewhere in the madness she'd devolved into.

*Such a fool.* Weariness settled into his bones, as did the knowledge that Nan was right. The road they'd taken would only lead to one outcome.

If only his sacrifice could be enough.

Duncan felt a presence fall in step behind him. Without turning, he knew it was Chiara. He kept walking, unwilling to face her after his abruptness earlier. She hadn't deserved that.

He felt a hand on his shoulder and let a mask fall over his features. He turned to face the Head Herbalist and Chiara winced.

She moved her hand from his shoulder to his cheek and gave him a searching look. "Don't hide from me. We're long past that."

Duncan dropped his gaze, trying to control his dread and the sense of foreboding threatening to overwhelm him.

"Hey. Talk to me," she murmured, her green eyes soft and concerned.

He swallowed his emotions and cleared his throat. "I shouldn't have run off like that. I apologize for my behavior."

Chiara frowned. "What were you and Abuela discussing?"

Duncan met her gaze for a moment before looking at the lake. "Whether or not I should turn myself into Myra."

Tension built between them in the silence that followed.

Duncan hazarded a glance towards her and met green eyes as cold as ice.

"How dare you." Chiara hissed when she found her voice. Her eyes flashed with hurt and anger. She crossed her arms and shook her head. "She will *kill* you, Duncan. You'd sentence yourself to the same fate as Andre when it didn't work the first time?"

Duncan felt his own anger flare at the dismissive way both she and Nan regarded his desire to protect his people. His eyes flashed, and he took a step closer. "I'm not a child, Chiara. I know what the consequences would be. But wouldn't the chance of ending all this outweigh one life?"

Chiara's anger turned to horror. "So this is about being the hero? Sacrificing yourself to save the rest of us, even though you know this world doesn't work like that?" Her eyes widened as she stood her ground. "Abuela was right. You are a fool." She whirled and walked away.

Duncan clenched his fists. Both women were right, but he found himself wrestling with his pride as he tried to admit it out loud.

"Chiara, wait." He called after her. The Herbalist kept walking as if she didn't hear him.

He jogged after her and put a hand on her shoulder.

Chiara turned, her cheeks wet and her face red with emotion. "If you're going to insist on walking willingly to your death, I don't want to hear it. I can't hear it."

Duncan gripped her upper arms and squeezed. "I won't. Myra will stop at nothing to destroy all of us, but you can't blame me for trying to find a way that ends in less bloodshed."

"Who says any blood needs to be shed at all? The Elven have stayed hidden for hundreds of years. Why can't we?" Chiara pleaded.

Duncan sighed. "That's not how this works. Myra and Vincenzio won't let us go that easily."

"But what if we tried?" Chiara's eyes were steel as she pushed against fate.

"Chiara, I—,"

"No, Duncan. Listen to somebody else for once. We can make a new home." Chiara tore from his grasp.

"And what about the ones we leave behind?" Duncan's voice was rough, weary from giving voice to the arguments he'd only had in his head.

Chiara stuttered, not having taken them into consideration. "We bring them here."

Duncan shook his head. "The Elven survived because they left the modern world without a backwards glance. That's what you're asking me to do and I can't."

Chiara frowned. "Then you doom the rest of us." She turned on her heel and left.

This time, Duncan let her go.

*If only my sacrifice could fix this.*

Luc pulled her coat closer and felt a shiver run down her spine.

*Who knew winter in the forest would be so much worse than winter in Heimat?* At least the city had solid structures to ward off the iciness of winter, unlike the tent city they found themselves in.

But the frozen lake was beautiful. She took a deep breath. And safety never tasted so sweet. Consequences be damned.

Her eyes caught on a familiar face, and her lips curled into a grin. "Zeke!" she called. "You look like a sheep that hasn't been sheared in years with all those layers on."

The fair-featured acrobat rolled his eyes at her. "Do you know how fuckin' cold out it is? Because that's how cold it is in my tent." He held out an arm to her when she got closer and pulled her into his side.

Luc let out a laugh and put her arm around his waist. "Oh no, poor baby. Sounds like you need somebody to warm your bed." She waggled her eyebrows at him.

"Shut up." Zeke lifted an arm and messed up her hair. Luc dissolved into giggles, trying to ward off his attack.

After a few moments, Zeke let her straighten, but kept her close to his side. "Don't forget, I'm still stronger than you."

Luc rolled her eyes but gave him a squeeze. "Yea, yea. Somebody's missing their beau." She shot him a smirk and danced away before he could retaliate again. "Ah, ah, ah. You can take it. After all the shit you and Rae gave Damien and me, you can take a little teasing." Her eyes glittered as she kept her guard up, prepared for the inevitable attack.

Zeke gave an audible sigh and held his hands in surrender. "Okay, okay. But Bane and I still haven't put a label on it. We're taking things slow until after things calm down a bit."

Luc shot him a look. "Call it what you want, but the two of you have been joined at the hip since Verdencia. Seems pretty serious to me."

Zeke rolled his eyes. "Think what you want, but nothing's official. I will say the more time I spend with him, the more I can't imagine my life without him."

Luc laughed. "About time you admit it." Her eyes softened as she held out her right hand, pointing her top two fingers and thumb towards the wind Crafter. "Truce?"

Zeke studied her and said, "You're lucky it's cold out." He matched her right hand, and they shook using the handshake they'd created as kids.

"And why's that?"

"Because I'm too worried about frostbite to put up a fight, and I forgot about the handshake. Call me sentimental or something," Zeke answered as he held up a hand and let a soft breeze twine through his fingers.

Luc feigned outrage at his forgetfulness and held a hand to her chest, her jaw dropping and keeping silent as if in shock.

Zeke lifted one eyebrow. "You've been spending too much time with Damien; his dramatics are rubbing off on you." His grin faltered when he saw concern and pain flit across her features. "Hey, what's going on? Talk to me." He grabbed at her hands.

Luc felt her eyes prick at his gentle tone and kind words. She squeezed his hands and fumbled for words, keeping her eyes on his. "Dame—, I can't...We—. Augh." She grumbled and took a moment to compose herself, toying with the pendant around her neck. With a frown, she continued, "It's hard to explain. But, I'm worried about Damien."

"Go on." Zeke kept his tone soft despite the tense set to his shoulders.

"He hasn't been the same since the battle in Verdencia." Luc chewed on the inside of her cheek, relieved to share her concerns with someone. "It's like he's here, but not at the same time. I try to ask him about it and his eyes fill with pain, but he still shrugs me off and gives me a bullshit answer. Zeke, he barely sleeps and when he does, he twists and turns and cries out. He's having nightmares and tries to fight sleep because of it. And he won't talk to me about any of it. He's refusing to share the burden of what plagues him." She hung her head and whispered, "And I don't know what else to do."

"Luc, I had no idea." Zeke pulled her into an embrace before pulling back to look her in the face. "This has been happening since the battle?"

She nodded.

"Have you talked to Chiara about it? She could probably whip up a sleeping draught, at least."

"I suggested that too, but Dame made me promise not to talk to his mom about it. He became hysterical when I mentioned it actually, saying he needed to be the one to talk to her." Luc paused as her heart thundered in her ears.

She hated feeling so out of control, without a plan or way to move forward. She recognized the relief in sharing her struggles with a friend and that, inadvertently, she'd been doing the same thing Damien had been. Keeping everything inside was the worst thing she could've done for both of them. But it was also more than that and she couldn't help but explain, "It felt like this was something we should handle on our own. So much was happening with you and Rae in the infirmary, my own recovery, and finding our way here. I thought once we were a little more stable, Damien would open up and we could move through it together." Luc said. She'd done a noble job of keeping the tears at bay, but thinking about the past few weeks opened a floodgate.

She leaned into Zeke's solid presence and felt his arms wrap around her. She held nothing back and let it all go. Luc let go of her frustration with and worry for Damien, the exhaustion that clung to her both mentally and physically, and the anxiety for their futures. Her frame trembled as sobs took over. She struggled to breathe as they became lodged in her throat and threatened to suffocate her. It took all she had and then some, her body's physical response freeing the chain that held her emotions and thoughts in tight.

This was what Luc needed to heal. She held tight to Zeke and gave herself permission to let it all go. Her own grief for those they lost escaped her in the form of wrenching sobs, loud inhales of breath, and snot that mingled with her tears. She let herself go for a moment more before forcing herself to take a deep breath. Zeke's arm still held her close and one hand stroked her hair while he whispered comforting words in her ear.

She took a last shuddering breath and squeezed him tight. "You were always so good at this."

"What do you mean?" Came the surprised reply.

"At knowing what to say to get someone to spill their darkest secrets." Zeke chuckled as Luc threw him a watery smile.

"I'll talk to him." Zeke hesitated. When Luc gave him a questioning look, he said, "It's because of the battle. You were in the infirmary the entire time dealing with your own shit. Luc, it was awful. There were blood and bodies everywhere you looked. Half the time, you didn't know if you were stepping on rocks or bones." Luc winced as a hollow look entered Zeke's normally vibrant eyes. It was the same look she saw when she looked into Damien's.

"I'm so sorry, Zeke. I'm sorry you had to see that, had to live that." Luc kept one arm around his waist and leaned her head on his shoulder. "Keep going," she insisted, recognizing Zeke needed this release as much as she did.

Zeke's eyes became far away, but he obliged. "You could taste copper in the air and the stench of death, but the worst by far were the sounds. The metallic clash of your sword meeting another's, the squelching as your blade pierced through flesh, and the screams of the dying will echo in my head forever." Zeke became lost in his memories for another moment before he met Luc's dark eyes. His own softened as he ventured, "He's probably not opening up to you because he can't. You weren't there and don't understand what we went through. It was a living hell."

Luc felt her face fall as she took in Zeke's words. She knew he was right, but hated that it made her feel like a failure. Her thoughts strayed to the conversation with Tyee at the start of their journey in the forest and the words he'd left with her.

*Either way, we'll learn a lot about ourselves as the changes keep coming.*

He'd soothed her blistered pride and feelings of uselessness after the attack from the Forest Shifters. To hear Tyee talk, every failure was an opportunity to prove yourself or learn something.

*This isn't about you. This is about helping your friends and Damien.* Her words to herself were a little harsh but necessary. She knew Zeke only spoke the truth, and even if it stung, he was trying to help her understand why Damien couldn't talk to her.

Zeke mistook Luc's silence for hurt and frustration. "Ah, Luc. Don't take it personally. It's not like you could've been out there and weren't. You were unconscious before the battle even started. Don't beat yourself up."

Luc rubbed at her face before patting his hand. "I know, old friend. There was nothing I could do at the time, and nothing I can do about it now. No sense in getting worked up about it." She sighed. "I look like a mess, don't I?"

Zeke took in her splotchy face and the long, dark hair that escaped her tie, now sticking out at odd angles. "You've never looked better."

Luc snorted and thumped his shoulder. "Liar." Sobering, she met his gaze.

"Thanks, Zeke. I needed that." She chewed the inside of her cheek and considered her next words. "I'd appreciate it if you'd talk to him. I think you're right in guessing that's the reason he won't talk to me. How could he when I didn't see the horror or the bloodshed?"

"You have my word." Zeke's voice rang with sincerity. "Will you be okay here?"

Luc looked around and realized they'd ended up on the path outside of camp. Her hand strayed to the pendant at her neck, gripping it like it was a lifeline. She took a moment to appreciate the stillness before nodding. "I might stay here a little while longer. The stillness will do my soul some good."

Zeke gave a nod and headed back to the city of tents, striding with purpose to find their fellow acrobat. Luc watched him go before turning back to the snowy forest-scape. She let her feet wander, but did her best to keep her mind blank.

Without Zeke around, the wind berated her cheeks and turned them pink. But the cold was a welcome distraction and a way to prove her grit to herself. Winter and the cold would never be her favorite, preferring the warmth of a campfire or the heat of a sunny summer day to harsh winds and icicles. But pushing herself to appreciate and admire what winter had to offer felt like its own victory.

Small victories were all she could hope for as of late.

The moment with Zeke left her feeling wrung out and emotionally exhausted. Most of it was from worrying about the man she loved, but she knew that wasn't all of it. Deep inside, she still struggled with the new reality she found herself in. Luc longed to return to the way things were. She wanted more days on the road, nights drinking by the bonfire, and time whirling in the sky on the trapeze. She loved the lights, the smiles on their patrons' faces, and the adrenaline in her veins when she performed.

Since Verdencia, life seemed mundane and monotonous. The Circus and its community lacked a clear purpose, leaving individuals to flounder and struggle with their own demons and self-doubts.

And the Mortal counterparts of the community seemed to take it the hardest.

Luc couldn't count the number of conversations she'd engaged in about how the other Mortals of the company felt inadequate or useless in their new normal. She did her best to reassure them, but could only do so much when she felt the same way. Her talents and expertise laid in contorting and flipping her body through the air, commanding the attention of an audience in the center of the ring. She could listen and bring their concerns to the Council, but needed to bring forth solutions or suggestions if she wanted them to go anywhere.

So what happened when she couldn't see a way forward and didn't understand her place in the new microcosm that was the Circus?

She let out a sigh and silently chided herself. *Keep your mind blank, remember?* She brushed the loose strands from her face and pulled her coat closer. Luc needed to figure something out before the bonds that held their community together fell apart completely. The Mortals were chafing at feeling useless and not being able to offer anything to their Magicae friends and family.

Luc furrowed her brows when Zeke's words came back to her.

*You weren't there and don't understand what we went through.*

Just like she couldn't sympathize with Damien or her friends and the horror of battle, the ones she was closest with couldn't sympathize with her about being Mortal. Well, Damien could, but he had an inner battle that prevented Luc from sharing her thoughts with him.

Rae, Zeke, Abuela, Javie, Chiara...even Duncan were Magicae and relishing their newfound freedom of not having to hide who they were. She needed to find someone to talk to in a circumstance similar to her own.

# Chapter Six

"This hawk will lead you to the lake. Try to keep her in your sights at all times, but she'll wait if need be. She won't be thrilled about it, though." Bane stroked the bird affectionately as he directed a look at Reg.

The man from Heimat gave a nod and pocketed the piece of cloth George sent for him. "Thanks, mate. I'll make sure we pack up as much as we can tonight and leave early tomorrow morning." Reg's eyes moved up and down over his muscular frame. He glanced around to make sure they were alone before asking, "How bad was it?"

Bane took a sharp inhale and let out a forced whistle before meeting Reg's eyes. "Worse than you can imagine. And not something I'm inclined to relive."

Understanding filled Reg's eyes. He clasped Bane's shoulder and said, "Battles are not something to be glorified. Thank ya again and safe travels."

Bane watched the man turn and head towards the camp at the edge of the forest. Those from Heimat that couldn't fight, primarily the young, the old, and the sick, had done what they could to protect themselves against the elements and those that meant them harm. But they were running out of the supplies they grabbed from Lockewater. They needed to meet up with the Circus as soon as possible.

Bane looked at the hawk still on his shoulder and met avian eyes that matched his own. He reached within his core and found the thread connecting him to the raptor. Through their bond, he impressed an image of Mantaga Lake and the settlement there. He also sent a picture of the group the hawk was to lead, emphasizing how slowly they would march through the forest.

When that was done, Bane withdrew from his core and refocused on the hawk's physical presence. She chattered her beak at him and ruffled her wings, but stayed perched on his shoulder. He stroked her head once more and whispered his thanks.

"This is the last I'll ask of you, old girl. Get them to the lake and have your freedom. I owe you a debt. Send me an image at any time and I'll come find you." Bane held an arm to his shoulder and waited for her to take a position on her new perch. "They leave in the morning. Wait by Reg's tent until he calls for you."

He sent one last image to her and propelled her into flight. He watched her glide through the trees, avoiding the branches and leaves with ease, before settling on a branch near Reg's tent.

Once satisfied the hawk understood what he asked of her, Bane glanced at the bush to his left. "You can come out now, Red."

His lips lifted into a smirk when the little girl let out a gasp. He heard her wrestle with the greenery before stumbling from the bush and landing at his feet. Bane gave a low chuckle and held out a hand to her. "No need to hurt yourself. There's no fire anywhere."

He helped the redhead to her feet and picked a leaf from her hair. The young Herbalist scowled at him and brushed the dirt and debris from her clothes. "How did you know I was there? I made sure the plants hid my steps."

Bane leaned down until he was at eye level with the five-year-old before answering her question. "Shifters have a sixth sense beyond the normal sight, sound, smell, taste, and touch. We can sense the auras and emotions of other living things. That's one way the Shifter Gift differs from your own Herbalist Gift. The Goddess gave each line of Magicae slightly different aspects of her power. The plants did their job, and I never heard you approach, but I did sense the cloud of emotions around you."

Gemma frowned as Bane straightened and stretched his back. "I have a cloud around me?" She looked at her arms and legs, searching for what Bane saw that she couldn't. After several failed attempts, she tried to twist in such a way that she could look at her back before giving up altogether. She looked at Bane with an accusatory glance. "Are you lying?"

Bane smiled and shook his head. "No, Red. I wouldn't do that to you."

"Prove it." Gemma crossed her arms in front of her and stared him down.

Bane's smile faded and his eyes softened. "It's as if green light emanates from within you. On our way to Lockewater and in the city itself, I saw everything from fear to pride to happiness within that green light. Your different emotions cause the light to form patterns, influence its brightness, and changes how green it looks. Throughout our travels together, I noticed how soft the light could be when you engage with the plants and how harsh it could flash when you felt fear. But I never saw the dim blue-green color of sadness that clings to you now."

Gemma's eyes turned glassy as tears gathered in her gray eyes. She hung her head and attempted to wipe the tears away, avoiding Bane's steady gaze.

Bane kneeled in the grass next to her, so they were at eye level again. He used a hand to lift the girl's chin and wipe a tear from her cheek. "It's just you and me, Red. Why are you so sad?" His eyes never left her face as she struggled for words.

A memory flashed in Bane's mind of his Da shortly after his Ma died.

*They were in the woods at a base camp they set up to ward off the chill and fear of the night. His Da had gone to find food, leaving the silent little boy to tend the fire.*

*But when he returned, the fire was reduced to embers and ash.*

*Bane lifted his head when Gar crashed through the underbrush, but let it drop when he realized who it was. His limbs felt like lead, and he knew his joints were stiff from sitting still for so long. Little children weren't meant to stay motionless for more than a few moments at a time. He remembered how numb and indifferent he'd been after losing his Ma.*

*It was as if something had ripped all the color from his world. Every aura around him was muted and even freedom on the wing couldn't clear the fog that surrounded him.*

*He'd expected his Da to yell or express his disappointment in how incapable his son was, not performing the one duty asked of him.*

*Instead, Gar dropped the rabbits he carried and went to work, stoking what was left of their fire in silence. When a modest flame, strong and steady burned in the shallow pit, his Da had kneeled next to him.*

*Bane avoided looking at him until the silence between them stretched so far he couldn't bear it. When he looked at his Da, the usual warm brown tones Bane associated with his Da's aura were replaced by angry burnt orange flashes of color. He'd held a hand out to the man that was a safe harbor in a wordless invitation.*

*His Da hadn't hesitated and pulled him in for a tight embrace.*

Looking back, Bane knew those flashes of light were the concern and fear Gar felt for him at that moment. His Da thought there was potential for him to lose both his wife and son at once. Gar's aura eventually returned to the tones of brown he was used to, but Bane never forgot how the emotions of others presented to him.

He opened his arms to the little girl and breathed easier when she took the invitation and wrapped her slight frame around his shoulders. He held her as she cried and waited for her sobs to ease. Once Gemma quieted and her heaving chest was reduced to shuddering breaths, Bane asked, "Do you miss your Ma?"

He waited as the girl stuttered and restarted several times. She took a moment to gather her thoughts and spoke in a low voice. "Yes, I miss Momma, but I miss Daddy, too. But everyone hates Daddy." She wiped her nose and gave a sniffle "They say he's why my Momma left me." Her voice broke on her last words and sobs racked her frame once more.

"Shh," Bane murmured as he rubbed her back. The Shifter held her close and rocked her back and forth. He waited for her sobs to subside before whispering, "Go on."

Gemma sniffled again. "Daddy wouldn't hurt me, would he?"

Bane's arms tightened around her. "Only your Da can give you that answer."

Gemma stiffened and pulled away from him. Her face was splotchy from crying, and horror shone in her gray orbs. "You believe the same bad things about Daddy." Her voice was scratchy, but her accusatory tone hit him like a wagon all the same.

"Red, I can only speak from what I've seen. My experience with your Da was not a pleasant one. He tried to hurt me and our friends. But it's hard for me to believe he would hurt you. And the only way to truly know would be to ask him. That's all I meant."

Gemma's eyes flashed, but she nodded, unwilling to keep arguing.

Bane studied her as the bright green flashes disappeared from the cloud around her and were replaced with the same dim blue-green color as before. He frowned when her gray eyes met his and their hollowness engulfed him.

"Is there anything else troubling you?" Bane asked, knowing something else plagued the little girl.

"Why does everybody leave me?" Gemma's hollow eyes bored into his, daring him to answer.

Bane sighed. The little girl still didn't understand the ways of their world. "Shucks, Red. We didn't abandon you. At least not in the way you think we did. Yes, we left to fight for our friends and our people, but that doesn't mean we weren't coming back."

"But you could've never come back." Gemma frowned. "I wasn't there to help and you could've gotten hurt."

"Red, I know you don't understand, but you will one day. You're hurting and can only see from your perspective, but that's okay. Just remember how much your loved ones care for you. Even when you feel alone, we are always right here inside your heart." Bane placed a gentle hand on her collarbone.

Bane watched as a single tear ran down Gemma's cheek and she didn't wipe it away. He looked into her eyes and watched some of the vibrance return. Sensing a change in her emotions, Bane expanded his observations to take in the little girl in her entirety.

The dim blue-green shifted slowly, but Bane blinked when he saw some of her aura shimmer. Thinking he was seeing things, he looked again and inhaled sharply. The shimmering spread until most of Gemma's soft green light twinkled with an ethereal shine.

Bane's eyebrows knitted with concern as he tucked away his observations for later. He had a feeling they would be important when he considered the occurrence later. A glance to the west confirmed he needed to get going if he wanted to make it to Heimat by morning.

Gemma was still struggling with the sentiment Bane was trying to convey. Her face scrunched as Bane lifted his hand and placed it on her arm. "You are a wonder, Gemma. Never forget that. But you're young and need time to develop your skills and control." His eyes hardened. "Hold on to your innocence as long as possible. I need to leave before the sun sets completely." He held a hand up when she opened her mouth to protest. "Please, Red. I have to do my duty; don't make this harder than it has to be. You'll see your Ma soon enough."

His last words gave her pause. She gripped his arm with trembling hands. "Momma?"

"Aye, she made it to the Circus before the battle began. Your Ma warned Duncan of the attack, or so I'm told. She's at the lake settlement with the others."

Gemma's eyes widened, and a sob escaped her throat. She threw her arms around Bane as tears leaked from her eyes again. Bane picked her up and swung her in an attempt to lighten the mood. He recognized the little girl was over-whelmed with emotions which manifested in all the tears. But the promise of seeing her Ma was meant to cheer her up and distract her from Bane's leaving.

He set her on her feet and gave her one last hug. "Chin up, Red. Soon enough, I'll be back and we can work on harnessing some of your skills. People can be cruel when they're scared or unwilling to understand someone else's point of view. Let their words roll off you like water because they don't understand your Da as you do." Bane put a hand into the coat Reg lent him and pulled out the feather he'd saved from when he'd Shifted to speak with Reg and the others. He offered it to the little girl. "This feather means we'll always be connected. Keep it in your pocket and if you're ever in trouble, grip it tight and I'll come find you. Deal?"

"Deal." Gemma took the feather with careful hands and put it in her pocket, making sure to close it before looking back at him. "I'll do my best to ignore the bullies." Before Bane could respond, Gemma threw her arms around his neck and gave him one last squeeze. "Safe flight, Bane." She held a pinky out to him with an expectant expression. "Promise I'll see you at the lake?"

"Promise," Bane said, extending his pinky to hers and giving it a shake.

Gemma flashed him a dazzling smile and skipped towards the camp, stopping once to look back and wave.

Bane waved his goodbye and watched her disappear down the path. *The resilience of children.* He thought to himself and turned to the south. He dropped the coat Reg had lent him and delved within to find the string that led to his avian form. With a pull, he felt his falcon form settle on his bones.

His body mass shrunk and his skin itched as feathers began poking through. Soon enough, a falcon sat where Bane had stood. He ruffled his wings and took off, beelining for the town of Heimat, where everything had gone wrong.

As he flew, Bane's thoughts returned to Gemma's strange aura and the déjà vu that came with it.

*Where have I seen that before?*

# Chapter Seven

*D*ays like these make me wish I was a fire Crafter. Zeke thought to himself as he pulled his layers close. He was used to having his wind Craft turn his blood to ice, but the cold this far north was unlike anything he'd experienced before.

And he hated it.

Rae and Luc were quick to point out the beauty in the frozen landscape and the peacefulness of nature's slower pace. But all Zeke saw was death and desolation. He longed for the hustle and bustle of warmer weather or even the reliable coziness of Heimat.

Anything but this awful chill deep in his bones.

Zeke let out a sigh and frowned when his breath turned to smoke. "Fuckin' cold," he muttered. His whole body shivered, and he rubbed his hands on his arms in a futile attempt to warm himself up. He kept walking, knowing that standing still wouldn't do him any favors.

As he marched through the camp, his thoughts returned to his conversation with Luc. His heart went out to both her and Damien and the pain they were experiencing on their own. Luc's outburst had come as a shock, because she never broke down like that. It meant she and Damien were struggling more than they let on.

And Zeke was appalled he hadn't noticed.

He knew the four of them had been in a weird place since leaving Verdencia. After the battle, they had taken time to reconnect and recover together, but now it almost felt like they tiptoed around each other. Hence why he never noticed how much two of his dearest friends were hurting. He needed to rectify this situation as soon as he could.

Which was why he didn't let himself stop at the various fires dotting the camp. He kept his eyes peeled for Chiara, hoping Damien's mother would know where to find her son.

"Someone's on a mission." Came an even-toned voice from behind him.

Zeke kept the frustration from his face and turned to whomever he'd walked past. Upon seeing Juno, the elephant Shifter, he made his way back to clasp hands with the older man.

"Sorry, J. I have a lot on my mind and wasn't paying enough attention to the world around me. I didn't mean to be rude."

J's brown, elephant eyes studied the flustered way Zeke responded, and the tense set to his body. He raised a hand to wave him off. "Don't worry about it. I think everyone has a lot on their minds these days. Anything I can help with?"

Zeke's eyes softened at the Shifter's question. This was what Zeke treasured the most about their community. The way they supported and looked after one another. He felt a twinge of regret at the way he stormed through the camp, recognizing others would've offered their help given the chance.

"Have you seen Damien this morning?"

J frowned and took a moment to think. "I can't say I have. Betsy was rounding up some archers to hunt for game and replenish her stores. Maybe she recruited him to help?"

Before Zeke could respond, something pelted them from the right.

J didn't hesitate and leaned down to gather snow as fast as he could. From his position on the ground, he looked up at the younger man with a glint in his eye. "Well, don't just stand there. Get down here and help me. We're under attack."

Zeke's reaction was visceral as he dropped to J's level, not quite understanding what was happening. He took a couple of deep breaths and scanned the area until he found their assailants.

"Geez, J. Give a guy a warning. I thought you meant an actual attack." He made to stand, but J yanked him back down and thrust a handful of tightly packed snowballs into his arms.

"No, no, no. You are staying here and helping me. You can at least hold them if you're not going to make more." J's tone left no room for argument as his hands worked like lightning to create more snowballs.

Zeke pulled his eyes from the furious pace of the older Shifter and glanced at the two young girls up the path. Eva and Wren were replenishing their own stores as fast as they could, only determination shining on their young faces.

The girls were posted behind two large oak trees, only visible when they bent down to gather more snow to form into missiles. They impressed him with their focus and drivenness in preparing for the retaliation bound to come.

Zeke couldn't help but crack a smile, his troubles forgotten as he became swept up in J's enthusiasm and the girls' determination. He leaned towards J and murmured, "What's our plan of attack?"

J flashed him a surprised grin. "We need to find a way around the trees, otherwise they'll just pick us off as we get closer."

"Leave that to me." Zeke used his wind Craft to levitate the snowball at the top of the pile in his arms.

"Excellent." This time, J's smile was wolfish, pleased with the turn of events. The girls would stand little chance with a wind Crafter against them. J made a few more snowballs and gave Zeke a nod.

Zeke pulled at the winds in his core until one came loose. It was too hard to control it with the snowballs in his arms, so he set them on the ground at his feet. Once his arms were free, he moved into the familiar positions he used to control the wind.

He bent his knees and held his hands in front of him, palms up to the sky. He lowered one arm and guided the wind to wrap around him. Zeke felt the icy power in his veins and let it permeate every part of him. The chill in his bones from the cold and snow dwarfed in comparison to the iciness of his wind Craft.

It was something he would never tire of feeling. He motioned for J to throw one snowball with his chin. Zeke watched it sail towards the trees and sent the wind in his hands after it. He aimed it at the base of the tree, giving the girls a warning of what was to come.

"Keep them coming, J. Give me five seconds in between and it'll be over by the time we get through all these." Zeke instructed, already reaching within for the next wind from his core.

J's response was to pick up another snowball and lob it towards his charges.

Zeke took a step forward and slammed the wind as hard as he could, propelling the snowball around the tree and into Eva's back. The men laughed when they heard her frustrated cry and readied themselves for a counterattack.

The girls' response came fast and furious as they pelted as many snowballs as they could.

Zeke was impressed by their aim and didn't use the wind to shield them, taking the hits they deserved. It was all part of the game and only fair to reward the girls for their persistence.

One hit J in the face and he heard both the girls scream in triumph. Deciding it was time to get on with it, Zeke called, "Alright, J. Let's make them wish they had found a different target."

J gave a grunt, snowball already in hand and poised to fire. "About time," he answered, his tone warm to soften his words.

Zeke reached inward again, this time pulling out one of the longer strands of wind. It would be harder to control once outside of his core, but it would be easier to get into a rhythm if he didn't have to keep pulling strands from within.

He took the bulky wind and forced it to bend around him. Once it circled his waist, he coaxed it through one hand, raising the other like a guillotine. When J launched the snowball, Zeke did the same with the wind and counted in his head. After three seconds, he made a slashing movement with his free hand and gritted his teeth, the hand by his waist closing around the wind from his core. After a couple of seconds, he let go again, propelling the strand of wind after J's next snowball.

Zeke let J do the aiming, trusting the wind to follow its arc and hit its intended target. He could hear the girls' shrieks of laughter as their snowballs found their marks. Before he knew it, Eva and Wren made their last push, rushing the two men and whaling snowballs as they ran.

Zeke felt the wind escape his grasp as he dissolved into laughter. The two girls were reduced to giggles once they tackled J, and he went down to the ground in a flurry of dramatics. Zeke watched the three wrestle as he caught his breath.

It was good for him to practice his Craft and build his endurance, but he'd misjudged how much his environment would affect him. The cold was the only thing he could think of as to why he felt so drained. He took in a deep breath and winced at the cold.

The wintry air was a harsh reminder of what Zeke was doing before Eva and Wren mounted their attack. His stomach dropped as his thoughts returned to Damien and the pain his friend was in. He leaned over, placing his hands on his knees, and forced himself to breathe.

After a couple of minutes, he looked up to see J's brown eyes studying him. The two girls stilled, their heads moving between the two men as they recognized the shift of energy in the air. They shared a look before Eva offered.

"What's wrong, J? Is Zeke okay?" Her voice was soft as she stared up at J from her position on the ground.

J gripped both girls by one hand and helped them stand. "Zeke is looking for Damien. It's important that he finds him as soon as possible."

"We saw Damien! This morning, we saw him at breakfast." Wren piped up with a smug smile, happy with herself for remembering a key piece of information.

Zeke's ears perked at the little girl's insight. "Did you see where he went after he finished his food?" He asked the two girls.

Wren crinkled her nose and Eva closed her eyes. Zeke was touched by how hard the little girls were trying to help. He gave them a few moments to think.

Eva opened her eyes and glanced at J. She motioned for him to lean down and whispered something in his ear. The Shifter frowned before smoothing his features into a neutral expression. When she pulled away from him, he gripped her arm to keep her close and whispered into her ear.

Zeke tore his gaze from the pair when he felt eyes on him. He met Wren's deep, jewel-toned blue eyes and smiled when she shrugged with a wry grin. "They do this sometimes. You get used to it."

He chuckled at her matter-of-fact tone and the easy way she accepted Eva's and J's bond. "What do you think they're talking about?"

Wren's eyes searched his face and Zeke held his hand out to her, guessing she was looking for the reassurance she could trust him. She took his hand, but kept her eyes on his face. Zeke waited until she found what she was looking for and spoke.

"Eva gets anxious sometimes. Her Papa would say things for her, but J told her she needs to try. So they made a deal. When Eva needs to, she can practice with J." The little girl narrowed her eyes. "But you can't tell anybody else. Eva doesn't want everybody to know." She held out her hand, pinky out toward the wind Crafter expectantly.

Zeke gripped her pinky with his and nodded, doing his best to remain solemn and keep the amused grin from his lips. *She's going to be a force. She's exactly what Eva needs in a friend.* Everybody understood Eva was shy and Zeke knew J was the right person to offer support while pushing her out of her comfort zone.

But Wren would do everything she could to protect and look out for her friend. Wren was the bold to Eva's caution and they would grow and learn so much from each other as time went on.

"Damien went into the forest after breakfast, but it wasn't to hunt. At least he left before the hunters did and never went to the chuckwagon where the bows and arrows. I can take you to the spot where he entered the woods." Eva took Zeke's hand before he could respond and pulled him towards the picnic tables where everyone took meals.

Wren grabbed his other hand and urged them into a run, shrieking with delight. They flew past the tables to an opening in the trees that led to a hidden path. Zeke pulled the girls to a stop and into a firm embrace.

"Thanks, Eva. This means a lot to me." He pulled back to meet the little Forger's eyes. "Thank you for speaking up. Keep your eye on Wren and head back to camp; I'll go on alone from here."

Eva's eyes searched his, and she asked, "Is Damien okay?"

Zeke could only answer with the truth, unwilling to lie to the children, but wanting to present it in a way that wouldn't terrify them. "Damien is struggling and needs a friend right now. But I'm hoping I can be that friend to him. Sometimes we all need a little help."

Both girls nodded at Zeke's words.

"J always says asking for help is a strength, not a weakness." Eva squeezed Zeke's hand before grabbing Wren's and pulling her back the way they came. "Come on, Wren. Let's go see if we can catch J by surprise again. It'll be easier without Zeke there to help him."

"Bye, Zeke!" Wren called behind her before letting loose what sounded like a war cry.

Zeke shook his head as his lips tipped up into a grin at the girls' tenacity in catching their mentor unaware. Their innocence and joy provided a needed contrast to everything the Circus had been dealing with since fleeing Heimat. It provided a small spark of hope that reminded him of their purpose.

He would fight for those little girls' futures with everything he had.

But his next battle was for his friend against the unseen demons Damien faced.

He used an arm to move branches and leaves out of the way as he headed deeper into the expanse of trees. *I'm coming for you, Dame.*

Zeke wandered the woods for what felt like an hour. He stopped to take a break and gather his bearings. Frustration built up inside as he gazed at the unending forest in front of him.

*There's gotta be another way.*

Zeke leaned against the tree and wracked his brain for an answer. A breeze made the branches around him sway and with little thought, he called it to his fingertips. Zeke let it slip through his hands, feeling the familiar way it glided over his skin like water. His focus drifted from thoughts of Damien to the feeling of the breeze beneath his fingers. An image flashed in his mind and caused him to tighten his grip on the breeze.

And just like that, the image was gone. Zeke forced himself to take a deep breath and loosen his grip on the wild wind, letting it flow once more. Like clockwork, the image flashed in his mind and he caught a whiff of pine, the damp smell of snow, and a faint trace of spearmint.

Zeke's eyes widened at the scent he associated with Damien. *Could it be?*

Too soon, the scent was gone, and the breeze slipped from his hands. Zeke had no doubt the smell of spearmint came from the dried herb his friend always kept on his person. Chiara always slipped bundles of the pleasant-smelling herb into his pockets to improve focus and keep away headaches. What had started when Damien was a child had become a habit in adulthood.

Zeke swiveled his head from side to side, trying to determine what direction the breeze originated from. Unable to know for certain, the wind Crafter paused and closed his eyes, willing another breeze to come his way. It took a couple of minutes, but Zeke felt the soft chill of a winter wind ruffle his silvery strands of hair. He closed his eyes and let the river of air engulf him.

His eyes flashed open as the faint scent of spearmint tickled his nose. He held a hand up and followed the wind in the direction it came from. Zeke let his fingers guide him as he kept his eyes on the forest in front of him, avoiding trees and rocks.

When the wind ran out, Zeke did his best to follow its assumed trajectory, hoping he would find Damien soon. He continued on in this way, only pausing to reorient himself when a fresh breeze blew his way, until he reached a clearing.

Zeke let out a sigh of relief when he spotted Damien's hunched form on a large rock in the middle of the meadow. He took a step toward his friend, but stopped before he broke the tree line. He studied Damien and felt his heart break at how fragile and defeated he looked.

Zeke's eyes blazed as he strode out of the woods and straight for his fellow acrobat. Damien barely acknowledged his friend's presence before Zeke knelt and pulled him into a tight embrace. Damien stiffened and didn't hug Zeke back, patting the other man's shoulder.

Zeke clenched his jaw but refused to release his friend. "I won't stop until you hug me back."

Zeke felt the moment Damien took his words to heart.

All the tension drained from his friend's frame and strong arms gave him a squeeze. Zeke held on a little longer, silently giving Damien permission to take as much comfort as he needed.

Damien was the first to pull away, rubbing at his eyes and taking a few shuddering breaths. He refused to meet Zeke's concerned gaze until Zeke put a hand on his shoulder.

"Come on Dame, talk to me."

Damien's expression was unreadable as he considered his words. "You spoke to Luc." His tone turned the statement into an accusation.

Zeke scrunched his eyebrows together and noticed the way Damien clenched both fists and leaned away from him. He got the impression Damien wished he were anywhere but here.

"Is it a problem if I did?" Zeke asked, raising one eyebrow.

Damien looked away instead of answering.

"Luc isn't the enemy," Zeke said, letting silence fill the air between them. Damien didn't seem ready to talk about what was going on with him, but supporting his friend didn't mean forcing him to talk.

Sometimes a physical presence was the only support a person needed.

While he waited, Zeke's eyes never left Damien's figure. He watched as the acrobat unclenched his hands, moving as if it took great effort to produce that simple movement. Once his hands were released, Damien dropped his arms, so they hung limply at his sides and pulled his knees to his chest. Damien rested his head on his knees and a shudder went through his whole body.

Zeke watched in horror as he took in the husk of the person Damien used to be. It was clear he had caught Damien in a moment of vulnerability, and he was unsure of what would be the best course of action. If what Luc said was true, Damien had been like this ever since the battle. Zeke noticed he'd been a little withdrawn as of late, but chalked it up as being Damien's way of processing everything from the past couple of months.

If he'd known how deep Damien spiraled, he would've pushed him to open up earlier. This was his opportunity to help his friend find his way back from the despair and horror he was trapped in. But Zeke needed the right words to give him a lifeline.

"Rae and I were terrified the entire time we were separated from the Circus. We reminded each other not to think about it, otherwise, it would drive us crazy. The worry and fear of something happening to the ones we love the most were enough to cripple us. But we held each other up and were strong for each other when we needed it." Zeke held his hands out in a gesture of peace, but didn't attempt to touch the other man. "I was reminded today that asking for help isn't a weakness, it's a strength." Zeke felt a small smile on his lips as he quoted Eva. "I can take it, Dame. We've been through too much to give up on each other now."

Damien swallowed and let out a long sigh, the tension draining from his entire body. After a few moments, he said, "I don't know if I can go through it again. I don't know if I'm willing to kill again." Damien still wouldn't meet Zeke's eyes, and Zeke could tell the effort it took for him to admit that. He stayed silent, hoping time would give Damien a chance to collect his thoughts and continue.

Damien lifted his head and spread his legs out in front of him, one finger drawing lines in the snow next to the rock he perched on.

"I never want to kill again. The faces of those I shot haunt me every night. With arrows sticking out of their backs, chests, and necks and blood running from their wounds. The sounds and the smells... Those soldiers were only following orders. They were wives and fathers and sons and daughters and I killed them. How am I supposed to live with myself?" Damien's voice shook as the words poured out of him. "But then again, how could I not? How do I sit by and watch my friends go to war without me? What am I supposed to do? It's a war between my principles and my morals, and I don't know the answer."

Damien hung his head as his hands shook with emotion.

"The ability to take a life isn't something to be celebrated. And no one will think less of you for refusing to do so," Zeke offered.

"But that's the catch, isn't it? If I kill someone, it's a mark on my soul, but if I don't, it's a slash to my heart."

Silence hung in the air between the two men after Damien's confession. This was the moment Zeke realized he was out of his league in trying to help Damien through this. It was an impossible situation with no right answer.

Damien ran a shaky hand through his hair and let out a breathy laugh. "Do you remember the first show we ever did?"

Zeke shot him a curious look. "The one where Luc fell?" Damien nodded. "What about it?"

"Do you remember that meeting we were forced to have with Duncan?"

Zeke furrowed his brows. "Vaguely, but just that we had one, not what was said in it."

Damien gave a terse nod. "Well, I don't remember much, but one thing Duncan said has always stuck with me. He told us we could never forget our priorities. Luc fell that night and we all froze. The only reason nothing terrible happened was because the nets were still up."

Zeke strained to remember that conversation and where Damien was going with this.

"He told us there would come a time when the nets wouldn't be there, when we had done the routine so many times we became convinced we didn't need any. But no matter how many times we performed a routine flawlessly, there would always be the possibility of danger. One wrong grab or flip could result in someone getting seriously injured. And the only way to make sure we were ready for that possibility was if our priorities were straight."

Understanding lit in Zeke's eyes. "That's right, and he went on to preach about how our safety meant more than anything. We were risking our lives to give cover to the Circus and save the Magicae, but some risks weren't worth it."

"Exactly."

Zeke shot another confused look at his friend. "But what does that have to do with anything, Dame?"

"Because, Zeke, that's what has to happen here. Our safety was always the top priority; more important than staying hidden or performing the routine." He toyed with the edge of his sleeve, still not meeting Zeke's eyes. He whispered, "I need to decide what my top priority is. My soul, or my heart. I have to put one first and it's killing me. But it has to be done if I want any chance of surviving this." Damien finally met Zeke's gaze with hollow eyes.

Zeke couldn't help himself as he leaned forward and put a hand on Damien's shoulder. "That can't be the only way, Dame. You shouldn't have to choose between your soul and your heart. You don't have to kill to prove your loyalty to us, and you don't have to sell your soul for me to know your heart."

Zeke willed Damien to understand as the sound of hoofbeats made them both look up. Zeke sighed as Damien made to stand up and meet Rae.

The moment was gone.

He could only hope his words had been enough to start the wheels turning and put his friend on a path towards healing.

# Chapter Eight

Naya pulled the hood of her coat down to cover more of her face as she moved through the streets of Fernwen. The sun set hours ago, leaving the city draped in torchlight. But Naya wasn't taking any chances.

She'd left the twins snuggled in all the blankets she could find on the corner of the Midnight Market, near enough to the bonfires for a bit of warmth but far enough to avoid detection.

At least, she hoped they were.

Being quick and getting back to them was the only surefire way to keep them safe. She didn't want to part from them, but visiting Ryker was too dangerous for the twins. Not when they were both Forgers and had murdered Battaglia with a flick of the wrist.

Best not to bring them around to the guardhouse where she'd find Ryker, the only other person she truly trusted in the city. But the Guard recruited Ryker once he turned thirteen, and it was a hard transition for both of them.

The last time they talked, she promised him she wouldn't visit the guard house again. He'd be furious, but some promises needed to be broken.

Ryker took her under his wing after her mom died, helping her navigate life as an orphan and teaching her skills she'd need to survive on the street. He was the older brother she never had and the sole reason she survived those first few years. Their bond was thicker than blood, and that was saying something for occupants of the Rook.

Fernwen was a capital city divided. It was located where the Mantaga River split into three branches, named for the three faces of their deity. The Huntress flowed to the Southwest and the heart of the Southern Woodlands. The Prophetess veered to the Southeast and the sea with several channel islands in its center. Rumor was the Prophetess placed them there to test the abilities of those striving to champion her kingdom of waterways. The last branch was named for the Goddess herself and flowed almost directly south of the city before reaching the sea.

Where the river broke into its three branches, three islands connected the banks of the river and its branches with a series of bridges. The Pearl of the Goddess was the old temple on the island lying in the arm of the Goddess. The island was nicknamed the Pearl, and only priestesses or initiates were allowed on it, with no bridges connecting it to the mainland. Only the most influential and important people in the city were invited there to worship. The other two islands held the Keep, where the government ruled from, and quarters for the staff and government officials.

Naya had never been across the bridges that connected the two government islands to the city, and she wasn't planning to.

The government was why she was in this predicament. She and Ryker became assigned to Battaglia three years ago when Myra passed a bill to get as many orphans off the streets as she could.

But words on paper were a far cry from the reality the dictator created.

Myra gave her newly appointed force of guardians complete control over the fates of hundreds of orphans residing across the Rook and South Bank. Each of them was given a number and someone to report to for all their basic needs. It was a publicity stunt because Myra and her enforcers were losing favor. Even Naya knew that, and she'd been seven. The streets were basically empty of orphans, as Myra intended, but not because they were well-fed and sleeping in warm beds. The guardians pocketed the coin for those things long ago while most orphans were sent to the Flesh Markets to be sold and traded like animals.

Naya had witnessed a lot in her ten years, but the Flesh Markets would always make her skin crawl. The one time she dared Ryker to take her there was a memory she'd sooner forget, but it was etched into her brain like a brand. There was no way to wash away the horror of children in cages, naked and shivering and crying out for someone to save them. The sight of leering men and women examining each poor soul had shattered what little innocence she had left. She knew the only reason it hadn't become her own fate was because of Ryker. In those first months after the bill came into effect, the pair took turns keeping watch should Battaglia go back on the deal Ryker made with her. He convinced her investing in the two orphans would give her more coin in the long run as opposed to a lump sum from a market sale. As long as they kept providing her with coin or drugs, they could keep their autonomy.

It was a damning deal, but it kept them alive and out of the hands of the wicked.

But Naya knew it was only a matter of time before Battaglia's death was discovered and reported. And that meant a new guardian would be appointed to her. Ryker was exempt as he now served on the City Watch, but Naya knew he had sent most of his salary to Battaglia on Naya's behalf. He was her biggest protector even now.

Shortly after Ryker reported to his first shift as a member of the City Watch, Naya stumbled upon the twins in a deserted part of the Midnight Market. Her heart broke knowing they had been left as offerings for the devils of the city. The pair had stared her down, brandishing broken kitchen knives and stiff grimaces. Their wills to survive coupled with their entrancing ice-blue eyes convinced her this was a moment where she could do something good. She did for them what Ryker had done for her and became their protector.

It took a month for them to warm to her, but now she couldn't imagine life without them. The fact they murdered the woman sheltering them from ending up in those cages was a slight hiccup she and Ryker could overcome. They would put their heads together and everything would be fine.

Naya glanced down both sides of the alley before stepping up and sounding three loud raps across the top of it. Her thoughts kept going in circles, always returning to the idea that once she saw Ryker everything would right itself.

She raised her fist to knock again, and the door flew open. Ryker scowled when he saw her, but pulled her in and glanced down both sides of the alley, shutting the door behind her.

A smile tugged at the corner of Naya's lips, despite Ryker's obvious frustration. She threw her arms around him and hugged him tight.

Ryker wiggled out of her grasp and held a finger to his lips. He took her by the elbow and led her to a back room coated in a layer of thick dust. He maneuvered them so they were out of sight of the doorway and motioned for Naya to crouch next to him.

"Why are you here?" Ryker hissed through his teeth.

Naya met his eyes and swallowed. "I know I'm not supposed to be here, but we're in trouble."

Ryker's eyes narrowed. "You mean you and I are in trouble? Or you and the twins?"

Naya shot him a look. "What's your problem? Jealous that I found friends after you left? Or is it something else?" Her voice rose as terror took hold of her heart. This meeting wasn't what she'd envisioned for untangling the mess she and the twins were in.

"Shh." Ryker chided, as his attention went to the open doorway. "Just because nobody comes back here doesn't mean they won't start. I wanted you to clarify if I was in danger so I could better understand what's happening. I figured it was bad for you to come by so soon after the market."

Naya blushed. Market days were the only time they could see each other without raising suspicion. It was an opportunity to catch up and gather supplies while forgetting about the circumstances threatening to overwhelm them. She'd seen him two days ago and left after accusing him of becoming like all the other City Watch they hated. Naya ducked her head. "Sorry, Ryker. It's too hard to see you in that uniform," she whispered, inclining her head to the dark blue clothes he wore.

Ryker's eyes softened, and he reached for one of her hands. "I know, Naya, but this was the easiest way to keep both of us from the Flesh trade. Battaglia was getting restless. We both know it was this or never see each other again." He squeezed and caught her gaze. "Tell me what's going on."

Naya launched into her story about coming home to Battaglia and what happened in the end. Her words came out in a rush, and she felt her cheeks flush with anger as she recalled what the old woman did to her.

"And good riddance is what I say. The old lady had it coming. If it wasn't the twins, it would've been someone else." Her tone revealed the relief she felt at being rid of the battleaxe of a woman.

The blood drained from Ryker's face and his fingers carefully danced over the bruises Naya couldn't hide. "So Hawk and Aurora are Magicae?"

Naya pulled back as if she was seeing Ryker in a new light, her expression hesitant. Every instinct told her to leave before she said something she'd regret. *But this is Ryker. I can trust Ryker.* She studied the boy and hesitated again. Every inch of his body was tense and he wouldn't meet her eyes, the blood still absent from his usual warm skin tones. "I—,"

Something crashed outside the doorway before she could say more. Ryker pushed her behind him and crept to get a better view. Voices sounded from the door to the alley.

"Yea, I know. Can't believe it me'self. Nobody thought Battaglia would ever die. But what does that have to do with the new orders?" The first voice was loud and rumbled with warmth.

"Well, did you hear how she died?" The second voice had a thin metallic tone that made it hard to make out what it was saying.

"She was strangled, eh?"

"Not exactly. There was metal found crushing her windpipe, as if somebody took the necklace she was wearing and used it like a rope."

The first voice boomed with laughter. "We got ourselves a Magicae hunt! Goddess, it's been how many years? Best news I've heard all day." The voices trailed away from the alley as the speakers moved further into the City Watch bunkhouse.

Naya felt her heart drop into her stomach like a stone. She made to stand and marched to the doorway; she needed to get to the twins. A hand on her shoulder made her pause.

"I'll do my best to stall, but you need to get them out of the city. They won't stop until they've found those kids." Ryker's eyes were filled with sincerity and fear.

Naya gave him a nod and pulled him close. The two young people took comfort from one another before pulling apart.

"Thanks, Ryker. Don't get killed." She shot him a smirk when she repeated the words they'd said to each other over and over again.

"Don't get killed yourself." He replied, completing the mantra despite the fear still pooling in his green eyes. He ushered her to the door and, after peeking around the corner, held the door open to the alley.

Naya wasted no time, squeezing his arm once before disappearing into the night.

Naomi shivered in the dank dungeon and let out the breath she'd been holding. It formed a cloud before dissipating into the cold air of her cell. Winter was the worst in the belly of the Keep as the stone felt every chill of the surrounding area. The Keep was the old castle Kamore royalty once resided in and was built on the biggest of the three islands in the middle of the Mantaga River. It was ancient and a symbol of a bygone era. Its stones held more secrets and memories than anywhere in the country.

And Naomi knew she was just one more for the stones to hold.

Unless she found a way out of this waking nightmare.

Myra was no fool, but she was arrogant. There had to be a way she could use that to her advantage. *If only I could get her to walk the gardens with me again.*

Naomi shuddered at the reminder of the regular contact she'd endured with the dictator she hated for years after her world shattered. But at least if she could leave the cell and its chains, she might have a chance at leaving it all behind her.

*And what about Mallick?*

Naomi clenched a fist and muffled her frustrated scream. Mallick was why Naomi was never a flight risk in those early days after the Uprising. She refused to do anything that could jeopardize the health and safety of her little boy.

Especially when he sometimes joined them on those strolls through the gardens.

Myra knew it was torture to be so close to the little boy and unable to treat him as her son. But the torture was worth seeing him. Even when he couldn't begin to understand the nightmare they were in.

But now... Mallick was a grown man with no idea of his true lineage. Maybe it was time for her to plant the seeds of doubt and drive a wedge between him and the woman he thought was his mother.

She bit her lip as her heart raced. Her hands dropped to her lap and the chains on her wrist rattled. The metal was so cold it burned her skin and limited the circulation to her extremities.

Naomi glanced at the door as her thoughts trampled through her exhausted brain. The glass of drugged water tempted her, and she averted her eyes. The fog was lifting from her mind, but withdrawal lurked just out of sight. She needed to think.

Myra was searching for Duncan based on the information she'd fed Mallick when he came to her last. She hadn't seen him since, but one word and he'd come running. He had the brashness and impatience of youth that meant he'd come as soon as she admitted they were all lies.

But when? When would she know the time was right to reveal who she was? Too soon, and Myra would have a chance to undo anything she set in motion. Too late, and her boy would never know the truth. And Mallick was their best chance at taking Myra unaware. If only she could find the words to turn him against the dictator.

*Goddess, give me guidance.* Her prayer was silent as she tucked her bony knees under her chin and closed her eyes.

She didn't want to fuck up her one chance at setting things right in the country she loved.

# Chapter Nine

Tyee blew out his breath in a huff as he scrubbed the floors of the greenhouse. He muttered curses and profanities to any face of the Goddess that would listen. Because there was no way he scrubbed another floor after the greenhouse.

Tota or whatever her name was had barely said two words to him before thrusting a bucket and a sponge into his hands and telling him to get to work. Every time he finished one room, Tota inspected it and, if satisfied, she'd point to the next room. If Tyee missed a spot, she clicked her tongue and told him to do it again.

He'd been scrubbing floors for almost two days now and couldn't stand to do another day of it. He'd tried to talk to the old woman and ask her questions, but she was more stubborn than Koko when he saw an apple tree. She'd either grunt or click her tongue, but refused to answer anything.

*Maddening old spinster. No wonder Fritz didn't want to come to the house, even if he could. The witch would've had him dusting while I scrubbed.* Tyee cracked a wry smile at the thought despite his sore back and wrinkled hands.

Moving his bucket for the last time, Tyee wiped the last of the dirt from the brick floor of the greenhouse and felt like collapsing. He braced himself with both hands and stretched his back out, cursing his aging body and the woman who put him through this.

With a grunt, he pushed himself up despite his protesting knees. Hunched over, he grabbed the bucket from his feet and turned to the entrance of the greenhouse to see the old woman smirking at him. Tyee glowered at her and made his way to her, a hitch in his step.

"It's done," he growled when he got within earshot of her.

"Maybe," said Tota as she brushed past him into the glass structure proper. She made a show of inspecting every inch of the place before turning back to the horseman. "It *is* done," she repeated his words back to him with another smirk. "About time."

Tyee snorted. "If this is how you treat all your students, no wonder they wanted nothing to do with you after they got what they needed. They grew tired of being your free labor and not learning about their birthright."

The old woman let out a cackle. "You speak as if you know me so well, boy, but you know nothing." She jammed a finger into his chest. "You'd do best to shut your mouth and listen."

Anger flashed in Tyee's chest at Tota's words. "I'm not a scared kid you can boss around as you like. I may not know much about you or your people, but I know a bully when I see one."

Tota scowled. "I don't make my students do housework so I get free labor. On the contrary, I test them on their mettle and meticulousness. To you, it was scrubbing floors, but to me, it was proving you have what it takes to master the runes and the power in your blood. Calling me a bully won't change the way I do things. I've been doing this too long to change my methods now."

Tyee felt a familiar wave of regret wash over him as Tota turned to exit the greenhouse through the door leading to her kitchen. He felt bad for making assumptions about the old woman and lashing out in anger. Tyee was frustrated with the lack of progress he'd made in learning about who he was, but that didn't give him license to take it out on his future mentor.

He started when the door closed shut behind her.

Tyee let out a sigh and picked up the bucket and its sponge. He looked around until he found a washbasin in the corner of the room. Walking over, he placed both inside and braced his hands on the stone structure. He took a moment to stretch his back before rubbing it with one hand. Spending two days hunched over on the floor differed vastly from spending two days in the saddle. It would take time for his muscles to loosen and recover from the strain.

With a shrug of his shoulders, Tyee lifted a hand and ran it through his dark hair. He felt the rough cut he had gotten in Verdencia and sighed inwardly. His hair was a mess, but it was better than having it in his face all the time.

The sound of the door swinging on its hinges made Tyee start. Tota's voice sounded from inside her kitchen. "I said you were done, didn't I? If you want supper, get in here and help me make the salad."

Tyee snapped to attention, hearing the impatience in the old woman's voice. He made his way to the door of the house but stopped to look back at the magnificence that was the old woman's glass house.

Tota's home was like those in the trees of Verdencia in that its heart was grown out of the trunk of an old, massive oak tree. But unlike the tree houses of Verdencia, Tota's home had structures attached to the main tree at its sides and opposite the front door in the back. The greenhouse was opposite the front door, made of panels of glass of all sizes. Most of the pieces were clear, but others were tinted blue and yellow and pink, giving the space an unearthly glow when the sun shone brightest. The glass and its colors were pretty, but what gave the glass house its charm was how it was constructed. The panels were not joined by stagnant lines of wood or metal, instead, they were held together with what seemed like roots of a tree, giving the house a patchwork of curving lines and jagged edges. It was a moving tapestry that even Tyee couldn't stop looking at

With one last look at the gorgeous structure, Tyee walked through the door and into the tree trunk, proper. It was hollowed out to house the enormous kitchen and hearth Tota needed for processing the plants she grew in the green-house and acted as a gathering place for guests. One side held the hearth and prep tables, while the other contained a massive table with two long benches in place of chairs. Tyee presumed this was where his lessons would take place. To the left and right of the kitchen sat rooms dedicated to housing others, complete with several bunks to accommodate students and guests alike. And lastly, the winding wooden staircase at the front of the trunk led to Tota's bedchamber and her personal library.

Tyee rinsed his hands in the washbasin near the door and looked at Tota expectantly.

She was stirring a pot at the hearth and directed Tyee to the table next to her. "Cut the greens and vegetables for the salad."

Tyee did as instructed, catching a delicious whiff from the hearth. He felt his mouth water at the thought of a warm meal. Tota left a sandwich out for him the previous night when he finished scrubbing the main floors of the first level. The sandwich was filling but not soul-soothing as the scent of the stew promised.

They worked in silence, Tyee chopping the vegetables as Tota adjusted the seasoning of the bubbling pot. Once satisfied, she moved to grab two bowls from a shelf and brought them to the table.

Tyee finished the salad and looked for something to serve it with.

"In the drawer to your left."

Tyee grabbed the flatware and salad and brought them to the table, taking a seat across from the old woman.

"Let's give the stew a moment more to settle while we enjoy some greens." Tota raised an eyebrow at him. "What happened to the man brimming with questions?"

Tyee flashed her a smirk and said, "Biding my time until I could catch you unaware."

The old woman let out a bark of laughter and shook her head. "You'll be waiting quite some time, then." A wicked grin graced her features. "I've been around too long to let a young pup like you catch me unaware. But alas, you're my first student since Hugo's youngest and I grow weary of silence. I will give you three questions tonight. One for each of our courses this evening."

Tyee furrowed his brows and considered her words.

"But I warn you, after we finish the salad from our plates, your opportunity is wasted."

Tyee glanced at both their bowls and blurted the question he'd been pondering since discovering he was to be sent to this old woman. "Why do you live so far away?" At Tota's puzzled look, he continued, "From Verdencia. Why do you live so far from the rest of your people?"

Understanding flashed in her eyes. "Ack. That viper of a queen gets no worship from me. I am content to leave them to the treetops and out of my hair."

Tyee considered her words. "I can understand the pull of solitude, but surely the dangers of the forest make you wary."

"Clever boy." Tota clucked her tongue at his way of asking another question through a suggestion. "Since it's in the same vein, I'll allow it. The forest is a friend to those who wish it well. Queen Ulla exploits this as much as everyone, but she's also vain. And running scared of people we once shared this world with. But disappearing doesn't do us any good, it only erases us from the world we once loved."

The old woman's words struck Tyee. There was a deep sorrow in her tone, belaying the weariness she felt with the world. Before Tyee could offer a response, Tota grabbed their empty plates and went to the pot on the hearth. She ladled the heavenly-smelling concoction into their used bowls, not bothering to dirty more dishes.

Tyee felt his mouth watering as he appreciated the old woman's practicality. Especially since he would be the one doing the dishes. Tota set their stew on the table and took her seat again. Tyee nodded his thanks and lifted the bowl to his mouth, inhaling the smell of something warm and soothing

"It tastes better than it smells." Tota croaked at him with a smirk.

Tyee chuckled and dug in with his spoon. The stew was filled with cubed vegetables from her greenhouse, chunks of meat, and an earthy broth flavored with comforting and homey spices. Tyee couldn't help himself from downing half the bowl before his next question came to mind. He chewed for a couple more minutes and mulled over how he wanted to ask the next question.

"The Elven call you Tota." The old woman grunted in response. "Fritz said your name was lost to time, so Tota became your new moniker. He said you are the oldest Elven on record and why you're revered as the best rune teacher they've ever seen."

Tota stared at him. "Ask a question or don't, boy, and stop expecting me to confirm or deny statements. It's not part of the deal."

Tyee lowered his gaze, knowing he'd pushed too hard. The old woman was giving him a chance; the last thing he needed was to alienate the only person willing to give him answers. He thrust down his pride and asked the question she'd least expect. "What's your real name?"

The old woman narrowed her eyes at him. After a moment, she returned to her stew as if ignoring him. Tyee waited, not taking his eyes off her.

"It's Andriette." Her voice was quiet, but when she met his eyes, hers glistened. "Nobody's asked me that in decades." She sighed. "But you of all people should call me Tota."

Tyee raised a brow. "And why is that?" He struggled to remember what Fritz said about the title of Tota.

"Because I'm your teacher and you would do well to do as you're told." She snapped and made to rise for the next course.

Tyee held out his hand to stop her. "That stew is the best thing I've had in weeks. Thank you." He grabbed her empty bowl and stood. "Let me get the next one."

Andriette nodded, saying, "I moved the apples to the front so they wouldn't burn."

Sure enough, the ceramic dish sat as far forward from the embers of the waning fire as possible. Tyee placed their dishes in the washbasin and grabbed two smaller bowls from the shelf. He took the lid off the dish to reveal two baked apples, dusted with what smelled like cinnamon and sugar. He used a spoon to put one in each bowl and brought them to the table.

"It's been years since I've had dessert."

Andriette clucked her tongue. "It's wrong to deny yourself the simplest of pleasures of this life. Moderation goes a long way in bringing joy and happiness to this world."

Tyee snorted. "You speak as if I had a choice. A lot has been going on in the world beyond the forest and sometimes simple pleasures are replaced with what's needed to survive."

"Then why are you here?" Her eyes were hard. "No one is making you stay. If you have more important things to do, then by all means, the door's right there."

Tyee glared over his dessert. "Trust me, I would leave if it was that simple."

"It is. You're the only one making it complicated."

Tyee's head pounded as he argued with the old woman. He rubbed his temple with the palm of his hand as Andriette fixed him with an accusing stare. "I have no choice if I want to make a difference for the people that gave me a home." Rae's face flashed in his mind. "I promised someone I'd get my answers and return to her. I need to learn about the Elven part of my heritage to understand what it all means."

Tyee turned his palm over and looked at the angry red lines that formed a rune on his skin. Andriette caught the mark and inhaled sharply. She yanked his left hand towards her and tilted it at different angles to get a better look at it.

When she met his gaze, she cursed, "Fjols. Don't tell me this woman you speak of bears the same mark." Taking in Tyee's shocked reaction, Andriette cursed again. "You fool. What have you done?" She released his hand with wild eyes.

Tyee was tongue-tied at the old woman's response. Dread coated his insides like ice. He'd made that mark in desperation after Rae used the last of her life energy. He had no idea what it meant or what it did, but the fact that Andriette knew Rae carried the same mark made his skin crawl. Tyee had a bad feeling about whatever he'd done to warrant this reaction.

But it gave Rae a chance to save herself. Whatever the consequences, he clung to that and cleared his throat. "It was all I could do to give her a chance at living. I trusted my instincts, and that's where they led me."

Andriette narrowed her eyes and slumped in her chair. "This is going to be harder than I thought." She pushed the half-eaten apple away from her and rubbed her temple.

The movement caught Tyee's attention, reminding him of their bargain. A hundred different questions came to the forefront of his mind, but his conversation with Fritz burned brightest. He couldn't face the answers she'd give him about the mark on his palm and the twin on Rae's palm, so he opted for another. "What are the Vandrere?" He winced, knowing he botched the pronunciation of Fritz's title for Rae.

Andriette's eyes snapped to his. "You mean the Vandrere as in van-drah." She considered him a moment. "And where did you hear that word?"

"Fritz called someone I know one of the Vandrere." Tyee did his best to copy Andriette's pronunciation of the foreign word.

The old woman gave him a shrewd look. "Is this someone who I think it is?" She glanced at his palm and back up at his eyes.

Tyee clenched his jaw. He'd barely known this woman for two days and hesitated to trust her with his secrets. But she was his best shot at getting answers. "Just answer the question. We made a deal."

Andriette huffed and shot him a glare. "Mind your tongue, boy. That's no way to talk to your great-grandmother." Her eyes widened when she realized what she'd said, and one hand covered her mouth. She closed her eyes before forcing them open and dropping the hand from her lips.

Tyee watched her in stunned silence. *Great-grandmother? But how?* More and more questions piled in his mind, but he pushed them aside. *Answers. I need answers first. It doesn't matter who she is as long as she can give me what I need.* But Tyee knew that was a lie.

The blood that tied people together in Kamore meant little when someone was willing to turn you in for a few coins. But when they weren't willing to do something so heinous, it meant everything. A part of Tyee's heart he thought was long gone panged sharply in his chest. He'd left his mother years ago and never wondered what became of her, but to have someone else he could call family... This change of events overwhelmed Tyee.

Clinging to the purpose that drove him here, he repeated. "Please, Tota. Fritz called Rae one of the Vandrere because she can call all four of the Crafts from the Goddess. But what does that mean?" He deliberately used the Elven title for grandmother, acknowledging what she'd said without making a big deal of it.

Andriette nodded her thanks. It seemed they had more in common than not. With a sigh, she answered. "The Vandrere were the original Magicae that came to Kamore a long, long time ago. Our early ancestor met with and assisted them in finding their place in Kamore." Her whiskey-colored eyes met his. "They had considerable power and, as I understand it, were anomalies even in their world. So much so, they kept it from their people and almost lost everything. Our ancestor, Elma, was her name, put them on the path to peace and prosperity." She shook her head slightly. "But the world is a cruel place. I've been around long enough to see some of the worst things it can do to people. Magicae, Mortal, or Elven, it doesn't matter. Wickedness strikes them all the same." Andriette rose from her chair with a groan. "But it's too late for these old bones. I trust you've washed a dish before?"

Tyee shot her a look. "Once or twice. You want me to leave as much food caked on as possible, right?"

The old woman rolled her eyes and moved towards the stairs, only stopping to squeeze his shoulder before ascending to her bedroom.

The horseman stayed seated until the sound of her footsteps faded. He let the shock of discovery wash through him, trying to convince himself it didn't change anything. That he'd learn what he needed and never spare this place another thought.

He let out a long sigh and braced his elbows on the table. Tyee stood and gathered the plates, taking them to the washbasin and putting his mind on the task at hand instead of the emotions threatening to overwhelm him.

# Chapter Ten

Rae's heart pounded in her chest, and her palms began sweating. She wiped them on her breeches and kept moving. She had to get there in time.

Crashing through the trees, she reached the circle of benches the Governing Council used for their formal meetings. Thoughts of Damien's tortured expression threatened the words she'd rehearsed since they'd left Verdencia. She shook her head as she joined the throng of people watching the proceedings from a distance. The Governing Council meetings were always open to the public, but rarely got this type of attention.

Being this far from traditional civilization raised the stakes too high for anybody to be indifferent. Everyone wanted a front-row seat to the decisions their elected officials settled on.

Rae glanced at those around the Council and Damien's face flashed in her mind again. *How many more are going through something similar? Who am I to ask them to sacrifice more?*

Those questions made her hesitate. Her heart squeezed as she gazed at faces she'd known for years; people she'd laughed with, danced with, cried with, and grown up with. Tears pricked her eyes at how unfair the world was.

*Some things cannot be changed.*

Rae clenched her fists as she tasted bitterness on the back of her tongue, brought on by the memory of her father's words. She hated how those words tainted her image of him.

But she couldn't deny the truth. Her father had been human, and she refused to make the same mistakes Andre Freeman did. He hadn't been the leader they needed to unite the Mortals and Magicae of Kamore.

Now was the time for her to become that leader.

Duncan laid the groundwork, providing a space for Magicae and Mortals to coexist and work together towards a common goal. However, Duncan and the elders of their troupe were tired. It was up to Rae and the other young adults to bring about the change they wanted to see in their country.

Taking a deep breath, Rae pushed her way through the crowd and strode into the middle of the circle of benches.

Midge stopped talking as the Council turned their attention to the acrobat.

Rae inclined her head towards the old seamstress. "Sorry Midge, I didn't mean to interrupt." Rae took a moment to gaze around the circle and meet the glances of the Governing Council. Her eyes ended on Duncan's. His gaze was weary and his mouth turned down in a slight frown.

Rae ignored his apprehension and continued, "I'm sorry to all of you for interrupting. It's not my place to interfere with the decisions of our elected officials, but I need to speak my peace. Furthermore, I feel it's important to encourage everyone to make their voices heard. All of you have served us extraordinarily, given the events of the past few months. Let me be clear, I do not doubt your capabilities in making decisions, nor your intentions for the good of the Circus and its people.

"I look around this place and I see a miracle. This is what my friends and I have yearned for, what we talked and dreamed about for so long." Rae met Luc's chocolate eyes. "A place to call home that's full of peace and opportunity. Somewhere children can grow without fearing for their survival. A place where we do not have to hide who we are and who we love. This is everything we've wanted for so long. Yet I can't deny the sinking feeling in the pit of my stomach.

"I can't stay here when Myra still terrorizes our people outside the forest. And I know a lot of you have that same incessant feeling, but not everyone."

Rae turned to the crowds of people surrounding the Council. She looked into the faces of fathers, mothers, children, and the elderly, knowing many of them were unwilling or unable to fight for the other Magicae of Kamore.

She clenched her fists and projected her voice.

"Nobody thinks less of those craving peace and rest. Our community has saved thousands of people across the country and we deserve to be proud of our efforts. But just like Duncan and so many of our elders in the months following the Uprising, there are a lot of us unsatisfied with the events in Heimat and even Tiva. The tragedies that took place in those cities speak to the larger picture of what the future holds if we do nothing.

"And I am determined to do anything I can to bring change to this broken place. My purpose in bringing this up now is to implore the Governing Council to be open-minded in their next major decision. We all know today is about deciding where we go from here. The stakes have never been higher and the decision about whether to stay or go couldn't be more polarizing."

Her eyes found Luc's and she let her friend see the sadness she was hiding. "One of my best friends has been struggling ever since the battle in Verdencia, torn between wanting to help and being unwilling to take another life. What I'm asking the Governing Council to consider is instead of staying or leaving, think about how can we honor our people's needs and bring about change in Kamore. I propose we let everyone split into groups, defined by what each group is willing to do and how they can best use their talents to overthrow Myra and create a better Kamore. Give our people a third option that allows them to further the Resistance without fighting or killing. Give them a chance to serve their people in a way that doesn't go against their morals."

Rae ended her speech and met Duncan's lavender gaze. The crowds of people were silent as they looked at the Ringmaster and driving force behind the Circus. Rae forced herself to unclench her fists and take a deep breath, willing the flames just beneath the surface to stay in check. She'd said what she needed to and could only hope Duncan and the others understood. Everyone waited with bated breath as Duncan gathered his thoughts.

Duncan held up a hand as some of the Council members talked amongst themselves. "We appreciate your thoughtful words, Rae. I would invite anyone else to speak now before we deliberate further."

Duncan looked at the crowd expectantly, raising one eyebrow.

The crowd shuffled as one person pushed to the forefront.

"I'd like to add that a lot of us from Heimat have family and friends still there dealing with Vincenzio. I respect your authority as elected officials, but know that once the snow melts, I have no choice but to return for my loved ones." George's face was stoic as he said his peace. Several heads nodded in the crowd, echoing his sentiment.

Rae met George's eyes and inclined her head in a rare moment of shared purpose. They weren't each other's biggest fans, but Rae knew their loyalty to their loved ones united them, regardless of how they felt about one another.

Rae felt another wave of fire threaten to overcome her control. She frowned and swallowed the panic rising in her chest. She had to stay in control of her Craft or else she'd need to face the unthinkable. There was no way the Crafter's Curse could still have a hold on her power. She glanced inward and heaved a sigh of relief.

Her flames were still contained in the ordered plait she'd braided them into. They were only responding to her emotions.

A commotion at the edge of the crowd captured everyone's attention. Rae craned her neck to see what was happening when a familiar voice sounded.

"Where's my Momma? Bane said my Momma was here. Can you help me?"

Rae didn't hesitate and left the Council circle, pushing through the crowd. The shock of red hair brought her to her knees as she exclaimed, "Red! You made it."

Gray eyes met hers as the little girl ran into Rae's open arms. Rae held her close and thanked the Huntress for keeping the young Herbalist from harm.

Mirabella marched along the edge of the lake, wringing her hands and cursing the cold. It had become a ritual for the lonely middle-aged woman as she waited for news of the little girl she'd sent away. Somehow, the monotony of walking the same path day after day kept her mind from dwelling on unpleasant things.

She winced as she remembered the whispers that seemed to follow her when she moved around camp and the furtive glances many gave her. Mirabella could only imagine the rumors her brother's people had started about her. Nobody announced she was Duncan's sister, the one that made the Uprising possible, but she knew the speculation and whispers were closer to the truth than they realized. Gossip spread fast in the small community, and she knew those from Heimat at least recognized her as Vincenzio's wife. It didn't take much to connect the dots from there.

Mirabella sighed, watching her breath form clouds in the chilly air. She traced a spiral pattern on her hand, letting regret and shame wash over her. It was hard to be in Duncan's community when she was faced with the repercussions of her choices everywhere she looked. The part of her she'd buried for so long struggled to reconcile itself with the lives she'd affected.

Mirabella dropped her head in her hands and let out a scream, using her thick mittens to muffle its sound. She couldn't bear living with this guilt for another instant.

A voice from far away pricked her ears. Her head whipped towards it and she strained to hear more, but the voice didn't continue. A child's cry propelled her feet into motion before her brain registered what she was hearing.

*Gemma.*

Mirabella sprinted toward the sound, reaching the crowd gathered for the Council meeting. Blood pounded in her ears as she searched, her eyes wild and her movements jerky. She strained to hear her daughter over the sounds of the crowd and let out a cry when she heard it.

With one last push, she reached where Gemma clung to Rae and choked down a sob of her own. Her hands shook as she took in the little girl's thick clothing and tangled dirty hair. Nothing mattered except that Gemma was safe.

Her throat was thick with emotion as she met the Crafter's golden eyes. The two women never spoke on the journey from Verdencia, but Mirabella knew Rae was integral in getting her daughter to safety after the boat left Heimat's harbor. Her debt to the young woman was something that could never be paid, but Mirabella didn't care. Understanding flashed in Rae's eyes and she leaned down to whisper to the little girl in her arms.

Mirabella felt tears prick the corners of her eyes as time slowed and she watched Gemma turn in Rae's arms. Mother and daughter stared at each other for a long moment before Mirabella crouched down and opened her arms.

It was the only invitation the little girl needed, and she launched herself at the woman she loved most. Mirabella let the tears fall as she scooped the little girl into her arms and spun her, crushing her tight and not quite believing she was finally holding her baby girl again. She cradled Gemma's head close and burrowed her face into dirty and tangled copper curls, breathing in the scent of earth and greenery that always clung to the young Herbalist. Mirabella lifted her head to meet Rae's gaze and mouthed the words 'thank you' to the acrobat. She watched Rae nod before whisking her daughter to the tent she shared with Duncan.

"Oh, wildflower. I missed you so much." She whispered in Gemma's ear and squeezed her tight, reluctantly softening her grip when the girl wriggled in her arms. Gemma's cheeks were tear-stained as she looked into her mother's face. Her little fingers were light as feathers as they danced across her mother's cheeks and touched her bleached hair. Questions swirled in her gray eyes, but she buried her head into her mother's shoulder instead of seeking answers, letting comfort and warmth be enough.

Mirabella rubbed Gemma's back and stroked her hair, whispering warm words in her daughter's ear as the little girl sobbed. "Shh, little one. I'm right here. Let's get you inside where it's warmer. You're safe, baby; you're so safe right here."

She shifted her daughter to one hip and used her free arm to move the tent flap aside, crouching as they entered the modest space. Two cots sat on either side, raised off the frozen ground and piled with blankets. Mirabella laid her little girl on one of them and tucked the exhausted Gemma in tight. The Herbalist let out a cry when her mother moved from the bed to tend the small stove radiating heat.

Mirabella stroked the girl's cheek. "Hush, wildflower. I'm not going anywhere. Let me stoke the coals and I'll be right back." Mirabella smiled softly as Gemma mumbled something incoherent and closed her eyes. More tears rolled down her cheeks as she placed a kiss on her daughter's forehead. She couldn't blame the little girl for drifting to sleep after the upheaval of the past few months. Duncan had relayed some of the journey Gemma and the others made, but the roller coaster of emotions from living on the road to being reunited with her mother had to be exhausting. No wonder she couldn't keep her eyes open.

Mirabella used the poker to stir the glowing embers and ignite low flames in the stove outfitted by the Forgers of the caravan. She marveled at the simple luxury and pulled her coat closer. They avoided using the stoves during the day to conserve firewood, but reuniting with her daughter called for a special treat. Mirabella wanted to be selfish for one more day and spend the next few hours with the daughter she loved more than anything.

After today, she could work on redeeming herself into a woman her daughter could be proud of.

She climbed into the cot next to the little girl and snuggled in close. As Gemma curled into her, Mirabella let the warmth from the coals and her daughter lull her into a doze.

The sound of footsteps padding around the tent woke Mirabella in a hurry. Her eyes snapped open to the low light of the tent and met Duncan's lavender gaze filled with worry. She sighed and looked at her daughter, sleeping soundly in the blankets next to her. Duncan proceeded to stoke the fire in their shared stove and sit on his cot. The only light came from the flames now flickering inside.

Mirabella met his gaze again, and he winced, regret and pain filling his lavender orbs. Dread spread like ice over her insides as she did her best not to jostle the sleeping five-year-old next to her. She narrowed her eyes and pursed her lips as she made to sit next to him.

The brother and sister had shared a tent since leaving Verdencia as a practicality. Neither seemed able to cross the expanse that divided them and heal what was broken. Too much time and too many betrayals hung between them. She was asleep before him most nights and woke to solitude in the mornings, doing her best to stay in the warmed tent as long as possible before returning to her silent vigil around the lake. They avoided each other around camp, piquing the interest of many onlookers. Mirabella avoided him because he was the starkest reminder of her faults. She regretted everything about the past two decades, except for the little girl sleeping soundly in her bed. If it wasn't for Gemma, she would've given up years ago.

With trepidation, she sat next to her brother and asked, "What? What is it, Duncan?"

He sighed and leaned on his elbows, refusing to meet her concerned gaze. "I have something to ask of you." He glanced at the sleeping little girl and sighed again.

Mirabella frowned and her tone turned icy. "She's not part of this Duncan. She's an innocent little girl who doesn't deserve to pay for the sins of her mother."

"Goddess, do you think I'd be that cruel? I said I have something to ask *you*, not the child." Anger colored Duncan's tone as he rubbed the back of his neck.

Chided, Mirabella held her tongue as fear made her hands tremble. She had a feeling she knew where this was going and hated that he felt he could ask it of her. A glance at her daughter resolved her. No matter what, she'd do anything Duncan asked as long as he kept her little girl safe.

Duncan swore and looked her in the eye. "I need you to return to Heimat."

Mirabella's stomach dropped. She could read between the lines; Duncan wanted her to spy on the husband she'd vowed never to see again. Her eyes wandered to Gemma's sleeping form, and she gulped. "Why?"

"We need ears in Vincenzio's keep and you're our best shot."

Mirabella let his words wash over her as she chewed on the inside of her cheek. She whispered, "He won't trust me, Duncan. I—, before I left, I wrote a letter that most people would take at face value, but not Darren. He'd have been able to infer what I didn't write down. The only way to make him trust me again would be to bring Gemma with." Her voice cracked, but she kept going. "I can't let that happen. I refuse to bring Gemma back there, so don't ask me to."

Duncan held up a hand. "I would never ask you to risk the girl."

Mirabella was close to tears, but she forced the words out. "I don't want to leave her, but I'll do it if you ask me to. I regret so much in this life, but regret fixes nothing. If I want to be someone she can look up to and be proud of, I need to atone for my past transgressions by doing something." She forced her watery gaze to meet his. "I can try, Duncan, but I can't promise I'll be much help once I'm back in that wretched city."

Duncan winced. "You have more power over him than you think. I'll make sure someone is close at all times. George says infiltrating the keep was the next thing on the city leaders' agenda after we evacuated the children." He grabbed and squeezed her hand. "You're stronger than you think."

Mirabella pulled her hand away and hung her head, unable to form words to make him understand. Returning to Darren would destroy her, but Duncan didn't know that. She'd never told him what she'd suffered as Vincenzio's wife and had no intention of doing so. Mirabella would have to find the strength to return to the monster she married and destroy him first.

A noise coming from her cot thrust her into motion. She was halfway across the tent before she noticed Gemma was in a sitting position, rubbing her eyes.

Her daughter yawned. "Why'd you leave Momma? It's too dark out."

Mirabella's heart panged at the thought of leaving her again. Gemma would be crushed. And if she didn't return... Mirabella shook her head. Those thoughts could wait until morning. There were more pressing matters to contend with.

She held a hand out to her daughter and said, "Come here, wildflower. It's time for you to meet your uncle." She guided the little girl, so she was in front of the Ringmaster.

Duncan met her steely gaze, and they shared a look. This was the first step in healing what was lost between them. They couldn't recreate what they'd once had, but maybe something new could blossom between them. Maybe they could be family once more.

Duncan crouched down and stuck out his hand. "Call me Uncle Dunc."

Mirabella nodded when Gemma looked at her and the little girl didn't hesitate. She gripped his hand with hers and replied, "My name's Gemma, but you can call me Red."

# Chapter Eleven

T he feeling of wind beneath his wings would never get old.

Bane could feel the change in the air currents as he got closer to the edge of the Great Northern Forest. The currents became wilder and unrelenting the closer he got to the end of the protection offered by the massive trees.

He let out a cry and brought his falcon form up above the treetops, trying to get a better view. He knew he was on the right track, but couldn't be sure his flight path was a direct shot to the intended city. Normally, he would've spent most of the journey above the trees, but a storm pushed him back beneath the cover of the forest.

He'd made up as much time as he could, but hated how far behind he felt. His orders were to check in with Rich and bring information on Heimat's fate back to the Governing Council. The sooner he made it to the city, the sooner · he could return to the people he loved.

Zeke's face flashed in his mind and he instinctively reached for the line connecting him to the feather he'd given the Crafter. The magic running in Bane's veins held mysterious power. For as long as he could remember, he'd been able to keep tabs on the ones he loved by using some of the loose feathers from his animal form. Based on his discussions with other Shifters, this wasn't something common among those blessed by the Goddess with an animal form.

He could only guess the lines leading to Zeke, his Da, and now Gemma were because of the strange magic separating him from the rest of his kind.

The differences between him and the other Shifters he met still unnerved him. Having power that was long forgotten made his stomach churn and his mind uneasy. He wasn't one to express himself or dwell on his feelings, yet this unease kept rearing its head deep inside. It put Bane on edge, not being able to brush it off and move on. The regret of not realizing it sooner and the fear of what it meant for the future weighed heavy on his mind.

He reached the sky and was assaulted by the acrid smell of smoke. Bane's eyes burned as he forced himself higher, seeking relief for his heightened senses. Too late, he realized he should've gone lower and dove as fast as he could, holding his breath. Bane's lungs burned from the lack of oxygen and the smoke permeating every part of the canopy. Knowing he needed to regroup, Bane landed on the lowest branch he could find and studied the trees surrounding him.

His stomach dropped as he considered what the smoke meant and the direction it came from.

*Heimat.*

Not willing to waste anymore time, Bane braced himself for what was to come and took off towards the city. The smoke became darker the closer he got to the outskirts of the northern city. His lungs burned and his eyes watered, but he pumped his wings faster, pushing through the pain.

He broke through the trees.

And couldn't help but scream in agony.

The forest was gone.

Bane felt his heart being ripped from his chest as he took in what remained of tall oaks, delicate birch trees, and sturdy maples. He barely registered himself landing on a blackened stump as he took in the horrors around him.

His avian form didn't use its tear ducts to express emotion, but he found himself unable to control the keening his scream devolved into. Bane hadn't heard that sound since his Ma's death and burial. He'd been so young when it happened. When his Ma put herself between her little boy and the soldiers trying to capture him. Her last words echoed in his head.

*Fly fast and true, my boy. Don't look back until you've found your Da. Go now.*

*With her last words, she'd kissed his brow and pushed him to the back door, picking up a pitchfork and turning to face the pounding of marching boots coming up the drive.*

*Bane had wanted to protest, but the fear in his Ma's eyes and desperation in her tone had him doing as she bid. He'd flown into the forest, searching for his Da, who was on a hunt. Seeing his son in avian form spurred Gar into action, knowing his wife would only send the young boy after him for one reason. He hadn't asked Bane for an explanation, simply sprinted towards the humble homestead, praying he wasn't too late.*

*His Da yelled at him to stay, but Bane couldn't help himself and followed at a distance, taking care to stay in the trees once he reached their home.*

*It was burning.*

*The soldiers killed his Ma and set the only home he'd ever known on fire. He watched his Da take out the two soldiers posted in case the boy came back and rush into the burning house. He returned with his wife's bloody body and collapsed to the ground.*

*Bane hadn't been able to control the scream that ripped from his throat then or the keening sound that followed as he grappled with the power in his veins, trying to Shift but knowing he couldn't. Too little time had passed since he left his human form. He'd flown to his Da and nuzzled his mom's still figure, that awful wailing sound never stopping.*

Those moments stuck in his falcon form when all he wanted was comfort in the form of human touch would always be the worst ones of his life. It was the cruelest torture to be unable to express his feelings to his Da and gain comfort from the only family he had left.

And this felt as horrific as then.

This part of the forest once housed innocent life in the form of trees, shrubs, grasses, and all the animals that called the flora home. The monstrosity of such destruction took Bane's breath away. His connection to the forest and its creatures through the power running through his veins made the loss that much more devastating. Bane looked at the charred remains of stumps and blackened carcasses of animals and felt grief tear through him anew.

He let himself grieve for several minutes until the wailing of his falcon form quieted. Bane was still a little ways from the city proper and on the forest side of the Mantaga River, but knew he couldn't be too careful. Vincenzio would have eyes everywhere and be on high alert after the battle in Verdencia. As much as Bane longed to Shift into his human form, he had a long way to go before his mission was complete. He couldn't risk Shifting nor did he have the time to wait in order to Shift back.

Taking stock of his surroundings, he let out a last cry and promised retribution for the flora and fauna that lost their lives unjustly. The forest and its inhabitants had done nothing to deserve this destruction. Their only crime was thriving next to a place controlled by a power-hungry general.

He would make Vincenzio and his soldiers pay for this latest atrocity.

Sticking to the cover of shadow provided by the still-standing trees, Bane made his way to the city he'd once considered a haven. Most of it sent black tendrils of smoke to the sky and Bane felt rage settle into his broken heart.

Vincenzio deserved to rot in hell for everything he'd done in the name of Myra and the suffering he'd spread across the continent.

This devastation couldn't go unanswered.

Darren Vincenzio studied what was left of Heimat from the roof of the former city hall. A feral grin transformed his features as he took in the destruction he'd caused and the pleasure he'd taken from punishing those foolish enough to defy him. He'd crushed the opposition like ants and made good on the threats he'd delivered to the Magicae of this putrid city.

His soldiers went door to door and purged Heimat of its vermin and the traitors that sympathized with them. Heimat would go down in history as his greatest feat and serve as an example for all of Kamore. The people rebelled, and he'd brought the city to its knees.

He took a deep breath of smoky air and exhaled with a sigh of contentment. Victory was the only thing that could fully satisfy him.

"Sir? I have a new report for you." Zander, his steward and the man he trusted most, hazarded to interrupt the general from his thoughts.

Vincenzio faced him with a manic grin. "In a minute, old friend. Take a moment and witness what we've accomplished." He spread his arms wide, gesturing to the city in shambles from his soldiers.

Zander did as he was bid with a hesitant expression.

Vincenzio caught his steward's reluctance and growled, "What is it?"

Zander gulped before looking his leader in the eyes, never being one to shy away from the volatile man. "Two more men died from complications during the battle with the Circus."

Vincenzio's expression soured, and he clenched his fists. Through gritted teeth, he said, "The Circus will pay for what they've done." He gestured to the still-burning city. "Heimat is only the beginning of what horrors await them. I'll burn the entire forest down if I have to."

Zander nodded his agreement. "I would expect nothing less, sir. Shall I gather your officers?"

Vincenzio took a moment to think before shaking his head. "Let them revel in their spoils for another night. I'll call them to the war room in the morning."

Zander inclined his head and waited for dismissal.

"That is all, Zander. Take the rest of the day off. It's going to be a busy next few days."

"With pleasure. Thank you, sir." Zander took the stairs to his quarters within the former city hall. Vincenzio knew he would head to the Wharf and find a card room and a beer to take the edge off the past few days.

Vincenzio went back to the edge of the roof and took in what was left of the city.

His thoughts turned sour as he thought of Duncan and his band of vermin.

*It's only a matter of time before they return for vengeance. And we'll be ready to rid the country of these pests once and for all.*

The sun was setting as Rich trudged up the path into Heimat. He carried a pack laden with preserved vegetables, dried meat, and fresh bread grown and made at the farmhouse where Tommy's and George's mother resided at.

Diane was a remarkable woman, willing to provide sanctuary when they desperately needed it. She welcomed Rich, his wife Anna, and their two grand-daughters with open arms, as they escaped before Vincenzio's men came knock-ing.

Her generosity knew no bounds as she insisted upon sending as many extra supplies as she could for those unable to leave the city.

Rich shouldered the burden of delivering these supplies as Tommy, Rob, Simone, and Eddie were still hiding with the Magicae of Heimat in some of the surrounding small towns. In addition to Rich, Anna, and their granddaughters, Diane also housed Sara and her three little ones. Needless to say, it was a full house with five unruly children, three grandparents doing their best, and a very pregnant mother about to give birth any day.

Most of the time, the children ran wild in the snow, only stopping to help bake bread, dry meat, and clean the vegetables from the cellar, harvested in the fall. Rich and Anna turned it into a game so the five rascals didn't realize the work they were putting in. They created a lovely oasis, several miles from town, but Rich knew it was only a matter of time before the soldiers came knocking again.

In the first batch of raids, only a few soldiers were tasked with checking the farms on the outskirts of Heimat. By the luck of the Goddess, the soldiers were still young and lacked the blood thirst many of their older counterparts thrived on. They checked everyone's eyes and made slight cuts on each individual's hands to confirm the entire lot of them were Mortal. They did a thorough search of the property and went on their way, satisfied with leaving them to tend the farm and animals.

Rich knew more soldiers would come and there was no telling whether they'd be as willing to leave them in peace.

As the only leader left in the city, Rich felt it was his duty to do what he could to help those living in what was left of Heimat. The risk of being captured was high, but Rich was banking on his age and what he carried to keep him from harm.

While the city still smoldered, there was little chance Vincenzio would fill the town with Mortals loyal to Myra, especially as winter tightened its grip. Rich was sure the only people left were Mortals able to hide their ties to the Magicae but unwilling or unable to leave their homes. Tommy and the others had gotten the Magicae out, and Rich knew many of their family members followed in their footsteps, unwilling to face the destruction left by Vincenzio and his soldiers.

Whoever was left deserved any help he could provide.

He took a horse as far as he could, but left it before he reached the city. It was a gamble that nobody would take the old mare, but riding into town on a horse would only bring unwanted attention.

Rich took lumbering steps as he entered the city. He kept to the shadows and alleys, wearing the threadbare shawl that hid his face under a hood. It covered his back, giving him the appearance of a poor old beggar with a hump and a limp.

Again, Rich was doing what was needed to provide relief to those left in the Heimat community.

Eventually, he made it to the boarded-up bakery, and his heart squeezed as he gazed at the still-smoking building. Most of Heimat was charred and smoking.

Witnessing the place he'd grown up and where he'd raised his daughter reduced to such a state caused a swell of emotion. The bakery would never be the same, no matter how much they rebuilt.

It was common practice for the soldiers to set fire to any building or home they found abandoned, as if they had orders to raze as much of the city to the ground as they could. It was despicable and enraging, but Rich knew he could do little in retaliation without a force behind him.

The time to fight would come, but until then, Rich would do what little he could to make life a little easier.

The cry of a falcon almost gave him whiplash as his head swiveled to find its origin.

*Well, I'll be. If this little guy isn't a Shifter, you can call me a cobbler.* The old man thought to himself as the falcon flew to his shoulder.

"I need to put this in the cellar," he whispered. "I'd say you could return to your human form once we're there, but it's probably best to wait until we're out of the city. It'll be just a moment."

The falcon left with a flap of its wings and stayed hidden in the shadows of the alley. The old man watched him go and gave a nod.

Rich opened the door and descended the steps into the bakery's basement. What was left down there originally was looted during the raids, but the pack he'd left a couple of days ago was empty with a note of thanks in its pocket.

He pushed the shawl on his shoulders to the side and took off the pack he was carrying, grateful to be rid of such a heavy load. Rich pulled the empty pack onto his back and touched one of the beams supporting the old structure. He whispered his thanks to the building that still provided amidst all the destruction.

He ascended the steps and fixed his shawl to hide the now empty pack he carried.

"There are eyes everywhere. Best to keep to the shadows until we're out of town and to keep our distance should anything happen. Less of a chance of discovery that way," Rich murmured to open air.

The falcon gave a quiet cry and waited until the old man took the lead. Luckily, they reached the outskirts of town with little incident.

As soon as they reached the place where Rich left his horse, the old man whistled and held out his arm. "There's a farmhouse south and two clicks to the east. You can't miss it if you follow the path and take a left just past the grove of apple trees. You should go on ahead to limit suspicions."

The bird chattered his approval and took to the wing, disappearing into the night sky. Rich mounted his horse and urged her into a slow lope, trusting her to find her way in the dark.

Before long, Rich made it back to the farmhouse.

He dismounted and brought his trusty steed to the stable, where Tommy and Sara's eldest grabbed the reins.

"I can take care of her, Uncle Rich." The young girl looked around before whispering, "I think there's a visitor inside who needs to talk to you."

Rich squeezed the girl's shoulder. "Thanks, young lady. I'll see what they want."

He opened the door to the farmhouse and found a trimmed young man with broad shoulders and large hands sitting at the table with a glower on his face. Diane was heating some of the leftover stew from supper in the hearth. As Rich stepped into the small kitchen, the man stood up.

"No need to stand, lad. I'm sure you've had quite the journey and could use the rest. Let Ms. Diane get you a bowl and we can talk as you eat," Rich said kindly and sent a nod to the generous woman. "Diane works wonders in the kitchen and your stomach will sing her praises shortly."

The woman shot him an amused smile. "I see right through you, Richard. Lucky for you, flattery gets you far in my house." She grabbed another bowl from the cupboard and ladled two sets of steaming bowls. Setting them in front of the two men, she patted Rich on the cheek. "The contractions started about an hour ago. I better get upstairs to make sure everything's ready for the new baby."

Rich caught her wrist before she could leave. "The baby's coming? How wonderful. Let me know if you need anything from me."

"That's sweet of you, but too many people can be as much of a problem as not enough. Just keep an eye on the kiddos when they come in from the stable. It should just be the two older ones. They can sleep on the sofa for tonight." She said as she extricated her wrist from his hand and hurried up the stairs.

Rich turned to the young man across from him with bright eyes. "The miracle of life doesn't stop for anything. It's incredible to have such moments of joy despite the hardships we face."

The man paused his inhaling of the delicious stew to meet Rich's gaze as he swallowed. "Babies do seem to come at the most inconvenient times," he responded tightly in a deep baritone.

Rich gave a chuckle. "Aye, that they do." His expression turned somber. "Am I correct in assuming you come bearing news from the Circus?"

The young man nodded. "Duncan sent me here to update you on your people and to gather information to bring back." His eyes filled with sorrow. "He destroyed everything, even the forest on the other side of the river." The young man pounded his fist on the table, restraining himself from doing more despite the pain in his eyes. "This is unacceptable. We can't let him win."

"I agree, son, but there's nobody left here. The adult Magicae that were left in the city were evacuated shortly before the raids happened. The only ones remaining are Mortals who could hide their ties to their loved ones. Everyone else is gone." Rich's expression was hard, as he didn't sugarcoat the reality of their situation. The young man in front of him had the passion of youth and needed a dose of reality before he did something stupid. "What's your name, lad?"

The Shifter battled his emotions as he did his best to regain his composure. He took another bite of stew before answering. "Bane. And you are?"

Rich could tell this Bane didn't like what he heard, but understood the magnitude of the situation at hand. "The name's Rich."

Bane gave a nod and opened his mouth to ask a question.

A scream sounded upstairs and the two men shared a look. A voice called down the stairs. "Rich, can you get the water? It's on the hearth."

"This will have to wait for a moment. Finish your stew and we can continue talking." Rich used a towel to grab the pot of water from the hearth and made his way up the stairs.

A new baby waited for no one.

# Chapter Twelve

"You call that a straight line? Even Fritz could sit still long enough to produce one better than that. Again. And keep going until you can do it in your sleep. Elven children learn the most basic of runes before they can walk. If they can do it, surely you can too." Andriette harped as she stooped over Tyee's shoulder.

"I understand that. But my childhood didn't exactly leave room for much reading or writing." Tyee responded with a growl. He'd been sitting at the table for hours and couldn't believe he'd reached the point where scrubbing the floors was sounding more appealing than sitting here. With a sigh, he dipped the metal stylus into the inkpot and started again.

Andriette had given him a list of the five basic runes and their meanings, instructing him to practice writing them out before memorizing what they meant.

But every time he put ink to paper, his hand wouldn't cooperate, and the letters came out wobbly.

*This is the biggest waste of time.* With that thought, he dropped the piece of metal and pushed away from the table.

"I need a break." He announced to the old woman and left before she could say anything. Without a word, he strode out the front door and headed to the lean-to serving as a stable, snow crunching beneath his boots.

Andriette housed one of the forest ponies favored by the Elven and a few other livestock, keeping them in the paddock surrounding the humble shelter.

Tyee had trusted Koko to the low walls of the structure, knowing full well the stallion could leave at any time. Hell, Tyee was pretty sure the small forest pony could clear that low of a fence.

But they stayed.

Tyee put his bare hands on the rough wood despite the chilly afternoon air. His fingers passed over a smooth section, and he looked down. A string of symbols crisscrossed the wooden post. He studied them, recognizing several as he traced them with a finger. Frustration welled inside as he was reminded of his failure that morning.

The old woman had demonstrated the combinations of lines with a flick of her wrist, making it look like the easiest thing in the world. But writing wasn't something that came intuitively to the horseman. As the head hostler at the stable, he'd memorized enough words to get by, but nothing more. And writing? Forget it. He'd always dictated his responses when needed to the stable hands; a precedent started by the man that held his position previously.

Tyee roused himself from thoughts of the past and let out a whistle, expecting Koko to clear the fence in one bound. But the horse came to his rider and pawed the ground, letting out a snort and sending Tyee an expectant look.

Tyee frowned and shook his head in disbelief, assuming the stallion was being stubborn.

"The runes prevent them from leaving."

Tyee clenched his teeth to prevent the frustrated sigh from escaping his lips. Once sure his face wouldn't betray him, he turned to meet the old woman's knowing gaze.

"Was riding always as easy as it is now?" Andriette shot him a pointed look.

Tyee met her gaze with a glare, understanding where she was going with her line of questioning. Andriette raised one eyebrow, waiting for his response.

"No," he admitted with a flat tone.

Tota's eyes glittered at his discomfort. "Give me as much attitude as you want, but we both know I speak the truth. Learning and using the runes is the only path to unlocking the power of your birthright. But nobody said it was going to be easy. As with everything in this life, you have to go through the hard stuff before you can reap the rewards. If you don't put in the work, it'll never get easier."

The old Elven woman waited for a response that wasn't coming. Tyee knew he had to put the work in despite his feelings of inadequateness if he wanted to leave by the spring. But he knew himself. If he didn't take the time to give his emotions an outlet, sitting at that table would be an exercise in frustration.

The silence stretched between them until Tyee gave her a grunt in reply, unable to form words to describe the insight he had.

Her eyes softened. "Go. Remind yourself of the fruits of hard labor and come back ready to work. Clear your mind and connect with the brother of your heart." She cocked her head to the side and studied the midnight stallion. "Your connection comes from the Elven blood in your veins. I've never taught one with both Elven and Mortal blood. We'll work together to discover how to access your sjel evner. Ride safe and fast, Nakni."

"Nakni?" He shot her an inquisitive look.

Tota smiled. "Grandson," she replied. "And don't get lost. I won't come to find you." She flashed him a wink and walked into the forest, humming a tune as the greenery swallowed her figure and a crow lighted on her shoulder.

Tyee watched her leave before opening the gate and gesturing to Koko. The horse trotted to him and bobbed his head in delight at the promise of freedom.

Tyee chuckled as the horse danced in place, trembling with anticipation while he tried to brush and saddle the beast.

"Shh, now. It's been a while, so let me check you over, ya brute." He gave the stallion a gentle shove and leaned down to check one of Koko's hooves. The horse let out a snort but quieted his limbs to let Tyee search for stones and thorns that lodged themselves within the softer inside of his hoof.

Tyee finished his inspection and removing dust and dirt from the horse's thick winter coat before setting his saddle and pad in place on the stallion's back. He tightened the cinch that circled Koko's belly and fitted the leather bridle over the horse's face. Most bridles included a bit that went into the horse's mouth, using pressure points to communicate the direction and speed to the horse. But Tyee hadn't used a bit on Koko for years now.

Their bond was strong enough that he didn't need such a tool. The bridle he used was a series of straps that circled the horse's snout and ears, with braided and looped rope as reins. The pressure on either side of Koko's snout was all he needed for Tyee to communicate his wishes.

Koko would always do his best to please the man who gave him everything, and Tyee would never ask the stallion to do something he couldn't. The trust they shared was unlike anything Tyee had ever experienced in a relationship with another person.

Although the budding relationship between him and his great-grandmother held the promise of potential. She seemed to understand him with little explanation on his part. He was starting to wonder what else he had in common with the old woman.

Only time would tell what could bloom between them. The pull of family was magnetic and Tyee wondered how different things would've been had his mother returned to this place instead of living on the streets of Kamore. Would he already be versed in these rune things? Would he still be as skilled in the saddle?

*Would I have ever met Koko?*

*Or Rae?*

Tyee shook the what-ifs from his head and led Koko away from the wooden paddock. In one smooth movement, he mounted the tall stallion and snapped the reins, leaning down over the horse's muscular neck.

"Let's fly, Ko," Tyee whispered into the horse's ear, bracing himself as he gave Koko his head.

In an instant, the horse was moving through the trees, gaining speed as he found a game trail, its snow packed down from use. The pair weaved swiftly in and out of the trees, losing themselves to the wind and the thrill of the ride.

Tyee let his focus hone in on matching the horse's movements, keeping his seat and letting his heartbeat in tandem with the big horse's breathing. He let himself become one with the brother of his heart, letting his frustration and shame wash away with every hoofbeat.

No matter what happened, Tyee would always have this to fall back on. And that was all the power he needed.

The Queen of the Elven steepled her fingers as she stared at the depiction of her father above the hearth in her quarters. Her father was the first of his line and the ruler she aspired to be. He had been cunning and ambitious, lifting Elven society to new heights, never seen before. Their cities flourished in the Highlands and the Forest, enjoying feats of engineering and rune work unlike anything they'd ever built.

He brought about a golden age that left as quickly as it came.

In the twilight years of his reign, war broke out across the twelve tribes of Kamore, and the Elven became caught in the crossfire.

As her father's general, she'd been called upon to lead the armies and fight for their cities. She tasted early success and became beloved amongst her people. But victory wouldn't last.

Her father took an arrow to the heart during a routine visit to one village in the Highlands. With his last breath, he begged her to save their people.

With the weight of the crown on her head and the Elven people's fate on her shoulders, she'd done what she could. She led battles against heathens and raiders and had the scars to prove it. A nick to her inner thigh proved almost fatal when it severed the artery just below her skin. After that disaster of a battle, she'd made the difficult decision to call for a retreat.

Ulla refused to taint her father's legacy and did the only thing she could to ensure the Elven lived on. They prospered in the forest and Verdencia echoed the ingenuity of the cities built during her father's rule. But change was coming, and the young Elven were becoming restless.

She sighed and gave her father's image one last look, pressing her fingers to her lips and placing them on his unmoving cheek. "Give me guidance and strength from beyond the veil, Papa. And I will bring back the golden age we lost so many years ago."

With a sigh, she stood up and strode to the doorway of her chambers high in the trees. Opening the door, she bellowed, "Send for my general. Let her know to meet me at the Mother Oak."

The guard nodded and made his way across one of the bridges in the treetops towards her daughter's quarters. With a nod to the remaining queensguard, she grabbed her staff from its place by the door and descended the ladder to the forest floor.

Without waiting to see if her guards followed, Ulla strode into the forest to the Mother Oak standing guard to the north of the city. Her thumb traced the symbols etched into her staff and they glowed beneath her touch. The Queen gave a wicked grin and pressed one rune, moving swiftly and silently through the snow.

Talon, the alpha, and leader of the Forest Shifters, sent a messenger asking for an audience with the Queen and her general. For what reason, Ulla hadn't a clue and her curiosity made her accept.

The Elven and the Forest Shifters were reluctant allies at best. This clan of Shifters had lived in the forest almost as long as the Elven had, giving up the ways of Mortals in favor of embracing their animal forms to their fullest. The two peoples lived in peace since the Elven sought permanent refuge in the forest, keeping to their own parts of the wooded landscape.

Talon was a gruff mountain lion Shifter with a thirst for blood and had never been her biggest fan, but sharing the protection of the trees meant she had no choice in answering the Shifter's plea. She only hoped her daughter would keep her wits and temper her slivered tongue.

Sylvia was an acquired taste, but as the sole heir to the Elven throne, Ulla had no other choice than to prepare her daughter as best she could. She'd hoped time and an iron fist would change her unruly daughter, but it only seemed to make her more defiant. Ulla gave another sigh as she reached the tall and sturdy oak. She ran her fingers along its bark before stopping at a knot in its rough skin.

"I'll never understand the significance of this tree to your people." A gravelly voice sounded behind the Elven queen.

Ulla's hand clenched into a fist but didn't leave the knot on the old oak. She forced herself to take a deep breath and focus only on the mighty sentinel in front of her. It was bad form to meet at the tree without acknowledging the Mother Oak herself.

Ulla quieted her mind and reached within until she felt the drumbeat of the tree's song. Closing her eyes, she lost herself in the mighty rhythm and felt her heart slow to match the power of the music. Ulla gave a sigh of contentment as the drums faded and a wind ruffled the limbs of the old tree, dropping leaves on her and the Shifter both.

Her duty done, Ulla's eyes flashed open, and she spun to face the pack leader of the Forest Shifters. Talon was in her half form, standing on two legs but still covered with fur, nails sharp enough to draw blood, and cat-shaped ears too far forward on her head.

Ulla hid her disgust at the unnatural half-breed form Talon insisted upon meeting with, but barely. The first time they'd met like this, Ulla was sure Talon saw the horror on her face, but only flashed her fangs at the Elven royal. It was hard to understand the Shifter's grating voice, but Ulla had conversed enough with the feral leader to no longer need time to pick up on Talon's words.

"This is the mighty Mother Oak. She was planted by some of the first Elven to reach these shores and has looked after us ever since her branches could provide shade and her trunk was too big to fit inside a single embrace. She offers us protection, wisdom, and connection to the forest around us." Ulla answered the woman's question, meeting her yellow feline gaze.

Talon snorted. "Pretty words that mean nothing. You and I both know the tree is little more than a symbol." She held up a hand when Ulla hissed her disapproval. "Hey, no judgment here. A leader has to use whatever they can to keep the masses in check." Her lips curled into a smirk. "Although if the rumors are true, you and your ice princess are barely keeping your people in line. Looks like you need any help you can get it." Talon made a low grating sound deep in her throat.

"Can we get to the point of why you called a meeting? Or did you bring me here for your own amusement?" Ulla snapped, knowing the Shifter was laughing at the position she assumed the Elven Queen was in.

"Ah, I kid, Your Grace." Talon gave a mock bow, the smirk still firmly in place. "Lighten up and laugh a little, my Queen. It does wonders for the wrinkles."

Ulla's skin prickled at the Shifter's words, but before she could find a retort, another voice sounded in the clearing.

"You'd do well to remember that, Talon. The only reason your pack has survived for this long is because of the Queen's tolerance for your kind. Your petty and inconsequential insults mean nothing to the glory of Her Majesty, the Queen." Sylvia's tone was sharp and dismissive, cutting the Shifter to the bone.

Ulla couldn't help the way her lips curled at the edges when she faced her daughter. She kept her tone neutral as she addressed them both. "No need to come to my rescue, General. Talon was about to inform me of the reason for her invitation to meet. Isn't that right?" Ulla turned her hardened gaze to the Shifter in her half-form.

Talon bared her fangs as her eyes flitted between the two Elven royals. Her gaze settled on Sylvia and she retorted, despite the Queen's unvoiced warning. "Yes, General. Nice of you to show up to something as dull as a diplomacy meeting. I hear your pet decided to stay but wants nothing to do with you. Must sting to know your bed will remain as cold as your icy heart for the time being."

Sylvia bared her own teeth and let out a hiss. "Your sources are incompetent if they told you my bed remains empty. Suitors line up to have a chance at proving their prowess in pleasure to the Princess of the Elven."

"Enough. Cut the shit, Talon. Why are we here?" Ulla's voice was steel as her glare glittered and the symbols on her wooden staff flashed.

Talon let out her guttural chuckle again. "I like your daughter, Your Grace. She has mettle and a tongue that bites deeper than a blade. You should be proud of her. She'll rule your people with an unwavering iron fist."

"Yes, she will do well. Now get on with it." Ulla said through gritted teeth, keeping a tenuous hold on her temper.

Talon tsked. "Testy now, aren't you? No matter, I'll make it quick. My people and I agree, the Circus is unnatural. Magicae and Mortals? Bah, they make me want to retch. Mortals can't be trusted under any circumstances." Her eyes narrowed as they met Ulla's. "But the battle for your city proved we don't have to settle for the peace Duncan and the others want. True peace will only come when the Mortals have been driven out of Kamore once and for all. An alliance between our peoples would mean we could start purging the North from this infestation of weaklings."

"I'm in." Sylvia held a hand out to the Shifter with a wicked grin and blood-thirsty eyes.

"Wait." Ulla put a hand on her daughter's arm. "Let me talk with my general and we will have an answer for you by the new moon." The Queen paused and pursed her lips. "To be clear, you're suggesting we destroy the villages just south of the Forest's border?"

"And start expanding the Great Northern Forest itself. Yes, that is what I'm proposing. With your kind's connection to the trees, it should be simple enough. By expanding the forest, we expand our stronghold and begin the long road to extermination." Her cat ears flicked back, and she ran a tongue over her canines that still showed even when her mouth was closed. "I look forward to your formal acceptance of my proposal and discussing strategies for our warriors to work together." Her last words were garbled as Talon Shifted into her mountain lion form and bounded into the underbrush of the trees.

Once the Shifter disappeared, Sylvia whirled on the Queen. "We have to accept this, Mother."

"The only thing we have to do is proceed with caution." Ulla's tone was frosty as she regarded her daughter and general.

Sylvia let out a growl of frustration. "But don't you see? This is the answer we've been looking for. We both know our people grow restless. Let's give them a purpose for their idle hands. Let's take back what was stolen from us all those years ago." Her eyes gave her mother a sideways glance as she added, "Let's take back what Grandfather lost."

Ulla let out a hiss. "Mind your tongue, Daughter. I will not be goaded into a decision that risks our people's lives. Remember that I am still Queen, no matter how much you wish it wasn't the case."

Sylvia had the decency to drop her gaze. "Of course, my Queen. I meant no disrespect."

"You are dismissed, General. I will see you at Council this afternoon." Ulla lifted her daughter's chin until glittering dark eyes met hers. "Be sure to keep this to yourself until then."

Sylvia's eyes flashed, but her tone was submissive. "Your wish is my command."

Ulla released her daughter's face and watched her retreat towards their city in the trees. With a sigh, she placed her hand on the old oak and closed her eyes.

"Give me strength, Great Mother. Help me see where we go from here."

With one last pat, she nodded to her guard and followed her daughter. The advisory meeting would be more interesting than usual, it seemed. She mulled on Talon's proposition as her feet brought her back to her people unbidden.

*Maybe it is time for a change.*

# Chapter Thirteen

Naya furrowed her brows as she watched her two sleeping charges. She'd grabbed them from their hiding place at the Midnight Market and whisked them to one of the safe houses for orphans like them. There were a handful scattered across the capital city, but "safe" was a relative word. It was understood these places harbored the poor and hungry, but only until their expiration dates. The longer you stayed in one, the more likely it was you'd end up on the wrong side of the Flesh Market.

They'd been here for one night and already Naya's skin was crawling. But Raj claimed Corbin would come the next day with word of an open post at one of the merchant's houses in Bayside. And that was something Naya could work with.

Ryker told her to leave the city, but Naya had never been to the wilderness. No way she would survive out there on her own. Let alone with two little kids to look after. Naya was worried about her and the twins' safety, but she didn't have a death wish. Maybe Ryker could live out there with his fancy guard's training and conditioning, but Naya didn't know how to hunt or even shoot a bow.

But she could steal. And she was damn good at it.

If she could get them into a merchant's house, they'd be safe for a while at least. The merchants lived to the north of the city proper, away from the dirty streets filled with the poor and hungry, but also free from the roving guards and their cruelty.

At least, that's what all the older orphans talked about. The ones that left their guardians and the hovels they provided to live in places Naya only dared to dream about. A lot of the merchants employed them because they were cheap and didn't compromise their morals like the slaves from the Flesh Markets did. The only problem was they only employed older children and didn't include room and board for any younger charges.

Naya needed to talk to Corbin and figure out which family was hiring and what the staff quarters looked like. She needed to know if she could sneak the twins in or if she'd need to charm the family into letting her bring her charges.

She glanced out the small window and tapped her foot on the dirt floor.

Morning couldn't come fast enough.

With a sigh, she stretched her hands over her head and rolled her back out. She knew sleep was pointless while thoughts swirled inside her head.

Her gaze drifted to Hawk's and Aurora's faces as she quietly slipped out of bed. They trusted her like nobody ever had. Without a doubt, they would follow her to the ends of the earth with grins on their faces and a spring in their steps.

No pressure or anything.

Naya pulled the scarf around her shoulders, making a hood to hide her hair and face in the predawn light.

She needed some air and a walk to clear her head. It was dangerous and Ryker would not approve, but she needed space in her head too. If this whole thing fell through, she had no other backup plan. Naya had to make this work, or else all three of them would lose what little freedom they had. She needed to make a list of everything it would take to reach the merchant's house and secure a place in his or her staff.

She pulled the scarf tighter around her head and opened the door, realizing she needed new clothes. *Anything but a dress. Maybe I can pass as a boy.*

Naya shook her head, knowing she could only afford one secret, and that was the twins. She looked down the alley, and finding no one, slinked to where it met the cobblestones.

Reaching the bustling street, Naya dove for the shadows as two guards strolled by. Engrossed in their conversation, they didn't notice the orphan in the alley.

*That was close.*

Naya looked both ways on the street and recognized she was two blocks from the market. Fishing in her pocket, she found two coppers and sucked on her teeth. Two coppers might get her a handkerchief if she was lucky. She'd have to steal a dress if she wanted to make the right impression on one of the merchants.

*This is going to end badly.* Naya knew the cloth traders at the market, and they weren't the kind of people you wanted to mess with.

Worse yet, they never opened early.

Some traders and merchants set up shop before the market opened and the guards arrived. Those were Naya's favorite vendors because it was easy to palm small goods and food in the twilight before sunrise.

These cloth traders felt their bolts of fabric and freshly sewn pieces were worth too much to risk setting up before the guards could catch any early thieves. Naya knew it was a long shot but she figured there was no harm in checking, just in case they strayed from their usual routine. To her delight, the family was there early.

*Maybe my luck is changing.*

Naya kept to the shadows and blended in with those setting up for a long day of sales. Her heart pounded as her palms sweated despite her fingerless gloves. Winter sucked because her fingertips were always cold, but gloves were too clumsy for the delicate art of pick-pocketing.

As Naya approached her target, she promised herself she would grab the first dress she saw and not look back. Even if the dress was three times too big, something was better than nothing. At least with something she would have a shot at fitting in at the merchant's house.

Naya crept closer. The two young people she'd seen before were nowhere in sight as she came close to the tables, already filled with cloth and clothing. She reached to grab a forest green woolen dress when the rustling of shoes had her diving under the table.

She heard voices above her.

"Come on, Leo. Mom said we must be set up before the sun rises. If your experiment is going to work, we have to do it properly." A voice shrilled from behind the table.

Naya held her breath as another voice sounded.

"Calm down, B. What Mom doesn't know won't hurt her. Besides, it'll be close enough." Unlike the first voice, this second one was warm and inviting. It sounded closer than the first and Naya realized its owner wouldn't be moving anytime soon.

She swallowed hard and made her decision. In one swift movement, she grabbed the forest green dress and threw her two coppers at the second voice, yelling, "Thanks for the dress!"

Naya took off running and didn't stop until she zigzagged across four blocks of alleys. Her heart hammered in her chest as she crouched low near a broken crate. Pounding footsteps sounded behind her and she gripped the dress close, hiding it against her body.

Boots slammed the cobblestones of the alley in rhythm with Naya's heightened heart rate. The young girl squeezed her eyes tight. She sent a plea to whatever gods or goddesses would listen and snuggled closer to the broken crate.

The alley quieted, and Naya slitted one eye open. A young man stood inches from her crate, staring at the dead end ahead of him.

"Blast it all to hell. Brigid is going to be crowing about this for years." The young man muttered under his breath before turning around and exiting the alley.

Naya kept her breathing even and willed her eyes to stay open, assessing as much as she could from her place behind the crate.

*Next, you need to hide the dress and make your way back to the safe house. All before the guards are out in numbers looking for the green dress and the favor that comes with it from one of the city's most wealthy merchants. Great.*

Naya did her best to hide the dress under her shirt and tucked it into the waistband of her pants. After making sure it was held tight, she repositioned herself and took a deep breath. She waited a few more minutes, listening to the sounds of the waking city, and fidgeted. The dress was finer than anything she'd ever owned and she found herself checking if it was still secure under her layers.

There was no telling when she'd need to run, and she sure as hell wasn't losing something so fine after the trouble she went through. Not to mention the two coppers. It might not seem like much, but those two coppers could be the difference between a full belly and going hungry again. Naya was an accomplished thief, but it always paid to have a backup plan on these streets.

As the surrounding air became lighter and lighter, Naya decided she couldn't wait any longer to make sure the coast was clear. Tentatively, she eased herself away from the broken crate and kept to the shadows as she looked down both sides of the main road.

More people were milling about, which was good and bad. More people meant it was easier for her to slip away unnoticed, but it also meant more people to possibly place her in the vicinity. And more witnesses meant a higher chance of guards knowing where she could be found. It wasn't ideal, but she figured with the scarf, there wasn't too much danger. Besides, being an orphan meant people ignored you all the time. She was just another hungry face among hundreds.

Naya slipped behind an elderly woman and melted into the crowd. She walked the two blocks to the alleyway that led to the back entrance of the safe house. Slipping inside, Naya couldn't hide her smile as she closed the door.

"Still grinning like a little girl at solstice with a handful of stolen honey treats."

Naya's head whipped to the thirteen-year-old boy who could pose as nearly fifteen. Without a second thought, she launched herself into his arms and laughed when he spun her around.

It was true that the only person Naya really trusted was Ryker, but growing up on the streets was impossible without a pack. Raj and Corbin had both been part of her pack at one time or another. She hadn't seen Corbin since he'd left to work on one of the horse farms just outside the capital.

"Corbin! About time you show your face around these parts again." Naya's grin was huge as she poked him in the ribs. "I almost didn't recognize you without all your bones poking through. If my eyes aren't deceiving me, I'd say you're almost fat."

Corbin let out a bark of laughter and put her in a chokehold. "Same Naya, never know when to keep a tight hold on that wit of yours." The boy studied her ebony skin and dark, wiry hair that hung limp from her scalp. "You look a little ragged. What's going on? Are you not doing well since Ryker left?"

Naya's heart clenched, knowing she'd have to lie, or at least not divulge the full truth to her former pack mate. "I—I need some help. I gotta get out of town, and the merchant houses seem to be my only option. Unless the horse farms could use another set of hands?" Her voice tapered off, knowing her last question was a long shot. She'd never touched a horse, much less rode one, but she could learn. Maybe. Her eyes drifted to the cot in the corner, and she sucked in a belly full of air.

The twins were gone.

Her senses went into overdrive and her head whipped around, looking for any clues as to where they'd gone.

Naya rushed to the pile of empty blankets and let out a cry. Her eyes were wild as she paced the small room. "Where are they? I wasn't gone for more than an hour. What did you do with them?" Naya did her best to keep her voice from shaking, but knew there was an edge of desperation she couldn't hide.

"What are you talking about? The little guys? Raj took them to McGrath for some fruit. Calm down." Corbin frowned at her with what seemed like concern, but Naya didn't miss the smugness in his tone.

*All an act.* She knew the games they were playing. No matter how sincere someone seemed, coin would always make somebody talk. She needed to find Hawk and Aurora *now*.

Naya's hands shook before she stuffed them in her pockets. "Which way did they go?"

"Naya, Raj, won't let anything happen to them." He placed his large hands on her shoulders and made her sit on one of the old rickety chairs. "Raj thought it would be good for you and me to talk without them here. Give us a chance to catch up. They'll be fine, trust me."

A sinking feeling took hold of Naya as she looked into her former friend's eyes. Corbin knew how dangerous this world was. He was trying to stall her. "I can't. Which way did they go?"

Corbin inclined his head to the left, and Naya shot out of the chair, taking care to stay out of reach of his long arms. The last thing she needed was for him to detain her by force. "Good to see ya, Corbin. Gotta run!" Naya called behind her. She didn't look back until she spotted Raj's tall figure in the distance.

Rounding the corner, she grabbed both Hawk's and Aurora's hands and pulled them into the nearest alleyway, taking care not to alert Raj to her presence. Clutching them close, she whispered, "Never do that to me again. The only person you go anywhere with is me. Got it?"

Hawk and Aurora looked at her with wide eyes and nodded, sleep still holding them in its firm grip.

With a yawn, Aurora asked, "Are we going to the merchant's house?"

Naya couldn't shake the suspicion from her heart, and she shook her head. "The only choice we have is the Pearl." She took a cautious glance at the market and saw Raj looking high and low for the two kids.

*Good. Serves him right for trying to do who knows what with the them.*

Hawk and Aurora shared a look at Naya's pronouncement, but didn't question their protector.

They were going to serve the Goddess.

# Chapter Fourteen

Myra pounded a fist on her desk and glared at the messenger across from her. "Well? You gave me the message. Now *go*. Before I decide I could use another privy cleaner." Her eyes glittered as she stared down the young girl.

The messenger knew better than to linger. She left with a salute and closed the door without a sound.

"At least the girl had sense. Can't say that about most of the degenerates in the service these days." Myra's tone was tinged with bitterness and cruelty. She knew it was unwise to speak of those below her in such a manner, but it was only her and her son. If anyone could handle her true self, it was him. He was cut from the same cloth despite not sharing a single drop of blood with her.

All the benefits of having an heir without actually being pregnant. The corners of her lips curled slightly as she met Mallick's gaze. She faltered when she saw his expression.

"Now what?" She snapped, annoyed at his lack of humor at her statement.

Mallick frowned and shot her a questioning look. "I beg your pardon?"

"Don't play coy with me. I saw the horror in your eyes. You think I was too harsh, don't you?" Myra's tone was clipped as fire blazed in her eyes and she stood from behind her desk.

Mallick was taken aback. "Mother, I meant no disrespect. If you saw horror in my eyes, it was only because you spoke the truth. Our forces are not what they once were and from your response to the letter, we seem to be in a situation where we need better troops, not worse."

Myra took a deep breath and exhaled slowly, beating back the retort on her lips. She knew what the boy was hinting at and a glance at the crumpled letter had her realizing he was right. If she wanted to win in the North, she'd have to send Mallick and his personal squadron. The Blades were the most skilled and ruthless fighters they had, and they only served their commanding officer. Myra was hesitant to give Mallick such power but seeing the way he drilled and prepared them she knew she'd made the right choice in entrusting them to her adopted son.

But she couldn't make it easy for him.

She needed to be sure he wouldn't die in the first battle he saw, or her captive might not be so compliant. Naomi wouldn't chance anything while Mallick was at risk, but if he died, so would her leverage against the former First Lady.

"I see where you're going with this, son. You've bested me three out of the past five times we've sparred. But do you have any idea what a battlefield looks like? Sounds like? Or smells like?" She cocked one eyebrow at the young man and stalked towards him, stopping to lean on the front of her desk.

"I only know what I've heard from the stories you and the senior officers have told. I respect your decision as my commanding officer and my mother. If you deem me unprepared, then it must be true." Mallick's tongue was trying to spread honey over her frustration, and Myra shot him a feral grin.

"Pretty words, son, but words mean nothing in the face of action. Report to the fighting pits and don't leave until you've been crowned the reigning champion."

"The fighting pits?" Mallick struggled to contain his disgust.

"What? Too good to grace the place I learned to fight with your presence? Don't be soft, soldier. I raised you better than that."

"Yes, ma'am." Mallick screwed his expression into stoicism but couldn't hide the hardness in his hazel eyes.

Myra gave a sharp laugh and thumped him on the back. "Convincing, but your eyes give you away every time." She shot him a wink as his expression fell. "Chin up, boy. Become a master in the pits and you will lead the Blades to battle in the North." She nudged him with her shoulder. "The pits are the closest thing we have to a battlefield this close to Fernwen. Prove your mettle and ability to get down and dirty and you will go to the front lines with my blessing."

Mallick's hopeful expression made Myra's heart swell in a rare feeling of pride for the young man she'd created. He wasn't her blood, but he was hers in every way that mattered.

"I won't let you down, Mother." Mallick gave her a salute and hurried out the door, readying himself for his tryst in the famed fighting pits of the Rookery.

Myra watched him go before returning to her desk. She gave a growl of frustration and smoothed out the letter from Vincenzio. He was whining again about not having enough soldiers should the Circus mount a counterattack. He had the audacity to use the soldiers she'd sent to sack the city without a coherent plan for defense. Heimat hadn't been built to withstand battle, and Darren grew lazy in his old age.

She was about ready to march herself, but her advisors would never allow that. There was too much unrest in the capital for her iron fist to leave them in charge. The merchants alone would riot and demand fairer taxes or other nonsense.

But sending more soldiers would leave her shorthanded. Unless she sent the Blades. It was the only way to keep her numbers bolstered and clean up the mess Vincenzio was making of the North.

*So hard to find good help anymore*

Myra drummed her fingers on the desk and considered her next move. *I know what will cheer me up.*

She smirked and strode to the door of her office. Without acknowledging the guards tasked with shadowing her, Myra made her way to the dungeons.

Naomi deserved to hear it from her that the boy would leave within the week.

Naomi shivered. Not from the cold, but from the lack of food and water, and the drugs she'd relied on for too long. She pressed her fingernails into her palm to distract herself from the waves of pain and nausea rolling through her. She unclenched her hands when it didn't work and wrapped them around her abdomen, curling in on herself to try to ease as much of the pain as she could. The shock of her cold metal chains against her bare arms made her cry out and tears ran down her cheeks.

Only thoughts of her baby girl and what was at stake kept her from reaching for the forgotten trays of food at the door of her cell. She needed to get through this if she wanted to do right by both her children.

Boots pounding on stone echoed outside her cell while fire lit inside her belly and she forced herself to sit up. Using the backs of her hand, she wiped away the tears and took deep breaths. This could be the opportunity she was waiting for, and she wasn't going to fuck it up.

A commanding voice sounded on the other side. "I don't have all day. Oh, forget it. Give me the key and wait over there while I do it myself."

Naomi groaned inwardly as the lock on her door turned. She braced herself for another meeting with the woman responsible for the nightmare that was her life.

Myra forced the door open with a loud bang, and Naomi's uneaten trays of food went flying into the stone wall. The imprisoned woman winced as a loud clattering echoed in the small space.

Myra smirked. "Good Goddess Naomi, is that your stench or just the rotting food? How do you live in these kinds of conditions?" Myra ended with a chuckle, enjoying the way her words cut at the once elegant woman's pride. The madwoman crossed her arms and shot her a look. "But honestly, you really let yourself go." She leaned down and ran her fingers through Naomi's stringy and dirty locks.

Naomi bit down on her tongue to keep from saying something she'd regret. The key to the game they played was never showing your hand too early. She needed to bide her time until she knew why this terrible woman was here.

If Naomi wanted another shot at Mallick alone, she needed to handle this interaction with the utmost care and keep Myra from guessing her intentions.

Naomi turned her head and averted her gaze, her hair falling free of the swordswoman's callused daggers. She knew it was a risk to chance inciting Myra's temper, but it let her get away with not speaking for a few more minutes.

A rough hand gripped her chin, forcing her gaze to meet Myra's. The woman was furious as she spit in Naomi's face. "Don't you dare look away from me when I'm speaking to you. That's not how this works. In another lifetime, you could get away with dismissing me, but not now." Myra wrenched her chin to look at the scattered trays of food and water. "Why aren't you eating or drinking anything? If this is a last-ditch hunger strike or something just as foolish, you have less sense than I give you credit for. If it's a cry for attention, then you have your wish. I'm all ears. Start talking or waste away. It's your choice. Your usefulness has just about run its course."

Naomi's eyes widened as Myra released her chin. The dictator gave away more than she realized. If Myra was willing to let her die, they had either found Duncan or something happened to Mallick. She needed to tread carefully if she wanted answers.

Myra frowned and spat on the ground. She tapped her foot with impatience as her eyes bore into Naomi's face.

The imprisoned woman sighed. "Why eat or drink when I betrayed the only person left to come save me?"

Naomi relaxed ever so slightly when Myra reacted the way she hoped. The dictator let out a cackle and thumped Naomi on the back.

"Glad to see you've still got your winning sense of humor. But the information you gave my son..." Myra's eyes glittered with malice as she let her words drag out. "It was useless. Clearly, whatever information you had was outdated. I could've guessed it would be, but I wanted you to have one more moment with your baby boy."

Naomi's heart stopped at Myra's words. *Did I miss my chance?*

The former First Lady kept her expression neutral and asked the question she was afraid to know the answer to. "Did he realize you weren't worth the time anymore and leave?"

*Crack.*

Naomi saw stars as her head ricocheted from the power of Myra's slap.

"Listen here, you little bitch. Mallick loves me and I've molded him into the perfect soldier. He may share your blood, but he is *mine.*"

Now Naomi spit blood on the floor and met her captor's gaze. "Only time will tell if that's the truth."

Myra shook her head and gave a low chuckle. "Classic Naomi, never knows when to shut the fuck up. No matter, you will be happy to hear I'm sending your precious baby boy to the front lines. Once he's crowned champion of the fighting pits, he marches with the Blades to do battle in the North. He'll lead the charge against Duncan and his excuse for followers." Myra's eyes glinted, and she gave Naomi a feral grin.

Naomi felt her hands get clammy and her heart race. Myra had no intention of giving her another moment with her son. She couldn't give the dictator any inclination she was desperate to see him one more time. She needed to play her cards right if she wanted an opportunity to tell her son the truth and apologize for not being able to protect him.

Naomi's voice shook, but she let the emotion through, hoping it would convince Myra of her false sincerity. "Maybe it's true. Maybe there's nothing left of me or Andre in him."

"I forgot how much I enjoyed our midnight rendezvous. Maybe we should start those again." Myra laughed as Naomi squirmed. "If you entertain me enough, I'll let you see your little boy one more time before he heads north."

Naomi felt her stomach drop and reminded herself this was what she wanted to happen. Her hands shook at the thought of spending more time with this wretched excuse for a human being. The woman's cruelty knew no bounds. She was more of a monster than any Magicae Naomi had ever met. She caught the look in Myra's eyes and time seemed to slow. Naomi shot her a questioning look, and Myra let out another bark of laughter.

"I wasn't going to tell you this, but it seems fitting. I was going to save it for when you really needed to be broken, but we've hit an all-time low." Myra gestured to the plates of food scattered on the stone floor. "Safe to say I finally shattered the formidable Naomi Freeman."

Naomi kept a level gaze, but inside ice coated every part of her. Her husband was dead, her son was brainwashed, and she betrayed the only friends she had left. There was only one other person Myra could use to break her. "What do you mean?" Naomi knew Myra wanted her to beg, but she'd have to make do with the question.

"Vincenzio's original report included mention of a powerful fire Crafter with hair as golden as the sun. She was the reason the vermin escaped on those ships. Pity he didn't note her eye color." Myra's words were biting as she taunted the emaciated woman.

Naomi's stomach clenched, and she gritted her teeth, willing herself to stay calm. She was sure if Myra had confirmation of the girl's death, she wouldn't hesitate to share. Myra couldn't even be sure the girl was Rae; she could only share her musings to get a reaction from her captive.

Naomi forced herself to take a deep breath and release the tension in her jaw. She'd be no use to either child if she fucked up now. Myra wanted a response, and she had to give it to the deranged woman.

Naomi reached out, her chains clanking as she gripped Myra's forearm.

"Leave her out of this, Myra. I beg of you. The girl has done nothing to you." Her insides boiled as she did the one thing she swore she'd never do. Even if it was all an act, shame took root in her heart as she begged for her daughter's safety.

The satisfaction on Myra's face let Naomi know she'd been convincing. She hoped the dictator would let more slip before she left.

Myra shook off Naomi's grip and went to the door. "Too bad the family reunion will end in bloodshed." Naomi paled as Myra stepped through the doorway. "Mallick has orders to kill the girl on sight. Oops, I guess he'll never get to know his older sister."

She left with a cruel smile and the slam of the cell door.

Naomi couldn't help but let out the scream she was holding inside. Tears slid down her face as she wailed, giving all her pain, frustration, and fear an outlet.

Whether or not she'd done enough to have another opportunity with her son, the time had come for Naomi to fight back or die trying.

# Chapter Fifteen

Rae slipped out of her tent in the middle of the night, pulling Tyee's leather coat tight to ward off the winter chill. The smell of horse and worn leather stilled her frantic heart. Once she reached the outskirts of camp, she snapped her fingers and let her fire light the way.

A smile graced her lips as she moved deeper into the forest. Her world was in shambles, but at least she still had the warmth of her flames as winter raged on. She felt a shudder move through her, thinking about how she'd almost been forced to bind it.

Rae gave herself a shake. She'd lost all signs of the Crafter's Curse after she'd harnessed her other three Crafts. It was no use dwelling in the past when the future had enough problems of its own.

She let herself look inward for a moment to make sure all four of her Crafts were still within the confines she'd placed on them. Rae would be remiss to deny she checked three or four times a day to make sure they stayed in their places. The last thing she needed was to lose control and be unable to regulate her power again.

Finding all four pulsing contently at her core, Rae gave a sigh of relief.

"That's quite the sigh, Sparks. Do you need a minute with that coat of yours?" Zeke flashed her a smile and cocked an eyebrow as he stepped from the shadows.

Rae gave him a playful shove, her heart pinching at their easy banter. She'd always feel guilty for using Zeke in pursuit of power, but used that guilt to ensure she never took him or anyone for granted. War was coming and more would die, but tonight was about reconnecting with her closest friends.

"No need for any of that, sicko." She winked at him, earning a chuckle. "Did you get the whiskey?"

Zeke scoffed and put a hand to his chest. "Do my ears deceive me? Or did my best friend ask the stupidest of questions?"

Rae rolled her eyes. "I'll take that as a yes. All I'm going to say is it better be the good stuff because it's fucking cold out." She looped her arm through his and continued to the clearing the four agreed to meet at.

"Again, why do you think so little of me? Only the top-shelf stuff for a night like tonight." Zeke sobered at his last words.

Rae shared a look with her trapeze partner.

This was the first step in healing the space between the four of them. In making new memories and dreaming for the future. She and Zeke missed so much being away, and it showed.

Especially in her relationship with Damien.

She couldn't believe Luc would hide something like that from her. But on the other hand, they'd rarely spent time just the two of them after leaving Verdencia. Luc was busy with her duties as Head Mortal and Rae had spent every spare moment practicing with her other three Crafts.

Maybe it was her fault they hadn't found time to connect. Even during all those years on the road and performing in the Circus, they'd found time to slip away just the two of them and a bottle of wine. Rae's heart hurt as they made it to the clearing and the pile of kindling they'd set up in the light of day.

Without a word, Rae went to the pile of sticks and offered the flame from her fingers. The sticks blazed brightly before settling into a warm glow. Rae met Zeke's eyes and gave him a sad smile.

"Z, what did we do wrong?" Her voice wobbled a bit, but she got the words out as emotions crashed through her.

Zeke pulled her into a one-armed hug. "Nothing. We did nothing wrong. Time and space make strangers of the best of friends. All four of us have new scars too deep to explain with words. You can't fault them for not sharing everything when we didn't either."

"I always thought I'd know when something was off with just a look. It breaks my heart to know Damien was hurting, and I never noticed a thing. How can we get back to the way we once were?" Rae searched Zeke's face for answers. Before he could respond, another voice sounded in the small space devoid of trees.

"We can't get back to the way things were before. There's no use in trying because we've all been through hell and back." Damien's baritone rang with truth. "And I'm fucking sick of pretending like everything is like it was before." He met the eyes of the woman he draped an arm over and pulled her close, before glancing back at their friends. "We can't go back, but we can move forward. If we're all willing to see what happens next."

Rae's eyes filled with tears and rushed to embrace the ebony-skinned man. Luc gripped her side as tears stained her cheeks, and soon enough, Zeke joined the group hug, too.

The four of them stood for several minutes, taking comfort from each other.

Eventually, Damien pulled back first. "Alright, alright. You're going to wrinkle this fine fur coat that Midge made for me."

Rae and Zeke laughed as Damien's sense of humor shined through. They pulled back and moved to sit around the fire. Zeke pulled the bottle of whiskey from his coat and passed it to Damien.

"Same rules as always. Each pull equals a secret. Should we say anything within the past two years?" Zeke asked.

"Ha, you'd think we'd have run out of secrets by now. I don't think we need to limit how far back the secrets are from."

"I agree with Luc. Drink up, Dame!" Rae nodded and flashed Damien a grin.

But the young man shook his head and passed the bottle to Luc. "I sure as hell ain't going first. You lot need to be more drunk before I'll start spilling."

"Boo!" Rae called, and Zeke joined in.

Luc shook her head and smiled, taking a long gulp of the burning liquid. She wiped her mouth with her sleeve and met the expectant stares of her friends.

"Dame wasn't my first kiss. Kaiser was."

"What?!"

"No!"

Rae shrieked and Zeke yelled before both whirled on Damien.

"Did you know this?" Zeke demanded.

Damien shrugged. "It's in the past. And besides, she's bagged a much finer man, if I do say so myself." He winked at the woman he loved and earned a giggle.

"Here you go, Rae." Luc passed her the bottle, still giggling as she snuggled closer to Damien's side.

"Geez. I have half a mind to pass it on while my world's been turned upside down." Rae smirked at Luc as she rolled her eyes.

"Get on with it, Hermana. Don't be a coward like Dame."

Damien shook his head as Rae shot Zeke a look. Rae had two options. First one was to follow in Luc's footsteps and choose something lighthearted to start with. Second one was to take the conversation deeper. She knew it would be better to go deeper before their heads were spinning, but she hated to be the one to kill the mood. She passed the bottle between her hands until she made up her mind.

Rae took a long pull from the bottle and felt its heat race down her throat. She swallowed the liquid courage and her eyes found Zeke's. "I tried to push all of my wind into Zeke and nearly killed him. He forgave me but it's a shame I live with every day. I was selfish and committed the worst atrocity to a fellow Crafter and my dearest friend. I used him and the power in his veins without his consent." Rae met Luc's questioning gaze and hung her head as silence descended on the quartet of acrobats, only the noise of the crackling fire breaking the stillness.

Rae felt arms wrap around her and she leaned into who she assumed was Zeke. Thin arms held her tight and Luc whispered, "Do you wish to say more, or should we move on?"

Rae hugged the other woman tight and found Zeke's silver gaze. "The last thing I'll say is that I learned my lesson and will do everything in my power to make sure it doesn't happen again. I'm already working with the younger Crafters and will continue to emphasize the importance of consent in everything we do with our Craft, from sharing life energy to using someone else as a conduit."

Zeke gave a nod and held his hand out. "Couldn't have said it better myself. Thank the Huntress you weren't my teacher, though. That would've been a nightmare." Rae flashed him an appreciative smile and handed him the bottle. Luc kept her arm around Rae, but shared a meaningful look with Damien. Rae knew the pair had sensed a shift in her and Zeke's relationship and could now connect the dots between their observations and what happened.

Zeke downed a mouthful of the contraband whiskey before he waggled his eyebrows and looked around the fire, holding out a feather for the group to see. "Bane gave me a feather."

Rae snorted and Luc broke out into loud laughter.

Damien closed his eyes and shook his head. "And what the hell does that mean? You spend every waking minute with the guy. I hope he's given you more than a feather. When are you going to make it official?"

Zeke's eyes glittered. "I've never been one to kiss and tell."

"Oh, come on, Zeke. You can't honestly believe showing us a feather from your could be lover is worth a mouthful of top shelf whiskey. Give us more than that." Luc protested.

"Alright, alright. Keep your shorts on. I will not comment on our relationship or lack of one, but I will tell you the feather is a way for him to always know where to find me." Zeke's eyes softened at the memory.

"Blah," Rae stuck her tongue out and pretended to barf into the fire. "Talk about nauseating."

"Oh yeah? What about that coat I caught you sniffing and moaning to?"

Luc looked scandalized and scooted away from the Crafter. "Gross! At least keep it in your tent."

Rae did her best to protest, but dissolved into laughter with the rest of her friends. As they sobered, Zeke offered the bottle to Damien. "Are we drunk enough for you yet?" he asked.

Damien responded by taking two big gulps from the bottle. "It'll have to do for now." He coughed twice and stared into the fire.

The other three acrobats waited in silence for Damien to release some of the hurt inside. There was a tension buzzing in the air and Rae felt the hairs on her arm stick up in anticipation. This was the real reason they'd done this. Rae, Zeke, and Luc concocted a plan to get Damien to loosen up and find a way to take action. He'd already admitted so much to Zeke, but this would be an opportunity for him to take another step in healing with all their support behind him. They just needed him to take the leap.

Damien kept his gaze trained on the dancing flames as he confided. "I hear their screams every time I close my eyes. I see their lifeless gazes and taste the tang of copper on my tongue from all the blood." He crouched forward so his elbows rested on his knees. "And there's nothing I can do. I killed them. I took their lives without a second thought and turned into a monster."

He turned until his eyes found Rae and understanding passed between the two of them. Luc moved closer to him until their shoulders were touching. He leaned into her steady support and continued, "Their ghosts haunt me and the only way to let them rest is to commit to never taking another life." He clenched his fists. "But I feel like I'm letting everyone down. Rae and Zeke, you don't deserve to live a life in hiding. I should be able to pick up my bow and say to hell with all of those bigots, but I can't." Damien's face was tormented as he looked at the two Crafters. He turned to the woman at his side. "And mi amor, you deserve a man that would fight to the death for you and the people you love. I'm sorry I can't be that man." His voice cracked as a tear fell from his eyes. "I'm so sorry, to all of you."

Rae kneeled beside him and gripped his hand, waiting for him to meet her eyes. "There is nothing to be sorry for. You make that commitment and heal, Dame. Your well-being is worth more than a million bows. You don't have to kill somebody to be an asset to the cause."

Damien swallowed and squeezed her hand, overcome with emotion.

Zeke sat on his other side and put an arm around his shoulder. "You're worth more to us alive and at peace than, Huntress forbid, dead or battling within yourself. Vow to never take another life, but don't stop there. Take another vow to do everything you can to further the cause in other ways. That's the only way you'll be able to move on and let go of your guilt. It won't happen overnight, but let the healing begin."

Damien's body started convulsing as his tears flowed freely.

Luc put a hand on his cheek and pulled him into a chaste kiss. Zeke's arm dropped as she pulled him into a fierce embrace. "Mi amor, you are more than man enough for me. It takes true strength and courage to admit what you need and pursue your peace. You don't have to kill someone to prove yourself to me. Not being able to stomach killing again proves more to me about your strength and character than anything else ever could. Rae and Zeke are right. Take an oath and swear another. Find your peace, mi querido."

The three stayed close as Damien's convulsions slowed and he cried himself out. He rubbed a gloved hand over his face and sniffled. "Anybody got a handkerchief?" Damien stilled when three hands held out what he needed. He narrowed his eyes as he accepted the one from Luc. "If I was a betting man, I'd say you three were plotting this all along."

Luc batted her eyelashes at him and put a hand to her chest. "You wound me, amor. How could you think so little of me?" She echoed his words months before, and everyone chuckled.

"Thank you." Damien's voice rang with sincerity before he blew his nose. Finished, he looked up at three expectant faces. "What?"

"Are you going to do it?" Rae asked, pulling a dagger from her boot.

"Do what?" Damien narrowed his eyes, noticing the weapon.

"Take an oath. Or oaths I guess."

Damien looked at Zeke and Luc. The former nodded, and the latter shrugged as if to say it was his call.

Damien swallowed and held out his forearm. Rae met his eyes and waited for him to nod before she placed the blade against his skin.

"Huntress, hear me from this place within the trees.

"We call on you to bear witness to this oath.

"With blood from the testifier and three witnesses,

"Let your presence be known."

Rae drew the blade against Damien's dark skin and a thin line of red followed her dagger. Keeping ahold of the weapon, Rae tilted Damien's arm, so the blood dripped to the frozen earth beneath them. As soon as the first drop hit the snow, a mighty wind blew through the clearing, putting the fire out in an instant.

Rae met Damien's gaze again. "The Huntress is here. Speak your vow and know the consequences should you break an oath said before one face of the Goddess."

Damien nodded and looked at the stars. "I am humbled by your presence, Huntress, and the presence of my three witnesses. On this winter night, I, Damien Rutter, swear on my life to never again steal the spark the Goddess has given to another human being, Mortal or Magicae. Accept this blood to seal my oath and set the terms." Damien squeezed his arm to make more blood drip to the ground.

The wind tore through their circle once more, this time lighting the fire instead of putting it out.

"Holy shit! I forgot how unnerving that can be." Rae felt a lingering presence rush through her before disappearing into the midnight air.

Luc rubbed Damien's back and offered him a piece of cloth to wrap his arm in. "How do you feel?"

Damien took a deep breath and exhaled slowly. "Better. Shaken, but better."

"Should we all take the second oath?" Zeke asked, looking around at the group.

"I think that's a great idea." Rae wiped her dagger on her pants and washed it with snow before sending Zeke a questioning look. He pulled up his sleeve and offered her his bare forearm. Rae made a shallow cut and wiped the blade again. Before she was done, Luc held out her bare arm with a smile. The Head Mortal winced as Rae made a small nick but nodded to let the Crafter know she was all right.

Rae cleaned her blade one last time before pulling up her own sleeve. She watched as the blood welled to the surface, escaping through the line she made with her blade. She looked around the fire and nodded to Damien.

"Goddess, Huntress, and Prophetess. Three faces for one deity. We come before you with a blood oath. Hear our pleas as we make promises to each other and our people." He met Rae's gaze, not sure of what else to say.

"I promise to do everything in my power to bring about peace and justice for the Magicae of Kamore." Rae's voice was strong and clear as she tilted her arm to make her blood drip onto the snow.

"I promise to protect those that can't protect themselves and fight for a more equitable Kamore." Luc mirrored Rae's movements.

"I vow to never stop trying until our people can live without hiding and in fear for their lives." Zeke's voice was quiet but strong as he watched his blood drip to the earth.

"And I take one more oath to do everything I can to give my friends and the Magicae of Kamore a place in this world. I vow to use everything I can to bring about change in this broken world without taking another soul." Damien squeezed his arm to force more drops from the almost dry cut and only relaxed when blood sprinkled the ground at his feet.

Three winds ruffled their coats before disappearing into the trees.

He looked at his three dearest friends and his voice cracked. "Thank you." He stopped and cleared his throat. "Thank you for doing all this. I am forever grateful for our friendship and your support."

Zeke thumped him on the back after he finished winding a piece of cloth around his arm. "Speak for yourselves, but I was only making sure I didn't break the blood oath we all made as kids. Not helping you means I'd be stuck with warts all over my face." He gave an exaggerated shudder to make the other three laugh at the memory. Young Zeke had been terrified of getting a wart on his face.

Rae laughed and grabbed the forgotten bottle of whiskey from the snow. "Yeah, yeah. We all remember. But now I want Luc to spill more secrets about this forbidden kiss with Kaiser." She held it out for Luc to take, and the game continued.

They stayed out until dawn, finishing both of the bottles Zeke stole from Mac's private stash and laughing until their sides hurt.

No one noticed that the blood they'd spilled was nowhere to be found in the pure white snow as they stumbled back to their tents.

# Chapter Sixteen

"That's enough for today."

Tyee gave a start. This was the third day in a row he'd spent from sun up to sun down working on writing and memorizing the runes. He'd mastered the first two sets of five she'd given him and moved on to the next set of seven. These were more complicated with multiple lines and specific ways lines crossed each other.

It was enough to give a man a headache.

He looked up from his place at the table and moved his head to one side and then the other, working out the kinks in his neck. "Just yesterday you told me I would spend every waking hour at this table until my fingers fell off, if that's what it took. What's with the change of heart?"

Andriette gave him a hard look. "The change of heart is because I'm bored just watching you. I think you would benefit from a little motivation." She pointed to the rows and rows of the first ten he'd done over the past couple of days. "You've learned the essential ten and your depictions of them will pass, but you need to see what the runes can do for you. Besides, it's the winter solstice and everybody deserves a treat on such a day. We're going to Oakenrock where the runes originate from." She pinched his cheek and smirked. "Look at that great-grandson, you've earned yourself a field trip."

Tyee scowled. "What do you mean, where the runes originated from?" He wiped off his metal stylus and set it next to the paper riddled with symbols he was starting to recognize.

"Oakenrock is the oldest city in Elven history and was the former capital. It was abandoned long ago, but not before the great Adrian Sweetwater discovered a way to harness the power from our veins. You've noticed the connection you have with animals, no?" Tyee nodded as he stood up and she continued, "You have that same affinity for plants. You may not have realized it, but the forest sings for you too."

Tyee's mind flashed back to that night in the woods, before Heimat was sacked and when Rae hurt Zeke. He'd found and cut some willow bark to help Zeke's headache. Tyee always assumed he'd learned that somewhere, but could it have been the magic of his Elven blood?

"Let me grab my coat. Are we taking the horses?"

"No. I think the walk would do us both good. These old bones need to be used if I expect them to keep doing their job. Bundle up, boy. Tonight we spend the night under the stars." Andriette ascended the stairs to her room to grab what she needed for the journey.

Tyee felt a slight increase in his pulse as he thought about getting the answers he'd wanted for so long. There were so many questions he had for his great-grandmother, but the only time she let her guard down and allowed for them was at mealtimes. And because they only ate dinner together, Tyee hadn't gathered nearly as much information as he would've liked. He knew it had only been a week or two since Fritz dropped him off at the old woman's door, but it felt like an eternity.

He'd learned a little about the old woman's family history and what happened to his grandparents, but not enough about the Elven people as a whole.

He'd learned that his grandmother was Andriette's only child, and she'd perished along with her husband in the battles before Verdencia was founded. Her death meant their baby girl, his mother, was left without someone to care for her.

Andriette had done her best to raise the girl, but she became wild and would leave for weeks at a time. When she came back pregnant, his great-grandmother threw her out for such recklessness.

Andriette had grown quiet after that admission, as if the guilt weighed heavily on her shoulders. Before Tyee could offer words of comfort, she confided that she'd been at her wit's end and hadn't known what else to do. If she'd known the girl would leave Verdencia altogether, she never would have thrown her out.

The rumors were she'd met a young man in one of the northern villages and was having an affair with him.

Shortly after those rumors surfaced, his mother's name was banished and Andriette never saw her again.

The old woman became silent after that and insisted on cleaning the kitchen herself.

That happened last night and Tyee could sense there was something else his great-grandmother needed to share with him.

He changed into warmer clothing and pulled the fur coat he still wasn't used to over his shoulders. He grabbed his pack from the corner and brought it to the kitchen to fill with dried meats and fruits, besides the blankets already inside.

His Tota joined him shortly after with a matching pack.

She nodded in approval, watching as he stuffed in more food. "How are you with a bow?"

Tyee shrugged his shoulders. "Good enough to get by. I wouldn't use it in a fight, but I won't starve if I have one."

Andriette grunted and slung the bow and its quiver filled with arrows over her shoulder. "I'll let you do the skinning then. Come now, we don't want to waste the daylight." The old woman walked out her front door without a backwards glance.

*Don't worry, I'll make sure we don't starve out there. Or freeze our asses off.* He grumbled to himself and, grabbing one more blanket, he tied his pack and followed Andriette out the door. Tyee found her at the paddock, stroking her forest pony. He watched the old woman and noticed the way she softened to the shaggy, dark brown equine. Andriette entwined her fingers in the pony's long mane and whispered low in his ear. With one last hug to his neck, she turned to face him.

"If you painted a picture, it would last longer." The old woman's sharp reply reminded Tyee of his frustration with the tactless crone.

"But then I'd never be rid of your disapproving gaze." He growled in response, harsher than usual.

She let out a cackle. "Your tongue is as razor-sharp as mine. Say goodbye to the brother of your heart and join me in the meadow."

Tyee sighed as the old Elven woman left him with the animals. He went to the fence and whistled, smiling when Koko materialized on the other side of the fence next to him. They'd been going for early morning and late night rides, so his presence in the daylight was unusual. Koko tilted his head and let out a whinny, before mouthing Tyee's gloved hands and jacket.

The horseman gave a low chuckle and rubbed the stallion's neck. "Greedy little thing, aren't ya? This will be the last carrot for a couple of days, so enjoy it while you can." Tyee offered the treat to the large animal and Koko bobbed his head in appreciation. His hands rested on the paddock and his fingers traced the runes protecting and caging the animals.

He started when he recognized the rune known as Teiwaz, a straight line with two smaller ones that formed a hat at the top of it. This was the rune for discipline and duty. It meant sacrificing for the greater good and bravery in the face of obstacles. With a frown, he traced more symbols, finding the single straight line that was Isa, representing ice.

Puzzled, Tyee wracked his brain for the other meanings of the ice rune. After a moment, it came to him. Isa also represented a forced pause, necessary before rebirth or renewal just as winter forced all of nature and civilization to slow down before the new life of spring.

Tyee's shoulders began to ache with the weight of his pack, and he readjusted the leather straps to get some relief. He reached for the stallion once more.

"This is it, old friend. I'm going on a trip with the old lady. If we don't return in two days' time, it is your duty to come find us." Tyee watched Koko's dark brown eyes, hoping his words would be enough to spur the horse into action should something go wrong. The last thing he wanted was for the horse to starve in the paddock, unable to leave because of the runes in the wood. The horse blinked once and rubbed his head against Tyee's chest.

Tyee took that as confirmation the stallion understood. With one last pat on Koko's neck, Tyee turned to follow his great-grandmother.

*Time for some answers.*

He meandered his way to the meadow, where Andriette sent him to forage for mushrooms in celebration of mastering his first rune. He'd been happy for the break but made the trip quick to continue working on the last four. Tyee had mastered two more that evening and another seven the next day. It felt good to be making tangible progress, but his Tota had a point. Just because he could draw a rune and recite its meaning didn't signify he was any closer to unlocking the power of his Elven blood.

Part of him was worried this trip would be a waste of time if he didn't have enough power to make the runes work. Andriette herself admitted he was the first half-blood she'd taught and couldn't be sure his blood was strong enough to use the runes until he learned to harness them himself.

Tyee rubbed his chin and shifted the heavy pack on his shoulders. His thoughts strayed to his time in captivity under Sylvie's fist. He'd used Luc's life energy to make the runes on his bindings release. And when Rae used the last of her life energy, he'd used his own blood and the runes he'd scratched into their palms to relight her spark. Surely he had some power to control the runes if he'd been able to do all of that.

*Except you almost killed Luc and yourself. Maybe you can use the runes, but is the cost worth bothering to use them?*

The palm he'd slashed to save Rae itched, and he struggled to relieve the sensation without taking his thick gloves off. Unable to satiate his skin, Tyee removed both gloves with a hiss as the frigid air hit his bare hands. He scratched his scar and narrowed his eyes when the tightness of the angry red marks didn't alleviate.

He rubbed his bare hand on the rough bark of an oak tree, but quickly removed it as if he'd been burned. With a bewildered expression, Tyee placed his hand back on the rough wood, this time gingerly, as if the tree would bite if he moved too fast.

Emotions flickered across his face before disbelief won out. Tyee kept his hand on the tree but leaned back to try to take in the oak's full profile.

He heard it.

Or rather, felt it.

He felt the song of the oak tree deep in his bones. It was a pounding drumbeat, accompanied by a buttery voice singing in a language foreign to his ears. His lips pulled up into a soft smile, and he closed his eyes.

This was the strangest and most amazing thing he'd witnessed in all of Kamore. It made everything pale in comparison to discovering he could hear the heartsongs of the trees he'd always found refuge in.

He kept his hand on the tree as the drums sped up and the singing came to a crescendo. And then silence.

Tyee opened his eyes, but it was no use. The tree was quiet.

"You've discovered the sound of the oaks I take it."

Tyee whirled to face his great-grandmother and stuffed his hands inside his gloves. Too late, he saw Andriette's open expression cloud as she caught sight of his palm. She sucked in some air and let it out slowly, releasing the tension from her face and softening her expression.

"There's nothing like the first time you hear it. Tell me what you heard."

"It was a drumbeat with a voice as rich and warm as fresh butter. They started out slow but built until all at once, both the drums and the voice went silent." Tyee recounted what he felt, but kept his eyes on the oak tree.

She nodded. "So you can hear the voice. In the journals from our ancestor Elma, she talks of how the Magicae could only hear part of the song. This is another powerful sign you should be able to use the runes." She took his arm and walked him towards the opening in the trees. "When it took you so long, I figured something happened. I walked back and found you with your hand on the tree, and I knew." She placed her free hand on his heart. "This is where the sjel evner comes from. This is where the power from your soul can be found."

Tyee met her whiskey-colored eyes and inclined his head. "Tota, can I ask you some questions? You may not have all the answers and I've appreciated everything you've already shared, but I'm not learning fast enough. It's already the winter solstice and I feel like I'm still miles away from where I need to be."

"Of course, nakni. That's what this journey is for. You have a lot to learn and something tells me demanding you to read it from a book wouldn't help much."

Tyee snorted as they continued walking. "And that's an understatement. I can read enough to get by but am in no way literate."

"And the books are in Elvish, so you wouldn't have a prayer." They both chuckled, and Tyee shrugged his shoulders with a smirk.

"Who knows? Maybe that's the problem. I can only read Elvish."

Andriette let out a howl and rubbed her eyes, clutching at her side. "You're going to give this old bird a fit if you keep at it. If you can't handle the written Mortal word, I doubt written Elvish would make much sense. I'm afraid it's a lost cause either way."

"Worth a shot." Tyee smiled at her, warmth spreading through him as he enjoyed the camaraderie that came inherent among kin. The old Elven woman could be a bear when she wanted to be but moments like these reminded him that there was beauty and power in finding the family that shared your blood. It meant something that he'd lowered more of his guard in the past two weeks with the old woman than he'd ever done after years in the Circus. There was still time for the other shoe to drop, but the more he got to know his Tota, the more convinced he was that she genuinely wanted to help him find what he came for.

"The journey is more often than not, worth more than the place you're trying to find. The biggest mistake we make is wishing the journey was over and not paying attention to the lessons along the way. I will answer your questions, but you may not like or be satisfied with the answers I can provide." Andriette raised her brow and shot him a look.

"Understood." Tyee stuck his gloved hands into the fur-lined pockets of his coat. "Is there a rune for heat? Or thicker gloves at least?"

She snorted. "If only it were that easy. The twenty-four runes are nothing like the woman you pine after. She's a Crafter, no?"

"Aye." Tyee gritted his teeth to remind himself to ignore the way she spoke about Rae. The only way to change her opinion of the Crafter would be to arrange a meeting. And that wasn't happening anytime soon.

"Good to know this old mind of mine can still remember some things. Anyway, your woman can call her magic or sjel evner with a snap of her fingers. Elven magic doesn't work like that. It ebbs and flows like water in a stream. It is as constant as the mighty Mother Oak and as fickle as the seasons. It's as sturdy as a boulder and as soft as a cub's fur."

"So this sjel evner or whatever is just as bad as a woman? Can never make up her mind and needs attention before she'll do anything?" Tyee deadpanned.

"Sounds like you've been running with the wrong kind of women."

"You don't know the half of it." Tyee looked towards the trees as thoughts of Sylvie crowded close.

"I heard about what the general did to you." Andriette squeezed his arm. "You don't have to share, but I'm here to listen if that's what you need. When you're ready, we can trade captivity stories."

Tyee returned his gaze to hers, one eyebrow raised. "You were imprisoned?"

"Don't act so surprised. Your great-grandmother was quite the spitfire back in the day. It was a way to—but that's a story for another day." Tyee noticed the way her eyes clouded as she winced.

"Can we go back to Elven magic? And why the runes don't work the way Crafter magic does?" Tyee changed the subject, knowing the old woman would open up in her own time. She'd already admitted the guilt she felt for the loss of his grandparents and the banishment of his mother.

Some wounds weren't worth revisiting.

Andriette smiled her thanks. "Yes, of course. As I said, Elven sjel evner is like nature. It's as powerful as it is unruly. In the beginning, the Elven rarely used their magic for anything besides helping the plants grow, connecting with our brother and sister animals, and coaxing the trees to create shelters for us to live in. It was a peace unlike anything seen in Kamore." The old woman's face turned wistful. "I grew up hearing those stories and how easy life would be if the world was simpler. But alas, that reality is long gone. As always seems to be the case, a few individuals grew unhappy with their station in life and went searching for something better.

"What they found was they could use their sjel evner for much more than what we'd used it for previously. But once they released it, they couldn't rein it back in. Instead, their sjel evner destroyed them from the inside out. Adrian Sweetwater lost his father this way and vowed to find a way to control our power.

"He was the one that developed most of the runes we use now. The idea is there's a combination of runes for any and every situation. Every rune has multiple meanings and *feelings* associated with it. Therefore, two different Elven are unlikely to use the same combination to accomplish the same task." She paused to let Tyee absorb what she was saying.

"That makes sense, but what do the runes actually do?"

"They act as calling cards for our sjel evner. The more feeling and emotion you put into them, the more powerful they become." She grabbed his left hand and shook it. "That's why this is so dangerous. You say you did this on instinct and if that's truly the case, you're worse off than I thought."

Tyee wrenched his hand from hers and stuck it back in his pocket. He was quiet as the reminder made him reach for whatever connected him to Rae. The bond was still solid as he gave it a squeeze, knowing Rae would feel it wherever she was. He hissed when the mark burned with Rae's response, but couldn't keep the small smile from his face at the continued connection.

"Tyee. This is not a joke or a charming love story. The rune you drew is known as Algiz, revered for its association with protection and providing sanctuary. But the two of you shared blood, no?"

Tyee nodded. "It was the only way to give her the life energy she needed rapidly enough. She was dying, Tota. I had to do something." He met her gaze with pleading eyes and whispered, "I couldn't imagine a life without her."

The old woman pursed her lips and averted her gaze. After a moment, she sighed. "Before young Elven can walk, they are warned of the consequences regarding drawing runes with blood. That's how the First Ones released the power in our veins. They slit open their skin and called to the Elven blood itself. What you did was reckless and could have ignited your own blood. Drawing the rune was probably what saved you. But now you've entwined your fate with this woman for eternity. You drew the rune of protection, and your blood will give everything to keep that promise to her. By marking her skin with the same rune, you may have placed the same burden on her, given the shared blood between you. If one of you gets into trouble, the connection between you will drain the life energy of the other."

Tyee paled at Andriette's admission. "But you can't be sure of that."

"I've seen it happen before, nakni. Many lovers take the same marks, unwilling to watch their beloved die. But forcing it upon her without the choice? It's not right. You didn't know any better, but this is why we're making this journey. You need to see the consequences should you disregard the rules of the runes again."

Tyee quieted as ice drenched his insides. He'd only been trying to give Rae a fighting chance. There had to be a way to reverse this. A tingling sensation made him look at his gloved hand. Rae was stroking their bond as if she could feel his agitation. Tyee let the comfort sink in before snapping his hand into a fist. He'd fucked this up before they'd had a chance to start. If he didn't want to lose the hellfire of a woman, he'd need to learn as much as he could about the power in his blood and the runes that held it in check.

*I'll make this right.*

"Will you help me undo what damage I can?" His voice was a whispered rasp when he finally spoke.

Concern knitted his Tota's brow as she responded. "Of course, nakni. We'll work something out."

Tyee nodded, and they continued in silence, the only sound their boots crunching on the snow covering the path. They walked for a couple more hours before making camp for the night.

The winter solstice ended with a dusting of snow as the song of wolves howling filled the air. It was a solstice Tyee would never forget.

# Chapter Seventeen

Naya fidgeted again as the rough spun wool of her hooded cloak made her itch. The haughty priestess in charge of the new postulants already gave her a lecture on the importance of stillness in the Goddess's presence.

A glance at Sister What's-her-name confirmed she'd seen Naya's movements by her pinched lips and tight expression.

But honestly, what else was she supposed to do? She was itchy but too warm to wear long sleeves underneath. She longed for the fur coat she'd left with the twins, but knew her threadbare desperation convinced the priestesses to accept her as a postulant.

Naya averted her gaze from the priestess and studied the elaborate woodwork of the pew in front of her.

The temple known as the Pearl of the Goddess was magnificent, with elaborate and beautiful structures. It sat on the largest of the three islands in the Mantaga and had no bridges connecting it to any other parts of the capital city.

On the outside, the front entrance had stone steps leading up to a set of large wooden doors. The doors themselves entranced with swirling patterns etched into the gorgeous wood. Side doors echoed the two main ones on either side in shape and style but were locked at all times. The doors were set into stone archways within the impressive feat of engineering. The pieces that made up the temple itself fit together so well that it was impossible to tell where one piece ended and another began. The result was a looming structure with carefully carved details and motifs, complete with stone columns and recessed stained glass windows.

Three terracotta domes crested the roofs of the structure, one for each of the Goddess's faces, with spikes for points. Three pearls sat atop those spikes, a large pink one on the middle and largest dome, while one white and one black topped the other two smaller domes on each side. Hence the name for the sanctuary.

Behind the Pearl, were the dormitories that housed the priestesses and postulants, the kitchens that fed them, and the land where they grew food and raised animals to sustain themselves. Naya had only explored a small part of the living quarters, kept busy by Sister What's-her-name but thought she saw a door leading to the basement with five different locks on it. It piqued her interest, so she'd avoided it like the plague. The only thing she needed to worry about was keeping the twins safe.

Naya had hauled the twins to the island after the debacle with Corbin and Raj. That night was a mess, but the three of them made it. And that was the only thing that mattered.

The temple rarely accepted girls as young as nine and never accepted boys, which was why Aurora and Hawk were stashed in a cave at the southern end of the island. Naya was loath to leave them on their own, but they needed food, water, fuel to make a fire, and warm clothes if they expected to survive the rest of the winter. She had no choice but to leave them and become part of the temple itself.

She spent her days cleaning, sweeping, dusting, and praying

As they were doing now.

Again.

It had only been a few days, but Naya knew the praying was what would do her in. Sitting still in silence would never be one of her strengths. It went against every instinct she had. On the streets, standing still meant you were an easy target. Those that didn't move quick enough most often ended up for sale. Naya would be damned before she let some fat lazy master own her very existence.

If only freedom wasn't so Goddess damn hard to keep.

Naya pushed herself onto the balls of her feet, wishing that was enough to relieve the burning on her skin.

"Sister Helga is going to beat you if you don't knock it off." A voice whispered from her right.

Startled, Naya said the first thing that came to mind. "Well, maybe if they learned to treat the wool the right way, it wouldn't be so damn itchy." She kept her voice low, but by the way so many heads turned in front of her, Naya knew she'd spoken too loudly. "Goddess damn. It'll be cleaning duty again," Naya hissed.

The postulant next to her vibrated with silent laughter. "I think you have a death wish."

Instead of responding, Naya tucked her arms into the oversized cloak and itched her skin as hard as she could. She earned some relief, but slowly the burning returned. The girl let out a low groan and heads turned again. She glanced at, Helga, was it? Naya knew she'd fucked up. The woman's eyes glittered with disapproval and her face held a scowl.

*Here we go again. I'll be the only one cleaning this gigantic place for my 'indiscretions.'*

Naya's thoughts were bitter as the past two nights replayed in her head. The first night she'd been caught trying to sneak out and was forced to join the cleaning crew on duty as punishment.

She'd felt bad as she mopped the floors on her hands and knees, thinking about how the twins would feel spending their first night away from her in months.

Hawk and Aurora wouldn't know where she was and didn't have their familiar tools, should something go wrong. But she knew she'd make it up to them with sweets she'd plucked from the kitchen on her way out. If only she could find a way to escape the prison that was life as a postulant at the Pearl.

Last night, she'd stubbed her toe on the way out of the temple after prayer and swore loud enough for the entire order to hear.

Sister What's-her-name relished doling out her punishment a little too much after that incident. She'd scrubbed the floors until her fingers were bloody, but at least dinner was waiting when she returned to her room.

Naya could tell she was in for another penance, but at least she knew the sisters in the kitchen were generous, even to those whom life was hardest on.

"Damn it all. Looks like I'm in the doghouse too." The voice had a weary tone but echoed louder than before, turning heads, but not because of Naya.

The young girl looked to her right and met sapphire blue eyes. She wore the same gray wool cloak as Naya, indicating she was also a postulant for the priestesses of the Pearl. The girl's eyes danced with mirth despite the trouble she was in, as if she couldn't care less about what Sister What's-her-name would do to her. The girl was at least four or five years older than Naya and gave off a magnetic presence the ten-year-old couldn't resist.

"Well, if I'm stuck on cleanup duty, I might as well make it worth it." The older girl shot Naya a wink as she shrugged off her uncomfortable robe and fell to her knees, hands clasped together and her lips moving in silent fervor. She closed her eyes and tilted her head back so her face was in line with the statues of the three goddesses, each holding a giant freshwater pearl.

The Huntress had a bow slung over her shoulder, a quiver full of arrows at her back, and the purest white pearl in her outstretched hand. The Prophetess appeared as if she came from the sea itself with waves clinging to her thighs, her clothes and hair dripping wet from the water and a bandanna over her eyes. She held a shining black pearl in one hand and a compass in the other. Lastly, the Goddess herself stood between them in a flowing white marble robe with a crown atop her head. Her lifeless eyes somehow held understanding and power within. The Goddess held out the largest of the three pearls, a rare creamy pink one, as if in offering, while her other arm swept wide to welcome everyone to her place of worship.

Most people thought these three marble statues depicting the faces of the Goddess and the pearls they held were the most stunning pieces of art ever created.

To Naya, it all seemed like a waste.

She looked at the statues and all she saw were opportunities to sell off their parts and pieces to get money for food and water. The Pearl always seemed to have an air of entitlement and arrogance around it and the priestesses it housed, but seeing it firsthand made Naya sick. With another glance at the girl next to her, Naya followed suit.

If she was stuck on cleaning duty, the least she could do was take off the suffocating and scratchy robe.

With a shrug of her shoulder, she let the itchy wool pool around her feet as she hit her knees. She closed her eyes and clasped her hands as if they were the only lifeline she had left. For one last effect, she let out a low keening sound as if she yearned for something only the Goddess could provide.

*Take that Sister What's-her-face. You can punish me for talking, but nobody will be able to say I'm not devout after this performance.*

Naya held her position and punctuated the still silence with her wailing every so often. The prayer and adoration continued for almost another hour. By that time, Naya's knees threatened to give out, and she almost wished she'd suffered through the wool robe. At least then she'd have the option to stand or sit after the bell tolled.

Finally, the Head priestess known as the Mother Superior walked to the front and struck the bell with her wooden staff. Its clear and crisp sound reverberated in Naya's chest, quickening the pulse at her wrist and making her head hurt.

The old woman turned to face her fellow priestesses and projected her voice. "My beautiful, loyal sisters. Your constant vigil and fervent devotion makes all three faces of the Goddess smile. We are blessed with each other's presences along with those of our very special guests."

Naya's blood ran cold as she looked toward where the Mother Superior gestured and caught sight of her worst nightmare.

Myra and her entourage sat only a few rows ahead of her in the middle section of the hard wooden benches lining the temple's interior.

She reached for her robe, desperate to hide herself before the dictator could catch a glimpse of her. The last thing she wanted was to face the woman that allowed Fernwen to devolve into what it was now.

She wasn't quick enough.

"Myra and her son grace us with their presence and support, and I thought it only fair to show them what their investment has already returned. Will our newest postulants please come forward?"

The girls and young women around her stood up, and she got lost in the tide pulling her to the front.

"Keep your head down and she won't even notice you." The older girl whispered in her ear, guessing at Naya's reluctance.

Naya trembled but didn't respond, tucking her chin and keeping her eyes downcast.

But she knew nothing would save her from Myra's attention. She and the older girl were the only ones without those dreadful wool cloaks and were sure to catch the tyrant's eye.

The dozen or so postulants made to stand in front of their Mother Superior beneath the three statues of the Goddess and her two other faces.

Naya did her best to position herself as far from the dictator as she could, hoping to hide amongst the others, even with the lack of a cloak.

"Mother Stella, you are too kind. My son and I are happy to fund efforts as noble as yours." Her gaze studied the young girls just starting their journey in serving the Goddess. "However, I can't help but notice that two of them seem to be missing their habits."

*Shit.* Naya never heard of a cloak being called a habit before, but she knew when she'd been caught. Her stomach clenched so hard she had to bite her tongue to keep from crying out.

"Ah, yes. You must forgive them in their zeal for serving the Goddess. Ophelia joined us from the Merchant's Guild two weeks ago and Kaia graced our shores merely two days ago. They are young and filled with a passion to serve the Goddess and their sisters. But their passion has not yet been tempered and they sometimes lose themselves." She gave a small smile. "Do not hold it against them until they've spent enough time with us to learn self-control. Come forward, Ophelia, Kaia. Let our brave and generous patron get a better look at you."

Naya grimaced at the name she'd given the sisters that she'd first encountered. In the heat of the moment, she'd said the first name that came to mind instead of her own. Every time someone said it, she had to do a double take and almost blew her cover in the process. At least it was close enough to her own that she always responded to it.

Or at least almost always responded to it.

Regardless, now was when she'd be forced to face the tyrant herself. Naya didn't know what she feared more, the woman, or what she'd do once she stood before the dictator responsible for so much poverty. She was to blame for every hardship and every hurt incurred by the orphans and beggars on the streets.

Naya wasn't a fool.

She knew a single person couldn't be responsible for all the evil in the world, but she did it, anyway. It always felt like an easy way to explain away every awful thing that happened to her.

At least it had been before she'd put herself in this precarious position.

A gentle tug on her arm brought her back to the inevitable. Naya's belly clenched again, and she stumbled forward until she stood in front of the Mother Superior.

Naya gave a start when she noticed how young the head priestess was. She couldn't be more than thirty, much younger than what Naya would have expected for the leader of these pretentious and self-righteous so-called sisters.

The Mother Superior plastered a smile on her face but couldn't hide the apprehension and anger from her eyes. It was plain to see that behind her calm facade, she was furious at being made to look incapable before her benefactor.

Naya took a gulp and remembered the older girl's advice, bowing her head and averting her gaze. She clenched her teeth, willing herself to remain quiet and not forget about the two kids counting on her. Attacking Myra wouldn't do them any good.

Naya and Ophelia stood in front of the head priestess with heads bowed and hands folded in front of them. They were the picture of devout postulants ashamed by the passions that urged them to this point.

"Please forgive us, oh magnificent Mother. I felt the Goddess moving through me and couldn't contain myself." The older girl dared to meet the head priestess's eyes. "I never meant to cast doubt on your capabilities or bring dishonor to the Temple."

Naya kept her head down, not trusting herself to speak until she felt Ophelia nudge her arm. Feeling eyes on her, she croaked, "Please forgive us, your excellence."

The Mother Superior gripped both girls by the shoulder and turned them to face Myra and her retinue. "I am not the one you distracted with your antics. As touching as your words are, they do not fall on the right ears."

Naya's pulse quickened, and she felt blood rush to her cheeks. She kept her head down and let Ophelia take the lead again, grateful for the older girl's quick thinking and confidence in speaking before such a crowd.

"President Myra, please forgive us for the lack of constraint we demonstrated during the service. Kaia and I are new to the Order and eager to learn from the sisters of the Pearl and our Mother Superior. Regardless of our passions, we should have taken more care to respect you and your son's time for worship. All we can do is offer our sincerest apologies and earnest assurances we will do better in the future."

"A silver tongue and a silver face." Myra assessed both girls with a frown, but her gaze kept training on Ophelia. "Mother Stella claims you hail from one of the Merchant's Guilds, but one as young as you must be from one of the ten families." Her words didn't form a question, but her raised eyebrow made it apparent she expected an answer all the same.

"Aye. You are correct, Your Excellency. I hail from the Starski family and am the youngest daughter to Quinn and Mel of the Armory Guild."

A hush descended over the people gathered.

The Starski family had a reputation for being unyielding and ruthless when it came to their business in creating and selling armor of all sorts. Quinn and Mel had never seen eye-to-eye with Myra but didn't let that stop them from signing a contract to be the military's sole supplier of chain mail, armor, and every weapon under the sun. They held a position of power that Myra refused to acknowledge.

Even Naya knew this would get them in even more trouble.

*Damn rich people. Worried more about politics than saving their own skin.*

Before she lost her nerve, Naya spoke up. "Your Excellency, please excuse my fellow postulant. We are taught that once we enter into serving the Temple, we must leave behind everything from our past lives. Ophelia may be of the Starski family, but all ties to them came undone the moment she donned her gray robes. Please have mercy on two girls trying to serve the Goddess in any way we can." Naya's voice wobbled, but she kept it from cracking. Her voice was directed to the dictator in front of her, but her eyes stayed glued to the floor. No way in hell was she letting Myra memorize her face.

"Mother, if I may?" A deep voice echoed within the hallowed place and almost shocked Naya into looking up but she caught herself, digging her nails into her palms as a reminder to keep her wits about her.

Myra gave a nod, and her son projected his voice. "You girls bring dishonor on your mentors when you act in such a manner. If you were in the army, you'd be flogged for such disrespect despite your intentions. We will return in one month's time and will expect to see vast improvement or else you will both serve two years in the army. That will straighten your paths if the Sisters of the Pearl can't temper your spirits." He shifted his attention to the woman still standing behind them. "Mother Superior, can we move onto the blessing you promised me before I fight tonight?"

The head priestess guided Naya and Ophelia to the side. "Of course. Postulants, please take your seats as we send prayers to the Goddess to protect Mallick in his fight for glory."

Naya only heard blood rushing in her ears as she followed the other postulants to their place at the back of the Temple.

"Whew, that was a close one."

Naya jumped when she felt lips near her ear and processed the words Ophelia said. "You're lucky I saved your ass. I knew Clan Starski was brash, but I didn't expect them to be stupid." The girl hissed as they returned to the pew where their itchy cloaks lay on the ground. Naya grabbed hers and shoved it over her head before anybody could stop her. The sooner she could dissolve into the crowd, the better.

"I like you. We're going to be friends. I can just feel it." Naya heard the smile in the older girl's voice and bristled as Ophelia donned her cloak as well.

"Don't hold your breath."

A look from Sister What's-her-name made them fall silent as the Mother Superior started Mallick's blessing.

Naya knew if she wanted any hope of staying out of trouble, she had to avoid this girl at all costs. Hawk and Aurora were depending on her to keep up the charade at the Temple for as long as possible.

Befriending a Starski would only lead to trouble.

# Chapter Eighteen

Bane landed on the branch of a tall birch tree, its paper-white and flaky skin a beacon in the dark forest. Getting back to the Circus's settlement at Mantaga Lake was taking much longer than the trip to Heimat. He knew it was from draining his life force at Diane's farmhouse.

But Goddess damn, he could barely fly a mile before having to stop and catch his breath. He should've stayed the night as Rich suggested, but he'd been stubborn and desperate to get home to his loved ones and the comfort they could provide.

His heart still clenched every time he thought of the blackened remains of the forest across the river from Heimat. Thoughts of those ruins spurred him onward as he spread his wings and launched himself from the towering branch.

He glided through the woods, keeping his senses alert for the sounds of predators and heathens. Few animals would dare swipe at his animal form since falcons themselves spent little time in the forest. They preferred the heights of the mountains and cliffs to the forest thick with trees. But his Da drilled it into him at a young age that being alert meant staying alive. It was an unconscious precaution at this point.

The heathens were the mercenaries and zealot citizens searching for the Circus. Rich confided there was a bounty for anyone who could lead the general to where the Circus ended up. Once Vincenzio knew where they were, it would only be a matter of time before he took his revenge on those he held responsible for his missing daughter and destroyed city.

Classic narcissist blaming everyone but himself for the situations he found himself in.

Bane's blood boiled as he found another branch to land on. He knew the best thing would be to bed down for the night and continue in the morning when his life energy was recovered. He'd cover a lot more ground in much less time if he gave himself a break.

But the rage simmering in his blood wouldn't let him. He'd keep going until he physically couldn't fly anymore. That was the only way he'd rest before reaching Duncan and the others.

Bane let the falcon part of his brain take over, trusting it to stay on course and stop when needed. His thoughts returned to the night before and subsequent morning.

*Rich ran upstairs with the hot water, but the screaming continued.*

*Bane was by no means an expert in anything regarding children or the labor needed to birth them, but a feeling in his gut said something was wrong. The couple of births he'd seen on the road with the Circus included moaning and groaning from the soon-to-be mother, but not this blood-curdling wailing.*

*Something wasn't right.*

*Torn between his duty to do what Diane asked of them and the instinct urging him to act, he hesitated.*

*The two eldest girls walked into the house with concern on their faces.*

*"Is it the baby? Is it here?" Asked the one Bane presumed to belong to the woman in labor.*

*"Not yet. It sounds like your mother's in pain, so I'm going to see if there's anything I can do to help. You two should stay down here and make yourselves comfortable on the couch."*

*Before the girls could protest, Rich came down the stairs holding the youngest boy in one arm and tugging on the hand of another little girl, who was pulling a second younger girl.*

*Rich's face was white when he looked at Bane and shook his head. Something was definitely wrong.*

*The two older girls crowded the old man.*

*"Is my Momma okay?"*

*"What's happening Grandad? Did Auntie Sara have the baby yet?"*

*Rich shared a look with Bane and made his way into the living room. "Come on, girls. The seven of us are going to have a sleepover in the living room while your Momma finishes having the baby. No need to be scared; the birth is just taking a little longer."*

*The two girls shared a look before following the old man into the living room.*

*Another scream echoed through the modest farmhouse.*

*Bane shot another look at Rich, his instincts screaming at him that something was wrong. "I'm going to run upstairs and see if I can help." Bane didn't wait for Rich's response and took the steps two at a time.*

*He followed the screams down the hallway to the third door on the left. Inside, Anna and Diane were doing their best, but the grim expressions on their faces gave insight into how dire the situation was.*

*Sara's legs were propped up on the bed and spread so Anna could sit between them, offering encouraging words. "Come on Sara. I can see the head, just push a little more."*

*Diane paced the room, alternating between checking the towels submerged in Rich's pot of hot water and going to squeeze Sara's hand or wipe the sweat from her brow.*

*Sara herself had tears running down her bright red cheeks and eyes filled with pain as screams tore from her throat.*

*Diane was the first to realize his presence. She walked to him and attempted to turn him around. "I'm sure you're only trying to help, but I assure you, this is the last place you want to be right now."*

*"Something's wrong. Tell me what's going on." Bane pulled out of her gentle grasp and strode towards Anna. "I've never heard a woman scream like this during birth. She's in pain. Something's not right; let me help."*

*Anna looked at him with a scowl. "What can you do? Have you ever helped a woman give birth?"*

Bane moved to Sara's side and gripped her hand. "I can't say I have. But something is telling me she needs life energy. My instincts have never been wrong before. Let me try." He met the gazes of both women and waited for their approval. Once they nodded, Bane turned to Sara. "This is going to be uncomfortable for you. I'm going to send some of my life energy to you through your bloodstream, okay? I'm going to have to make a small cut on your hand so my blood can mix with yours, and the life energy has a direct route to where it needs to go. The baby is stuck and this life energy should help give you the force you need to get the baby out. It might hurt, but it will only be for a short while. Does that make sense?"

Bane held on to Sara's hand tightly, ready to give her the life energy she needed but unwilling to proceed without Sara's consent. As soon as she inclined her head and gave a slight nod, Bane did what his instincts had been screaming for him to do for almost twenty minutes. He made small nicks in both of their palms and placed his large hand over hers. He closed his eyes and concentrated, letting the gift in his veins trickle into Sara slowly. Overwhelming her now was too dangerous for her and the baby.

Bane knew that sometimes babies got stuck in the birthing canal. It happened in humans and animals both. It was dangerous to use his life energy to help Sara force the child out, but it was more dangerous to let the baby linger in this position. He looked at Sara and asked, "Do you feel that?"

Sara nodded and let out another scream.

"Okay, on three, I need you to push. Can you do that for me, Sara? When I say push, I need you to push as hard as you can and we'll get this baby out sooner rather than later, okay? I need you to nod or say something so I know we're on the same pa—."

"I got it," Sara gritted out before another scream sounded and she broke into sobs.

This time Bane looked at the two older women and said, "I'm going to help her get the child out, but it's up to the two of you to figure out what to do with it. As we've already established, I have no experience, but I do know we need to work fast."

"We'll be ready," replied Anna. Diane nodded and went to grab the towels.

"Alright, Sara, one, two, three, push!" Bane sent a shock of life energy through Sara's body as she groaned. She gritted her teeth and pushed as hard as she could.

"Great job. You're so close. One more push and the babe will be free. You're doing so well." Anna held the towel, ready to catch the little one when it arrived.

"All right, Sara, one more time. I'll do the same thing, so don't be surprised when you feel it. One, two, three, push." Bane sent another shock rippling through the young woman. This time, Sara screamed as tremors racked her body. As soon as her cry ended, another began. This one coming from the little boy Anna wrapped in a towel.

"Hush, now, little one. I know it's scary coming into a new place. Welcome to the world." Anna beamed at Sara, but her expression fell when she noticed the woman's limp form. "Diane, something's wrong. Can you get the smelling salts?"

Diane rushed to the side of the room and grabbed a container, bringing it to Sara's side, opposite Bane. The Shifter kept his grip on Sara's hand and felt it loosen. His eyes widened as he watched Diane wave the container underneath Sara's nose.

They waited a short while, but nothing happened.

"It's not working. Is she bleeding?"

Anna held the now quiet baby boy in one arm and checked under the sheet she'd put over Sara. She gasped. "There's a lot of blood."

Bane's heart pounded in his throat. Sara was going to lose her life if they didn't act quickly. No one in this room was a Herbalist, or even a doctor. Bane racked his brain, trying to think of the herb his Da used for that one sheep.

"What about yarrow? Doesn't it slow the bleeding?" Bane asked, hoping Diane would have some in the house. If they didn't have any on hand, it was doubtful Sara would make it through the night.

"I have some in the cupboard, I'll go get it." Diane rushed downstairs.

Anna shot him a look and asked, "How did you know about yarrow?"

Bane shrugged his shoulders. "It's what my Da gave an ewe when she lost too much blood during delivery. I'm going to keep giving her life energy until Diane gets back and she's stable."

*"Thank you,"* Anna said, her eyes shining with sincerity.

Bane felt the exhaustion in his limbs and realized it was too dangerous to continue. His falcon form had taken him as far as he physically could. He flew to the top of a pine tree and settled in for the night.

*Diane did have yarrow in her cupboards and brought it back to the young mother. It took over an hour for the herb to stabilize Sara's condition. By the end, Bane had used most of his life energy to keep her life-giving functions going. It was one of the hardest things he'd ever done, but when she finally woke with tears in her eyes, he knew it was worth it. He'd left the room when Sara took her baby boy into her arms for the first time.*

*It was dawn by the time Bane made it down the stairs and Rich met him in the kitchen, baking bread for breakfast. "How's she doing?"*

*"She's going to be okay. They're both okay. She'll need rest for the next few weeks, but there seems to be enough hands for that." Bane sighed. "We need to talk and I need to leave."*

*"Boy, you look beat. Maybe you should get some rest and leave tomorrow at the crack of dawn. Give yourself some time to recover." Rich offered.*

*"I thank you for the hospitality, but Heimat doesn't have time to spare." Bane shot him a pointed look, reminding the old man of what was at stake.*

*They spent the rest of the morning and a good chunk of the early afternoon talking about what had happened to Heimat, its people, and the forest it once shared the land with. Rich told him about Vincenzio's promise and the destruction he racked on a city already reeling from so much loss. He told him about Johanna's legacy and how Tommy, Simone, Eddie, and Rob brought the last of Heimat's Magicae to some of the surrounding towns.*

*Bane's head had spun with all the information Rich shared, but it only hardened his resolve to leave at once.*

*The Circus needed to exact vengeance on the evil that was Vincenzio and his soldiers.*

He'd flown as far and as hard as he could but now, Bane resigned himself to rest, knowing he'd wake once his life energy was strong again and he could fly high above the trees to maximize his speed.

It was time for the Resistance to take a stand.

Mallick threw his opponent a cruel smile that showed all his teeth. Sweat covered his chiseled and exposed torso despite the chill of winter. The press of bodies and giant torches ensured all the fighters felt was heat as they faced each other in the recessed pits.

Mallick spit and rolled his shoulders out. Cuts, scrapes, and bruises covered almost every inch of him as he lifted his eyes to meet his opponent's gaze. This was the last adversary between him and the title of champion. One more fight and he'd leave this Goddess-forsaken city for the open road and the battlefield. He'd finally be out of his mother's shadow and prove his own prowess when it came to combat and strategy. Mallick was sick of playing war games on a table.

The time for fighting had come and Mallick would be damned before he let lesser men take the field before him.

His mother was never one to coddle. Hell, she'd been the exact opposite. Cool and aloof most of the time, it took a lot for Myra to offer any sort of praise. But when she gave it, you felt like the king of the world. Mallick hadn't minded his childhood nor held anything against his mother being aloof. Love and affection were for the weak.

And that was the one thing Mallick was not.

Weakness had no place in this world, and he would forever be grateful to his mother for driving it out of him at a young age. It was the best thing she could've done for him and what he would spend the rest of his life striving to repay her for.

If he was a fool, he would've thought his mother's reluctance to have him join the front lines was a sudden show of affection in response to possibly losing him. But Mallick knew that was the farthest thing from the truth. Myra had a reputation to protect. She wouldn't let him embarrass her on the field after training him herself. Mallick needed to be the best of the best if she was going to release him into the world.

The man in front of him was solid muscle and a few inches taller than him, but Mallick wasn't worried. The six other opponents he'd faced were of similar builds and went down easy enough. They were small enough to be fast, but built enough to do some damage when they landed a hit. The trick was to match their movements and be quick enough to avoid their blows.

Each match seemed harder as Mallick's strength flagged, but something about facing this last man gave him new vigor. He was out to prove something, and this man was a fool to think he could stand in the way of Mallick's future.

They circled each other in the deepest of the fighting pits, the crowds jeering and taunting the opponent they bet against. Mallick tuned them all out as he waited for the bell. There was only one rule in the pits and that was the fighting didn't start until after the bell tolled. Anybody throwing punches before the bell was immediately disqualified.

If they started early, that meant less time for the bets to go through.

Mallick was tempted to look and see whether his mother was in the crowd, but didn't dare lose his focus. He wasn't taking any chances with this last fight. Besides, she'd been strange ever since the blessing at the Temple. He'd chalked it up to nerves about him fighting but when she'd left him at the front door of the warehouse-like structure, she'd only told him not to wake her when he got home. They would discuss his leaving in the morning. His mother had hurried off without a goodbye or a second glance.

But that wasn't the cause for his concern.

He was worried she'd disapproved of the way he'd handled those two stupid girls. He'd started sitting in on the Advisory Board meetings but was still naïve when it came to the games his mother played with the politicians and wealthy of the country. Mallick knew the Starski family was renowned for the pieces of armor and weaponry they distributed and had a suspicion they wouldn't take kindly to the way he'd addressed one of their own.

His mother seemed distracted as they marched through the streets, only increasing Mallick's sense of wrongdoing. But Myra wasn't one to keep her thoughts to herself. If Mallick fucked up, he would've heard about it.

His mother was plotting something, and he needed to know if that plot interfered with the future Mallick had planned. Defeat the best fighters of the pits and leave the only city he'd ever known. Join the battle for the North alongside Darren Vincenzio and rid Kamore of the Magicae once and for all.

His mother insisted on bringing them to the capital, but Mallick thought it better to get rid of them.

The dead couldn't launch a counterattack after all. And their people were successfully seduced into believing a potential rise of Magicae would mean the end to Mortals. Fear was the most powerful weapon a general could command, and Myra was a master in using it to her advantage.

Something Mallick aspired to do. Which was why he shot his opponent another feral smile.

*Ding-dong. Ding-dong.*

Mallick didn't hesitate and attacked first, determined to end this as quickly as possible. He leaped and tackled the man standing between him and freedom.

The crowd roared as the last fight of the night started in full force.

# Chapter Nineteen

"Duncan, you can't expect me to up and leave when Gemma just got here. The poor little girl finally has her mother back and you're sending her away?" Mirabella's voice cracked as she looked at her older brother. Her brother's impassive expression only made it harder for her to hold it together.

It had been a day since Gemma arrived at the Circus, and Duncan was already asking the impossible. Mirabella resigned herself to returning to Heimat and the man who made her life a living hell, but she hadn't expected to leave so soon. She'd assumed she would have until spring to love on and watch her daughter grow.

It was happening too fast and her heart was breaking all over again.

"Bella, you know I wouldn't ask if it wasn't important. Gemma is a special little girl, she'll be okay. Conrad will travel with you through the forest and once Bane returns, I'll have him send a falcon as a messenger. We need eyes on Vincenzio if any of this is going to work." Duncan's expression turned pleading as he leveled his lavender gaze on hers.

"Duncan," Mirabella's voice cracked again as a sob escaped from her throat.

"Bella, talk to me." Duncan put a hand on her shoulder and pulled her into him.

Mirabella sobbed into Duncan's shoulder, unable to form the words to describe the life she'd be returning to. Her brother whispered soothing words into her ear and rubbed her back, letting her cry it out.

"I promise that no harm will come to your little girl while you're away. She'll be safe, Bella. Once we know what Vincenzio's planning you can come home."

Mirabella only cried harder. Duncan was doing his best, but it only reminded her of everything she had to lose. If she went back and Darren didn't believe her, he would kill her. There was no doubt in her mind.

But that's not why she cried. She'd risk her life to help the people she'd hurt, as it was the least she could do. She cried for the daughter who could potentially lose her mother.

Gemma was a smart girl, but her youth made everything more complicated. The girl only saw in black and white, not the shades of gray that her parents resided in. She wouldn't understand why her mother would return to her father without her. Mirabella's greatest fear was her Herbalist daughter would realize the part she played in destroying what the Magicae once had. She needed to do everything she could to make up for her transgressions before her daughter understood what she'd done.

Mirabella had no choice in going back to the man who turned her world into a nightmare. It made her skin crawl even considering being in his presence again, but she'd do it for her daughter.

And herself.

She deserved retribution from the man who manipulated and abused her for years. Even if it meant enduring it all over again.

But how could she explain all that to Duncan?

Her thoughts were all over the place as her mind raced a mile a minute. She sobbed harder, letting Duncan continue to comfort her. After another few minutes, she quieted and the last of her tears dried. She took a couple of shaky breaths and pulled away, avoiding Duncan's questioning gaze.

"I'm scared, Dunc. You—you don't know what it's been like the past few years. Darren used to—it doesn't matter." She sighed and took another deep breath. "My life with Darren has been a nightmare ever since Gemma was born and I fell apart. At first, he was only helping, but it turned into controlling every part of my life." Her voice was a whisper.

"Bella, I had no idea—,"

"Please, just listen." Mirabella cut him off, afraid if she didn't get it out now, she never would. "When you first asked me to go, I dreaded going back and resuming my sentence in his prison.

"But it's the perfect way to atone for the crimes I committed against the Magicae. Ever since Gemma's birthmark became more pronounced, and she grew into her power, I've struggled with how to explain her father's hatred of her people. Not to mention my part in the Uprising and everything that followed. I will do what you ask and return to the man who broke me, if only to reverse some of the hurt and death I've caused. All I ask is that you keep her safe if anything happens to me. It breaks my heart to leave her again, but the thought of her growing up without her mother terrifies me. I will give my life for this cause if it comes to that, but I'm scared for what damage that would cause my baby girl. Promise me you'll raise her and protect her if this goes south."

Mirabella met his lavender gaze with fire in her eyes. Gemma was the only thing that mattered. That brave little girl brought so much light to world, and she'd shielded her daughter from as much as she could. But the time for shielding was past. Gemma needed to learn the truth if she was going to survive in this cruel world while Mirabella was away.

Duncan's gaze was pained. "Bella, I wouldn't ask if there was any other way. The abuse you suffered is unacceptable. I'll make sure help is always at hand, but this is the way that leads to the least amount of bloodshed. If I could take your place, I would in an instant. Say the word and we'll find another way, but if you're willing, we need you to do this."

"I can do it. I can go back and be your eyes and ears in the castle, but Gemma needs to be taken care of first. It's a good plan and I'm your best shot at getting into those meetings behind closed doors. Darren will want to put off a united front and keep me by his side until he determines if he can trust me."

"Be careful of the dangers in store. And if you ever find yourself in a position where you fear for your safety, promise me you'll call for help." Duncan's expression was hard to read and only made Mirabella more frustrated.

"Stop treating me like a little kid. This is exactly what happened back then.

Trust me to do this. I've been playing the part of a dutiful wife for years now. I can last another couple if need be. Just promise me you'll do right by Gemma." Mirabella's voice shook with frustration as she stared down her older brother. She wasn't letting history repeat itself and would demand the respect he'd denied her all those years ago.

Duncan was quiet for a couple of moments. He met her gaze once more and pulled her into a fierce embrace. "You have my word. Gemma will be safe. But promise me you won't take any unnecessary risks. I lost you once, and losing you twice would ruin me." He whispered in her ear before releasing her.

Mirabella nodded as silent tears leaked from her eyes.

"When do I leave?"

"Tonight, so make today count." Duncan gave her one more hug before leaving her to find her little girl.

Mirabella watched him go and gave a long sigh. She'd gotten little sleep the night before as she wrestled with the idea of returning to her abuser. She may have accepted her fate, but disclosing it to her daughter was another story. Mirabella would put that conversation off for as long as possible.

Mirabella walked back to where she'd left Gemma with some of the other children at the picnic tables. She smiled when she spotted her daughter's telltale copper curls bouncing as she laughed at the little girl next to her with soft brown waves of her own. An older girl sat with them with mousy brown hair and slight frame. She was rolling her eyes, trying to hide the smile on her face as the younger girls kept laughing.

Mirabella felt tears prick at the corners of her eyes. Gemma rarely spent time around children of her own age because of safety concerns from her father and the fear of discovery from her mother.

There were plenty of wicked people in the world thirsting to see how far they could push Myra's right hand. If anybody knew the truth about Gemma, it would only be a matter of time before the people demanded action and Darren decided what truly mattered to him.

Mirabella would never be willing to give him that choice.

"You're not who I expected would be responsible for the demise of an entire people." A sleepy voice startled her.

Mirabella looked over and met eyes of liquid gold. She studied the woman's face carefully, recognizing her as the one Gemma ran to when she couldn't find her mother. She knew the woman's name was Rae but hadn't talked to her, or anybody really, on the journey to the lake. Duncan suggested it might be easier for all parties if she kept a low profile, and Mirabella found she couldn't disagree.

But something seemed so familiar about the woman in her early twenties.

"But then again, you should never judge a book by its cover, eh?" Rae flashed her a mocking smile and Mirabella froze.

She'd seen that smile a million times before in what seemed like another life. The mother studied the Crafter and found bits of Naomi and Andre in her face, her expression, and the way she held herself.

"You're Naomi and Andre's daughter." Mirabella blurted out before she could help herself.

"And you're Duncan's sister. The one that got my father and so many others killed," Rae said with narrowed eyes.

*Ouch.* The accusation stung, but Mirabella accepted it without complaint. "I am one and the same and it's my biggest regret and deepest shame."

Mirabella learned long ago not to waste words. Saying less gave more power to the words she did use. And kept her out of trouble when she was around those who wished her harm.

Rae gave her a once over before inclining her head. "We all have things we wish we could've done differently. Is it true you're going back to Heimat to be our inside woman?"

"Aye. Duncan suggested it and I found there was no reason to say no to such an opportunity to make amends." Mirabella still felt wary of the blunt blonde but appreciated the chance to explain herself.

Rae frowned. "Does Gemma know?"

"Know what, Momma?"

Mirabella's heart stopped when she heard her daughter's high-pitched voice filled with innocence. Her panicked eyes met Rae's apologetic ones, and she sighed inwardly. There was no use in putting off the inevitable when her daughter looked between the two of them with suspicion edging on fear.

"Let's go for a walk, wildflower. We can talk as our feet move." Mirabella held an arm out to the young Herbalist.

Gemma looked like she was about to protest when Rae picked her up and spun her.

"Don't look so glum, Red. Your Momma will explain it all to you while you're exploring. There's nothing better than exploring, is there?" She ruffled the little girl's copper curls with a smirk.

Gemma giggled. "Nope! You'll still find me later, after lessons with Miss Chiara?"

Rae held out her pinky. "It's a promise." Gemma wrapped her smallest finger around Rae's and they shook on it. Gemma wrapped her arms around the Crafter's legs and squeezed before taking her mother's hand.

Rae mouthed an apology that Mirabella waved off. It didn't matter when she told Gemma she was leaving, the little girl would be devastated. Rae only ensured she couldn't take the coward's way out and wait until the last moment to deliver the difficult news.

She gripped her daughter tight and whisked her into the woods and onto the path she'd taken so many times around the frozen lake.

Gemma usually squirmed until she was set free to explore and observe all the greenery of the forest. But today, the little girl was quiet and clung to her mother's arm.

The night she left Gemma at the bakery flashed in Mirabella's mind. Her heart broke for her gorgeous daughter and what she was obliged to say next. Looking around, the woman spied a fallen trunk with only a dusting of snow on it. She tugged on her daughter's arm and brought her to the once mighty tree.

Mirabella wiped off the snow and lifted her daughter to the makeshift seat so she was at eye level with her mother. The two stared at each other for a long moment and Mirabella put a hand on either side of her beloved daughter. Gemma's lower lip trembled as her watery eyes met her mother's. Mirabella gave an inaudible sigh and her breath formed clouds in the icy winter air.

This was the moment. Mirabella's mouth went dry, and she had to swallow twice before she could get the words out that could destroy everything.

"Wildflower, how much do you know about Herbalists, Magicae, and their place in this world?" She caught the little girl off guard, evident in the way her eyes sharpened and how her lips formed a small frown.

"I know I'm a Herbalist because of what I can do with the plants." Gemma let out a giggle when she noticed some of the surrounding greenery reach for her. She continued with a smile, "I know there are four types of Magicae; Herbalists control the plants, Shifters turn into animals, Crafters shoot elements from their fingers, and Forgers make stuff from rocks and metals and stuff." Gemma beamed at her mother, proud of herself for all that she'd learned in her time away.

"Very good. And what of their place in the world?" Mirabella prodded, a knot forming in the pit of her stomach.

Gemma's smile faded, and she scrunched her eyebrows together. "Place in the world?" The little girl went quiet. Her lower lip trembled again and her voice became a whisper. "Is this about Daddy?" She searched her mother's face. "The other kids told me Daddy was a bad man. That he wanted to hurt me and that's why you sent me away," Her little voice cracked, and she choked down a sob "They said you weren't coming back for me..." Mirabella could barely hear her daughter's last words despite moving closer.

When her brain registered what the young Herbalist said, she pulled her into a swift embrace. "Hush now, my darling girl. Get those words out of your pretty little head." Mirabella rocked her as Gemma sobbed into her shoulder. Mirabella rubbed her back and whispered comforting words into her daughter's ear, the pit in her stomach momentarily forgotten.

Gemma's crying quieted and Mirabella pulled away, keeping her hands on her daughter's shoulders. She wiped the tears from Gemma's eyes with her gloved hands. "Gemma, I have some very important things to tell you and you may not understand all of it right now, but promise me you'll always remember how much I love you. No matter what you hear today or in the future, promise me you'll never forget I love you more than anything in this world."

Gemma, still upset and unable to form words, nodded her head so hard her curls bounced long after the movement stopped.

Mirabella gave a soft smile and kissed the little girl's forehead. "That's my girl. I love you to pieces, wildflower, which is why these next words are so hard to say." Mirabella sighed and screwed up her courage. "A long, long time ago, your Momma made a mistake. A big mistake that I wish every day I could take back. But it's important you hear it from me and know the truth from the lies people like to say."

Mirabella paused, giving Gemma time to process her words and preparing herself for the inevitable.

"At the time, I was very young and impressionable. I let bad people tell me what to do, and I ended up hurting a lot of people. I tricked the president into getting into a fight with his wife and distracting him so the military could take over. My actions made it necessary for the Magicae to hide. I'm the reason you have to be so careful with the plants."

She watched her daughter process her words and felt her heart shatter. If this little girl lost faith in her, what else was there to live for?

Gemma scrunched up her nose again. "It's okay, Momma. Rae and Uncle Duncan will beat the bad people once spring comes. They'll make everything okay." She leaned forward and hugged her mother before pulling back again. Mirabella saw the little girl's chin wobbling and felt her stomach drop, knowing what was coming next. "And what about Daddy?"

"Your Daddy loves you very much, wildflower. But your Daddy can be cruel to the people he doesn't like. I know deep in my heart, he'd never hurt you, but his position as general of Kamore means he'd have no choice but to turn you in." Gemma's eyes welled with tears and Mirabella's heart broke all over again. She pulled her daughter close and rocked back and forth.

After Gemma wore herself out crying, she sniffled and looked at her mother. "So everything they say about Daddy is true? That he's killed more Magicae than anybody else?" Her little voice dropped to a whisper. "Is it true you kept my magic a secret because Daddy is one of the bad men ?"

Mirabella was at a loss for words. She was torn between telling her daughter everything and letting her keep the innocence of childhood. In the end, she knew there was only one choice if she wanted Gemma to have the knowledge she needed to survive in this awful world.

"Wildflower, I don't have all the answers you need, but I know your Daddy could be ruthless when he wanted to be. After you were born, I struggled with the transition of not having you with me all the time. Some days, I couldn't even get out of bed. Your Daddy helped me get out of bed and made the decisions I couldn't bring myself to make. At first, I thought it was sweet and helpful, but even after I got back to my old self, your Daddy kept ordering me to do certain things or wear my hair a certain way. He became controlling and mean when we were alone."

"Did he hurt you?" Gemma asked with wide eyes when her mother paused in her recollection.

"Not physically, wildflower, but he hurt me in ways you can't see."

Gemma grew still and quiet as she processed the words her mother confided.

Mirabella shivered and rubbed her hands on Gemma's arms, willing warmth into her trembling hands. She had one more thing to say to the little girl before they could move on with their last day together.

She took a deep breath.

"I have one more thing I need to tell you." Gemma's eyes filled with pain and her lower lip trembled. Mirabella held her close and stroked her copper curls, knowing the little girl had guessed this news from the start. "Your Uncle Duncan needs me to go back to Heimat to spy on your Daddy."

The silence that followed was deafening.

And then Gemma's cries filled the winter air.

Mirabella tried to pull her close, but the girl squirmed out of her arms and put space between them, glaring at her mother from underneath her hood.

"You told me you'd never leave me again. You lied to me." The betrayal in Gemma's voice sent splinters through her heart. Mirabella stepped closer but kept her hands up to indicate she wasn't going to force her touch upon the young girl.

Gemma regarded her with suspicious eyes but didn't move away again, crossing her arms and sending her mother a pointed look.

Mirabella took this as a sign to try again. "This is what you won't understand, wildflower. But it's okay. When you're older, you'll know why I had to do this. I can use my position with your Daddy to gain information about his plans that nobody else could. Your Uncle Duncan and Rae need my help to get that information and help them win their fight. I have to do this to help them and make up for my mistake."

Gemma's gray eyes softened and filled with concern as her shoulders sagged. "Will he hurt you again?" she whispered.

Mirabella couldn't take it anymore and pulled Gemma close, rubbing her back. "He might, but it's a risk I have to take."

"Don't leave me, Momma." Gemma was past the angry phase and moved on to the begging phase. She clung to Mirabella, and the mother found herself wavering and trying to justify staying.

But staying wouldn't soothe the guilt and shame in her heart.

Pulling away so she could look into her daughter's eyes, Mirabella said, "I'm leaving tonight, wildflower. Remember what you promised me. No matter what happens, you're to always remember that I love you to pieces. You don't understand why I have to go, but you will when you're older. This is my chance to make things right with the people I hurt all those years ago."

Gemma wailed and clutched at her mother again, fury and anguish leaking from her eyes.

Mirabella held on and rode out the tears with her daughter, stroking her hair and humming soft lullabies in her ear. At last, Gemma's cries subsided, and she looked up at the woman she adored.

"Momma, promise me you'll come back to me. I made a promise to you and now you have to make a promise to me."

Mirabella's heart squeezed, knowing what her daughter asked was something she couldn't promise and that she'd do it, anyway. "Of course I will. As soon as Rae and Uncle Duncan win back Heimat, I will come home to you."

Gemma gave a slow nod and hugged her mother tight.

"Now, enough of this serious talk. We have one last full day together, so let's make it count." With those words, Mirabella scooped the little girl from the fallen tree and set her on the path.

"Bet you can't catch me!" Mirabella yelled, hoping to distract herself and her daughter from the looming separation.

Mirabella ran from the girl and the future she'd chosen.

The present was a gift and Mirabella refused to waste it. She'd spend the day spoiling and showering her daughter with love, giving them both one last happy memory to hold on to.

# Chapter Twenty

"You wouldn't know it by looking at these ruins but Oakenrock was once the hub for learning and invention for the Elven." Andriette stroked what was left of a stone wall covered in moss and lichen, only chest high in its present state of decay. Tyee waited for her to continue.

"This place was filled with artists and scientists and dreamers. It's where the runes were born and where we flourished. I spent every summer right over there."

Andriette inclined her head and drifted in the direction she indicated. Her breath came in puffs of smoke, the only indicator she was having a tough time. Tyee couldn't be sure whether it was the walk or the memories that took such a heavy toll on the old woman. He followed her, attempting to picture a city amongst the ruins.

Easier said than done.

There was a strange, ominous air about the place. Stone structures had tumbled over leaving nothing more than rubble scattered around foundations overtaken by weeds. Tyee was surprised there was little evidence of the wooden structures like those in Verdencia. He held his tongue to keep from asking the questions forming on his lips. Andriette would tell him when she was ready.

"This was the two-room house I spent every summer in. One bedroom that my Ma and Pa shared while me and my siblings had full rein of the larger living and dining room." Andriette's eyes grew misty. "I can picture it like it was yesterday. It's been so long since I've seen any of them." The old woman rubbed at her face as tears leaked down her cheeks.

Tyee wandered into the remnants of the stone structure, giving his great-grandmother a moment to compose herself. He'd never seen her this vulnerable before. Even the night she told him about his grandparents and mother, she'd kept her dry sense of wit. It was bewildering to see the firecracker so subdued.

Something terrible happened here. You could feel it in the air. Tyee scanned the ruins and finally realized what made this place feel so off.

There were no trees.

Only bone-white trunks and stumps stripped of their bark remained, keeping silent watch over the stones and rubble of a once bustling city. Some weeds and shrubs dared to encroach on what was left of the city, but no new trees.

Tyee looked at his great-grandmother and met eyes that mirrored the horror in his own. "Unspeakable things happened here. Didn't they?"

Andriette sighed. "It started as a cough, but within three days the afflicted person was gone." Her hands clutched at one of the rocks still standing from what remained of where she grew up. "My Pa let out such horrible screams when the disease came for him. My Ma was by his side every moment. When she started coughing two days after he passed, she told me to take my two younger siblings and leave the city. She locked herself in the room she'd watched my Pa die in and refused to open it, no matter how hard we pounded or cried out for her."

The old woman fell silent. Tyee stayed quiet in respect of the pain she was sharing with him.

"When I heard her screams, I grabbed everything I could and told my siblings to hold hands as we walked to the main gate. But the gates were locked from the outside. They quarantined the city and left us with the sounds of people coughing and screaming," Andriette bit her lip and hung her head

This time, Tyee decided it was better to prod and help lift the weight of so much grief off of her. "How did you leave?"

"I didn't. I took my siblings back to the house, back to the garden my Ma once tended with such care, and we hid in the shed. The plague ripped through Oakenrock as if it were paper. After two weeks, the gates were opened, and the streets combed for any survivors. Only three dozen of us survived that awful, awful disease. And the worst part was, that was the last time I ever saw my siblings. As soon as the people realized my parents were among the casualties, they took me to one of the cities deep in the forest for protection and so I could learn how to become a true leader." Andriette rubbed her thumb over the weathered rock as Tyee gathered his thoughts.

"What do you mean, learn how to become a leader?" His eyebrows scrunched together as he frowned, not following what his Tota was saying.

The old woman started as if she snapped out of a trance. "Come, this place holds too many dark memories. Let's go to the market square and discuss what we came here to." Without waiting for a response, she turned and marched towards the center of the ruined city.

Tyee followed with a suspicious heart. There was something Andriette wasn't telling him, and he was unprepared for how much that realization stung.

"This is where the merchants and artists gathered on market days. There were always musicians playing merry tunes and people dancing in the street. It's one of my fondest memories and why Verdencia will never be home. This is what home is." Andriette sank to her knees as her voice cracked.

Tyee found his head and his heart at war, seeing the old woman reduced to this. His head was telling him to help the old woman, but his heart still prickled at the thought of her keeping something from him.

Tyee knelt next to his great-grandmother and asked, "Tota, what is it you're not telling me?"

She gripped his forearm. "Don't ask me that, nakni. I promise I will tell you everything, but we need more time before I can do that. It will distract you from learning the runes and take away our freedom. Don't make me do that just yet." Her eyes pleaded with his as her arm shook.

Tyee put his hand on hers. "I trust you. Have we seen enough? This place weighs heavily on both of us. I think it's time to leave."

Andriette shook her head. "I feel it too, nakni. We must do what we came here to do. Help these old bones."

Tyee kept his hand on hers and stood, reaching down to grip her elbows and lift his great-grandmother to her feet. He felt the wiry muscles in her arms, even as her legs wobbled. He frowned, recognizing the frailty of the normally steely woman.

He followed her, a hand ready to catch her should she fall until they made it to where the main gate must have been.

"I want you to look at the runes here. Despite the destruction and decay, these runes have stood the test of time. What do you recognize?"

Tyee brushed dirt from the stone and traced the symbols with a finger. His body gave a shiver as he felt the ancient power in the line of runes. "Gebo means sacrifice, Tiwaz means bravery, and Algiz means protection." He winced at the reminder of the lines on his palm.

Andriette nodded, ignoring his wince. "Exactly, and if you kept going, you'd see so many more. When the plague first hit, nobody knew how to combat it. They couldn't determine what caused it and reacted in kind instead of taking the time to follow it back to its source. Instead, they created a line of runes meant to protect against all dangers. But the sequence has too many meanings. They meant it to be symbolic when different people wrote each rune, but it also meant different feelings for each rune written. This line of symbols ensured no one could leave to face the dangers outside the city. We could only leave when the plague ran its course and the danger of starvation grew too great. To this day, no one knows how the plague started or whether it could come again. It's why Ulla brought our people to the trees instead of trusting in our protections. People lost faith in the runes after the destruction they wracked in our beloved capital. But people are fools. The runes are only as strong as the people who draw them. Whenever you etch a rune, you have to be clear on your intention. The more vague you are, the more destruction you can cause, understood?"

Tyee nodded. "I understand, Tota. The magic in our blood is extremely powerful because it resembles the energy of nature, correct?"

"Aye. It's a little more complicated, but you get the gist."

"Right. But how does this help me understand what the runes do? Are they simply catalysts for what's inside?"

Andriette pursed her lips. "It's more like they act as a conduit that gives our magic boundaries and a purpose. Follow me."

Andriette walked into the forest and Tyee sighed in relief, happy to be leaving the dark and dreary place. He took one last backwards glance at the once fine city and gave an involuntary shudder. He had a feeling the plague had never truly left.

"We always start the learning process with Isa; the single line rune that stands for ice, the challenges we may face, and the time we spend feeling stuck in place before big transitions. Take out your knife and scratch Isa into this tree, making sure to only think of the ice part of her meaning." The old woman commanded when Tyee caught up with her.

Tyee threw her a look. "Isn't that everything you're against? Harming the trees and whatnot?"

"If I had wanted your opinion, I would have asked for it," she snapped. Tyee couldn't keep the smile from his face when the old woman's fire returned. Things still felt fragile between them after Andriette's admittance she was keeping something from him, but with the return of her briskness came a sense of familiarity.

Instead of replying, Tyee stepped to the tree and lifted his knife. He took a deep breath and willed his hand to stop shaking. When that didn't work, he passed the weapon to his other hand and shook out the one he wrote with.

"Today, boy. Some of us have better things to do than sit here and watch you get the shakes."

Tyee rolled his eyes but didn't turn around. This was the first time he'd be scribing a rune on anything other than paper. Paper was easily destroyed when he made a mistake, the tree not so much.

With another deep breath, he sunk lower into his heels and let them ground him. With a silent prayer to the Huntress, he let the knife bite into the flaky and rough bark of the young oak. Before his knife left the bark, Tyee remembered he was supposed to be infusing emotion into his cut.

His breath hitched as he slowed his progress and closed his eyes. Tyee pictured the snow falling after he'd left Heimat and the coldness he felt at Rae's absence. He thought of the frozen water floating in his waterskin and the sound they made when they knocked into each other as he bounced on Koko's back. He thought of the ice coating his insides when he'd realized Sylvie was the one imprisoning and separating him from the people he respected.

With that final thought, he hissed and finished the rune.

Spiderwebs of black frost crisscrossed the tree's skin and dark crystals formed at the edges of the lines.

Tyee felt a hard pull on his life energy and he let out a gasp, clutching at his chest. He whipped his head to face his great-grandmother and met her surprised gaze. Slowly, her lips turned upwards into a smirk.

"Well, that's all the answer anybody needs." She strode to the tree, wielding a small knife meant for gathering herbs. Tota made quick work of slicing three symbols into the tree.

When she stepped back, the dark lines of black ice seemed to light from within and burn away all traces of the dark spiderwebs.

The tree looked as if nothing had happened. The only trace left was the three runes Tota had carved. Even the rune for ice he'd sliced into the young tree was gone.

Tyee's eyes widened, and he looked at his great-grandmother. "How did you do that?"

Tota's eyes sparkled as the wrinkles at the corners of her eyes became more pronounced with her smile. "That, boy, is why we study the runes. Ulla and so many others lost their faith in the ways runes can direct our power, but if you know what you want and have a way to translate that into a line of symbols, you will be unstoppable. Look at the three runes and tell me what emotions I fed them."

Tyee did as he was told and stooped to get a better view of the symbols she'd carved. He traced them with his fingers before looking back at her. "The one that looks like a C is Kenaz, the torch and a rune for controlling burning fire. It's what you used to burn the ice without harming the tree. But the second rune is Gebo, the one that looks like an X, and I don't understand why you would offer the tree a gift." He shot her a frown, but she gestured for him to continue. "And this last rune means nothing to me. I have no idea what it means or what it's for."

The old Elven woman traced the rune that looked like a B and smiled. "This is Berkano. It represents rebirth, healing, and growth. You are correct that Gebo represents a gift, but it also expresses gratitude and receiving through sacrifice or offering." She met Tyee's gaze and inclined her head. "Now put it all together."

Tyee looked at the sapling and studied the symbols once more. "You chose these three runes to chase away the ice with fire, express your gratitude for the tree's sacrifice for my benefit, and offer healing and growth in exchange for what it endured." He looked at her with expectant eyes. "Right?"

Tota grinned widely and slapped him on the back. "That's it! Good work, boy. You—," the old woman interrupted herself, coughing and bending over so her hands were on her knees.

Tyee acted on instinct and thumped her back, offering her some of his waterskin. "Take a sip, Tota. Maybe it will clear your throat."

Andriette held up a hand and let out a few more coughs before gripping the waterskin and taking deep, greedy gulps from it. Tyee waited for her to clear her throat and took the empty waterskin when she handed it back to him.

"Thanks, nakni. I forget the toll strings of runes can take from a person."

"What do you mean?" Tyee tilted his head and listened intently.

Andriette gave another couple of coughs before moving to an open rock. She sat and took several deep breaths. Tyee watched her with concern, having never seen the formidable woman in such a state.

"The more runes you use, the more complex your wishes are. In order for your intention to manifest, the runes have to draw quite a bit of power from your life energy. I forget that in my old age, even using one rune can be taxing.

Let's rest a minute." Andriette's face was pale, and she hid her hands in her traveling cloak, trying to hide their tremor.

"Tota, you don't look so good. We need to get you inside." Tyee sat next to her and put an arm around her. "Huntress, you're freezing." He moved, so he knelt in front of her and took her wrinkled hands in his, rubbing some warmth back into them. "How far are we from the cabin?"

"There are moments when I forget you didn't grow up with your people. Every time you invoke their Goddess and her faces it smacks me in the face. If you're going to use the runes, you need to know about Skaber, the creator of the Elven."

Tyee cut her off before the old woman could launch into her tale. "Tota, we need to get you out of this cold. We can talk about Skaber after we get you inside. How far is the cabin? Should I call for Koko?"

Andriette let out a heavy sigh. "If we walk about ten minutes to the east, we will reach Verdencia. But don't expect me to climb into one of those treehouse things they have there. My feet belong on the ground or the solid wood of my house."

"Understood. Lean on me and we'll stay at the cottage I was in before Fritz brought me to you." Tyee stooped and pulled Andriette's arm over his shoulders, leading her to the east and the promise of warmth.

Tyee looked at his sleeping great-grandmother and breathed a sigh of relief. The fire in the hearth was roaring, putting out more heat than Rae when she was angry, and Andriette was wrapped in all the blankets he could find. He went to the window and looked toward the city proper, his gut churning at not letting anyone know they'd be staying there. The last thing he needed was for some of the guards to come barging in with a death wish for any trespassers.

His only saving grace was they were in the cottage he'd used before leaving.

Hopefully, somebody would put two and two together before it came to blows.

He glanced back at the old woman and shook his head. *Stubborn fool.*

*It's not like you're any better.*

Tyee clenched his fists to clear the traitorous thoughts from his head. Blaming Andriette wouldn't change their predicament.

The front door opened with a creak and Tyee threw his hands up, moving in front of the exhausted woman.

"It's only me and Tota. She overexerted herself in the woods and needed a place to get warm. Verdencia was closer than her cabin, so I brought her here. There was no time to inform anybody, and I apologize for barging in. I mean no disrespect." Tyee forced the words out quickly to try to avoid any sort of combat.

"Never thought I'd hear the halfbreed admit he needed something from me." The voice purred from behind the door.

Tyee's stomach dropped when he recognized the haughty tone.

"Sylvie," he hissed, reaching for the knife at his belt.

"Uh, uh, uh. Pulling a weapon on the royal family is punishable by death." Sylvie slinked into the room and shut the door behind her with a cruel smirk. "But I'd make sure to draw it out as long as possible." She gave him a wink.

Tyee bristled and felt his hands start to tremble. Flame shot through his palm, but Tyee ignored it. He wasn't losing focus while Sylvie was within striking distance. No way in hell would he let her catch him unaware again.

He took a deep breath and loosened his stance, returning the knife to its place at his hip. He refused to give her an excuse to take him into her custody again.

"If you didn't come here to fight, then why are you here?" Tyee demanded.

"Oh, Stableboy. You really are a lost cause, aren't you? Or has the great Tota failed to clue you in on your family history?" Her eyes glittered with danger as she watched him for any type of giveaway that she'd hit a nerve.

Tyee kept his face a mask as his palm flared with pain again. He refused to even grimace in an effort to keep Sylvie from guessing he was hiding something.

Sylvie gave a pout. "What, no time to play our little games anymore? Too embarrassed to do so in front of your precious Tota?" She spat those last words.

"You would do well to remember you are a guest in this place. And no matter how much you learn or how many people you charm, you are still a halfbreed and an outsider." The cruel smile was back in place on Sylvie's tanned face.

Tyee felt his hackles rise at the insults she kept throwing, but kept his mask in place. Sylvie was a bully, and he would not give her the rise she wanted. Instead, he kept his voice even. "Yes, Sylvie." A thrill went through him when he saw her wince at his use of the name she'd traveled under all those years ago. "I am only half Elven and yet I didn't see you drinking at the bonfires with your people. Seems like you're a little out of touch if you think I'm the outsider here."

Sylvie let out a growl and paced back and forth in front of him. An uneasy feeling took root in Tyee's belly at her agitation. He'd wanted to get under her skin but hadn't thought through the consequences. He'd need to hold his tongue if he wanted to evade her wrath.

Andriette's even breathing changed ever so slightly and Tyee took comfort in knowing she was awake. At least she'd be a witness if the worst happened.

Sylvie stopped her pacing and looked him straight on, curling her lip back to bare her teeth. "You're lucky you have the Queen's favor. If you didn't, you'd wake up with a knife to the heart courtesy of yours truly." Her voice was like ice as she sent him a sneer. "Besides, we have more important things to worry about now that the raids have been planned."

"Raids?" Tyee struggled to keep the concern from his voice. Raids didn't sound like anything good. "What do you mean?"

"Talon and the Shifters of the Forest presented us with an idea too delicious to ignore. Although my mother hesitated at first, she's come around. In two day's time, we attack the Mortal towns at the edge of the forest and watch them burn. Kamore will fall and every Mortal will perish. Even your dear ole Da if he's still alive." Sylvie's face was as deadly as it was beautiful, filled with passion and bloodlust as she talked about the fates of so many innocent people.

But Tyee couldn't care less about their fates, he thought instead of the people he'd come to call family. The Circus was created to protect Magicae, but it went beyond that. The tapestry of people wouldn't be the same without both

Magicae and Mortals. If Sylvie was on a warpath to kill all Mortals, the Circus would be in danger.

"And the Circus?" Tyee's lips formed a tight grimace as he forced the question out, knowing how much it would please Sylvie to know she'd struck a nerve.

The Elven general preened, stepping too close to him. Tyee stepped back, but felt his legs hit Andriette's cot. Sylvie came closer, careful not to touch him but close enough to charge the little space between them.

"Don't worry, Stableboy, your plaything is safe. For now, at least." She showed her teeth. "We agreed the Circus would be a problem best dealt with after we've taken the country." She reached her hand up and traced his jawline, using one finger to lift his chin.

Tyee wrenched his head from her grip and used both hands to move her back until she was pinned against the wall.

Sylvie let out an icy laugh. "If you were lonely, all you needed to do was say something. Remember now, the rougher the better."

Tyee's hands felt like they were on fire as memories of the two of them flashed in his mind. He released her as if he'd been burned and felt the familiar prick of pain in his left palm. He rubbed it on his trousers and realized his mistake too late.

Sylvie lunged for his hand and turned it over, revealing the red lines of the Algiz rune etched into his skin. Recognizing what it meant, she gave another feral grin. "Tsk, tsk. Creating a blood bond when you're already spoken for? Poor girl is going to get her heart broken." Her eyes met his shocked ones. "Good luck with surviving the fire sprite's rage when you break it off. See you soon, Stableboy." She winked at him before leaving as quickly as she'd come.

*My bed's always open when you decide you're ready for a real woman.*

Sylvie's words grated in his mind and Tyee lost consciousness.

The last thing he heard before he blacked out was Sylvie's cruel laughter.

# Chapter Twenty-One

Luc made her way to the large community tent in the center of camp. The Governing Council was holding a closed session to decide on what they would do next. Duncan instructed them to take a week and consider what they'd heard from their people, then come ready to make decisions at this meeting.

Luc could feel nervous butterflies forming in her stomach, despite how much better she felt after the night with her friends. The battle put a strain on her and Damien's relationship, but Luc was cautiously optimistic they were finally on the right track. The winter solstice brightened Damien's mood considerably, and she'd been able to see more light in his eyes and warmth in his tone. He was finally returning to himself and all Luc could do was praise the Huntress in relief. Only time would tell if the deadness in his eyes returned, but for now, Luc was ready to face what happened next.

She'd taken the past couple of days since the solstice to be honest with herself. Most of the Crafters, Forgers, and Shifters would be hungry for a fight. Luc was unconscious for most of the battle at Verdencia, but even if she had her wits about her, she wasn't sure how much of an asset she'd be in a fight. She could do a lot of things, but wielding a sword was never something that interested her much. Luc knew more about healing and herbs, and what it took to combat disease than she did about slipping past someone's guard. She could flip and twist in the air and never lose her balance on a tightrope, but had no inkling of where to aim an arrow to cause the most damage.

Luc wasn't convinced it was a bad thing, but she could still feel a small pull of regret in her heart. The day they held the open session had hit her in the gut. The people she loved wouldn't care if she decided to stay at the settlement and foster their community or any wounded they sent back. Nobody would think less of her for not bearing arms.

If it was true for Damien, it had to be true for her as well.

But that wasn't why her stomach was flip-flopping within.

Rae's solution to provide a third option was why her blood roared in her ears. Luc wanted to take the lead when it came to creating a network of spies and carriers that would further their efforts without needing to kill someone. The carriers would provide transportation for the sick, wounded, supplies, and others that needed a safe place while the spies would infiltrate Myra's most intimate areas and pass along information when they could.

Luc was confident she'd be exceptional in the role, but it meant she wouldn't be sent anywhere to do either. If she went into this meeting, guns blazing, she would be asked to head the committee.

And she'd be separated from Damien and her friends. She played with the pendant around her neck, silently asking her father for guidance.

Which she didn't know if she could handle. She'd already spent over a month without Rae and Zeke, and it almost killed her. Nobody but those closest to her could pick up on her heightened irritability and shortened temper, but they were real consequences due to her worry for those she loved. She didn't want to imagine what would happen to her if she was separated from the two Crafters and the man she loved.

The sacrifices she'd need to make in order to step into that role were significant, and she needed to be sure she was willing to make them. She'd wrestled with these thoughts for days now and was no closer to an answer.

But time was up.

Luc had to decide whether she helped her people or stayed with her friends and the love of her life. Luc paused with her hand on the tent flap that would bring her to her inevitable choice.

But she knew who she was.

She knew it wasn't really a choice.

"And with that vote, we have our three heads for our three planning committees." Duncan said with a flourish and a soft smile. "Chiara will lead the
home front committee with Nan and Jay, Luc will lead the communications
committee with Midge and Gar, and I will head the front line committee with
Conrad and our newly elected Vera. The goals for today are to determine the
directives for your group, what sort of prep needs to be done before springtime,
and any training your people will need before they can do their job effectively.
Questions?"

Luc shook her head with the others before turning to Midge and Gar. They'd
already spent almost an hour and a half hammering out a plan of action. It
was unanimous to take Rae's suggestions to heart, and they spent most of the
time creating a blueprint for three different groups. When it came time to form
committees, Chiara and Duncan immediately nominated themselves for the
home front and front-line committees, respectively. There was an odd tension
between the two of them that Luc didn't understand. She'd have to ask Damien
about it later.

That left the group they were calling the communications committee needing a leader. Luc hesitated only a moment before speaking up and putting her
name forward. The three nominations were received with glowing praise and
Luc hadn't missed the proud sparkle in her Abuela's eyes.

And now the hard part began.

Luc cleared her throat. "Midge, Gar. I appreciate your support and faith in
my leadership."

Gar gave her a thump on the back. "Anyone would be a fool to think you were
incapable, lass. What should we discuss first, directives?"

Luc and Midge nodded in unison, causing all three of them to chuckle.

"I guess that settles it. What are our directives for the communications group?" Luc asked as she pulled a leather-bound journal and ink pen from her pack.

"Considering the name, we should have communication between the home front and front lines as one of the first." Midge offered.

"Aye, along with communication between spies and the home front? Or the front lines?" Gar added.

Luc gave a small frown. "It would simplify things if spies only sent information to one place. I think it would be more beneficial if they sent their information to the front lines. That way, Duncan, Conrad, and Vera could make decisions with the most accurate information possible." Luc suggested.

"Couldn't the carriers also take information to the home front? Your logic is sound, cherie, but we don't want the people here blindsided should something happen." Argued Midge.

Luc tapped her chin. "Good point. Maybe we come back to that after we've decided on roles for the spies and carriers? We for sure need communication between the home front and the front lines and I'll leave a note saying we also need communication from the spies to the front lines and home front. We'll table that and keep going." Luc suggested, not wanting to lose momentum so early in the discussion.

"Good idea, lass. Let's move on to the spies. Their aim is to gather information, yeah?" Gar obliged her.

Luc smiled. "Seems pretty simple, right? And for their safety, I think it's best they focus on doing just that. As time goes on and people get more comfortable, maybe there would be room for interference but for now, let them focus on building trust and passing on any information they can."

Midge and Gar nodded their agreement. Luc wrote furiously before looking up again.

"Okay, and then the carriers. They need to transport supplies, weapons, and new troops to the front lines." Luc initiated their next topic of discussion.

"We also need to transport the wounded from the front lines and other

Magicae in danger to the home front. Just because the Circus is no longer running, doesn't mean there aren't people out there who still need saving. It hurts my heart to know there are babies out there alone and living in fear. It makes my soul ache, knowing we can't continue to save those people." Midge's eyes were misty as she finished.

Luc put a hand on her shoulder and squeezed gently. "Absolutely. And I think that's a super important point. The caravan has always had people who would rather stay in Heimat and those who want to do more, but wouldn't pick up a weapon and fight. Our community has been fueling this Resistance for years. And more people will be willing to help in this way than I think we realize. So, we also need carriers taking wounded from the front lines, and Magicae from the cities back to the home front. This is going to be a lot of moving parts, and we need to rework the strategy we've used for the Circus in the past."

"What do you mean, lass?" Gar asked. "I understand we can't be the Circus on account of that Vincenzio fellow, but couldn't we do a different traveling show?"

"No, I think any sort of traveling band is going to rouse suspicion. We need to do smaller groups doing completely different things than the Circus did. I don't think it's even safe for people to perform the same act as they did in the Circus. I'm sure anyone claiming to be an acrobat will be sent straight to lockup, whether or not they're Magicae." Luc countered.

"What do you suggest instead, cherie?" Midge asked with a frown.

"I think we limit our groups to two or three people strong. That will arouse much less suspicion than a group of ten or twenty. And gives us room to pick up people along the way without worrying about group size.

"For example, say there's a group of three, an old couple traveling with their granddaughter will arouse less suspicion than three clowns, or even two women versed in embroidery with a mercenary for protection. We need less flowery identities and more simple ones to keep suspicion off the carriers and let them do what they need to." Luc's mind raced as she considered the possibilities in front of them.

"Yer brilliant, lass. What else should we decide on?"

The three of them dove into more specifics and what training would look like before dividing the rest of the different tasks between the three of them.

As the bell for supper rang, Luc left the tent motivated and filled with purpose. Talking things out with Gar and Midge helped her realize they, too, understood what it felt like to not be able to fight on the front lines effectively. The three of them had created something magnificent without needing to lift a bow or swing a sword. Anytime she felt useless, she'd remember this day and know she could talk to Gar or Midge about it all. She couldn't wait to see Damien and tell him everything they'd come up with and discussed.

A pang of guilt swept through her at the thought of Damien, but this was the only way to stay true to herself. An idea struck and Luc veered from her path towards the tent they now shared, making for the forest instead.

It was hard to find in the snow, but eventually, she found a piece of knot grass and made for her Abuela's wagon. She stole some beeswax and mineral oil from a side compartment before heading to their tent.

She almost dropped what she was holding when Damien strode out of the tent.

"Luciana, mi amor mas bonita and keeper of my heart. I was coming to find you." Damien gave her a lopsided grin and reached for her.

Luc avoided his hands with a sparkle in her eyes. Damien gave a frown and crossed his arms, suspicion in his gaze. He raised one eyebrow.

Luc slipped the wax and oil into her coat, so the only thing left in her hand was the piece of knot grass. She met Damien's eyes and felt hers express the love and adoration she felt for him. Her heart thundered in her chest and she could feel sweat on her palms inside her gloves.

*Now or never, Luciana.* The voice inside her head urged her forward, and she sank to one knee.

She took Damien's left hand in hers and met his questioning gaze.

"Damien Rutter, will you do me the honor of becoming my husband?" Luc's voice trembled and she could feel tears prickling in her eyes, but Damien's shocked expression was worth it all. He dropped to his knees and captured her lips with his, tasting of spearmint and chicory. She could feel every inch of emotion as Damien deepened the kiss and set her whole body on fire.

"So I take it that's a yes?" Luc asked breathlessly when they came up for air.

Damien pulled her to his chest, and she could feel it rumble with laughter. "I already proposed to you. Of course it's a yes!"

Luc tied the knot grass around his ring finger with trembling hands before holding him tight.

If they had to be separated, at least they could hold on to this promise.

Night fell as Bane returned to Mantaga Lake. His falcon form had woken with renewed vigor after he'd given in to the sleep he needed. The rest of the journey passed as quickly as could be expected.

But Bane was ready for some companionship. He'd forgotten how lonely it could be on the road.

Bane was proud of being a Shifter and using his Gift to serve the Circus and his people. He hadn't always been as open to lending a helping hand, but once he and his Da found the group of performers and rebels, Bane had changed.

It was the kids that made him think twice about whether he was doing everything he could to help the Circus. After that revelation, he'd been more willing to run messages between the Circus and Heimat or other cities as needed. He'd gotten to know the scouts pretty well and cherished the camaraderie he shared with them.

But those trips took hours, not days. And he'd been communicating with his friends, not strangers. Even at Diane's, he'd felt a little outcast. Not quite in the fold, but appreciated for what he could bring to the table.

After the destruction he'd seen in Heimat and the forest across from the city, he'd yearned to share his rage and despair. He'd discussed it with Rich, but it wasn't the same as talking to someone he loved.

The three feathers pulsed in his mind's eye and he flew faster, the icy wind whipping by. He flew by the light of the moon, three days after the solstice with stars dancing as accents to the little sister of the sun. To the north, green lights shimmered in the distance; a sign the Goddess and her other two faces were near.

Bane wasn't the suspicious or religious type, but believed it couldn't hurt to offer the deity respect and worship, just in case. He believed in a higher power but wasn't convinced the Goddess and her faces were the only options when it came to the beyond.

Regardless, it didn't matter, anyway. Vincenzio had still burned the forest and destroyed thousands of lives. The Goddess, or whoever was up there, hadn't interfered to stop that, so why would she or he or it stop the slaughter of his people? He'd act in deference to the Goddess, but he wasn't leaving anything to chance. The only way to ensure his people thrived was to urge them into action.

They needed to do something before Vincenzio burned down the entire forest looking for them. The man was just as bad as Myra and wouldn't stop at anything to extract retribution for the embarrassment he'd faced losing in Verdencia.

Vincenzio was out for blood and the Circus needed to ready their people.

Finally, the lake came into view and Bane swooped low, keeping his eyes peeled for the settlement. He spied the tents and let out a cry.

He beelined for his Da's tent, knowing the older man would be cross if he wasn't the first to know Bane was back. As he neared the entrance to his Da's tent, Bane let out another cry and almost crashed into his half-awake Da.

"Whoa there, lad. You'll give your Da a heart attack if you come in any hotter."

Bane balked and spread his wings wide, directing his momentum to land on his Da's shoulder. He chattered at the man and nipped his ear affectionately.

Gar swiped at the falcon and grumbled. "You know I hate it when you do that. And quit your chattering. You're still my boy and you'll listen even if you don't want to. You're old enough to know that your old man's not a blowhard.

If I say something, I mean it. Now get in here and tell me everything."

Gar brought Bane into the tent and gestured for him to take a perch on the large trunk. "You Shift into something that can answer me and I'll nip some food and whiskey from the cantina. Then you can tell me all about what you've seen." His Da strode to the tent flap and looked back at him. "You did good, lad. The others made it back from the coast safe and sound, if not a little hungry."

With that, he left to deliver on the food and liquor he promised.

Bane let all the tension from his avian body melt away as he drank in the warmth from the coals in the tent stove. There was nothing like returning home and getting out of the cold.

He reached inside and pulled the cord that would take him back to his human form. His bones grew in length and density as his feathers retreated. Bane felt his beak and claws flatten and lose their sharpness while his wings shifted position and coiled together before elongating into arms.

Once he returned to his human form, Bane shook out his muscles and cracked his neck. He opened the trunk and rifled inside for clothes that would fit him.

No sooner had he dressed, than his Da returned with a bowl of something that smelled like heaven. Mice and rats were sustenance enough, but Bane couldn't deny his preference for eating in his human form. Spices and vegetables brought such flavors to a dish that raw meat couldn't compare.

He lunged for the bowl of stew and his Da laughed.

"Betsy was still up when I got there. She insisted on heating it up when she heard it was for you and not thirds for me." His Da flashed him a smile.

Bane could only grunt as he inhaled the rich and warming concoction. Gar poured two mugs of whiskey and set them on the small table next to his bed. The tent was crowded with the two stocky men inside, but neither would change it for the world.

When Bane finished, he rubbed his sleeve over his mouth and reached for the glass. He took a long gulp and hiccupped.

Gar chuckled. "Slow down, lad, we got a bottle. Now sit next to me and tell me everything."

Bane did as he was bid and began with his search for the others, finding Gemma and her questions about her Da, and then leaving for Heimat. He relayed the destruction he found near the river and how hard it was to stay the course and not go for Vincenzio himself. He shed a tear when he described the bones and carcasses and charred earth.

It felt so good to share the horror with someone who loved the forest and its creatures as much as he did. Gar spent his life hunting in the woods and had a deep respect for its inhabitants that only came from depending on them to sustain himself and his family.

Bane told his Da about the city that was still on fire, meeting Rich, traveling to the farmhouse, and how he saved a woman in childbirth and her little boy. He confided about how he'd still felt like an outsider even at the farmhouse and what a relief it was to be back home.

He left out how long it had taken him to return and how he'd pushed himself to near exhaustion. His Da would only lecture him and there was someone else he needed to see before he could sleep for the night.

Gar shot him a sympathetic look. "The road is as lonely as it is winding. I just thank the Huntress you came home safe." He squeezed his son's shoulder. "We had a Council meeting today about the path forward. I know you'll want action this second, but our plans won't be ready until the spring." He held up a hand before Bane could interrupt. "I know how strongly you feel, but we're at a disadvantage with all this snow. It's best to wait and make sure our people are trained and ready, as opposed to hurling them at something they're not prepared for."

Bane frowned but nodded, recognizing the wisdom in his Da's words despite his impatience. He'd rather ensure a win and the opportunity to rebuild than lose before they really began. "Aye. When is the Council announcing their plans?"

"Tomorrow after breakfast." Gar pulled his son into a one-armed hug. "Go see the lad and then get some sleep." A knowing smile lit his face when Bane pulled out of the embrace.

He shook his head. "As you say, Da. No promises, though."

Gar laughed as Bane hurried from the tent, reaching for the second feather and the man it connected him to.

He reached the tent and opened the flap a crack. "Zeke?" he whispered.

The Crafter stirred and cracked an eye.

Quick as a whip, he threw the covers off and rushed to the entrance of his personal space.

Bane took that as his cue, slipping into the tent and reaching out for the man he'd come to adore. The Shifter pulled Zeke into a kiss and backed him onto the cot.

He felt the man in his arms rumble with laughter before pulling away.

Bane let the rumble in his throat communicate his displeasure as he captured Zeke's lips again. He felt hands on his chest, and this time, Zeke pressed against him, creating space between them.

"Well, hello to you too." The Crafter threw him a cheeky grin and Bane chuckled despite himself.

"Sorry. I didn't realize how much I'd miss you or how long that would take." Bane admitted.

Zeke yawned and sat on his cot, gesturing for Bane to join him. When he did, Zeke said, "I want to hear all about it, but in the morning. You'll just have to repeat yourself if you try."

"Deal." Bane threw him a questioning glance. "So what do you want to do, then?"

Zeke sighed. "We should get some rest. Tomorrow's another day. Stay with me?"

Bane watched emotions flit across Zeke's face and knew this meant something important to him.

"What aren't you telling me, Crafter?"

Zeke gave him a hard look. "My friends keep asking me what we are to each other. I don't need to call you my heartmate or partner or anything, but we need to be on the same page."

Bane studied the man next to him before giving a nod. "Aye, as it should be. I can't promise we'll be together forever, but right now, this is what I want." He clasped Zeke's hand and willed it to be enough.

Putting words to his emotions would never be one of his strengths.

Zeke pulled him in for a chaste kiss. "That's enough for me, Shifter." He laid on the cot, moving over to give Bane room before rolling onto his side.

Bane smiled and laid his head to rest, slinging an arm over the man he'd missed dearly and thanking the Huntress for leading him home at last.

# Chapter Twenty-Two

Heavy footsteps echoed outside her cell, getting closer and louder with each step. Naomi trembled, knowing who to expect. Myra had taken her for a walk in the gardens the night before, and Naomi worked the magic Andre used to praise her for. Her diplomacy averted many a crisis when her husband was president.

Just not the biggest one they ever faced.

Regardless, by the end of the night, Myra insisted Naomi prepare for one last visit before Mallick went to the front lines. She'd claimed it was the last chance the prisoner would have to share any information to keep her son safe.

Goddess, she hated that woman.

But at least her plan worked. Mallick was coming to see her again, and she'd have another shot at making things right. She needed to tell him who he was without making him confront Myra. She needed to convince him she was his mother without the young man acting brashly and lashing out or informing Myra. If she was to persuade him to switch sides, he needed to understand the importance of playing the part.

Naomi couldn't care less what happened to her, but she still felt the need to protect the boy with her blood in his veins.

She heard a key rattling outside her cell and felt her heart race.

*Shit.* It was now or never, and she still didn't have a plan. Naomi knew the water had been a risk this morning, but she'd been so thirsty and only took a sip. It was enough to knock her out for a couple of hours, and now she was out of time.

The door swung wide, and her handsome boy filled the doorway. She squinted in the light and thought she saw bruises and scratches on his face. He stepped inside, and she let out a gasp. A massive scar marred his cheek and both of his eyes were black and blue.

Naomi reached for him, but the clanging of chains brought her back to reality.

Mallick let out a humorless chuckle. "You should see the other guy." He frowned, as if realizing too late what she'd been trying to do. "Mother said you wanted to talk and I don't have much time. Say what you need to say and let's be done with it." His voice drawled as if he was bored with the conversation before it fully started.

Naomi's eyes became slits, and she tried to make herself as small as possible. She wanted him to think she was as weak as possible.

The words she had to say would come as more of a surprise then. But she had to give him something.

She sent a silent apology to Duncan and spoke with a rasp. "Duncan has an old injury in his right leg. If you hit him on that side, he's more likely to go down."

Mallick blinked slowly. His face turned into a sneer and he backhanded her across the face. "You little *bitch*. That's all you have to say? My mother was there when he got that injury. I've been training for months using hobbled wind Crafters as practice. I delayed my send-off feast and celebration for *this*?" The young man hissed as tears welled in Naomi's eyes.

Maybe there was nothing left of her boy in this wretched and cruel man. She studied his face as the stinging in her cheek cooled with the silent tears streaming down. The realization he'd never turn on Myra settled on her shoulders, weighing her down.

*It was never supposed to be like this. Me, Andre, Rae, and our baby boy. We were supposed to be a family. How can I still love this boy when he's hurt and killed so many? Including me.*

*Maybe I should let him go.*

Mallick spat at her feet and turned on his heel towards the door.

The face of a little girl with golden hair and golden eyes flashed in her mind.

She could pretend like she didn't care whether her son lived or died. It was a lie, but she could pretend that she saw nothing of her or Andre left in him. What she couldn't do was turn a blind eye to the danger her daughter was in. If Mallick had been charged with killing Rae, Naomi needed to make him hesitate.

"Wait. That's not the only thing I have to say." Naomi made her voice tremble, as if she was scared to say more after he slapped her.

Mallick paused with his hand on the door. He turned to her and lifted one eyebrow, keeping his hand on the latch.

"I can tell you about the fire Crafter...about my daughter." Naomi swallowed hard. Her mind whirred, knowing this was the only way to keep Mallick from leaving.

The young man let go of the door and took three steps toward her. "I'm listening." He furrowed his brows. "But why would you give me information that could get your daughter killed?"

"It took me a long time to see Myra's logic, but after our walk last night, I realized my baby girl would be safe if she'd been locked up years ago. If I'd only listened, maybe things would be different." The words burned as they left Naomi's lips, but she saw the glint in Mallick's eyes.

He believed her.

She pushed forward, knowing if he got a word in, she'd lose her nerve. "I only beg you not to kill her. Capture her and bring her back to Fernwell. Bring her home."

Mallick let out a bark of laughter. "Ever the diplomat, aren't you?" He steepled his fingers and considered her. "If you give me a way to capture her, I'll bring her back alive. I can't promise she won't be injured but she also won't be dead." Mallick gave her a smile that showed all his teeth. "Now what is this miracle insight you have for me?"

Naomi felt bile in her throat, but she swallowed it down. The information had to be reasonable, but there was no way in hell she was giving him anything remotely useful. It just had to seem so.

"When Rae was little and her fire first came, the Herbalists gave us a tonic. They told us all we had to do was sprinkle a couple of drops onto her forehead and it would calm her flames. They gave us a whole jug of it and we stored it in her bedroom. If it's still there, sprinkle it on her and she'll be reduced to a Mortal for a time." Naomi watched Mallick process this information and hoped it would be enough to convince him to at least go look.

She wouldn't reveal the tonic had to be drunk and was only strong enough to affect a small child, but if Mallick thought otherwise, who was she to stop him?

Mallick considered her words. "And if you're lying?"

Naomi let her tears of frustration and anger at losing her vision of their family run down her cheeks. Her chains clanked as she gestured to herself. "Look at me. The only thing I have left is my daughter. Why would I give you false information if I knew it could lead to her death? And besides..."

She trailed off on purpose, hoping to spark his curiosity just enough.

It worked.

"Besides what?" Mallick took another step closer to her, his eyes hard as he tried to decide whether or not to trust her.

Naomi raised her chin and looked him in the eye; the first time she'd done so since he arrived. She didn't miss the spark of surprise that registered in them at her boldness.

"Besides, I couldn't bear it if you killed your own sister." Naomi held his gaze as the cell went dead quiet.

Mallick narrowed his eyes. "What are you trying to say?" His hands clenched into fists and shook with barely contained rage. "That *you* are my mother." The disgust in his voice as he spat out the words made Naomi wince.

But she didn't look away. If she was going to do this, she was going to do this the right way. She would not give Mallick the slightest room for doubt in the words she spoke.

This could be her last chance to get through to him. If there was anything left in him of her or Andre, she needed to try.

"That's exactly what I'm saying. You can go to Myra and she'll deny it tooth and nail, but it doesn't change the truth. I was five months pregnant with you when they threw me down here. Myra stole you from my breast and I couldn't risk not seeing you, so I kept quiet. But she's sending you into battle and I couldn't bear the thought of you not knowing the truth." Naomi's voice didn't waver as she let her words tumble out. She'd observed enough to know Mallick wouldn't respond to emotion, so she kept it locked up.

Goddess, what she wouldn't give to take him into her arms and forget everything between them.

Mallick gave her one last look before slipping out without a word.

Naomi collapsed in a heap and let everything she'd been holding back come to the surface. Violent sobs wracked her bony frame as the stress and weight of everything she'd endured and the family she lost came crashing down.

She let her despair consume her, not caring who heard or the consequences of what she'd done. If Mallick told Myra what she'd revealed, there was no doubt she'd be killed and any chance of helping her daughter, Duncan, and the rest would die with her.

Naomi couldn't bring herself to care, though. Myra was a sick son of a bitch for sending the only person she claimed to give a damn about, not love because Goddess knew she was incapable of that, to unknowingly kill his own kin.

She was the worst kind of evil, and Naomi was her prisoner.

*Why didn't she protest more when Andre appointed Myra his general?*

*How could she have been so blind?*

*Was it too late to stop such a monster?*

Naomi let herself cry as those thoughts and worries about her children filled her head. Tomorrow was a new day, so for today, she'd let herself cry it out.

Only time would tell whether Mallick believed her.

Naya checked behind her for what felt like the hundredth time, but still didn't see anybody. She'd finally been able to slip away after noon prayers were done. It was risky to leave during the daylight but Sister What's-her-name had been watching her like a hawk since the stunt she pulled in front of the Queen Tyrant and the Prince of Arrogance. Not to mention her new best friend, Ophelia.

That girl was going to get Naya's foot in her face if she didn't back off soon.

The older girl was worse than the smell of rotting fish guts down by the docks in the summertime. No matter what Naya did, Ophelia was always right there, ready and waiting as if she was obsessed or something. Naya wished she could shake her and knock some sense into her, but if Sister What's-her-name caught her fighting, there'd be even more hell to pay. She was already on thin ice for her stunt the night before, and the last thing she needed was another reason for them to want to get rid of her.

*I wonder if they've ever sent a sister to the flesh markets. I'm sure one would catch quite the pretty penny.* Naya felt those damned eyes on her again and whirled around, ready to bite someone's head off if need be.

Again, no one was there.

"Fuck the sisters and their bloody disaster of an island. If only it was summer. Merchants always need more help in the summers." Naya muttered under her breath. She found herself doing that a lot lately, working on her self-control. At least if she muttered it, there was less of a chance someone would hear her. She took one last glance around and slipped into the cave's entrance.

"Hey!" The twins chorused together. They ran to the ten-year-old girl as if she were their savior, clutching at the gray robe she tied around her waist.

"Shh," Naya put a finger to her lips and glanced back at the cave entrance. She loved these two kiddos to pieces, but still had a bad feeling about potential threats to their safety. Naya ushered them further into the cave before pulling out the pack of food she'd brought for them. She dumped a feast of bread, hard cheese, apples, and as many sweets as she could carry. With a cry of excitement, the two five-year-old children lunged. Naya gave a soft smile, having known they would react in such a way. The twins had a sweet tooth something fierce.

Naya let them have first pick and watched their innocent faces light up with delight at the sugary goodness. She felt her stomach grumble and tried to quiet it with a touch. Most of the food came from her own rations, since she was still trying to figure out when the kitchens were unoccupied. The couple of times she went in the middle of the night, they had still been roaring with life and laughter. So, until she figured that out, she would go hungry before she let the little ones suffer.

She looked down and her stomach grumbled again.

"Here, Naya, there's plenty here." Aurora handed her one of the honey cookies. Naya began to refuse until she noticed the eclectic collection of metals, wood, and cloth in the cave's corner.

"What have I told you about these inventions of yours?" she hissed through gritted teeth. "You know what would happen if somebody found these. I know you think I can protect you from anything, but if someone realized you were Magicae, there's nothing I could do to stop them from taking you."

Aurora looked a little sheepish, but Hawk gave her a look of defiance. He put his hands on his hips and squared off opposite her.

"What do you want us to do, just sit here? We're bored. If we can't be with you, the least we can do is create new inventions. Besides, if it weren't for us, you wouldn't be here." Naya was taken aback when Hawk threw her an I told you so look.

"I know this is boring, but it's for your safety."

"We're sick of being told it's for our safety. If they come for us, Rory and I can take them." Hawk moved his hands from his hips and crossed them in front of him, doing his best to look down his nose at her. If she wasn't so scared for them, she would've laughed at the way he was acting. But at the present moment, laughing was the last thing she needed.

"Hawk, you don't know what you're saying. The two of you could probably take on a couple of guards, but you can't take out all of them. And then where would you be? In a dungeon, wishing you'd listened to me. So eat your damn cookies and put the shit away. Let me remind you, this island isn't that big and I don't know how often they come check these places. The two of you need to be ready to leave or hide at a moment's notice. If you're not, then I can't promise you'll be here when I get back next time." Naya winced, knowing she was being a little harsh, but sometimes Hawk could really get under her skin. He acted like so tough when he had no idea what the real world really entailed.

*I wonder if this is how Ryker felt about me when I insisted on doing something stupid.* The thought brought an amused smile to her lips, softening her expression. She looked at the two kids before her and grabbed both their hands.

"I'm sorry I yelled. That wasn't fair. It just bothers me I can't be with you guys all the time. Things will be better once we can leave this island and head to an estate or even the country. Just a few more months and we'll be out of here, I promise. Then we'll spend so much time together you'll get sick of me, deal?"

Hawk and Aurora nodded their heads with sober expressions. Naya released their hands and pulled them into a bear hug.

"Nay-Nay, if we promise to hide our inventions, can we keep experimenting?" Aurora asked with an open expression.

Naya gave her a small frown. At the old house, the twins had a hidden compartment where they could hide their trinkets and the things they practiced their Forging with.

Naya didn't know much about the Magicae or Forgers but she knew how much they scared the Queen Tyrant and her soldiers. Only bad things happened to the Magicae, with the likes of her in charge. Because of that, they never spoke of Forging, only their inventions. It was a way to make sure no casual listeners overheard something they shouldn't. In times as hard as these, anybody would turn their neighbor in for a chance at the reward.

But the twins were kind, bold, and innocent. The only people that had to worry about the two of them were the ones that got between them and their honey cakes.

How anybody could think they were dangerous or in need of being locked up, Naya would never understand.

But the danger was always there.

She looked at her sweet Aurora and defiant Hawk and let out a sigh. She'd never been able to deny them anything, no matter how hard she tried. They'd opened a soft spot in her heart she never knew existed and if something happened to them, the young girl wasn't sure her heart would ever recover.

Which was why they needed her to be stern. She was only ten years old, but to them, she'd always be their protector. No matter how many looks Hawk gave her.

But they were kids, alone and in a cave for hours at a time. They needed something to keep their minds off of everything and working on their Forging was a surefire way to keep them occupied.

She gave them both a hard stare. "If you promise me you'll hide them as soon as you hear the slightest noise, you can keep working on your inventions."

The kids jumped for joy and threw their arms around her with a cry of excitement.

Naya shushed them and pulled back, taking in Aurora's dimples and Hawk's smirk. She raised a finger at them.

"But I mean it. If I come back and can find them within five minutes, you have to get rid of them all. And you heard me, all of them will have to go."

Aurora nodded her head so hard Naya worried it might fall off. "We promise, Nay-Nay! You won't regret it." The little girl kissed her cheek and Naya pushed her away with a chuckle.

"Gross. Stop slobbering all over me." Her smile let the girl know Naya didn't mean it, but it fell when she realized she needed to get back. "Now, I gotta get back to the Sisters before they notice I'm gone. I've probably already risked more time than I should have."

At their protests, she pulled them into a group hug again and messed their hair. "I'll be back as soon as I can. Tonight, if possible, tomorrow afternoon at the latest. Make the food last until then and I'll be sure to bring more honey cakes. Stay safe, little ones."

She squeezed them before getting up to leave. As she turned away, she felt a tug on her long skirt and looked down. Hawk stared into her face with a serious expression.

"I'll take care of Rory. She didn't wanna hurt the Bat lady, but I told her we needed to stop her before she killed you. She didn't like it but could do it. I'll make sure she doesn't have to."

Naya studied the young boy and inclined her head. "You're very brave, Hawkman. Just remember to let her take care of you, too. We're stronger when we work together." She glanced at the sensitive little girl. "But you're right, Rory shouldn't have to kill if she doesn't need to. Hide first but fight if it doesn't work, deal?" She held her pinky out.

"Deal," Hawk echoed, entwining her finger with his.

Naya gave one last smile and left before they could convince her to stay. She was risking everything as it was being so late. She'd have to run if she wanted a shot at returning undetected.

Throwing the blasted robe over her head, she took off at a light jog, struggling to get the thing situated so she could see.

"So this is what you're hiding."

Naya tripped on her robe and plummeted to the ground as she was surprised by a familiar voice. She turned to face her assailant and almost ripped the hood off her cloak. Naya glared at the black-haired beauty.

"I'll rip your tongue out before you say anything, mark my words." Naya's heart thundered in her chest as her worst nightmare came true.

Ophelia knew about the twins and where they were located. One conversation would be all it took to make Naya's world come crashing down.

Her hands trembled as she moved to stand.

Ophelia held her hand out with a smirk that Naya ignored. Once she was upright, Naya squared her shoulders and raised her fists.

"Give me one reason I shouldn't clock you right now." She spat on the ground and rubbed her mouth on her sleeve. The key to winning a fight with a bigger and older opponent was to never show fear. The more you talked, the more they screwed up. Plain, simple, and it worked every time.

Naya wasn't going to leave until this girl swore on everything she held dear that she wouldn't breathe a word of this to anybody. And even that might not be enough.

Naya wasn't a stranger to violence, but she avoided it as much as she could. Every injury was another obstacle in her way. And Naya already had enough shit to deal with.

The girl held up her hands but couldn't hide the smirk still on her face. "Down, tiger. I won't breathe a word of your stowaways. That's what friends do; keep their secrets safe, right?" Ophelia gave her a wolfish grin.

Naya's skin crawled at the other girl's insinuation. She'd have to play this rich girl's games if she wanted to keep the twins safe.

She narrowed her eyes, realizing Ophelia was waiting for an answer. "Of course. And real friends tell each other stuff, right? So what secrets are you hiding, O?"

Ophelia let out a bark of laughter. "I knew I liked you for something. That spunk will get you far, girl." She paused as if to consider something. "Well, except here. The Sisters disapprove of anything that doesn't look like blind obedience." She rolled her eyes in a conspiratorial way.

Despite her fear for the littles, Naya couldn't help asking the question that came to her mind. "Why did you come here if your family's rich?"

"Questions like that reveal how young you are. Best to keep those thoughts to yourself." Ophelia's expression didn't waver, but Naya noticed a new hardness in her gaze.

She had to play this right if she wanted something to hold over the girl to keep her quiet.

Naya bit her lip and let her eyes water, making herself as small as possible. "Sorry. I grew up on the streets and this place seems like heaven to someone like me." *Lie.* Naya kept her thoughts from her face, willing herself to look as innocent as Aurora. "But the way you talk makes me think you hate it here. So why would someone from one of the merchant families come here?"

Ophelia studied her for a long moment. Naya felt her skin crawl again, but she kept her face neutral under the older girl's gaze.

"Some questions don't have easy answers." Ophelia looked to the river. Her blue eyes snapped to Naya's brown ones and narrowed. "Let's just say my parents and I don't always see eye to eye. And this was the compromise we could come up with." The sigh she gave sounded frustrated. "Sometimes I wish I'd gone with my sister when she'd offered to take me on one of the trade routes. But I was in love with a boy and couldn't be parted from him. Gah, only a fool lets a boy determine her future." She shook her head and grew quiet, knowing she'd said too much.

Naya wasn't sure if this information would help her, but she filed it away just in case.

Ophelia glanced at the sky and let out a shriek. "We need to get back, Kaia. Come on!" The older girl grabbed her arm, and Naya let Ophelia pull her along.

Guess she wouldn't be able to shake the girl after all.

It looked like they would become best friends, whether Naya liked it or not.

# Chapter Twenty-Three

Tyee paced the inside of the cottage just before dawn. He only stopped to confirm his Tota was still sleeping. He'd passed out after Sylvie spoke to his mind again, waking up on the floor with a crick in his neck and a terrible headache. Tyee had considered leaving in hopes the fresh air would clear his head, but resigned himself to staying until he got the answers he needed.

Sylvie was cruel, but she'd never been a liar. She'd held back bits of the truth plenty of times but never lied.

So Tyee's only option was to accept what she'd said as truth. The Elven and the Shifters of the Forest had created a new alliance in order to take back Kamore and weren't above killing any Mortals in their way.

Tyee frowned as he resumed pacing. There was once a time when he wouldn't have cared about what the Elven and Shifters did, as long as it didn't affect him. But things were different. Tyee had changed.

Kamore was filled with innocent people trying to make ends meet and children who learned hate from their parents. Killing them all wasn't the way to make this place better or safer.

He needed to talk to the Queen and send a message to Duncan. They needed to put a stop to all this as soon as they could. Freya, one of the Herbalists from the Circus, had stayed back with him to learn more from Hugo and his team of Healers in the Elven infirmary. She'd have a way of contacting the Circus if he could find her.

Hopefully, Fritz was still living in the cottage three doors down. He'd be able to put Tyee in touch with his father and Freya. Plus, he'd be able to escort him into the treetops without much fuss. He needed to find the talkative guard as soon as possible. Andriette would be okay for a few hours alone. Maybe Freya or Hugo would have suggestions on what to give the old woman to speed up her recovery.

His mind made up, he went to the door and caught sight of the darkness through the window.

*Damn. Probably too early to drop in unannounced on Fritz.* He chewed the inside of his cheek and began pacing back and forth in front of the door again.

"You're making me dizzy just looking at you." A voice rasped from the bed.

In an instant, Tyee was crouched next to his great-grandmother and offering her a glass of water.

"Here, Tota. Drink as much as you can. Your body needs water to heal."

"Stop fussing like a mother hen. I'll be the one to tell you what I need." Andriette took the offered water and drank deeply. Her expression was sour when she looked back at him. "She tried to speak mind to mind, didn't she?"

Tyee pursed his lips and gave a tight nod. Not trusting himself to speak.

"So that must be where your Mortal blood limits you." Andriette mused out loud with a frown.

"What exactly do you mean, mind speak? Like actually being able to communicate through your thoughts?"

His great-grandmother sighed. "Only the most powerful Elven can send their thoughts to someone else, but all the Elven can receive them. It's used mostly on the battlefield with officers sending silent commands to their soldiers. However, some of the royal line find it amusing to use it on those least expecting it."

Tyee offered her more water, and she waved a hand, fixing him with a knowing stare.

"I heard every word last night and when you fell, I tried to get out of bed to help you. But when I saw stars, I figured me sleeping on the ground with you wouldn't help anybody. In fact, it would only make me more of a bear to deal with." She held up a hand. "And no, I wasn't fishing for some half-baked compliment. Ask what you want to know and let's be done with it."

Tyee inclined his head, acknowledging his great-grandmother's bluntness.

"What did Sylvie mean when she said I was promised to someone else?" Tyee felt the pit in his stomach grow bigger at the memory of the Elven general spitting those words at him. Sylvie had been toying with him and he hated not knowing what she meant by her cryptic answer.

Andriette shot him a look. "Because by Elven tradition, you are." She held up trembling hands. "Let me start from the beginning and it will make more sense." She motioned for the water he'd placed on the table next to her. When he made to hold it to her lips, she took it from him and downed the liquid. Andriette returned the cup and smacked her lips. "Better. Now let's go back to Oakenrock. My parents were in line to inherit the Elven throne from my paternal grandparents at the time. They'd chosen to spend their summers in Oakenrock, among the people and in humble dwellings ever since they'd married. Getting out of the castle helped them recenter what was important to them and gave them insight as to what the Elven people were struggling the most with.

"And the Elven people adored them for it. They were beloved and respected by all, which meant we, as their children, were also beloved. My grandparents and their advisors were on their annual parade of towns where they went and visited the countryside to strengthen the bonds between all Elven. Nobody wanted to return to the time of the clan wars. But alas, they were gone when Oakenrock fell.

"Since I was the eldest of the King and Queen's only child, their advisors made sure I was brought to a safe house for my own good. My siblings were split up and sent to various great aunts and uncles in the country. The advisors claimed splitting them up would keep them safe."

Andriette's eyes misted, and she gasped for breath, a hand on her chest. She coughed and swiped at her eyes.

"But splitting them up only made them easy targets." The old woman whispered as ghosts from her past played before her. "While I was holed up in the safe house, both my siblings perished. I didn't learn the truth until nearly two years after they passed. If I'd been less focused on learning everything I could about becoming an effective queen, maybe I could've seen the chess match they were playing around me."

More tears streamed down her cheeks, but Andriette didn't stop. "At sixteen, my Tota passed in her sleep. My Grandfather was heartbroken and passed soon after." She hung her head and her hands gripped the covers.

Instinctively, Tyee reached out and squeezed her hand, offering comfort for her loss. She squeezed back and continued. "I ascended the throne at sixteen with the youngest of my grandparent's advisors and Ulla's grandfather named as my regent. This meant I was a figurehead for the people while my so-called advisors made all the decisions behind closed doors. Half of the official council meetings I wasn't even invited to.

"I grew angry, understanding what was happening even if I didn't see how the deaths of my siblings and grandparents played into it all. I needed to find a way to take my power back or else I would lose my throne and sense of agency. So I went for a walk. I walked right out the front gates before anybody could stop me and started talking to the people. I remembered the way the people adored my parents for their willingness to live amongst them, even for only part of the year.

"And I did that every day until my eighteenth birthday, when the people flooded the area around the castle to catch a glimpse of my coronation. Check and mate." Andriette shot him an amused smile. It faded as she continued. "My first act as reigning Queen was to dismiss every one of my advisors. Ulla's grandfather protested the loudest and the longest, but I put them in their place when I appointed my own council with people they never knew existed in their own city. The look on their faces when I appointed bakers, teachers, and doctors to their positions was worth every hardship.

"You see, I learned later that these advisors were about to take a vote on who to marry me off to. Guess who was at the top of their list?"

Tyee narrowed his eyes. "Surely not Ulla's grandfather."

"The very same. And once I heard that, I knew I needed to marry and produce an heir as quickly as possible. Your great-grandfather was a lovely, lovely man. We lived a long and happy life but only had one daughter, your real Tota. And I've shared their story and how awful your grandparents' deaths were, but I left out one thing. Ulla's father proposed marriage to my little girl as soon as was socially acceptable. She denied him, of course, but he stayed salty since that incident."

Andriette gave a heavy sigh. "When your grandparents died and left a baby girl barely one year of age behind, I broke. The people were devastated by the loss of so much life and I lost the favor I once knew. I looked at that little girl and the wolves sniffing around her and made the hardest decision I've ever faced. I abdicated the throne.

"I realized my fate would end up being the same as my grandparents if I didn't. There's no doubt in my mind that Ulla's grandfather had my grandparents poisoned to make it easier for him to take power. He thought I was young enough to assert his will over mine, but I proved him wrong.

"Ulla's ambitious and cunning father wasn't going to make those same mistakes. My baby granddaughter was the definition of someone impressionable to anything she was told. He would get rid of me, declare himself regent, and then rule through her or silence her in favor of his own child. I couldn't let that happen, so I left. I took your mother and went to my quiet cottage in the woods. We were happy for a long time, just the two of us. But as a child grows, they crave the company of their peers. I couldn't deny her that, so we moved back to the city. And that was where the downfall began.

"It started in the orchard where the children would play for hours. Your mother heard whispers of her being the true princess even though her Tota had given up the throne. She became obsessed with it and the man who claimed it for himself.

"See, Ulla's father had offered to take the throne as an interim ruler until the council could decide on the next course of action. But soon he started referring to himself as the King and making decisions without the council. He built cities and brought the Elven into the forefront of Kamore. And soon enough, he named his daughter as the crown princess and heir to the throne.

The people appreciated everything he'd done for them, so they kept their unease to themselves for the most part. But the Elven appreciate tradition and order, and this transfer of power had no ceremony or tact. It was a hard pill to swallow for most.

"Which is why your mother heard about it from her peers. She asked me and I told her the truth. As you know, I don't sugarcoat anything and I think I scared her a bit, what with the poisoning and deception." She gave another sigh and motioned for more water. After taking another drink, she picked up right where she left off. "What I didn't realize is that she became even more obsessed. She befriended Ulla without my knowledge and spent much of her time in the staterooms of the new crown princess. Your mother grew and became unruly, disappearing for days at a time.

"Before long, she started showing and dodged all my questions about who the father was. Ulla was pregnant at the same time and they spent hours talking about and hoping they had babes of the opposite sex so they could pledge them to each other.

"Ulla gave birth to Sylvia and, several months later, you were born. They pledged you together, as is the old custom and the people were elated."

Tyee had gone ghost white. Fuck the traditions. There was no way in hell he was tying himself to the likes of Sylvie. His palm flared, and a smirk lit his features. *Looks like Rae agrees. This pledging thing is bullshit.*

"Now, when you were six months old, your mother disappeared with you in the middle of the night. I'd long returned to my serene cottage in the trees, leaving her to her own devices. I have no idea what went through her head or if she realized what would happen should the people find out you were half Mortal. Again, the only woman that knows isn't here to tell us. Ulla herself almost broke my door when she came banging and looking for your mother." She paused as she noticed her great-grandson's pallid color. Andriette squeezed his hand. "Pledging isn't something that's upheld in Elven tradition anymore. You are as promised to her as you are to this cottage. And as for her knack of knocking you unconscious, we'll practice warding your mind and maybe ink your skin with protective runes. They'll sap your life energy, but will be stronger than any mental barriers you create."

Her words settled him a bit before he remembered the other words Sylvie had uttered.

"And what about Ulla's alliance with the Shifters? Do you think she'd actually send forces to destroy towns and kill Mortals?"

Andriette met his gaze and gave a slight wince. "She's capable of anything. And I'm sure she feels threatened by the claim you have on her throne. Sylvia is disliked by many who would see almost anybody else on that throne. This type of forward momentum would give Sylvia a chance to prove herself as a successful general and maybe endear her more to the Elven people."

"Tota, I'm not my mother. I have no desire for the throne or the shit storm that comes with being any type of leader. I have my own people to return to." Tyee's voice left no room for argument as he glanced at the now-lit window. "Besides, I'm a halfbreed. Nobody will take me seriously once that comes out." He put a hand up to quiet her protests. "What was the expression you used? I'm not fishing for any half-baked compliments?" He shot her a smirk and continued when she offered a smile and a nod in return. "Now that it's not so Ungoddessly early, I'm going to have Fritz bring me to the Healers to get you something for those tremors and the weakness you've been feeling." He inclined his head to her hands.

Andriette snuggled into the blankets and grunted her approval, worn out from her emotional tale.

Once Tyee was sure she was comfortable and there was fresh water beside her, he left the quaint cottage and headed to what was once Fritz's place.

# Chapter Twenty-Four

Fritz led the way up one of the ladders, climbing with sure feet and fingers. Tyee followed, taking his time to find hand and footholds. As he reached the top, he paused and let his fingers linger on the tree. The song of the mighty maple was softer than the drumbeat of the oak, but no less clear. He closed his eyes and waited for his heartbeat to match the rhythm of the tree. He let himself get lost in the music and gave a sigh. The noise made him open his eyes, and he heaved himself onto the wooden platform.

"Started hearing their heartbeats, eh?"

Tyee looked up and found Fritz offering his hand with a bright smile. He grunted in answer and accepted the help into a standing position.

"Touchy this morning, aren't you? I didn't think you could be wound tighter than when I dropped you off at Tota's. But turns out I was mistaken." He studied the tense set to Tyee's shoulders and shook his head. "You don't have to tell me what's going on, but learning about the Elven shouldn't make you defensive. Being Elven is the best thing in the world; just give it a chance."

Tyee studied the younger man and considered confiding in him. As soon as the thought crossed his mind, he dismissed it. He had two things he needed to do: get help for his Tota and warn Duncan about what the Elven and Shifters were planning.

There was no time to spare, so he shook his head.

"Maybe another time. Right now I need to see Freya."

Fritz accepted his answer with a nod and a smirk. "Well then, let's get to it.

Won't accomplish anything standing here."

Tyee bumped his shoulder and held his arm out with a wry smile. "Lead the way."

"Are you telling me you don't remember how to get there after spending all that time with your firebrand?" Fritz shot him a wink and turned towards the bridge that led to the infirmary.

The humor drained from Tyee's face at the mention of Rae and the mess they were in. His guilt coated the inside of his mouth and his palm felt like a brand. She didn't even know what he'd done. Their fates were tied, and he wasn't sure there was a way to fix it.

Again, he shook those thoughts from his mind. He had a job to do. He followed Fritz into the expansive structure and took a deep breath. Tyee blinked as he adjusted to the low light and the bustling of Healers and patients.

"I think I see them over there." Fritz raised his voice to be heard over all the noise.

Tyee didn't wait and strode towards where Freya was laughing with some of the younger Elven Healers.

She met his gaze and called out when he could hear her. "Looks like my dreams are finally coming true. Excuse me while I talk to tall, dark, and handsome here."

Tyee wasn't phased by Freya's flirting. They'd talked a handful of times on the road, and he knew it was harmless.

"Let's step outside for a minute." His tone was unwavering as he inclined his head to the door he came from.

Freya shot him a conspiratorial look and gestured behind her. "I got just the place." She looped her arm through his and pulled him in the direction she'd indicated. "Now, if we put our heads together, they'll think we're up to something indecent." She leaned her head towards him with a smile.

Tyee let out a humorless chuckle and gave her a nudge. "I'm too complicated for you, Freya."

Freya shot him a look. "You're too pretty to say something like that. Regardless, Rae's a friend. I can't be getting between my girl and her man." She cracked a wicked grin. Seeing his expression, Freya rolled her eyes. "Huntress, Tyee. Relax a little, I'm only kidding. You know that. This must be really serious if you can't take a joke." She frowned. "Come on."

She opened a door behind a curtain on the back wall and pulled him through to a little balcony off the backside of the infirmary. It was secluded from the rest of the settlement, surrounded by branches and lined with benches. There was even a small place for a bonfire in the center.

Freya closed the door and pulled a latch to lock it. When Tyee gave her a look, she shrugged. "Something indecent, remember?" She gave a small smile, trying to offer an olive branch. She took a seat and patted the place next to her. "The Healers use this as a decompression room. It's understood that if the door is latched, the person behind it needs a break. They'll respect our privacy while we talk and no curious Elven will walk by and interrupt." She gave him a once over. "And it looks like we're going to need all the privacy we can get. So talk, before I need to get back."

Tyee sat next to her and put his head in his hands, letting the stress of the past twenty-four hours wash over him. He let himself feel overwhelmed before he forced his head up. He looked straight into Freya's dark eyes and let it all out. "I don't have a lot of time to explain everything, but foremost, Tota is in a cottage down below, the ones you stayed in with the Circus, and she's hurt. I think she used too much of her life energy when she was using the runes." He saw the confusion in her eyes but didn't explain more. "I know that makes little sense to you, but maybe Hugo or somebody has a better idea of what it could be. Bottom line is, she needs help."

Freya held up a hand. "I've been learning about the runes and how they work, but I've never heard of something like that. I'll get Hugo to go down and check on her." She hesitated for a second. "But if that was all, you should have gone to Hugo right away. We both know whatever this Tota has is over my head."

"You're right." Tyee's face was hard as he glanced at her and then at the door. "I need you to send a message to Duncan. I trust you have a way that's secure?"

Freya frowned. "Course. But it's not between Duncan and me. There's an old Herbalist code Chiara tweaked a little just for this purpose. The deal is it's only between her and me, so you have to give me more than that."

Tyee chewed on the inside of his cheek and considered. *Will it get there in time? Will Freya make it urgent enough?*

The horseman had no choice but to trust the two women. "The Elven and the Shifters of the Forest have found the common cause in ridding Kamore of its Mortals. Their first attack starts in two days' time. The plan is to take the border towns and work their way south."

Freya gasped. "No. I've met the Elven. They're peaceful people and only want harmony amongst all of Kamore. The Healers would never—"

"This wasn't the people's decision, Freya. Sylvie and Ulla did this on their own." Tyee interrupted, conscious of the time ticking away.

"What about the Circus? What about our people?" Freya had terror in her eyes, something Tyee never thought he'd see. She was a formidable young woman in her thirties, with a thirst for travel and knowledge. She was the kind of person you could count on in a crisis to lighten the mood with a joke or quip. Freya didn't scare easily.

"They're safe for now, but our contacts aren't. We need to get word to Duncan and maybe he can do something."

"Tyee, it's the dead of winter. Will Duncan be able to do anything that far north? I'll send a letter, but we need to do something now. You should go talk to the Queen. You're half-Elven, right? That's the rumor I heard, and if it's true, you have a better shot at getting her to listen than I do. I'll talk to the Healers and the patients that come in, but the Queen won't give someone like me the time of day."

Tyee's stomach dropped, but he nodded. "I don't think she's too inclined to listen to me either, but I'll do my best. We gotta try, right?"

Freya stood up. "Exactly. I'll get a letter to Chiara and Duncan." She unlatched the door into the infirmary and gave a half bow, gesturing for him to go first.

Tyee couldn't help the smile that formed on his lips as he followed the Herbalist. "And don't forget about Tota."

Freya turned back and replied. "Never would I forget about someone in need. Good luck, Tyee; speak softly and stride with purpose." She laughed at his puzzled expression. "I'll let Tota explain that one to you."

Tyee shook his head and exited the infirmary, heading to the Queen's quarters.

"Queen!" Tyee bellowed and pounded harder on the door.

"I think that's enough, sir. If the Queen wanted to see you. She would've opened the door by now." The guard next to him snapped, moving to position herself between him and the door.

Tyee frowned, but was forced to back away. He knew the Queen was in there because three of her personal guards stood outside the door. How could he make her speak to him? He was ready to barrel past the guard when the door cracked open.

He watched the guard's expression. Tyee knew the Queen was giving her direction despite the lack of sound coming from the door. Ever since Andriette told him about the Elven's ability to speak mind to mind, he'd paid closer attention to those around him, trying to identify when it happened.

He shuddered, wishing his Tota had given him the ink before he came to see the Queen. Knowing his weaknesses only made Tyee work harder to minimize them, which made this position especially hard to be in. There was nothing he could do to prepare himself before meeting with the Queen.

He started when the guard spoke again.

"The Queen will see you now." Her expression belayed nothing except her displeasure, letting him through after his outburst.

Tyee nodded as his only response, gathering his courage and resolving not to leave until he convinced the Queen to see reason.

*Thank the Huntress she's not Sylvie.*

He squared his shoulders, took a deep breath, and strode into the receiving chamber of the Queen's quarters. Freya's words flashed in his head and he vowed to do whatever it took without raising his voice.

*No matter what the Queen does or says, she needs to put an end to the raids. I'll find another way if I have to.*

Tyee felt his palms sweating as he sat down across from the Queen of the Elven. He felt the pressure to keep his temper in check and make the Queen change her mind. If only the Huntress could make Ulla see how foolish this direction was. She and her people knew nothing about the world outside the Forest and attacking without sound intel would end in more Elven bloodshed than was necessary. If she would work with the Circus, they might have a chance at creating something great. They might actually have a shot at taking down Myra in the capital.

Killing was inevitable, but a massacre would never be the right answer.

"What can I do for you, Tyee?" The Queen's tone was icy as she looked down her nose at him. Her gray hair was almost white and provided a stark contrast to her tanned skin.

Tyee bristled at her tone but kept his voice even as he asked the question that could get him in even more trouble. "Is it true you will soon start attacking the Mortal towns along the northern border?"

Ulla narrowed her eyes and glared at him. "And where did you hear that rumor from?" She hissed, before adding, "Let me guess, my daughter paid you a visit when you sought shelter from the cold."

"It doesn't matter who I heard it from. Is it true?" Tyee insisted, clenching and unclenching his fists in his lap, trying to keep his tone in check.

Ulla regarded him carefully and drummed her fingers on the worn desk between them. "I assume she also told you the Circus is off-limits. Your people will not be harmed by myself or Talon or our soldiers. Their Mortals proved themselves as assets and will be rewarded for their loyalty."

"And what of the Mortals that would prove the same if given the opportunity? How can you justify killing so many innocent people?" Tyee asked through gritted teeth. He tried and failed to keep all the emotion from his voice.

"You forget who you're talking to. I am the Queen of the Elven and you will take care to address me with some respect. I have no obligation to explain my actions and decisions to you, nor will I. Mortals have ruled for too long and it's time they pay for their transgressions against those they don't understand. They deserve to pay for what they've done to us." Ulla's eyes blazed with fury unlike anything Tyee had ever seen. He recognized the barely concealed power underneath her skin for what it was. He felt a sense of awe at how much her power resembled the very forces of nature in all their glory and magnificence.

A twinge of regret panged in his heart at the thought that his blood could never hold such power. Being half-Elven meant his energy would only imitate the force that drove the wind and water and seasons.

But Tyee wasn't scared and wouldn't be cowed by the Queen, even in all her power. Thanks to Andriette, he had an ace up his sleeve.

"It seems you forget who you are talking to. Tota claims you and my mother were friends, but I see no evidence that you cared about her. Queen Ulla, please, I'm begging you. At least have a meeting with Duncan and come up with a way to usurp Myra and let the innocent live. Duncan and the Circus are planning a Resistance and they could use your help. Call off these attacks and come up with a bigger and broader strategy." Tyee hated the pleading tone in his voice, but he wanted to try diplomacy before he wrenched the Queen's arm.

"The time for mercy has passed. It seems Tota hasn't schooled you well enough on the history of the Elven. If she had, you'd know that the atrocities we've suffered more than justify these attacks. Duncan and the Circus fought admirably during the battle of Verdencia, but that doesn't mean I need to consult him about every decision I make."

A growl escaped Tyee's clenched teeth, and he placed both hands on the desk. "I may only be half-Elven, but I wonder how the people would respond if they knew what bloodline that half came from."

"Are you threatening me? This is the type of stunt I would expect for my daughter. Brash and not thought through all the way." Ulla's tone was icy again and her eyes shot daggers at Tyee for his insolence. "But let's think this through for just a moment.

"You're right, there are a lot of Elven that remember when Tota was Queen and they want nothing more than to put her bloodline back in power. Some couldn't care less who it was as long as my daughter doesn't inherit the throne. I know they whisper, but the truth of the matter is Sylvia will be the next Elven Queen. Because if you ever try to make a pass for the throne, you will start a civil war. The Elven will turn on one another as they fight over the line of succession because as many supporters as you would have there would be just as many naysayers who would never concede to a half-blooded king. The hate and disgust for Mortals runs deeper than you could ever guess. So before you take that step think through exactly what you want to put my people through."

"But a civil war among the Elven would mean the Shifters would have to stop their battles, right? If I made a claim for the throne, the Elven would be otherwise engaged and the Shifters wouldn't be strong enough to continue on with the plan. It would save millions of lives." Tyee felt sick to even suggest something like that, but he knew bluffing was the only way to get the Queen to back off. She would be just as at fault for sending the Elven into civil war if she didn't try to make peace before it came to that. He watched her eyes blaze with fury before softening as a smirk graced her features.

"I think I have the perfect solution."

# Chapter Twenty-Five

Rae was sweating despite the chill in the air. She panted and ignored the pain, pushing her body and Crafts to their limits.

With a cry, she whipped the wind around her and summoned rocks and earth from beneath the snow. Her blood felt icy from her wind Craft and sluggish from her earth Craft but she didn't let the warring sensations in her veins distract her from the task at hand.

She grunted as she forced the wind to whip faster, bearing the new weight of dirt and pebbles until a tornado raged around her. Seeing spots at the edge of her vision, Rae used her arms to direct the wind to a fallen log and watched as the rocks and earth pelted what was left of its decaying body.

Rae could feel her heart thundering in her chest and she gave herself a moment to recover. With a grunt, her hands became engulfed in flames and she plunged them into the snow around her. The frozen water hissed with the onslaught of sudden heat, mist wafting into the air. Keeping one flaming hand in the snow, Rae removed the other and used it to call the droplets of water to her palm.

When enough had gathered, she flicked her wrist, and the droplets became a thin line. With another flick, they soared through the air, slicing into the old tree trunk. She did this again and again until sweat rolled down her back and it hurt to breathe.

Letting out another cry, Rae called the wind back, removing her hand from the snow but not letting the flames retreat. She used one arm to control the motion of the winds, spinning them around her person, and brought her flaming fist to her lips. With a forceful blow, she sent a line of fire into the tempest of wind surrounding her.

The fiery ball of wind and flame flickered around the Crafter and Rae let a smile dance on her lips. This was the first time she'd been able to get this far through her combinations, and she couldn't deny the pride she felt at how far she'd come.

It had taken a lot of sleepless nights and almost blacking out a time or two, but she'd finally built up enough endurance to fight like this.

She was in awe of the power beneath her skin and relished finding new ways to combine and use them.

The Resistance was about to begin, and the Circus needed everybody to play a part in this next act. Rae would be damned before she became a liability for the ones she loved. Even after everything that happened, she still feared the Crafter's Curse was lying in wait for her to make a wrong move. She'd never admit it to anyone, but it was ever-present in the back of her mind.

The only thing that could quench her fear was working to master her Crafts and gain the control she once had.

Fire licked at her cheeks and Rae let out a bark of laughter. Using both hands, she swirled the fiery wind faster and faster, spinning with it until she almost fell over. At the last second, she directed it to the fallen log and watched it burn long and bright, fed by oxygen from the wind and sparks from her flames

She called the snow to form a barrier around the log, keeping the burning restricted to the dead tree and avoiding a forest fire.

As the log disintegrated, her fire quieted until all that remained was ash.

Rae made to grab more of her earth Craft from within but became dizzy when she gripped a spire of rock from her core. She let go of the spire and sat on a rock, close to where the old log once laid. She put her head between her legs and took deep breaths, trying to center herself as her life energy recovered.

*At least I know my limits again.* Rae chose to look on the bright side as she gave herself a break. Once she was sure she wouldn't pass out, she'd start again.

The only way to build her endurance even more was to keep pushing.

And defeating Myra was the only motivation she needed to keep at it.

The Governing Council had presented their plans and Rae was elated to hear they'd listened to everything she and the others brought forth. She didn't hesitate when they were told to self-select which group they wanted to initially align with.

She and Zeke joined Duncan, Conrad, and Vera with the other fighters. They'd discussed training and stations briefly with the promise of more information as they developed a broader strategy. Duncan had invited her and Zeke to the next Council meeting as leaders in the group.

Rae accepted without hesitation, but the weight of leadership crept onto her shoulders during the night. The time to fight was upon them and Rae found herself in a position to directly influence what happened next. She'd hungered for this for so long, but now that she had it, she was terrified. Her decisions could end in death for the people in her command.

Jess's face flashed in her mind.

*How can I ask more from the people I love? Risking the lives of others is way more daunting than risking my own.*

Rae gritted her teeth and shook the thoughts from her head. She'd failed Jess and refused to let it happen again.

That was why she couldn't stop training and finding better ways to use her Craft. She couldn't let somebody else die fighting if she wasn't there, too. Rae would be on the front lines with the rest of her people and she wanted to be as unstoppable as possible.

Taking a deep breath, she started to push off the rock beneath her when her palm tingled. She frowned and pulled the leather glove from her left hand. Once freed, she brought it closer to study the red lines that refused to heal.

Her fingers traced them lightly as she focused on the tingling that turned to tightness as she sat there.

Clearly, she and Tyee were bound in some way. She knew this tightness meant Tyee was agitated about something. She pushed harder on the lines, frustrated there wasn't more she could tell from this thing between them. Frustrated he was Huntress knew where and duty kept them apart.

Her palm flared and Rae let out a surprised cry, clutching at her wrist, afraid to touch the now tender spot. It sparked again with a flash of pain and Rae gripped her wrist tighter, wincing at the intensity of it. She looked around and plunged it into the snow, hoping for relief from the burning.

It didn't work.

She pulled her hand from the snowbank and cradled it to her chest. Rae pushed the panic down and reached for her water Craft, seeking the soothing feeling that entered her veins every time she used it.

But something was wrong.

She reached for her Craft but it slipped through her fingers. Rae saw spots at the edges of her vision and put a hand to her head.

She'd never had her Craft refuse her like that before. The only time she couldn't access the power in her veins was when her life energy was too low.

*Did I overdo it that much? I was using a lot but not enough that it wouldn't have time to regenerate.*

Her last thought was of Tyee as she slipped from consciousness in the middle of the forest.

"I can't believe the girl was out there for so long. The poor dear could've frozen to death." Nan gave a shudder and looked at Duncan. "Hasn't she been through enough?"

Duncan's eyes were weary. "I think we've all been through plenty, Rae especially. But the Huntress works in mysterious ways." He peered into the entrance to the building they were using as an infirmary. "Did you see the lines on her palm? I'm no Herbalist but shouldn't those have healed by now?"

Nan furrowed her brows. "Aye. But those lines are a type of symbol, no? It reminded me of the ones in Verdencia. I think there's more to them than we realize." Nan shook her head, wishing there was an easy answer to everything they'd faced these past few months.

*If only the Goddess was more plain in Her desires.*

Nan knew their deity and Her faces would show Their hands when the time was right. All they could do now was keep moving forward. The ghost of a tingling pain in her chest reminded her of how fleeting life was. She had to make whatever time she had left matter. There was no telling when she'd be called onward and she'd do what she could to make life easier for the ones she'd leave behind.

"The girl's a fighter. Chiara claims she'll watch her through the night and monitor her closely for signs she isn't improving. I know you worry about her, dearie, but there's not much else we can do." The old woman looped her arm through his and pulled him away from the infirmary. "Besides, there are a few more things we need to discuss regarding what else needs to be done here. The infirmary is almost complete. All we have left to finish is the addition for the outpatient center. Since we used what originally was the dining and gathering center for the infirmary, we need to start construction on those as soon as we can."

Duncan nodded. "Absolutely. Betsy, Mac, and Juno were drawing up plans the other day. I'll check in with them and talk to Jess—," Duncan's voice became strangled as he realized his mistake. Nan watched pain fill his eyes even as he pushed forward. "Excuse me. I'll talk to Vera about appointing one of the adult Forgers to head up the project."

Nan put a gentle arm on his shoulder. "It's okay to miss her. Jess was as much a part of the fabric of this place as you or I. It'll be a long time before the pain dulls."

Duncan heaved a heavy sigh. "Jess was my rock. Nothing was ever impossible when she was around. I knew I depended on her for a lot, but now that she's gone..." He trailed off and gazed into the long shadows created by the waning sun. The words he couldn't say speaking volumes.

The Herbalist rubbed his back. "Losing our own is never easy, but especially someone so close to you." She moved her hand to his chest and met his lavender gaze. "She's with you in here and we both know she isn't going anywhere. The Huntress decided it was time for her to move on and be reunited with the ones she loved and lost. We'll always feel her absence, but it's okay to let others fill her physical space. Rest easy knowing her place in your heart will never be filled."

Duncan pulled her to his side and draped an arm over her thin shoulders. "I know, Abuela. Grief is full of ups and downs and all you can do is weather the storm. I appreciate the reminder, though." He squeezed her close and gathered his words. "We're getting closer and closer to the start of the Resistance and there are too many unknowns whirling through my mind. I keep wondering if we'll be ready, but the truth is, it doesn't matter. Losing Heimat was the breaking point. If we don't fight back, Kamore will truly be lost for those of us with the Goddess's Gifts."

"Our people will be ready, Dunc. They've been hungering for this day for longer than you think. We're on the path the Huntress has laid at the behest of the Goddess herself. When the snow melts, we must be prepared to march. Trust in the Huntress and our people." Nan wrapped an arm around his waist and squeezed. She frowned and threw him a scowl. "Have you been skipping meals again? If I didn't know any better, I'd say you were a bag of bones by how thin you are. We need to visit Betsy's magical bubbling cauldron."

Duncan gave a low chuckle as Nan steered him towards the chuckwagon wafting something delicious their way.

*Good food nourishes the soul and heals the heart.* Nan couldn't believe how thin their Ringmaster had become and noticed the way his worry for Rae aged his face more than anything. Duncan needed to get some sleep and a good meal if he wanted to stay on his feet. *Maybe a day with a good friend. Anything to take his mind off of the stress of leading.* She frowned. *There's something wrong between him and Chiara. If only they had a chance to speak to each other and fix what's going on between them.*

Nan shook her head at the absurdity of the situation.

"Duncan! Nan! Wait up a second!"

The pair turned to the voice and saw Chiara running toward them with a letter in her hand. She reached them, panting, and placed a hand on Duncan's arm to steady herself. Nan raised an eyebrow at the look they shared and the way Duncan immediately moved to support the Head Herbalist.

*Maybe the chance to talk will come sooner rather than later.* A small smile crept onto Nan's face before she registered Chiara was speaking.

"—, it was written on behalf of Tyee." Her voice dropped to a whisper as she glanced around them. "He claims the Elven and the Shifters of the Forest are planning to mount a coordinated attack on the border towns. They mean to slay as many Mortals as they can."

Duncan's face went white and Nan could only hear a roaring in her ears.

This changed everything.

Rae felt as if she were floating.

Everything was pitch black, but warm and soothing, rocking her up and down as if she were cushioned by warm water.

Huntress, it'd been a long time since she'd been able to enjoy a nice hot bath. As in, take her time washing and letting the warm water heal her aches and pains. Since they'd left Heimat almost a year ago, she'd guess. On the road, there was only time to bathe in the streams and since they'd settled at Mantaga Lake, she hadn't allowed herself such a luxury, reserving that for the young and elderly who needed more relief from winter's chill.

She'd forgotten how lovely this could be.

Rae laid her head back and spread her arms out, lifting her hips and legs to the surface and relishing in her weightlessness.

A prickling at her palm made her frown.

Thoughts of the clearing rushed back, and she rubbed at the lines she knew would forever mar her hand. She felt something through the bond that connected her to Tyee and, on instinct, she pulled on it as hard as she could.

Weariness overcame her, and she let the darkness engulf her once more.

When she woke again, strong arms were hooked under hers, dragging her towards something. Instead of alarm, all she felt was a strong sense of safety and warmth. When she opened her eyes, the darkness was morphed into a rich maroon.

Soon enough, she felt sand beneath her and the arms lifted her as if she were a child. She leaned her head on the man's shoulder and inhaled the scents of leather and horseflesh. Her eyelids drooped, and she snuggled into his warmth.

The next time she woke up, it was to soft lips kissing her cheeks, nose, and forehead as salty tears splashed onto her. She tried to sit up, and those strong arms lifted her until she leaned against him. Rae squinted to see more of him, but his face was still obscured in the maroon mist that clung to everything around them. With a snap of her fingers, she called a single flame and raised it to Tyee's face.

What she saw made her heart break.

Tyee's eyes were filled with anguish, and his face was blotchy from crying. He was struggling to calm down and Rae did the only thing she could think of. She pulled him close and rocked both of them, whispering words of comfort into his ear.

Tyee's frame became wracked with sobs and he trembled all over, giving in to the comfort she offered. He whispered apologies to her over and over without explaining what he was so sorry for. As he ran out of tears and his trembling stopped, Rae put a hand on his cheek and turned his head to meet her gaze.

"Tell me what's going on, Drifter. What does all this mean?"

Tyee swallowed and tried to form words.

When he couldn't, Rae took a guess. "It's this bond between us, isn't it? Whatever's happened, you saved my life. Talk to me. We can figure something out, but you need to tell me what's going on if I'm to be of any use."

"I'm so sorry." Tyee's voice was so soft, Rae could barely make out his words.

"Tyee, I forgive you. Whatever this means, you saved my life. There's nothing to apologize for." Rae was alarmed at how distraught Tyee was. She'd never seen him like this, and it unnerved her.

He took her hand in his and traced the lines on her palm. "I didn't mean to."

Rae felt shivers at his feather-light touch and drew soft circles on his arm with her free hand. "I know you didn't. It's okay, Drifter, we'll get through it."

He seemed to relax at her touch and some of the anxiousness Rae was feeling released. The line connecting them seemed to loosen as they responded to each other's closeness.

Rae touched his cheek again. "What is this thing between us?" She spoke in the tone she used when Arwen was spooked or one of the kiddos was scared to jump into the net. It was gentle but unyielding, meant to encourage and reassure.

Tyee's dark eyes met hers and the torment still in them almost took Rae's breath away. Something was extremely wrong for Tyee to wear such an expression.

"It's a blood bond. I didn't know that's what I was making. You have to believe me." His eyes became pleading as he squeezed her shoulders. His tone was as desperate as a drunk for one more shot. Rae felt butterflies in her stomach at his words despite not understanding what they meant.

She knew what he needed from her and cradled his face with her hands. She pulled him into a quick and chaste kiss, pulling away to say, "I believe you, Drifter. You acted on instinct as I've done time and time again. I understand and I forgive you." Her eyes shone with sincerity, even as one eyebrow raised. "Is it serious, this blood bond?"

Tyee made to answer, but no sound came from his open lips. His frustrated expression made Rae laugh, and she felt sweet relief when he sent her a wry smile.

Seeing Tyee so upset and vulnerable was something she'd never thought she'd see. Her instinctual need to make him feel better had come as a bit of a surprise. It meant she could no longer deny the feelings she had for the dark rogue. Rae surmised that this blood bond meant their fates would be entwined for the rest of their lives, and she found herself not upset at the thought.

She opened her mouth to speak, but nothing came out.

Tyee shot her a puzzled expression and pulled her close.

His lips met hers with the force of a hurricane, his emotions making themselves known as he deepened the kiss and sent fire racing through her veins. Rae met him with her own passion, slowing the kiss down as if they had all the time in the world.

*You drive me crazy, Birdie. When this is all over, I hope you're prepared for what I have planned.*

Rae broke the kiss when she felt Tyee's husky voice in her head. Her wide eyes gave him pause.

*Can you hear me like this?*

Rae made to respond before remembering their predicament and nodded instead.

*Why don't you try?*

Rae lifted an eyebrow and shot him a look.

*Come on, Birdie. Never thought you were the type to be scared of a little challenge.*

*I am not scared.* Rae thought her response and grinned when she saw Tyee's wide eyes. *Turns out it's not much of a challenge after all.*

Tyee's shoulders shook with silent laughter. *This is so different from when Sylvie speaks mind to mind with me.*

Rae shot him another look and a smirk. *Isn't Sylvie your bitch of an ex?*

Tyee's expression turned serious at the mention of the cruel Elven general. *She is. Rae, there's something else I need to tell you.*

She furrowed her brows and gestured for him to continue, but his face began to fade, covered by maroon mist. Rae clutched at his hands, but soon even they were covered with the rich color.

In desperation, Rae threw her thoughts at him, hoping at least he could hear her. *Don't forget your promise, Drifter. Come back as soon as you can.*

*I need you.*

It was the closest she'd come to saying the words she knew were true and she couldn't know if he'd even heard them, much less what his response would be.

Before long, she was floating again in the warm darkness.

She closed her eyes and let unconsciousness take her once more. Thoughts of Tyee and the blood bond swirling in her head.

# Chapter Twenty-Six

Mirabella felt her heart flutter as she entered the city she never thought she'd set foot in again. Conrad had left her at the edge of the forest, after having a visceral reaction to what remained of the once mighty forest. She felt horror at the atrocities done to the thriving ecosystem, but she knew her feelings were nothing compared to those of the feline shifter, connected as he was to the natural world. Bane reported the devastation inflicted by the man she once loved, but witnessing it for themselves came as a shock.

The charred earth and blackened stumps brought sorrow to her heart and fueled the hatred she now felt for Darren.

And yet, she was still returning to her abuser.

She kept the image of Gemma's smiling face at the forefront of her mind to convince herself to keep putting one foot in front of the other. Her little girl was safe and would find happiness in the community she was now ingrained in. Mirabella would do this for her daughter and the other Magicae of Kamore.

This next piece of Mirabella's story would help her make up for her past decisions. She'd resume the role she once had as Vincenzio's meek and submissive wife, but behind closed doors, she'd fulfilled a purpose she'd only dreamed of.

Conrad had helped her distress her clothing, and splatter them with mud and grime. Mirabella knew she reeked and could still pass as gaunt and underfed, some bones still poking through at odd angles. She'd become thin after leaving Heimat and wandering the forest, and never regained her appetite with the Circus as she worried about her daughter's fate. She refused to eat much of what Conrad provided during their trek back to Heimat for fear of putting on too much weight. Mirabella knew Darren would scrutinize her appearance and every word she uttered. If she wanted to survive his questioning, she needed everything to be as believable as possible.

With that in mind, she pulled the scarf back from her head and rushed toward the barracks and the man she hated. In the letter she'd wrote, she took responsibility for losing Gemma and claimed she was searching the river bank for the little girl to make up for what she'd done.

Whatever that was.

But knowing Darren, he'd have some reason to blame her for what happened.

She was the one that brought Gemma to Rich's that night, but if everything had gone according to plan, Darren wouldn't know that was where she'd been. Mirabella rubbed her freezing hands together and blew to warm her exposed skin. She went through the words she'd prepared on their journey south.

*I can't screw this up.* Mirabella thought to herself as she stepped closer to the main part of the ruined city. She was confident she could pull off what needed to be done, or she'd die trying. Darren would watch her every move so she'd have to be careful, but Mirabella trusted Duncan would find a way to open communication between her and the Resistance.

When she reached the city proper, Mirabella collapsed in the first soldier's arms she saw. Playing the part of the grieving mother and damsel in distress, Mirabella insisted she be taken directly to her husband. She knew there was a small chance of the young man refusing on account of her husband's reputation for violence, but she figured it was worth a shot. The less she had to deal with his steward and dear friend Zander, the better.

The young man, boy really, took her to what was once the town's City Hall and knocked on the doors leading to the council chambers. This was the room her husband chose as an office and where she'd witnessed one of his last outbursts before she left. The boy raised his fist to knock on the door again, when a voice sounded behind them.

"What do you think you're doing?" The voice's tone was icy.

Mirabella gritted her teeth at a familiar baritone. In an instant, she remembered her purpose and spun around with wide eyes. "Zander! Thank the Goddess!" She threw herself into his arms and forced herself to weep. The more convincing she could be better. Zander patted her back awkwardly and Mirabella forced herself to shed some tears to keep the smile from her face.

She'd thrown the steward off-kilter by seeking comfort from him. They'd never been friendly towards one another even before she'd married Darren. She could feel the tension in the man's frame and fought to hide another grin.

"I got so lost. It was awful. And Gemma, she's gone. There's no trace of her anywhere across the river and that's why I got so turned around. I need to see Darren." Mirabella choked out the words and met her husband's steward's gaze.

Zander considered her with a shrewd expression. Instead of answering her, he turned to the guard who escorted her. "You're dismissed, soldier."

The boy gave a salute and rushed off as quickly as he could.

With the boy taken care of, Zander turned his attention to Mirabella. "You were a fool to leave, Mirabella. What happened to your hair?"

Mirabella almost swore under her breath. She'd forgotten about her hair. The cutting was easy to explain away, but the bleaching? She'd have to think fast. To buy some time, Mirabella played with the hem of her frayed sweater, keeping her gaze down.

"It was a tangled mess and would get caught in the trees, so I cut it with the sharpest rock I could find. I can only imagine what a mess I look like right now. And the color." She winced. "There was an open spot in the river and I attempted to wash it. But there must have been something in the water because now it looks like this." She let her voice crack and a sob escape on her last words, as if it had all been a horrible mistake. Goddess, how she hated that dull brown color Darren preferred. She swallowed the words on the tip of her tongue and met the steward's gaze with her own watery one.

Zander frowned but seemed to buy her story. "I will escort you to your room and see to it the general knows of your return. He's in meetings for the rest of the day, so don't expect him until later tonight. That should give you a chance to make yourself presentable again." He raised one eyebrow, as if waiting for her to challenge his instructions.

Mirabella averted her eyes and nodded, playing the part of the broken wife with ease. She let Zander lead her to her room and felt some of the tension release from her shoulders as she sank down on the uncomfortable cot after he left.

The actual performance was about to begin. She'd spend the rest of the day rehearsing what she'd say to the man she thought she would never see again and whom she needed to trust her as he once did.

She needed to become the woman he once knew, desperate to get her daughter back and willing to do anything to make it happen.

Even if it was the last thing she did.

Mallick took a deep breath of crisp winter air as he thundered across the countryside with his men, known as the Blades, to the masses. The Blades comprised the boys he'd grown up with, turned into fierce and unwavering men. They were his best friends and his fiercest competitors. They challenged him to develop his skills as a swordsman and tactics as a leader. They'd never been ones to curb their tongue and Mallick appreciated their blunt way of keeping him at his best.

They weren't afraid to question his decisions when it was warranted. They were loyal to a fault, and when pressed, did as they were bid, regardless of whether they agreed with it or not.

He looked behind him and gave his second a feral grin. The man answered with a matching one and let out a cackle, urging his horse faster.

Mallick turned his attention back to the land in front of them and spotted the bridge they were taking to get across. He held his hand up and signaled for them to slow, giving their horses a chance to catch their breath and ease themselves over the large bridge.

"That rush never gets old." Mallick turned to see his best friend and second in command still grinning wide as he ran a hand through his long light brown locks. "I'm still in disbelief that you left so early last night. Let me tell you, there were quite a few maidens disappointed you weren't there to deflower them." Laurent goaded him, his grin turning to a cruel smirk.

Mallick sighed inwardly, but gave his friend a matching smirk. "Who said they didn't find their way to my bed, anyway?"

Laurent laughed darkly and thumped him on the back. "Should've known. The golden boy always gets what he wants. Good thing too. Who knows when the next such opportunity will present itself?"

Mallick grunted in response. Laurent had made it very clear about how he felt, leaving the comfort and luxury of the Keep for the hardship and loneliness of the road. They'd argued for hours after Mallick told him how Myra consented, as long as he could become the reigning champion of the pit. But even Laurent conceded that once Myra set Mallick on the path, there was no way forward except through victory. He hadn't dared suggest Mallick throw the fight to make himself look weak.

Laurent wasn't happy, but his loyalty and dedication to Mallick meant he'd suffer through whatever his friend wished. But that didn't mean he wouldn't grumble about it.

They approached the bridge and an old codger stepped in front, blocking their path.

Mallick felt his temper flare at the man's audacity. "Out of the way, old man, or the Blades will relish the opportunity to use their skills against you."

The wizened old man locked eyes with Mallick, recognizing Myra's son. His voice shook as he scrambled to get out of the way. "My apologies, Your Excellence. I've been charged with checking anyone who passes for signs of Magicae. I was only doing my duty."

"If you want to do your duty, open your coffers," Laurent piped in, earning chuckles from the rest of their brigade. "Open your house and fetch us a fresh, hot meal and your daughters. It's been too long since we've felt the comforts of feast and flesh."

Mallick smirked as the old man's face drained of color. "Your reserves of grain and dried meat will do fine. Gather them together and make sure they find their way onto the wagons behind us. We'll stop by on our way back when we have more time and a victory to celebrate."

Cheers rose behind him, and Mallick raised his sword. "Onward, to the north!"

Without another glance at the frightened old man, Mallick spurred his horse into action, crossing the river and continuing on the journey that would lead him to his destiny.

Naomi's words rattled in his head.

*Besides, I couldn't bear it if you killed your own sister.*

He hadn't bothered to tell his mother about the lies the former First Lady whispered in his ear. Even after he'd won in the fighting pits, Myra had been cold to him. He'd thought the victory would attest she was right to trust him, but it seemed he had a lot more to prove before she'd recognize his usefulness. The last thing he wanted to do was give her a reason to doubt him and sharing the prisoner's words with his mother would be a surefire way to do so.

But there was a small voice fighting to be heard, pleading for him to listen. Pleading for him to consider the woman's words.

He pushed the voice away again.

They had thought Naomi Freeman was broken but turned out she still had a silver tongue. Even if the words she uttered had any truth to them, his destiny was clear.

The fire Crafter needed to die.

# Chapter Twenty-Seven

Tyee's hand shook as he forced himself to practice the last set of runes. Hugo insisted on moving Tota to the infirmary to better care for her, but Tyee felt sick at the thought of staying in the trees.

Not after Ulla's proposal.

He was in his cottage on the ground, doing anything he could to keep his mind off of the terrible choice he faced.

Tyee finished another row of wobbly symbols and set his stele down with a sigh. He'd come a long way in being able to write and understand the runes, but this last set was the most complicated and made his head swim.

It was no use to keep working when he couldn't focus.

Maybe a walk would do him good.

Tyee made to leave when someone pounded on the door. Without hesitating, he pulled the door open and came face to face with Fritz.

Tyee blinked in surprise to see the large man at his door.

"Fritz, I thought you were on duty for the next few days."

Fritz rubbed the back of his head and gave a sheepish grin. "Yea, I am. But my Da told me to come get you. Tota's awake and asking for you."

"Of course." Tyee didn't delay and pushed past him, shutting the door behind him. Outwardly, he kept a cool composure, but inwardly, he felt his pulse racing and his palms sweating. He wouldn't let anybody see, but being close to Ulla only made his choice more real.

Tyee marched to the ladder directly below the infirmary, not needing Fritz to lead the way anymore. He started to climb when Fritz's voice made him pause.

"My Da told me you know about who you are."

Tyee dropped to the ground and spun towards the young man. "Don't do that, Fritz."

"Do what?" Fritz's eyes widened with innocence.

"Don't suggest something we both know is unrealistic."

Fritz frowned. "Tyee, your family led the Elven for centuries. The Queen forbade me from accompanying you all the way to Tota's in fear of you realizing the truth. Her power is weakest that far in the forest and she couldn't be sure the runes she made her soldiers draw would hold. Ulla's become paranoid and obsessed with her legacy. You have more support than you realize, and you know how awful Sylvia is. Many people would support any reasonable candidate over her."

"Fritz, stop being naïve. I'm only half-Elven. Nobody would support my claim over a full-blooded Elven." Tyee gave a dark chuckle. "And besides, I don't know how to rule. I'm an outsider and the farthest thing from a royal."

"You're right, you are the farthest thing from a royal, but I think that's what we need. Everyone is so restless, especially our young people. It's time to get back out into the world and who better to lead us than someone who's been in that world." Fritz pushed back, trying to get Tyee to see what he did.

Tyee put a hand on the man's shoulder. "It would mean civil war. You know Sylvie won't let go of the throne for anything. Your people don't deserve that."

"You mean our people. I know you didn't ask for this, but the reality is you're our best shot at avoiding a future with Sylvia in charge. Nobody's asking for an answer now. Just think about it."

Tyee clenched his teeth to keep from blurting out Ulla's suggestion on the matter. He couldn't risk more people knowing about his predicament, no matter how much he wanted to trust the redheaded giant. He could feel his blood boiling and his skin felt too tight, but he turned and climbed the ladder, anyway. The sooner Andriette was fit to travel, the sooner they could leave.

And some distance was what Tyee needed to think clearly. He knew every delay meant more people could get hurt, but Tyee wasn't ready to sign away his future. No matter the cost.

If he agreed to Ulla's terms, his freedom would go up like a puff of smoke. He needed time to decide whether he was willing to make that sacrifice.

He made it to the top of the ladder and took the bridge to the infirmary.

"You must be Tyee. My name is Hugo and I'm one of the Head Healers." An unassuming middle-aged Elven held out his hand to the horseman.

Tyee shook it and asked, "How's Tota doing? Is she strong enough to leave yet?" Tyee gave a slight wince at how selfish his second question sounded, but he couldn't help asking what was on his heart.

"Tota is a beloved member of our community. Despite what she would have you believe," Hugo shot him a conspiratorial grin. "She's lived longer than any Elven on record and the power in her veins is strong for what you'd expect from someone who's lived for centuries. However, I can confirm she has rune sickness. In her younger days, Tota would've been able to string together lines and lines of runes without consequence." Hugo paused and gave Tyee a knowing glance. "If I ramble about things you already know, don't be shy." Hugo motioned for Tyee to follow him to the edge of the platform in the infirmary. He looked at the horseman with expectant eyes and Tyee gave him a slight nod.

"My understanding is you have very limited knowledge of the runes. I assume you understand the basic premise." Hugo paused again, giving Tyee an opportunity to respond.

"Aye. Each rune stands for something and has multiple meanings. In order to accomplish something, you can put the runes together and create different combinations for just about anything. It's different for each Elven, so how you interpret the runes will determine which ones you use for certain tasks." Tyee motioned for him to continue after proving what knowledge he did have.

"Very good. You understand the basics. Again, you may already know this, but whenever you use the runes, they pull from your life energy. Once the rune is carved into something, it must be charged in order to be used again. The first time you draw them, they work once. If you wanted to use those same symbols again, you would need to charge them before they would do anything. In this way, we make sure they're not continuously draining our life force. The more runes you draw, the more life energy they take. Normally, drawing three runes is child's play. There's enough power in our blood that children can use up to ten runes without fear. After ten, things get a little complicated, and you can run into opposite meanings. This can lead to drain out, which is why ten is the cutoff for most Elven, even as they grow into adulthood. Besides, most things can be accomplished with five or fewer runes."

Tyee took a moment to process this new information. Andriette had been more concerned with him learning how to draw the runes and understand their meaning than the mechanics behind how they worked. Or at least she never taught them to him. Before he could think about it, Tyee blurted out another question.

"What about something like this?" He held his bare left hand out so the mark of Algiz was on full display.

Hugo sucked in a breath and took Tyee's hand in his own, tilting it to get a better view of the rune. His eyes met Tyee's, and he said, "Blood bonds are entirely different. They're usually reserved for the one you become mated with. The blood bond is one of the few exceptions in that whoever wears the matching mark can call on your life energy whenever it's needed. If the other person is in danger, so, too, will you be."

Concern filled Hugo's eyes, but Tyee only gave him a terse nod. "That's more or less what Tota told me. Is there a way to undo it?"

Hugo frowned and tapped his chin. "The blood bond is a widely outdated practice among the Elven. If I remember correctly, there are a few texts on it in the library. I would check those out, otherwise, there is nothing I know of."

"I appreciate your help." He let his hand drop to the side. "I'm sorry, I interrupted. You were telling me about the rune sickness."

"Yes, the rune sickness. It's most likely Tota knew she had it, which is why she only attempted three runes. The disease has progressed enough that even three was too many for her. There will come a time when even one draws too much from her. What we hypothesize is the runes take and take and take without stopping. They only stop once all the user's life energy is used."

Tyee blanched at what Hugo was telling him.

Just last night, Tyee had attempted to use five runes to place a protection on his cottage to stop Sylvie from barging in whenever she wanted. As soon as he finished the last symbol, Tyee felt his life energy leave faster than even when he'd given it to one of the Magicae. Neither Rae nor the stable boy had taken so much, so fast. He lay down and shivered as if he had a fever. The night was miserable. But when he woke in the morning, he felt better.

As if someone gave him some of their own life energy.

Tyee's wide eyes snapped to his palm again. *Rae.*

"You okay there, lad? Maybe you should sit down. I know this is a lot to take in." Hugo attempted to herd Tyee to the chairs outside the infirmary, but stopped when Tyee held up a hand.

"Can this sickness affect anyone? Young or old?" He asked in halting tones.

Hugo scrunched his brows and shot him a look. "Aye. It's rare to affect the young, but not unheard of. Why do you ask?"

Tyee leaned his elbows on the rail of the platform and debated confiding in the Elven Healer. In the end, logic won out and Tyee responded. "Last night I tried to ward my cottage, but I felt the life energy drain dangerously fast after I finished the fifth rune. I must have passed out. But when I woke, it was as if nothing happened."

Hugo frowned. "How many runes have you drawn prior to the string of five?"

"One."

"Sure, but how many total have you drawn? Not how many you've done as a string." Hugo prodded.

Tyee felt his cheek warm as he repeated, "One. As in, I've only drawn a single rune. Tota had just started my education on using the runes for a purpose when she fell ill."

Hugo gave a low chuckle. "Well, don't jump to conclusions, then. One to five is a big jump when you're first learning. Build your endurance and try again." Hugo hesitated and met Tyee's gaze. "But I will say, most of our people don't know your story, Tota told me in case something were to happen to her. She didn't want your education to be lacking if Skaber called her home before it was done. As you are only half-Elven, I must warn you not to use more than five runes at a time. Ten is safe for most, but I would be wary in your situation. Especially with another tied to you." He inclined his head to Tyee's palm. "You most likely don't have the sickness, but repeated drainings could force your body into rejecting the runes. And when that happens, the runes gain the upper hand and start taking more and more."

Tyee said nothing for several long moments.

"Is that what happened to Tota?"

"It's hard to say. For someone as advanced in years as her, it may be her body is too weak to bear them anymore." Hugo placed a gentle hand on Tyee's shoulder. "Would you like to see her?"

Tyee nodded and followed the older Elven into the bustling infirmary.

Hugo led him to one of the back corners and pulled the heavy curtain back to reveal where Andriette lay resting. Tyee tried to catch a glimpse of Freya as they'd moved through the maze of beds and healing stations, but hadn't seen her distinct dark profile and shaved head. He turned his attention back to the old woman dozing before him. He felt relief wash over him when he noticed her color was better.

They were in a quieter part of the infirmary, but Hugo closed the curtain to give them privacy. He whispered words to the old woman and checked her vitals before leaving without a word, not giving Tyee a chance to thank him for the care and willingness to explain everything to him.

"Here to prison break me?"

Tyee smiled at the raspy tone and moved closer to the cot and his great-grand-mother, reaching for her hand.

"None of that now. I'm sick, not dying. We don't do sappiness." She swatted his hand away.

Tyee chuckled. "Of course. Your color looks better."

"Exactly, which is why you came to prison to break me." Her eyes revealed her weariness when her tone didn't. She studied his face and posture. "You wear the weight of the world on your shoulders. Let me share the burden, nakni." She patted the cot next to her.

Tyee hesitated, not wanting to hinder his great-grandmother's recovery. Andriette raised an eyebrow and patted the bed again, giving him a knowing look. With a sigh, Tyee sat and bared his soul to her.

"I spoke with Ulla."

"Address her as Queen when you're in the trees, boy. You know you're the last person who should be talking treason."

"Of course." Tyee started, with so much on his mind the royal's name had slipped out without a thought. "I spoke with Queen Ulla about the raids on the Mortal cities. And she confirmed everything Sylvie said the other night." Tyee trailed off, not sure how to explain the choice the wretched Queen had given him.

Andriette gave him time before nudging him with her leg. "The curtain is runed to prevent people from overhearing. Speak plainly and unburden yourself without fear."

Tyee sighed and met her matching dark gaze. "I was desperate. I begged her to stop them and when that failed, I threatened to expose and take my claim to the throne."

"Hmm, I take it that didn't go over well." Andriette shot him a wry grin, despite the concern in her eyes.

"That's an understatement. She—," Tyee swallowed, knowing this was it. Once he spoke the words aloud, the decision and its consequences would be real. But he was drowning. He needed to tell someone before it overwhelmed and destroyed him. "She told me she'd make a bargain to put a stop to the attacks. She said if I honored the pledging to Sylvie, she'd pull her forces immediately as a show of good faith. We'd be mated before summer's end." Tyee leaned his elbows on his knees and refused to meet his great-grandmother's gaze.

Promise himself to Sylvie and his people would be safe. Give himself to the cruelest woman he'd ever met and save thousands. Take the throne and sign his death sentence.

It was a choice between duty and freedom.

How could he be so selfish?

How could he not?

He felt a hand on his arm and met his Tota's gaze, seeing the horror that now filled it and knowing this was the last thing she wanted for him.

"You did *what?*"

Ulla put her hands to her temple at her daughter's shrieking tone. When she met Sylvia's blazing eyes, the Queen made hers as hard as steel.

"You'd do well to watch your tone. You're the one who told him about our plans. If you'd learned to keep your mouth shut, you wouldn't be in this situation." She snapped, her words as sharp as icicles.

"Mother, you can't expect me to tie myself to a halfbreed. This is a clumsy attempt at *our* throne and you're giving him everything he wants on a silver platter. Our people will follow him like ducklings in neat little rows, brainwashed by the Istaqa bloodline once more. We've worked too hard to let that happen. How could you?" Sylvia's voice didn't waver as she raced to convince the Queen before it was too late.

"Again. You're the one responsible for your circumstances. If you were more likable, I wouldn't have to marry you off to make people accept your leadership." Ulla hissed, frustrated with the way her daughter refused to take responsibility for her own actions that led them to this point.

"You expect me to have an heir with a halfbreed? You agree to attack the Mortals responsible for our retreat into the trees and then introduce their thin and powerless blood into our royal line?" Sylvia's voice was tinged with desperation, recognizing her mother had already decided what was to be. "No wonder Grandfather refused to give up the throne to someone as spineless as you."

*Crack.*

Ulla's hand stung from the force of her backhand. Sylvia placed a palm on her reddening cheek and glared at her mother. Ulla glared right back, seething.

"You little brat. I would never suggest such a thing. You've already proven more than capable at keeping the boy in line. I'm sure he'd be relieved not share a bed with you. Produce an heir with whomever you want and then you can get rid of the Istaqa however you want." Ulla pinched her lips. "I thought I raised you to have a brain. You call me spineless when you can't see what's right in front of you."

Sylvia shot daggers at her mother. "And what about Talon and the Shifters? They won't take kindly to your sudden change of heart."

Ulla's smile was as sharp as the knife at her belt. "Well, it'll be up to you to explain to them why you're not enough of a leader to rule on your own. Maybe a leash will do you good. Rein in that temper and tendency towards cruelty. Get out of my sight."

Ulla turned her back to her daughter in dismissal. She heard the woman scurry off, shutting the door with a bang behind her.

Once her audience was gone, Ulla collapsed into the chair behind her desk and wrung her hands. Her eyes strayed to the painting of her father and she whispered, "Father, give me strength. You'd always wanted to join our line with that of the Istaqa. Help me guide Sylvia to do what's right. Help me lead our people through this dark night."

She leaned back as her eyes drank in the likeness of her hero.

She'd do what she must to uphold his legacy.

Ulla wouldn't let her daughter be the reason the Elven destroyed what was left of their people

# Chapter Twenty-Eight

Nan held on tight to her grandson, praying to the Huntress she stayed on the back of the horse as it flew down the paths in the forest.

Freya's letter had been disturbing, to say the least. She reported Tyee had intel that the Elven and the Shifters of the Forest were planning to attack some of the towns that bordered the Forest's edge.

*So much death and destruction. When does it end?*

Nan insisted she go to implore the Queen and the Shifter Alpha to change their minds. She would make them see the benefits of joining the Circus in taking down Myra and her followers the right way. It was true, many Mortals were bigots and couldn't be reasoned with. They were the ones who would fight tooth and nail before they'd give the Magicae or Elven a place at the table. They would harass and threaten anybody who disagreed with them.

But other Mortals only wanted to live their lives. They couldn't care less about who they shared their space with as long as they could make a living and enjoy the years they had.

And some yearned to openly embrace their Magicae loved ones.

She thought of all the Mortals that helped them when they traveled the country as the Circus. She thought of those now fighting for Kamore and an end to the oppression and prejudices facing their world. Nan thought of her own granddaughter and how the Goddess hadn't blessed her with a Gift. Luc didn't have power in her blood, but she had the same spirit that her father did. She was kind, courageous, and full of positivity and life. Her granddaughter was a miracle and lacking in nothing.

There were thousands of Mortals across the country just like Luc. Those people didn't deserve to die because of the loudest of their kind. The country needed every kind of people if they didn't want to lose out on the diversity they'd built. There was a rich tapestry of lives that made up the history of Kamore. Losing one or more strands of that tapestry would be a shame.

*Ulla doesn't know what she's doing. We have to stop her.*

Nan held onto the back of her grandson and tried to move her body in rhythm with the horse beneath them. But it'd been years since she'd last ridden a horse. Her old bones weren't used to the jarring movements as the horse raced across the forest floor. They followed the path they took to get to Mantaga Lake in the first place. She trusted Javie to keep them on track.

He was a Herbalist after all, and could see paths among the vegetation along with understanding where they would lead. But Javie was abnormal in that the power running through his veins was so weak. He struggled time and time again to coax a plant to flower. It weighed on him to where he stopped pursuing his studies altogether. Only the threat of war motivated him to try again.

She feared he resented his Gift as he'd never fit in with the other Herbalists, choosing to pursue friendships with the young Forgers of the troupe. Nan knew they were good people, but worried there was something Javie was missing. She tried for years to help him understand it, thinking there was some sort of deep-rooted trauma after losing his parents at such a young age, but nothing worked. It was as if the Goddess only bestowed part of a Gift.

Nan couldn't lie to herself that she brought Javie purely for family reasons.

She wanted some alone time with the young man to talk about how he was faring and what group he wanted to join. Javie would be nineteen come springtime and could choose for himself how he wanted to take part in the Resistance. Her heart hurt to think both her grandbabies would be leaving her, but Javie would be an asset to wherever he decided to serve.

Nan was proud of Luc for stepping up and leading the carriers. There was a good chance she'd see much of Luc in the next coming weeks as she needed to stay behind to coordinate everything for the first batch of run-throughs. It would be a grueling few weeks, but Nan only felt pride for the way her nieta took to the leadership position. She'd proven herself in more ways than one, and Nan didn't miss the sparkle in her granddaughter's eyes.

Luc had found her place in the world, and it filled her with joy to see her doing so well.

Not to mention the celebration she and Damien were planning for the summer solstice. With the caveat that they could push it back depending on where the Resistance was. They were hoping to have reclaimed Heimat as a sanctuary by then. It would be a special day for the two young people.

The sun was fading in earnest and Javie slowed their mount to a trot. He squeezed his Abuela's arm and said, "We should find a place to stop for the night. It's getting too dark to see and we need some rest."

Nan squeezed his middle and chuckled in his ear. "I appreciate you saying we instead of you. If you get the horse settled and the mats out, I'll make us a fire and heat some of those rations."

"Deal." Nan could hear Javie's smile in his tone. As a kid, he'd always been relegated to finding sticks for the fire and relished every opportunity he had to get out of it. A walk in the woods would do the old woman some good and stretch her legs before bed. Goddess knew she'd have enough saddle sores for the next twenty years at this rate.

Javie found a clearing to the left of the trail and urged the horse to it. They both performed their assigned tasks in setting up camp and soon, sat beside a roaring fire eating dried meat, hard cheese, and vegetables roasted in the fire. There hadn't been snowfall in about a week and the chill in the air wasn't quite as debilitating as it once was.

Winter was ending. The time for rebirth was almost upon them.

Nan would welcome the warmer weather with jubilation, but felt her anxiety rise with the temperatures. Jess was only the first of many they'd be grieving by the end of all this. It made her weary thinking about the loss they would have to face.

She watched the smoke curling upwards into the sky and took in the sight of thousands of stars. Green and purple lights danced in the sky and Nan felt the haunting beauty as an ache.

She gave a heavy sigh. "Have you ever seen anything so beautiful?" She didn't take her eyes off the sky, drinking in the splendor of the Goddess's creation.

"I don't know, Abuela. The beef stew you used to make would give it a run for its money at a time like this."

Nan shook her head and met her grandson's hazel eyes. She chuffed him behind the ear, saying, "That's what you get for being a smart alec."

Javie gave her a playful push and laughed, "It's gorgeous, Abuela. Even in Heimat, the lights never danced as brightly as they do here." Nan stayed quiet, hoping her grandson would fill the space between them.

They sat for several moments staring up at the sky, letting the fire warm them before Javie spoke again.

"Abuela, can I ask you a question?" Javie's voice was hesitant, as if he felt awkward about what he wanted to ask.

Nan shot him a smile. "I think you just did, nieto."

Javie rolled his eyes, some of the tension leaving his shoulders. "Seriously. Can I ask you something that might be strange?"

Nan's curiosity was piqued at the way her grandson so hesitantly brought all this up. "Of course. You can always ask me anything. No question is too big or too small when it comes to the two of us. Your sister, on the other hand." Nan winked at her inflection, earning a chuckle from her grandson.

"You got that right." His smile faded as he formed the words he wanted to use to ask his question. "Have you ever seen someone or heard of someone with more than one Gift? Not like a Crafter having two Crafts, but I mean a person being a Crafter and a Herbalist. Is that even possible?"

Nan furrowed her brows.

"Rae and Bane are special cases we haven't seen in centuries. I saved some of the ancient texts during the Uprising, but they're very limited. There's only one that mentions such things, if I remember correctly. I've never come across anyone like that, though. Why do you ask?"

Javie gave a sigh and spread his fingers wide, refusing to meet her eyes as he studied the backs of his hands. "I think I have two Gifts."

Nan started, not expecting that. "Why would you think that?"

Javie swallowed and ran a nervous hand through his overgrown head of hair. "I, I'll just show you."

Nan couldn't keep the bewildered expression from her face when her grandson got up and went to the saddlebags next to his mat.

*Two Gifts? How is that possible? There are only Herbalists on my side of the family. There's no Forger on either my mom's or dad's side. Unless there is someone on his father's side.*

Javie brought back a lump of rusted metal and sat next to her. He met her gaze, and she only saw apprehension in his eyes.

She put a hand on his shoulder and gave an encouraging nod. "Don't be afraid, nieto. Just because I don't know about it, doesn't mean it isn't possible. Show me what you can do and we'll figure it out together."

Javie only nodded in response before turning his attention to the metal in his lap. He put both hands on it and closed his eyes.

Nan gasped in surprise as tendrils of metal grew from beneath Javie's hands. They grew up and up to the sky before the most delicate little flower popped from one of its buds.

When Nan didn't respond, Javie opened his eyes and viewed his work.

He swallowed again, this time with nerves. "Forgers can't do this. They can't create more of a substance. They can only manipulate the materials they have, but I can use it to grow things."

"This is a miracle. You are a miracle." Nan's shocked expression melted into one of pride. "How clever of you. You always told me it didn't feel right with the plants, but I never understood." Nan's eyes glittered, and she smiled at the young man. "Who knows about this?"

"I only showed Charlie about a week ago. She assured me it wasn't something Forgers could do, which is why I began to think I could have both Gifts. But if I try to manipulate the metal, it's just like trying to grow plants. It doesn't work."

Nan nodded, relieved Charlie, one of the Forgers his own age was the only one who knew. She was a genuine young woman and could be trusted with such a secret.

"When we're with the Elven, we'll look for something in that library about such an anomaly. Don't worry, nieto, we'll figure this out together. We'll help you master this miracle of yours." Nan patted his cheek, and they got ready for bed. She banked the fire and laid on her mat, praying to the Huntress they made it to Verdencia quickly.

Her new mission included finding out as much information as she could for her grandson, for Rae, and for Bane. The more knowledge they could discover, the better.

"Don't tell me that's all ya got, Georgie!" Reg yelled from the middle of the lake.

George gritted his teeth and took another step on the frozen water. *Damn bet. I'm going to wring his neck when this is all over.*

Cheers rose from the lake's shore, where many of their people watched in awe of the two men.

*Fools.* George thought to himself even as he sent them a grin and a wave. They cheered again, encouraging him to go further.

George still couldn't believe he'd let Reg talk him into doing this. *All because I had too many shots.* He blamed Tam for the shots.

"Come on, Georgie! The kiddies will laugh yer arse off if ya can't even make it to the middle of the lake." Reg cajoled him, already halfway across the expanse of frozen water.

George gritted his teeth and followed, listening for any sort of creaking or cracking beneath his feet. His steps were slow as he tested every piece of snow-covered ice.

"Georgie? Are you—," Reg's voice stopped and a large crash sounded in his direction.

George's blood ran cold as his friend's voice got cut off. He looked up and immediately started running, using Reg's bootprints as a guide.

His friend was nowhere to be seen.

He slid to a stop in front of a jagged hole filled with freezing water. Without hesitating, he lay prostrate and plunged his arm under the frigid water. The water was colder than anything he'd ever felt, but he persevered.

Reg's survival depended on it.

His hands bumped into something solid and scrambled for purchase on the object. Just as George was losing hope, he hooked something and pulled with all his might, taking care to keep his weight as dispersed as possible.

Realizing he had one of Reg's arms, he repositioned his hands so he gripped the man from behind and under both arms.

"REG! BREATHE!" He yelled as he pulled the freezing man out of the water. Once most of Reg's body was on top of the ice, George switched tactics and rolled him the rest of the way out.

The movement jarred Reg out of his shock, and he spluttered, water going everywhere as he gasped for breath. He coughed and curled in on himself, shivering from the cold.

"Reg? Can you hear me? We need to get you back before you freeze to death. Come on, let me help you up." George shook the man's shoulder and waited for an answer.

Still unable to talk, Reg motioned for help as he struggled to his knees.

George pulled one arm over his shoulder, while his other arm wrapped around Reg's waist.

"Come on, Reg. Let's be quick before we lose anything to frostbite.

Chiara was going to kill him. Both of them.

What they were doing on that ice only the Huntress knew.

They were lucky they both made it out alive.

"Again, if I catch either of you pulling another stunt like this, I won't heal you. And the rest of the Herbalists will have explicit orders not to help as well. It's about time the two of you grow up." She lectured both of them while they were stuck in the infirmary overnight for observation.

Reg had a very mild case of frostbite on a few of his toes but was otherwise unscathed after getting out of his wet clothes and warming up. George had no injuries.

But the two were grown men. They should've known better than to tempt the Huntress.

*What I wouldn't give to live in a world where men aren't driven by their hormones.* She gave the two a long look before leaving with a flourish.

Chiara left the warmth of the infirmary and headed to her tent.

She'd had enough work for today.

"Chiara! Wait up a second." A voice called behind her.

Chiara stiffened when she recognized the voice. *Speaking of men being stupid.*

She heard the steps get closer, and with a sigh, turned to face Duncan. "It can't wait until the morning?" Her tone came off harsher than she intended, and she gave a wince. "Sorry, it's been a long day."

Concern filled Duncan's lavender gaze as he hesitated. "I only wanted to apologize for our argument."

Chiara arched one brow. "That fight was days ago. So much has happened since then. Seems a little late for an apology. What game are you playing at?"

It was Duncan's turn to wince. "I know, and I regret that." He took a step closer to her. "Between the Council, Rae's condition, and now Tyce's letter, there has been no time." He looked her in the eyes and Chiara saw sorrow reflected in his light-colored eyes. "Or to be honest, I haven't made time to talk to you. For that, I apologize."

Chiara crossed her arms and suppressed a shiver. "Great, I forgive you. Let's move on."

"Something tells me you're still upset."

Chiara rolled her eyes. "What an observation."

Duncan frowned. "How do I fix this?"

Chiara sighed, letting some of her anger and hurt dissipate into the frigid air of winter. "Time, Duncan. I need time. I understand why you and the rest of the Council insist we fight. My idea to create a bubble of safety around this place was idealistic, but you could've at least pretended to entertain the idea."

Duncan reached out so his gloved fingertips trailed across her rosy cheek. "I already lost Jess. I can't lose you too." He whispered, his voice filled with emotion and cracking on Jess's name.

Chiara looped her arm through his and led him to her tent. "You haven't lost me, Duncan. We've had a row, that's all. But I need to get out of this cold."

"Chiara, I—"

"I know, Duncan. But we're friends first. Let's cross this bridge and go from there. Now let me rant about the men from Heimat who went through the ice." Chiara interrupted, opening the flap to her tent and inviting him in.

Duncan obliged, and the pair spent a better part of the night talking. When he finally left for his own tent, Chiara was left feeling warm with her spirit filled.

She sent a quiet prayer to the Huntress, thanking the deity for Her hand in the day.

# Chapter Twenty-Nine

Z eke collapsed on the ground, panting as his arms gave way. He lay there for a few seconds before forcing himself back into a pushup position, matching the pace Bane counted out.

"Seventy-nine." *Pause.* "Eighty." *Pause.*

They kept going and Zeke pushed himself to one hundred before collapsing again, his arms trembling. Bane kept going, voice unwavering and strength unflagging.

Zeke attempted to start again, but his protesting arms refused to listen. Instead, he took several moments to admire the physically impressive Shifter.

Bane managed to stay clean-cut despite the remoteness of the Forest. With his broad shoulders and strong brow, he wasn't what most people would call traditionally handsome, but there was a rugged allure to the no-nonsense young man.

He shared many characteristics with his father, but Zeke had spent the better part of winter learning the softer side of the Shifter. They'd shared their hopes, dreams, and fears over the past weeks, and Zeke had a better understanding of what lay beneath Bane's outward impassiveness.

Zeke marveled at the way Bane's muscles worked like a machine, never shaking or slowing, simply continuing in their movements. He watched Bane's face for any indication he was growing weary, but his tight expression never changed.

*I'd be throwing up by now if I kept at it like that.* Concern flashed in Zeke's silver eyes as he studied the man across from him. Guilt spurred him into another set of ten pushups, but this time, his arms gave out before he could lower himself to the ground.

He landed with a thud and a wince.

*Goddessdamn it. How am I supposed to be a warrior when I can't do a few pushups?*

Zeke wallowed in self-pity, missing when Bane finished his set and rolled closer.

"Being a fighter takes more than brute strength."

Zeke started and looked up, meeting Bane's knowing gaze. He rolled his eyes in answer and copied the Shifter, rolling onto his back.

"But it helps," Zeke mumbled.

Bane breathed heavily and closed his eyes, taking a moment to catch his breath before answering. "Maybe to an extent. But I expect you to keep most enemies at a distance with that wind of yours. You're an accomplished swordsman with that toothpick of yours, but the more you can keep from getting to you, the better."

Zeke heard the smile in Bane's voice as he described the thin rapier he preferred to larger broadswords. It was a weapon meant for thrusting and slipping between gaps in an enemy's armor. It required more skill and grace to wield, but Zeke loved how it felt in his hand. He'd spent days and days perfecting his skill with it while they were on the road.

"You're only jealous you've never learned how to use one."

Bane snorted in response and Zeke chuckled, rolling onto his side so he faced the man with animal eyes. Zeke propped his head on his hand and his gaze turned serious as he studied Bane's prostrate figure.

"Promise me you'll be careful." Zeke's voice was a whisper as he memorized every inch of Bane's serene face.

Bane's eyes flashed open, meeting Zeke's terrified eyes. Without hesitating, he pulled him into his arms and murmured. "Of course. It's going to take more than a war to keep me from returning to you. Remember what I promised you. We'll make it through all this, one way or another."

Zeke melted into Bane's embrace, letting himself believe those impossible words if only for a few moments.

Bane could've picked the front lines group or the communications group. He'd be an asset to either on account of his unique abilities to Shift into different animals. He would be a terror on the front lines or the enemy's worst nightmare as he lurked beneath their noses in the dead of night.

In the end, Bane decided he'd be of more use in the communications group. His ability to communicate with and direct multiple species would be invaluable in delivering messages.

But it meant they'd be apart again.

Zeke was dreading when they'd be separated, soaking in every moment he could. He'd selfishly hoped Bane would choose the front lines group as he had, but respected the other man's decision. Everyone had the right to determine where their skills would be most useful and what they were willing to do for the Resistance.

Zeke had chosen the front lines group without a second thought.

He'd fight for the Magicae's right to set down roots and join the tapestry of life in Kamore with his dying breath. There was no question whether this was a cause worth fighting for, and Zeke was determined to put the country to rights. It was time to retake what the Magicae lost all those years ago.

And the warmth on the winds meant winter was releasing its icy hold on the North. Spring was coming and so was the day they would march for Heimat.

But right now, Zeke would relish the time he could be in Bane's arms. He felt the other man stiffen and soon enough, his ears picked up on someone or something moving through the underbrush.

"Oh, I can come back if I'm interrupting something." The voice said in an unsteady voice, as its owner caught her breath.

Zeke immediately relaxed, recognizing the voice. He squeezed Bane and sat up, twining his fingers through the other man's. "Don't be silly. I can't believe you're already out of the infirmary. Chiara made it sound like she'd shackle you to the bed before she'd risk you leaving before you were healed."

He patted the space next to him and cocked an eyebrow.

Rae was too pale. She looked smaller, almost, as if the amount of space she once took up in the world had shrunk. He frowned as she maneuvered her coat to act as a barrier between herself and the still-covered snowy ground. When she sat, he pulled her into his side, offering her warmth and companionship.

Bane squeezed his hand and released it, moving to sit on Rae's other side.

"You look a little worse for wear, Crafter." The Shifter meant it as a joke, but Zeke caught the undertone of worry in his words. Rae must be really struggling for someone other than him to notice.

Rae grunted in answer and closed her eyes. "I figured the fresh air would do me some good. But then I got turned around..."

She trailed off, and Zeke shared a look with Bane over her head. Rae closed her eyes and leaned against Zeke's side, her brows furrowed as if she were concentrating on something.

Wordlessly, Zeke took one glove off and pushed her sleeve up to reveal bare skin. He gripped her wrist and opened a connection between them, letting some of his life energy trickle into her veins.

*She's low again. Chiara said her life energy was draining during the night, but I thought they'd helped her become stable. What's going on?*

Slowly, color returned to Rae's cheeks as Zeke's life energy revived her. Soon she lifted a hand to her temple and forced her eyes open with a wince.

"Ugh. My head is pounding. Anybody have a healing tonic by chance?" Rae's voice was soft as she straightened, no longer leaning on Zeke for support.

Zeke shot another look at Bane, understanding and concern passing between them with a single glance. Zeke felt a shiver work its way across his skin at the intimate way they could communicate. This type of relationship was unlike anything he'd experienced before. And he never wanted it to end.

Coming back to the present, he gave Rae a shrug. "We were doing some conditioning and didn't bother bringing any packs with us. Drink some water, maybe it will help." Zeke offered her his waterskin, and she took it with reluctance. He furrowed his brows. "Rae, what's going on? Why are you so low on life energy? Is it like what was happening in Windemere?"

Fear flickered on Rae's face before she could smooth her expression. She passed the waterskin between her hands, not taking a drink. "No, it's not like the Crafter's Curse. At least I hope to the Huntress it's not. But my Crafts don't feel any different." She hesitated before taking a deep gulp. "I think it has something to do with this."

She took the glove off of her left hand and held out her palm.

Zeke let out a hiss at the dark red marks cutting across her palm. He cradled her bare hand in his gloved ones and sent her a searching look, not understanding what it meant.

"It's my connection to Tyee. I had a dream..." Rae explained what she'd seen and felt in her dreams about the water and the man who dragged her to shore. She confided how distraught the usually composed horseman had been and the words he'd used to describe the bond between them.

"Chiara thinks we're connected in more ways than the thread I feel in my mind. She thinks we can share life energy and claims my dream only confirms it." Rae finished, extricating her wrist from Zeke's hand and using both to hug her middle.

Zeke saw red as he put two and two together. Tyee was responsible for what was happening to Rae.

"I'll wring his neck," he growled, reaching to pull her into him.

Rae vibrated with laughter. "Simmer down, Z. No need to go all Dad on me." Zeke felt the vibrating cease, and he looked at Bane again, seeking the comfort his eyes provided. "Besides, you'd end up killing me, anyway."

Zeke felt his heart drop as Rae uttered that sentiment. If she and Tyee were connected as Chiara suspected, anything that happened to the horseman would affect his best friend. Feelings of helplessness and rage warred inside the acrobat. Bane sent him a look that mirrored his own emotions, but he placed a hand on Rae's arm and spoke only to her.

"Abuela and Javie left for Verdencia just yesterday. I'll send a bird to them asking for information from Tyee. We'll sort this out, Rae."

Rae nodded her head and moved her arms from her middle, resting them in her lap even as she formed fists with her hands. "Regardless of what they discover, I need to learn how to deal with it. I'll train harder and build my stores of energy higher. This isn't the end, it's a new beginning."

"Your optimism is as inspiring as it is toxic," Zeke drawled. "If you train any harder, you'll kill yourself."

Rae arched one eyebrow, her golden orbs meeting his silver ones. "Weren't you the one that always claimed what doesn't kill you makes you stronger?"

Zeke snorted. "You know that was Luc. And besides, this is one of those things where you could die. It's not a game, Sparks." He added in a whisper, "Don't make me have to do this without you."

Rae took his hands in hers. "You will never have to do this on your own. We've made it through so much, Z. Look at me." She waited for him to lift his chin. "This isn't like the Crafter's Curse. I can still feel my limits. They just hit me a lot sooner than I'm used to. I have to assume Tyee is struggling with something as he learns about the power in his blood. It'll take some time for him to get the hang of it. But once he does, I would assume he wouldn't be draining me so frequently."

"But Rae, we don't have time for Tyee to figure his power out. Don't you feel that?" Zeke spread his arm wide, gesturing to the meadow around them and trying to make her understand the urgency they faced. "Spring will be here before we know it and then we march. Rae, the Resistance is fighting back, but I can't risk you in this present state. Maybe you should stay back and teach the young Crafters. At least until we have answers about this bond between the two of you."

Zeke let his concern and fear of losing her shine through his eyes. Suffering Jess's loss reminded all of them how real this was. Anybody could die on the battlefield and if Rae could be reduced to this in an instant, she'd be dead within an hour of fighting.

He couldn't lose her.

Memories flashed in his mind. Rae grabbing his hand and pulling him into the big top for the first time. Running through the trees until they reached the meadow where all four of them trained. Laughing until his sides felt like they'd split open. Teasing her when she got too drunk the first time they stole Mac's whiskey.

When she forced her wind Craft into him.

He winced at the shadow of pain that always accompanied that night.

But regardless of good or bad, Rae gave him a home when everyone he loved abandoned him. She could be hot-tempered, vexing, and more stubborn than a mule near water but she was also fiercely protective, loyal to a fault, and cared deeply about her people.

His entire world would shatter without her.

Zeke swallowed his emotions and hardened his gaze. Rae was stubborn, but so was he. If she didn't recover soon, he'd make sure she didn't risk more than what was necessary.

Rae noticed the change in his eyes and frowned. "I'm not letting my people do the fighting for me. I'm the strongest Crafter we have and I'd let the Goddess strike me down before I hid from this fight. Our people need me to be strong, so I will be."

"Getting yourself killed is the last thing our people need. You're the one who insisted there were more ways to serve the Resistance than on the front lines. Why can't you put yourself to use where you'll be safe?" Frustration crept into Zeke's tone.

"Because this is all my fault." Rae's voice cracked at her exclamation. Tears burst from her eyes and she hid her head in her hands as her shoulders shook.

Bane put a hand on her shoulder and shot Zeke a questioning look. Zeke's responding glance was hollow as he realized the burden his friend still carried.

"Crafter, what do you mean, this is all your fault?" Bane asked, rubbing soothing circles into her back.

Rae composed herself, wiping her nose on her sleeve.

Zeke's heart broke at how shattered she was.

"If my parents sent me away as soon as my eyes turned, maybe Kamore wouldn't be such a mess. They would've had more time to set things right and the Magicae would still have a place in the world." Rae's voice shook, but she forced the words out.

Understanding transformed Bane's features. He took her hands and made her meet his avian gaze. "A wise woman once told me there's no use in considering the what-ifs. She told me it was an exercise in frustration. The only thing we can do is move forward, keeping the past where it belongs but not forgetting the lessons learned or how we wished we'd have acted. Just as I can't take fault for my mother's death, you can't take fault for the demise of the Magicae. Got it?" He gave her a small smile with his question.

Rae took a deep breath and Zeke knew what she was doing.

"Don't push those feelings down, Sparks. Let them go and release yourself from their hold on you." He sent a breeze to ruffle her hair, suggesting she release her emotions to the wind he provided. "Fighting on the front lines isn't the only way to redeem yourself."

"Some things cannot be changed," she spat in bitter response and pulled her arms around her again.

Zeke gave an exasperated sigh and stood. Reaching down, he gripped her wrists and pulled her up despite her protests.

"Come on. Let's get you somewhere warm. Maybe then you'll see sense."

Zeke let out a cry when Rae's arms flashed with a searing heat. He dropped her wrists immediately and dropped into a crouch.

*If she wants to fight, then let's go.*

Using his hands, he spun some winds from his core until they formed a deadly wind tunnel and sent them barreling toward the fire Crafter.

He spared a glance at Bane and saw him watching with wide eyes. He'd never witnessed the two go head to head and, in fairness, they hadn't done so since they were kids. It was a way to get their emotions out and settle disputes between themselves.

Rae sidestepped the spinning winds when they came her way and pulled strands from them, whipping them around her body in a figure-eight pattern.

Zeke stayed in a ready position, watching her movements and not daring to give a second glance to Bane. Any distraction could end with a loss.

The winds in her hands lighted with fire and she sent them his way with a flick of her wrist.

Zeke was ready for her and countered with a wall of wind, dissipating the fiery air into sparks and wisps of wind. Once the threat was neutralized, he went on the offense, sending the wall of winds crashing into the trees above her.

Leaves, branches, and sticks rained down on her and she threw up an arm, bringing a shield of earth and rock over her person.

Zeke didn't hesitate and sent a gale straight for her chest.

Rae gave a cry of frustration as the impact left her in a heap on the ground.

"Do you yield?" Zeke asked, poised for his next attack.

"Never." Rae's breathless reply sent a wave of nostalgia through Zeke. This was the familiar back and forth from when they were kids. Neither would yield until they were close to passing out.

Zeke didn't hesitate, sending another twister Rae's way.

She arched her back and narrowly avoided the angry twister, her earth and rock shield disintegrating on top of it, knocking the winds apart. She struggled to her feet and threw one hand towards Zeke.

Too slow. Her jet of icy water hit him square in the chest and knocked him to the ground. Zeke threw out wind after wind, attempting to overwhelm his trapeze partner.

Rae blocked the first couple, but the rest had her on her knees. Tears streamed down her face as she fell to the ground, tapping twice to signal her defeat.

Bane sent Zeke a disparaging glance and went to the battered Crafter, helping her to her feet. Once she was stable enough, Bane pulled her arm over his shoulder and guided her to the path that would take them back to the lake and their settlement.

"Wait." Rae's voice was stronger than either man would have expected. She turned to Zeke with the familiar fire in her eyes. "This changes nothing. You can't keep me from fighting for our people." She held her hand out and Zeke went to her. She cupped his cheek. "Spar with me. Help me get my strength back and we'll both be better for it. We won't lose each other."

Zeke pulled her into a tight embrace and they clung to each other as if they were children in the dead of night, both afraid of the monsters beyond the walls of their tents.

"I'm scared, Sparks. It feels like something terrible is coming and nothing I do can slow it."

"I'm scared too, Z. But we can do it. Together."

"Together," Zeke echoed. He wrapped an arm around her waist and supported her as they followed Bane back to the warmth of the settlement.

# Chapter Thirty

Naya stifled her groan as Sister What's-her-name launched into another lecture on how important the work they were doing was.

*No mythical lady in the sky gives a damn about how polished the floors are in this monstrosity of a building.*

She let her head fall back, closing her eyes as if beseeching the Goddess herself. But really, Naya was trying to keep herself from rolling her eyes at the middle-aged woman's words. Eye rolling was the quickest way to being put on night duty, and Naya couldn't afford that again. She'd been off it for the past two nights and spent both with the twins in the cave. It was a balm to her soul spending so much time with them, reassuring her they were taken care of and still hidden.

Naya was determined to stay off of night duty as long as possible. Even if it meant she had to bite her tongue, close her eyes, and pretend to listen to the haughty woman in charge of the postulants.

*Finally. Let's get moving so she doesn't go into another rant.*

Naya thought the words and willed them to her fellow postulants, hoping they'd receive her wishes and act accordingly.

It seemed to work. The girls each grabbed a bucket and a mop, getting to work on making the floors of the Temple shine before the President's monthly visit to the evening service.

Naya felt unease bubble up at the reminder of Myra's inevitable return. As long as she kept her head down, there was no reason for the tyrant to single her out. She had to be on her best behavior for tonight's service.

Naya felt a sharp pain and looked down, seeing an elbow retract itself from her side. Naya looked to her right and met Ophelia's sapphire gaze.

"I have a project for you after service tonight." Ophelia hissed from the side of her mouth, keeping her lips as still as possible.

Naya mopped fervently, trying to ignore the older girl's summons. *Maybe if I don't say anything, she'll go away.*

Naya knew it was a long shot, but figured it couldn't hurt to try.

"Kaia! Did you hear me?" Ophelia brought her mop closer to the younger girl and waited for an answer.

*Guess that was too easy.*

Naya inclined her head in a slight nod, refusing to give Ophelia anything else. This girl posed a danger to the twins, so she had to be careful, but she also didn't trust her.

Naya walked a fine line between appeasing the girl and keeping her nose down. When the girl didn't step away, she shot her a look.

"What? I can't get in trouble again." Naya hissed under her breath.

Ophelia's eyes glittered and her lips turned upward into a smirk. "Don't get caught then."

With a flourish of her robes, Ophelia was gone.

Naya shook her head and focused on her mopping. The sooner this job was done, the sooner she could sneak into the kitchen and grab some food for the twins. She'd grown fond of the women who worked there and their way of looking the other way whenever she entered. It was the only bright spot in this whole ordeal.

Naya couldn't wait for the cold weather to leave, so she could make her exit with the twins. It was the last shred of hope she clung to on days like this when the work and prayers seemed endless.

Goddess, what she wouldn't give to be out of these infernal robes. Still itched like a dog with fleas, especially when she was sitting in the Temple, surrounded by candles and sweat dripping down her skin. As an outsider, the whole thing was laughable. Worshiping an old woman in the sky that supposedly had three faces? Only the desperate would believe such lies.

Naya couldn't decide whether the sisters believed that nonsense or were just hopeless. She couldn't imagine what horrors they'd have faced to end up in a place like this. Ophelia was a prime example. All the money in the world and she was stuck here? Something didn't add up.

Naya was going to get to the bottom of it.

Naya botched the words to the last prayer but kept her head down so Sister What's-her-face wouldn't notice. She kept her robe on, putting her hood up and down when prompted, and even stayed on her feet during the longest part of the service. She was sweating again, but at least she wasn't in danger of being put on the night crew. It was boring and several times Naya caught herself dozing, but she made it.

She heard a hiss behind her, followed by a poke in her back. Naya closed her eyes and willed herself not to express her frustration audibly. She could guess who wanted her attention and knew it would be wise to turn around, but there was a small part of her that insisted it best to ignore the girl.

*It's not like she can do anything, anyway.*

Naya felt the color drained from her face at the thought. There was actually a lot Ophelia could do to her. Against her better judgment, Naya glanced back at the dark-haired girl.

"Finally. The Temple steps as soon as you can."

Naya gave the older girl no indication she'd heard her, but committed the words to memory. Both she and Ophelia knew Naya would be there, if only to protect her two charges.

She could only imagine what Ophelia would ask of her. Probably something stupid like stealing liquor from the wine cellar or playing a prank on Sister

What's-her-face. Ophelia had that little rich girl vibe about her that set Naya's teeth to grinding. She was only a few years older than her, but Ophelia acted as if the universe bowed to her. It was a wonder she lasted this long as a postulant.

Her past must have been pretty dark for her to come and stay here. Especially when it was clear Ophelia believed in the whole Goddess bit as much as she did.

She risked a glance at the tyrant, her fifth time since the start of the ceremony. Naya had kept count, in an attempt to stop herself from sending so many glances Myra's way. It would be a disaster if the woman caught her looking, but as it was the end of the ceremony, Naya figured she could risk it.

*Five wasn't terrible*, Naya reasoned as her eyes slid to the middle of the Temple.

The little girl frowned. It was clear Myra was agitated about something. When she glimpsed the woman's face, she was wearing a deep scowl. And Naya could tell just by looking at her how much tension she held in her shoulders.

*What is she so anxious about?* Naya thought to herself. The woman was head of the country, with every single citizen at her disposal. There was nothing she had to worry about from the girl's perspective. Certainly, she didn't have to wonder where her food was coming from or where she'd lay her head at night.

Those were luxuries for most of the population of Kamore. She forced her gaze away as the tyrant strode past the sisters preparing to leave and straight to the dais where the Mother Superior sat. The two spoke in hushed tones before Mother Stella ushered her behind the sacristy.

*Weird. Wonder what that was about.*

Naya gave a start when she noticed she was the only one still sitting on her bench. She stood abruptly and shuffled out with the other postulants.

As soon as she knew Sister What's-her-face wasn't watching her, Naya slipped through the crowd and clung to the shadows in the entryway of the Temple itself. The sisters always entered at the back, despite their living quarters being closer to the front of their place of worship. It was maddening to think of how much more efficient they could be. At least it made slipping away that much easier.

The chaos and press of bodies meant the postulants were left to their own devices. The only exception being those stuck on night duty. But since they'd mopped the floors of the Temple that morning, the night crew was scouring the kitchens. Sister What's-her-face only went looking if somebody didn't show up to their night crew duties. Naya wouldn't be missed until the morning.

She stayed in the shadows until the rest of the sisters filed out. Once the Mother Superior's deputy doused the rest of the candles, Naya was drenched in darkness. She blinked a couple of times to let her eyes adjust to the inky blackness. The sister's steps faded as she returned her candle bower, or whatever it was called, and left through the door near the front.

*I knew it. I knew the sisters were lazy. If it wasn't for the Mother Superior, I bet everyone would take the easier way back to their rooms.*

Smiling to herself, she pushed against the heavy door and left the Temple, sitting near one of the stone walls along the top of the stairs to keep herself in the shadows.

"I was almost worried you wouldn't show." Ophelia drawled, moving to sit next to the ten-year-old.

"Sadly, I have no choice." Naya snapped.

Ophelia pouted. "But I thought we were friends. Friends don't force each other to do anything. You're here because you want to be." The older girl arched one eyebrow and gave Naya an expectant look.

Naya groaned, unwilling to give the older girl an answer

Ophelia chuckled. "Oh, come on. You're going to love this. Trust me." She jumped up and walked to the right of the Temple.

Naya furrowed her brows and considered leaving until Ophelia glanced back and beckoned her forward. She let out another groan and sprung from the steps, following the older girl.

They walked at a furious pace, their thin flat slippers slapping against the stone walkway. Naya was sweating again in her wool robe. She growled her frustration, causing Ophelia to let out a bark of laughter.

"Have you dunked it in the river yet?" At Naya's questioning gaze, Ophelia continued, "You know, give it over to the Prophetess, and she'll make it softer." She sent Naya a smirk and the younger girl snorted.

"You know that's a crock as much as I do. Don't pretend you believe in that shit." The girls slowed their pace as they talked.

"Language. What's Sister Helga going to think about that?"

Naya snorted again, unable to deny the things they had in common. If there was one thing they could agree on, it was that Sister What's-her-face was a demon sent from down below to torment as many postulants as she could.

"You hate her as much as I do." Naya hesitated and glanced up, meeting the other girl's sapphire gaze. She took the bait. "What are we doing?"

Ophelia put a finger to her lips and grabbed her hand, pulling her swiftly into an alcove, hidden by bushes and a tall oak tree.

Naya began to protest, but Ophelia raised another finger to her lips and pointed to a small door etched into the stone.

Naya felt her heartbeat quicken. They were at the front of the Temple at this point and only one person would be left inside.

*Two people,* Naya corrected herself in her mind.

She watched as Ophelia took a knife from beneath her robes and pried the door open. Naya winced in apprehension, assuming the old door would squeal.

Ophelia's shoulders shook with silent laughter as she studied Naya's expression.

*Right. Ophelia was here before.*

Ophelia gripped her hand again and pulled her into a hidden tunnel that went under the main floor of the Temple. It was at ground level as the Temple itself had been raised. Ophelia kept a tight grip on Naya's hand and led her through twisting and turning tunnels until they reached a spot where the warm light flickered through a large grate.

Naya felt a warm breath on her neck and jumped when Ophelia spoke directly into her ear. "Listen closely and don't make a sound."

Naya felt her heart thundering in her chest and scratched at the collar of her robe, still sweating from the race around the Temple. Ophelia tugged on her wrist and pulled her closer to the grate.

Naya strained her ears and heard voices above.

"What do you mean, they're not ready? My son has already marched, and you promised they'd be ready by now. What am I supposed to do with this?" Myra's voice was unmistakable as it rose loud enough for the girls to hear.

Another voice murmured something that they couldn't make out.

"Oh, for Goddess's sake. I would have killed the lot of them, but my advisors assured me our doctors and engineers developed a way to use the power found in the blood of the Magicae for our own ends. They ruined the last batch, and I need more. You will send them on the next ferry or pay the consequences."

Naya swallowed, her eyes wide. She registered what the two older women were talking about.

The Mother Superior was providing Magicae children for Myra to experiment with.

Naya wanted to scream, but clamped a hand over her mouth to keep from uttering a word.

Myra was a worse monster than she'd thought.

The haunting howling of the wolves filled the crisp air with the melody of the night. Their cries rang with sorrow and reverberated with longing.

Mallick had long identified with those fierce creatures. The way they read their prey, picking out the old, young, and sick with a glance and culling the herd to keep it strong. The way they would pursue a deer or elk for miles and miles, resorting to tiring the poor creature when all else failed. The way they could turn on each other if another became sick or injured.

Mallick was a wolf, for better or worse.

He closed his eyes and lifted his voice to match theirs. He let out a howl and joined the chorus. Soon enough, the rest of his men joined in, jostling each other and grinning like idiots.

Mallick shut them all out and focused on releasing the emotions he'd had since his last encounter with Naomi.

*Besides, I couldn't bear it if you killed your own sister.*

Those words rattled his brain ever since that night. He'd mulled them over more times than he could count, egged on by a small voice he thought he'd squashed years ago. The small voice that flailed at every cruel word, menacing snarl, and brutish torture. It was the voice that tormented him in the dead of night, no matter what he did.

Myra did everything to rid him of a conscience, but this information made it flare with new life. It was relentless in trying to get him to listen.

And only brought him more confusion.

He kept telling himself the woman's words didn't matter. Even if they were true, they changed nothing. He was still Mallick, raised to be ruthless by Myra, commander of the Blades, and on his way to crush the rebels in the North.

Nothing could change who he was or what his purpose was.

If they did, it would prove he was weak.

And a wolf was not weak.

He opened his eyes and threw daggers at the men around him. "You lot are a bunch of animals. Get to bed, you need the beauty rest. We ride at dawn."

Cheers rose from the hordes of men and they dispersed to their tents.

"You know they won't listen to you with the full moon on display to light their way." Laurent threw an arm over his shoulder and kissed his cheek as sloppily as he could.

Mallick shoved him off and wiped at his face, ridding himself of the other man's spittle. Laurent howled with laughter and doubled over, unable to keep it together.

"You should see your face. The horror!" He patted Mallick on the back and wiped a tear from his eye. "Goddess, how easy it is to get under your skin."

"Only you get under my skin like that, Laurent. You and that smell coming from Fig's tent. I swear he rolls in the mud and muck for fun and has never heard of a bar of soap."

"You nailed that one on the head. Fig is worse than all of us combined. Just be glad you never had to share a tent with him."

Mallick cracked a grin as they continued to discuss the flaws of Fig and the other members of the Blades. Laurent procured two brews from who knew where and they ended up sitting at the fire next to Mallick's tent.

They weren't the best models for what Mallick expected from his men, but the Blades were used to Mallick and Laurent being held to different standards.

Leadership had its perks.

And so did befriending the leader.

Mallick kept Laurent close for two reasons. One being he was the only person Mallick trusted to be competent enough to watch his back and two, to keep a close eye on the man who knew so many of his secrets.

They kept drinking until Mallick had a warm buzz and his tongue loosened. "Wanna hear a secret?"

The words slipped out before Mallick could stop himself. He had a feeling in the back of his mind this was not a good idea. His instincts screamed at him to stop the conversation before it could begin, but he ignored them.

Besides, by the look Laurent was giving him, there would be no point in shutting it down now. His wolfish grin and glittering eyes betrayed his excitement.

Laurent was like a dog with a bone when it came to something he wanted. He wouldn't let it go until he was satisfied.

Mallick knew in his heart he shouldn't divulge this information to anybody. It would only reveal his weakness in needing to get it off his chest. But Laurent was the one person he could risk it with.

The pair had been inseparable since birth, making it inevitable they both knew each other's deepest and darkest secrets.

One more couldn't hurt, could it?

Mallick's head pounded from the pressure building up at not confiding in anybody. He'd spent years learning that two heads were better than one. Myra always made him talk through his reasons for different battle strategies or ways to train. She insisted they act as a team to learn from one another.

As long as there was someone he trusted, Myra taught him to talk it through with them. A powerful leader was decisive and confident, but needed to keep from becoming so arrogant they underestimated their enemy.

These were the lessons Mallick took to heart. To the world, he was an unstoppable and immovable force, but to Laurent, Mallick was a young man trying to find his place in the world.

This meant Laurent earned a place of privilege at the son of the President's side. And he would not risk losing that position anytime soon. This was the perfect opportunity for the cunning brute of a man to secure his status to new heights.

And Laurent was not a man who wasted opportunities.

"Of course, I want to hear a secret." His reply came as slick as butter on a hot day.

Mallick instantly regretted his question when he met Laurent's calculating gaze.

"Nevermind."

Laurent gave a fake pout. "Come on, Mal. You can't tease me like that. You'd be no better than those waitresses at The Dove. Always so willing when a tip is on the line, but as soon as you've paid, they couldn't care less about you. Don't be like those girls, unwilling to put out when it counts." His wolfish grin was back, and Mallick could feel a compulsory need to prove him wrong.

Laurent had a way of sending Mallick back to that place when they were kids, and he'd needed to prove himself to everybody. He knew Laurent was trying to get a rise out of him and still, he took the bait.

"Maybe if you weren't a menacing creep, they'd give you the royal treatment. I can speak from experience when I say they put out just fine." Mallick flashed him a matching wolfish grin, unconcerned about the way he talked about the waitresses. They meant nothing to him or Laurent and only demonstrated how cruel both of them could be. It was a game they'd played since they were kids;

always trying to find the most outlandish things to say.

Laurent let out a bark of laughter. "Of course they did. Your mother paid them to keep the edge off. You were becoming insufferable."

Mallick knocked back his last swig of beer and dropped his empty bottle to the ground.

"We should go to bed."

"After you tell me your secret," Laurent countered and pulled a flask from his inside coat pocket. He pulled the cork from the bottle and took a long pull before offering it to his friend.

Mallick held up a hand to refuse, but Laurent forced the bottle into it, anyway. The young man rolled his eyes and took a small sip, letting the burning liquid race down his throat. It ate at his insides and made him feel like he was floating at the same time.

"Go on then. Else we'll be pissed drunk and hungover for our arrival in Heimat. You know the rules." Laurent shot him a pointed look.

When someone pulled out a flask, you drank or spilled your secrets. And the only way to stop the game was to spill your darkest one.

"Aren't we too old for this kind of nonsense?" Mallick asked, not taking his eyes off his friend.

Laurent took another pull and wiped his face with his sleeve. He smirked and held the bottle back out for Mallick. "Loosen up, Mal. No need to act as if we're old and boring. If you want it to stop, then tell me the secret."

He pushed the bottle on him again, and Mallick relented, taking the liquor bottle and knocking it back for a few seconds.

The fire water burned him from the inside out, and Naomi's words flashed in his mind again.

*Besides, I couldn't bear it if you killed your own sister.*

His orders were to capture or kill the powerful fire Crafter. A week ago he wouldn't have thought twice about slitting her throat, but now... Did it matter? Did their blood have significance? Or would she be another faceless Magicae?

Goddess, his head hurt again.

He took another swig from the bottle and let it drop beside him, missing the triumphant glint in Laurent's eyes.

"Naomi Freeman made claims to being my birth mother." Mallick's tone was flat as he delivered the impossible words.

Laurent's expression turned unreadable as he rubbed his chin. "Isn't that the former President's First Lady?"

Mallick nodded, studying the other young man closely.

"Does it change anything?" Laurent asked.

*Yes.*

"No."

"Then why'd you mention it? Are you trying to say you now have a heart or something?" Laurent raised an eyebrow expectantly at him.

*Because our mission may mean killing my sister, and I don't know if I can risk killing her before I know what the truth is.*

"Only the Goddess knows. I must be drunk." Mallick scoffed and tried to shrug him off.

Laurent narrowed his eyes, honing in on his friend's discomfort.

"Don't go soft on me now, Mal. We're so close to everything we've ever wanted. Naomi, or whatever her name is, would say anything to protect her daughter. She knew there was a chance she'd get under your skin and it's working. Don't let her do it. The Magicae must be eradicated at all costs. Right?" Laurent's gaze was intense and seemed to pierce his soul.

Mallick gave a terse nod. "It would take more than that to rattle me from our purpose. I just needed to get it off my chest and out of my brain. Nothing's changed, trust me."

Laurent chuckled darkly. "I don't know how it's possible to trust someone so completely, yet not at all. Speak plainly or take it to your grave. Whose blood runs in your veins matters to your subjects most of all. Don't fuck this up for me, Mal."

Mallick swallowed. "I've always wanted a sibling. What if the girl really is my sister?"

"She's one of the Magicae. Vermin, needing to be disposed of. That's all. Period. End of discussion. Even if she is your sister, you can't be tied to the Magicae if you expect to be appointed to Myra's general." Laurent's voice was like iron, leaving no room for argument.

"You're right. None of it matters because she's *one of them*." He put on a convincing face. "The only thing I need to focus on is climbing the ladder and figuring out how to cause Vincenzio's fall from grace."

Laurent slapped him on the back. "That's the Mal I know and love. Once we figure out what we can blackmail him with, darling Darren will meet an early retirement from his post as your mother's second in command."

"No room for two generals when one will do just fine." Mallick plastered a smirk on his face, hoping Laurent couldn't catch him in his deception.

The truth was, Mallick wasn't sure he could kill the woman who might be his older sister. His hand strayed to the pouch containing the tonic Naomi revealed would stun the Crafter.

*I need answers. And I won't get them if she's dead.*

*The fire Crafter needs to be taken alive.*

Mallick clenched his fists at his sides and forced a yawn. "I need some sleep if I want to spar successfully with Vincenzio tomorrow." He stood from the fire and made his way into his tent, not waiting for Laurent's reply and knowing his friend would keep watch over his person until the next guard change.

But he missed the calculating look Laurent gave the crackling fire.

Mallick wasn't the only wolf in his camp.

# Chapter Thirty-One

"I'll do it. I'll bond myself to Sylvie if it means you stop the raids on the border towns. But I have one more stipulation." Tyee cringed once he forced the words out. He struggled to breathe as he felt an imaginary cage draw tight around him. He kept his trembling hands in his pockets as he loomed over where Ulla sat behind her desk.

She laughed as a glint entered her eyes. The expression made Tyee flinch, unnerved by how similar it was to the look Sylvie used to give him. "You're not in any sort of place to negotiate, but go ahead. Let's see what else you have in mind." She leaned back in her chair and stared at him with a hard smile.

*Bitch.*

Tyee swallowed, keeping his thoughts to himself. "If you want to fight, pledge your soldiers to Duncan's cause. There were rumblings of rebellion when they were leaving Verdencia. If you met with him, I'm sure the two of you could find a way to destroy the Mortals that mean both our peoples harm."

Ulla steepled her fingers and studied him. Tyee felt his stomach tying itself into knots and sweat bead on his back. His heart felt sluggish as he willed the Queen to see sense.

The Elven stood to gain more than the Circus in such a union. The Circus possessed the resources and people to create a spy network unlike anything the Elven could come up with. They already had hundreds of contacts throughout Kamore they could draw from, not to mention the ways the Magicae themselves could blend into the crowd should they need to. The Elven didn't understand or have knowledge of the world outside the trees.

"If I agree to this, I need a date on when the bonding ceremony will take place." Ulla's eyes flashed with challenge.

Tyee's jaw clenched, and he gave a terse nod. His palm burned, and he could feel Rae's concern through the invisible string tethering them together. "Once the fighting is done, we'll be bonded."

"Not good enough. The Spring Equinox symbolizes new beginnings. I will make sure preparations are made and my daughter is ready." Ulla dismissed him with a wave and bent to read some papers on her desk.

"And when will you contact Duncan?" Tyee pressed, her apathy at his and her daughter's fates chafing against him.

Ulla sighed in frustration. "I will have Sylvia meet with Talon tonight and call off the raids. My summons for Duncan will be sent out by tomorrow." She arched one eyebrow. "Anything else you'd like to lecture your Queen on?"

Tyee fumed and shook his head, not trusting himself to keep his words in check.

"Good. I will see you on the Equinox." Ulla went back to her papers.

This time, Tyee accepted his dismissal and fled from the too-small room. He let the door slam behind him and scurried down the ladder as fast as he could.

He needed to go for a walk to clear his head.

*No turning back now.*

Sylvia wanted to punch something. Her blood boiled as she paced back and forth in front of the Mother Oak.

*She's a fool. I would kill her for this.*

Her thoughts were like venom, soaked in rage and dripping in malice. She knew she needed to pull it together before Talon arrived, but all she wanted to do was scream.

Ever since she was a little girl, Sylvia was preparing to take the throne. Every moment devoted to becoming the leader her people needed. Even if they didn't like what she'd turned into. She was strong, decisive, and maybe a little cruel.

But what leader wasn't?

Yet all that preparation and sacrifice were for nothing now. Her Mother had the audacity to give her throne to the *halfbreed*. Sylvia would kill him before he could even think about acting as royalty. She chewed on her lip and kept pacing.

*If it looks like an accident, maybe I could get away with it.*

She let out a strangled cry of frustration.

*I'm sure Mother has already told her advisors. Word will be out before the end of the week.*

*I'll have to do it after the bonding ceremony.*

*Fucking halfbreed.*

"Someone's in a bad mood." Talon's guttural voice startled the Elven general.

Sylvia recovered quickly. "You don't wanna know the half of it." She shot the Mountain Lion Shifter a smirk. "Although, maybe you could be the answer to all of my problems. Ever killed somebody on behalf of another?"

Talon was in her half form, standing on two legs but covered in fur with nails more like claws and teeth still as sharp as fangs. She made a low grating sound in the back of her throat that could only be laughter.

"I never thought you'd be the type that couldn't do her own dirty work." Talon's smile was a challenge.

Sylvia kept the smirk on her face but let her eyes glitter with danger. "Taking the life isn't the problem. If I want to keep my place in line for the throne, I can't have this halfbreed's blood on my hands. No matter how much I long to do it myself."

Talon threw her a matching smirk and drew closer. "So bloodthirsty. You should've been born a Shifter. Being Elven limits what you could become."

Sylvia's jaw clenched as she kept her features schooled against the remark. This wasn't the first, nor would it be the last time she'd be told she didn't fit the mold for the typical Elven. The Elven were industrious, hardworking, and even ambitious but they were also kind, protective of their loved ones and the trees they cared for, and in possession of unwavering loyalty. She fit the first three to a tee but lacked the last three, among others.

Instead of being kind, she was cruel, instead of protective, she was possessive, and instead of loyal, she was an opportunist.

Sylvia was many things but being proper Elven royalty never interested her. The world was too hard for her to be anything but iron and ice. Anything softer would bend at the slightest sign of opposition.

Her mother set up this meeting between her and Talon so she could explain why the raids needed to stop.

*Or do they?*

Sylvia had been toying with the idea of betraying her mother's wishes ever since the Queen gave her the command. She didn't agree with her mother's reasoning or plan to marry her off. Queen Ulla was only concerned about preserving her legacy. And that legacy meant shit if the people mutinied as soon as Sylvia took the throne.

Her mother was a fool.

Sylvia's smirk became feral. "My mother called this meeting so I could tell you the raids are off."

Talon spat on the ground. "Curse your mother. Why would she order such a backwards move?"

"Because she negotiated with the halfbreed to ensure we're bonded by the Spring Equinox." Sylvia was blunt, unable to hide her disapproval.

"Hence the need for someone to kill for you." Talon rubbed her chin and leaned back on the Mother Oak's solid trunk. Her cat eyes formed narrow slits as she followed Sylvia's every move. "You want to defy the Queen's orders."

The corners of Sylvia's lips curled upward into a smile that showed all her teeth. She closed her eyes and took a deep breath, taking in the damp, cold air and woodsy aroma wafting from the surrounding trees.

*Take the leap. Treason or your throne.*

*It's not like she gave you a choice.*

Sylvia's eyes flashed open, and she held her hand out. "It's high time Mortal blood spilled instead of ours. The raids must continue, but they'll have to be in secret. I have a handful of soldiers I can spare who are the bloodthirstiest of them all. But our attacks will have to be quieter, with more time in between them."

Talon flashed her fangs at the Elven general and gripped her forearm. "Thank Skaber you have more sense than your mother. For this, I will kill your halfbreed. Take it as a sign of my gratitude."

A deadly look entered Sylvia's eyes as she shook arms with the Alpha of the Forest Shifters. "He's on his way to the old woman's cottage. Do it before the Spring Equinox and I'll pledge more troops to the cause."

"How will you do that?" Talon cocked her head and released the woman's lithe arm.

"The Queen's seemed pretty frail as of late, hasn't she?" Sylvia's face was murderous as her lips tightened into a cruel smile.

Understanding dawned in Talon's cat eyes and she inclined her head with a grin. "I had the same thought the last time we met. Pity she hasn't been feeling like herself. If it gets much worse, you'll need to act in her stead."

"Yes, I will. Look for my people in three days' time. They'll be ready for something other than guard duty, so don't hesitate to use them."

Talon nodded once before bounding into the trees, Shifting into her full animal form as she went. Movement in the coniferous undergrowth indicated her hidden entourage followed her back to wherever the pack remained.

Sylvia clenched her fist and let out the scream she'd been holding for so long.

Birds took to the air and mice scurried to find hiding spots at the ear-piercing sound.

She fell to her knees and pounded her fists into the snow-covered ground.

*She didn't give me a choice. I had to do this.*

The Elven general hung her head.

Her throne was at stake and she wasn't going to give any of its power to someone like Tyee. Her mother would see it her way in the end.

Sylvia would take her place by force as she'd done everything else in her life.

*Unyielding and unrelenting are the only way to be when you're given a place of power.*

Her Grandfather's words echoed in her ears as she stood and made for the part of the forest where the hemlock grew.

Her mother wouldn't know what hit her.

The forest was pitch black and deathly quiet. Nothing moved or breathed other than the man, his horse, and the old woman with locked arms around his middle.

Tyee rubbed Koko's neck with affection. The large stallion arrived shortly after Tyee called him with the rune, Ehwaz, which meant horse and forward progress. Andriette was cleared for travel in the morning, so Tyee had carved the rune in the wall of his cottage, hoping it would do what he wanted.

The single rune didn't take nearly as much life energy as the string of five, but Tyee still became light-headed after feeding it some of the power in his blood. He'd sat on his bed and waited, only leaving when he heard the brother of his heart's familiar cry.

He'd settled the horse and then gone to check on his Tota one more time as the sun sank under the horizon. She'd insisted they leave at once instead of waiting until morning.

With the deal he'd made with Ulla still leaving a bitter taste in his mouth, Tyee wasted no time. He'd whisked her out of the infirmary before Hugo or anybody else could tell them otherwise.

Now they rode together on Koko, trudging through the snowy forest in the middle of the night.

"You're sure there's no rune that would warm us up?" Tyee called over his shoulder, his voice echoing in the silence of the darkness.

He felt the old Elven woman rumble with laughter and a wry grin graced his features.

She said something into his back but he couldn't hear her as the wind picked up.

Tyee urged the horse faster, knowing it was dangerous for both of them to linger in the icy wind.

Andriette touched his arm, and he strained to hear her over the buffeting gales.

"Take—, left for—shortcut."

The wind stole most of the wizened woman's words, but Tyee did as instructed and nudged Koko to the left. The two didn't speak again until the cottage came into view through the trees.

Tyee felt Andriette pinch his arm and release a warm breath on his neck.

"Something's not right."

The hair on the back of his neck rose as Koko's ears perked at something. The stallion breathed harder and danced against Tyee's firm hold on the reins. He peered into the inky blackness and gave a low huff.

Tyee placed a soothing hand on the horse's neck and squinted in the direction of Koko's ears. He couldn't see a thing, but the hairs on his neck still stood at attention. There was something in the air that didn't feel right. It was heavy with foreboding.

Tyee swallowed and slid off his steed's back.

"Foolish, boy. Get back on the horse." Andriette hissed.

Tyee handed her Koko's reins. "Steer Koko back the way we came. I'm going to see what I can find."

He whispered in Koko's ear and pushed on his shoulder until the large animal performed a one-eighty turn. Koko bobbed his head and blinked his eye, understanding passing between horse and rider. Koko snorted and started back down the path.

Andriette turned to watch her great-grandson, protests on her lips.

Tyee gave her one last wave and turned his back.

He would get his answers.

The horseman kept to the tree line and crept closer to the clearing housing the old cottage. He felt that tension in the air again and stopped to listen for anything that sounded out of place.

The crack of a shutter hitting the wooden exterior of his Tota's home set Tyee's teeth on edge. He took a few steps closer, sticking to the shadows. Andriette would never have left the cottage so exposed to the elements. He knew this sanctuary meant too much to the old woman to leave its survival to chance.

Somebody had been inside.

And could still be there.

*But who?*

Tyee's mind raced but couldn't come up with anyone who would wish his great-grandmother harm. She lived as a recluse and rarely saw any other Elven besides Hugo when he made his rounds on the Elven living outside the city.

His feet brought him to the place directly across from the worn wooden front door, still under the cover of the shadows from the trees.

He strained his eyes and ears, trying to find any trace of a break-in or sign someone was still inside. The bushes rattled not twenty feet away, and Tyee felt his heart thundering in his chest, the noise catching him by surprise. He kept his wits about him, staying silent and keeping his breathing even.

Sure enough, a massive wolf appeared from the bushes and turned his bright yellow eyes towards the path from Verdencia.

Tyee's heart skipped a beat as he studied the large canine. Something seemed familiar about the way the wolf held himself and Tyee swore he'd seen those yellow eyes before. He didn't dare move as those large eyes scanned the area again.

The wolf gave the air one last sniff before disappearing back into the undergrowth.

Tyee watched the spot with his eyes, still not moving an inch. After a few moments, the tension in the air dissipated and the young man breathed a little easier.

*But those eyes. I've seen those eyes before.*

Tyee eased forward and stepped towards the cottage's front door.

*CRACK!*

He swore under his breath at the stick he'd missed, now crushed beneath his boot.

There was rustling in the underbrush approaching the clearing.

Without time to think, Tyee pulled the short sword from his hip and crouched into a defensive position.

No sooner had he taken his position, than the sound of a body crashing through the tree line made him grit his teeth.

The wolf growled and snapped his teeth in challenge, circling around the horseman and looking for an opportunity to attack.

"I don't want to hurt you." Tyee held the wolf's familiar yellow eyes as he matched the canine's movements.

The only response he got was the wolf pulling his lips back further, showing all his teeth in a sinister caricature of a smile.

Tyee licked his lips, puzzled by the human response to his words, and focused on the animal's movements. The wolf had a slight hitch in his front right shoulder. If he could hit the old injury, maybe the wolf could be persuaded to leave.

It was the biggest wolf Tyee had ever seen. Bigger even than the wolf lieutenant of the Shifters of the Forest.

*The clearing.*

That's where he'd seen those yellow eyes.

The wolf didn't hesitate and lunged while Tyee was lost in thought.

The horseman acted on instinct, throwing his arm up to protect his face.

Tyee felt teeth slice through the fabric of his thick, fur-lined coat, skimming over his now unprotected skin. The sudden attack left him unsteady, and the wolf moved like lightning, taking advantage of Tyee's disoriented state.

Tyee lost his sword in the scuffle and it took everything he had to stay on his feet. Without the sword, there was no way to strike back at the animal. When the wolf lunged again, Tyee spun closer to the canine, sidestepping its snapping jaws and ending at its rump. With a quick sweep of his leg, Tyee took out one side of the wolf's legs, causing it to jump sideways and away from him.

Tyee pursued the creature, getting closer to his weapon and staying away from those murderous teeth.

The wolf spun fast and Tyee lost his position, landing in reach of the animal's deadly fangs. The wolf snapped at him and drew blood from the exposed skin in the arm of Tyee's coat.

Tyee let out a cry as pain raced like fire up his arm. He backed away, losing the ground he'd gained by risking the proximity to the wolf.

His arm was on fire, but Tyee didn't let the pain distract him. He inched in a circle closer to his weapon. The wolf mirrored his movements, circling his injured prey.

Tyee felt sweat bead down his back and his heart pound in his throat.

Just a little closer.

He was steps away from reaching the short sword.

His gaze glanced to where the sword was and the wolf lunged again.

Tyee dove on top of the blade, grasping for purchase of the sword's hilt.

The wolf missed his first lunge but geared up for another, this time leaping on top of the horseman and pinning him to the ground.

Tyee fought desperately to get one hand free, but the wolf was too heavy.

Hot and rancid breath blew in his face and Tyee felt like he was going to be sick. Those yellow eyes met his and Tyee saw his intent as clear as day.

The Shifter was going to kill him.

The wolf made to snap at Tyee's throat when a noise came from opposite the path he had sent Koko. With the shift in the wolf's focus, Tyee used his legs to force the animal off of him and reached for the sword.

Missing the wolf's teeth by inches, Tyee's fingers fumbled for the blade's handle.

As a dark shape burst through the trees, Tyee got ahold of the sword and raised it in front of him. With the wolf's attention diverted, Tyee plunged the metal into the animal's side.

A bloodcurdling scream tore from the creature's throat as it struggled to separate itself from Tyee and the weapon he held.

It took two steps before collapsing in a heap.

Tyee groaned but forced himself to his feet, sword held toward the dark shape hurtling towards him.

"Tyee?"

Before Tyee could make out the owner of the voice, his world went dark as he fell to the ground.

# Chapter Thirty-Two

Luc's deep brown eyes watched her fellow council members with interest, waiting for them to respond to the progress she'd reported.

She, Gar, and Midge had divided Kamore into three regions; Gar took the North, Midge took Central, and Luc had the South, respectively. They'd figured it would be best to split up the task of creating routes and identifying possible safe houses for their people. From there, they could go about assigning groups to travel those routes and drop spies in the towns they needed eyes in.

She'd informed the other two about her headway in creating feasible travel routes and given them a roster of who she imagined would travel them and become their eyes and ears in the cities.

"You want to send Damien to Fernwen?" Midge asked, with caution in her tone.

"Lass, that's a big sacrifice. Fernwen is a rough place these days. Ya don't want yer lad in a place like that," Gar insisted with an unreadable expression.

"It's no different from Bane going to Heimat. And it would be selfish of me to keep Dame from the action because I'm afraid for him. He's been through too much to insult him like that. He has the skills we need in the capital, so we'll send him where he can be of the most use." Luc's voice didn't waver despite the sharp pains in her heart.

She'd discussed everything with her fiancée the night before. She'd confided in him about her plans and where she knew he'd make the most impact. They shared their fears for what was coming and held each other through the tears.

Then they dared to dream of their future afterwards.

Since Luc's proposal, both of them started to wearing loops of knot grass around their ring fingers as reminders of those dreams.

Luc played with the stiff loop around her finger and added, "It wouldn't be fair to send someone else into danger when Damien's just as, if not more, qualified. We talked about it and it's the only thing that makes sense." She met both of their kind gazes and held them for long moments, willing the two older council members to understand. This was as hard as they could imagine, but the decision was made. Telling her it was the wrong one did nothing for her or Damien.

Gar placed his large hand on her shoulder and squeezed. "You're braver than me, lass. Your plans are sound; let's move on to Midge's proposition for the Central region."

Luc wiped the stray tear from her eye and listened to the Forger go over the routes and teams she'd drawn up. They went back and forth on a couple of teams of people but eventually settled on a compromise for which groups would serve which region.

Then Gar did the same with the North and the process repeated itself.

It took almost three hours, but by the end, everyone on their roster was assigned a task and region suited to their skills, age, and ability.

Just in time too, because they'd promised to post their people's assignments after lunch.

Luc walked to the bulletin board outside the half-built dining hall and posted the sheets of names. Most were bundled in groups of two or three as traveling groups. The three Heads decided it was best to have as many groups on the road as possible. It gave them more options for sending communications and supplies, and harboring the injured or sick to safety. And there was always more innate security in traveling with a group.

Only ten names were listed singly for spy assignments.

This was because of the danger and need for specific skills to be considered for such a position.

She posted the lists and stepped back, a grim expression on her face. She couldn't shake the feeling that not all those names would return.  Her eyes drifted from the board to the frozen lake and snow-covered trees.

Duncan and Chiara were determined to make this settlement a home, but Luc couldn't help feeling as if this place was anything but a home. It was too wild, despite their attempts to tame the snowy landscape. The lake and its surrounding trees were breathtaking; almost too pretty to justify marring such magnificence with permanent wooden structures.

But the ground they'd settled on seemed perfect for what they needed. Luc knew the Circus needed this haven while they fought for their place in the world, but afterwards? Maybe there would be reason to return this place to its wild state and find another sanctuary.

"The lists are up! Out of my way, lady!"

A young voice pushed her from her spot in front of the board as people crowded in, searching for their names and those of their loved ones. Luc became lost in the crowd, but managed to elbow her way to the side.

She searched for a friendly face and met Zeke's silver gaze. She cupped a hand around her mouth while maintaining eye contact with her fellow acrobat. Luc gestured with her other hand and waited for his eyes to fill with understanding. He moved one hand in a circle before pointing to her and nodding.

Luc spoke, her voice amplified by Zeke's wind. "I know you're all excited and nervous about your assignments, but please take note; we will hold a meeting tonight after dinner. Report to your region leader and we will go over the logistics of skills training and our dry runs. Spend the rest of the day with your loved ones because assignments start in the morning."

She uncupped her hand and nodded at the now quiet crowd. Luc felt guilty for springing that on them so fast, but knew sometimes it was best to cut straight to the point. She weaved through the people towards Zeke as the whispers started.

She tuned out the complaints about group members, region assignments, and all the rest, forcing herself to her friend's side. Zeke said something, but Luc couldn't hear him over the sounds of the crowd and gestured to a spot out of the noise.

"Sorry, Z, what were you saying?" She asked with a sheepish grin.

Zeke slung an arm over her shoulder. "I said nothing like a little of Luc's tough love to stir up a crowd."

Luc couldn't help but smile, even as she gave his side a playful shove. "Be nice. I figured if they knew their time was short, they'd make better use of it."

"And there's the famous Luc wisdom coming out to play."

Luc rolled her eyes and bumped his shoulder.

"Luc, I'm being serious! There's a reason you were the youngest person to ever be voted to the Governing Council. Everybody respects you and the way you carry yourself. Whatever you set your mind to, you do with flying colors. They may not see it now, but they'll thank you later." Zeke's eyes were earnest as he held her gaze.

Luc sighed. "Thanks for your kind words. It always strikes me how hard it is to be in charge. You don't realize it until you're the one making the decisions that affect so many. It's exhausting. I don't know why Myra would be so hell-bent on keeping control of something so taxing."

Zeke gave a dark chuckle. "That's exactly why you're such a good leader. Only the wrong kind of people thirst for power and control. The ones that don't want it know how hard of a job it really is."

Luc contemplated Zeke's words before nodding. "I guess. I have a couple of hours before I need to be back. Wanna come visit Rae with me?"

Zeke shook his head. "I just came from there. She shooed me out and ordered me to spend as much time with Bane as I could before he leaves."

Luc gasped and covered her mouth with her hand. "I am so stupid. Of course, why are you still standing here listening to me ramble? Go be with your love."

She pushed him towards the line of tents where the players slept.

Zeke gave a wave and continued on, not looking back as he went to the Shifter that held his heart.

Luc felt a stab of guilt at the thought of not being with Damien every moment she could.

*He's with Chiara. They deserve time, too.*

She chided herself as she made her way to the infirmary. She would check on her friend while her fiancée spent some quality time with his mother.

Luc was happy to give them the time they needed, but knew she'd have to do something to keep her mind off her worries. Her Abuela and Javie left the other night, so between worrying about them, Damien, and the rest of their people, she was ready for a distraction.

Maybe she could lose herself in helping Rae figure out how to combat this next set of challenges and distract her from worrying about her loved ones.

A woman could dream, at least.

Gemma swung her feet back and forth over the side of her cot. She'd gotten cold after playing in the snow with Wren and Eva for most of the morning and went back to her tent for a change of clothes.

The little girl was startled when she saw the man she was supposed to call Uncle banking the coals and releasing delicious heat throughout the small structure.

She'd forgotten again for a split second that this man was the only one sharing the tent with her since her mother had left. Gemma was still shy around him, especially since he still refused to call her Red. She'd asked him to, but he always reverted to Gemma. Instead of changing, she'd sat as close as she could to the makeshift stove and held her hands out.

When they'd warmed up enough, she'd done the same with her feet. But she'd gotten distracted by seeing how far she could swing them.

It was taking a lot longer for her toes to warm up.

"Maybe we should take those boots off. They might dry out faster if you took them off your feet." Gemma met her "uncle's" strange lavender eyes and cocked her head.

"But if I take them off, then I have to hold them over the fire with my hands. And me, Wren, and Eva were walking through the mud this morning. They'll be all gross." Gemma argued, swinging her feet harder. "Maybe if I move them faster, the wind will help."

She dropped the man's gaze and focused on her feet, unsure of what to say to the man she barely knew.

"Here, let me try." He moved his hands and thrust them towards her boots.

Gemma giggled. "That tickles!"

She felt the wind from his hands twine around her ankles and buffet against the thick leather of her boots. Her teeth chattered as Duncan's wind blew away the warmth from the stove.

Her uncle stopped as soon as he heard her teeth. He grabbed her blanket from the cot and wrapped it around her before putting more wood on the stove.

"Momma says we're not to put logs on the fire until it gets dark out." Gemma's expression was serious as she stared at her uncle, her teeth still chattering.

"I know, Gemma. And your Momma is completely right. We want to keep as much wood available as possible for when we sleep at night. But right now, you need to get warm. You're shivering too much after all that wind. Can we take those wet boots and socks off now?" Duncan's voice was gentle but firm, similar to when her Momma would tell her she'd had enough cookies.

Gemma closed her eyes and tried to wiggle her freezing toes. She'd thought they were getting warmer, but now she couldn't quite get them to move. "They don't want to wiggle."

Her uncle frowned. "Your toes?"

Gemma nodded.

Her uncle didn't hesitate and unlaced her boots, taking them off with care and setting them close to the stove. Next came her socks. When Duncan grabbed them from her feet his face became unreadable.

"Gemma, you're freezing." He tore the socks from her feet and threw them to the ground. He knelt by the cot and rubbed her feet.

Gemma squirmed, but didn't say anything. He was tickling her, but his hands were so warm against her frigid skin. She gave a sigh and let Duncan and the stove warm her frozen toes. She began to doze and close her eyes when her uncle said something.

Gemma started and blinked her eyes, willing them to open. "What did you say, Uncle Duncan?"

The older man smiled at her and tucked a stray curl behind her ear. "I asked if you could wiggle your toes now."

Gemma giggled again. "Oh! I almost fell asleep. My feet feel better."

"Good. Try wiggling those little toes for me to make sure." Duncan waited with an expectant smile.

Gemma furrowed her brows and concentrated on her feet. It took a moment, but then one toe moved, followed by the rest. Her face broke into a triumphant grin and she beamed at the wind Crafter.

"All better!" Gemma exclaimed, looking for her coat. She found it where she'd left it on the chair by the tent flap leading outside. She pulled it over her shoulders and looked for her hat and mittens.

"What are you doing, sweetheart?"

"I'm supposed to meet Eva and Wren at the dining hall for lunch. They may have already finished without me." Gemma said in a brisk tone. She'd forgotten about their plan until now, distracted by the heat from the camp stove. Now that she remembered, she was trying to hurry.

"Whoa, whoa, whoa. Slow down, Gemma. You almost lost those toes of yours. The last thing you want to do is risk them again."

"But I told them I'd be there and I'm already late. I need to go now if I'm going to catch up with them." Gemma gave up on the hat and fumbled for new socks. She stuffed them on her feet and reached for her shoes.

Duncan held out a hand to stop her. "I can't let you go traipsing around in those wet boots. Let me go find Eva and Wren and have them bring some food for you. Maybe the three of you could have a sleepover."

Gemma considered his offer. She glanced at the warm stove and sat back down on the cot. "I've never had a sleepover before." She licked her lip before chewing on it. The young Herbalist met his eyes and stuck out her hand. "Deal."

Her uncle shook it without hesitation and went to the stove. He poked the fire, making it burn bright again before adding another log.

"Keep an eye on this while I'm gone and stay under that blanket." He shot a pointed look at the blanket on the floor from when she'd hurried to get her coat.

Gemma felt a flush creep up her neck and she averted her gaze. "Yes, Uncle Duncan."

He waited for her to wrap the warm wool around her person before leaving by the tent flap.

Once he'd left, Gemma shrugged off her coat.

She missed her Momma something fierce, but she was starting to warm to this uncle of hers. He was nice, even if he was a little awkward.

*I need to get ready for this sleepover.*

Gemma busied herself with cleaning the small space, imagining all the fun they would have before it was time for bed.

*This is going to be awesome.*

# Chapter Thirty-Three

Mirabella bounced her leg as she waited for the man she once loved to send for her. She ran a hand through the close-cropped curls starting to grow back and itched her scalp. She'd never realized how itchy it was to regrow hair.

Unable to take the waiting anymore, she went to the window of her room overlooking the square outside the Barracks where the soldiers slept.

*So much destruction.*

The square was still black from where the fires raged. Most of the city stopped smoking, but ash still covered most of the walls, and the cloying smell of smoke still burned in the back of her throat.

It would be a long time before Heimat returned to its former glory.

A knock on the door gave her a start. The change in her expression was immediate. The cool indifference she'd worn like a second skin before her miscarriages and Gemma settled over her like water. Mirabella was surprised by the easy way her masks slipped back into place when she'd bid them to.

And Darren had been too willing to believe them.

She'd begged him to forgive her for her duplicity and the way she'd left without telling him. And then she'd laid it on thick. Mirabella went into a tirade about how Duncan and the rest needed to pay for taking their daughter. She made derogatory comments about the Magicae and how she'd been right to play her part in the Uprising and have them locked up.

Mirabella made sure there was no doubt where her allegiances lay. Gone was the meek mother cowering in the corner. If she was going to be privy to Darren's plans, Mirabella needed to be at his side as an equal. Or at least close to an equal.

Myra was the only woman Darren truly respected, but Mirabella could become the woman he'd loved once.

*Or pretended to love.*

She wasn't fully convinced Darren could love someone, but whatever positive feelings he had; she was determined to make him direct those at her again. Darren was a bully, and giving in to his ridiculous demands hadn't done her any good. If she wanted to survive this next stint with him, something needed to change.

And it worked.

Darren ate up every word she'd uttered, disbelief in his eyes. He'd questioned her until she was blue in the face but couldn't find a chink in her armor of lies.

Mirabella was a better actress than anyone knew.

Now she had to keep up the charade until she had the information the Circus needed to retake Heimat. She hoped that day would come sooner rather than later. Darren had already begun issuing gentle touches to her lower back and arms. It was only a matter of time before he made a move.

The thought made her skin crawl. But if Darren thought she was back to the person she'd been when they got married, he wouldn't be able to resist himself. And she wasn't ready to make that type of sacrifice for Duncan or anybody. She'd need a plausible excuse should he try something.

She opened the door once she reached it, burying her musings out of reach in her mind. Mirabella came face to face with a young boy dressed in the uniform of the city guard. She gave him a once over as he stood there, gawking at her and moving his lips without making a sound.

"Speak up, I can't hear you." She snapped at the boy waiting on the threshold of her doorway.

The boy turned bright red and averted his eyes. "The general demands your presence at once."

Mirabella tapped her fingers on the doorframe and narrowed her eyes.

"Those are the exact words he used?"

The boy did the impossible and turned even redder, then nodded wordlessly.

She let a glint enter her eyes before whirling around and returning to her place at the window. "Tell him I'll be down in a minute."

The boy's eyes widened, and he swallowed thickly. "But My Lady—, nobody keeps the general waiting." The poor boy was stuttering and Mirabella felt a flash of guilt in her heart, knowing Darren would take out his frustration on this innocent boy.

"What's your name?" She kept her tone icy, not dropping the charade of a woman wounded and hardened by the world and losing her daughter.

"Bram, My Lady." The boy whispered with his head down, still in shock at the thought of having to deliver such news to the cruel man in charge.

"Bram, tell the general I am on my way. I will be right behind you. I promise." Mirabella softened her tone just a little, trying to assuage some of his fear.

The boy nodded and closed the door behind him.

Mirabella looked in the mirror and rearranged the short copper curls so they were out of her face. She met her reflection's gaze and whispered, "Showtime. You can do this."

She took a deep breath and exited her chambers. Her stomach turned sour upon seeing the door to Darren's chambers so close to her own. He'd insisted she move closer to him for "security" reasons. Gemma was no longer in the nursery, so she hadn't protested the change in rooms.

Again, she'd find the perfect reason to refuse him if it came to that. Right now, she needed to focus on the task at hand.

The woman marched with purpose, letting her dark gray woolen skirts float behind her. She wore the color of mourning in honor of her daughter. It helped bolster her appearance as a grieving mother hellbent on exacting revenge from her enemies and those who wished her harm.

Her smart leather boots echoed against the old wooden floorboards of the former government building. Her feet took her to the council chamber room where she was to meet with Darren before his advisory meeting. Mirabella wouldn't be able to speak at the meeting itself, but she'd insisted they talk beforehand and come up with a plan.

She wouldn't be blindsided again if she could help it. Memories of the day Darren viciously informed her of Myra's kill order out on Duncan's head flashed in her mind. She could feel her heart pounding in her chest at the thought and she clenched her fists tight, feeling her nails bite into her palms.

*Keep it together.*

She repeated those words in her mind as she rounded the corner that would lead her to the chamber's doors.

"Mirabella. What a surprise."

Mirabella gritted her teeth at Zander's shrill tone. She kept her expression unreadable and met his gaze with blazing eyes. Zander was a bully just like Darren and she was done letting him push her around.

"Zander. I could say the same about you. I'm to meet my husband before the meeting. What business brings you here?"

The lanky man stuttered, unable to take his eyes off of Mirabella's. "Well, I mean... The general needs me to keep watch on the doors. Make sure nobody enters that he wouldn't want in there yet."

"Great. You keep watch and I'll see about what Darren plans to reveal to his advisors." Mirabella made to push the double doors of the chamber open when they both heard Vincenzio roaring at someone.

Mirabella winced, knowing he was yelling at the young lad, but didn't hesitate, pushing the doors inward and entering the large space.

"Really, Darren. There's no need to shout at the poor boy." Inwardly, she was trembling with fright at addressing him in such a way, but she didn't let her voice waver. When they'd been dating, Mirabella always told him his anger and outbursts were a consequence of the passion in his veins.

*Gag me. What a foolish girl I was.*

Mirabella arched an eyebrow at the raging man as she berated her younger self in her mind. Now she recognized that anger and his outbursts for what they were; consequences of an arrogant man not getting his way.

He was seething as his eyes rested on hers. She fought the urge to fidget, needing to keep her composure if she wanted to stand a chance against the brute.

"I was the one that told him I would be late. Dismiss the poor boy and let's get on with it. There isn't much time before your advisors arrive." Mirabella drawled, keeping her tone uninterested.

Vincenzio studied her with cool disdain. "And why, pray tell, were you not ready when I called for you? I agreed to meet with you as a courtesy. Don't test my patience, woman, you're already on thin ice."

Mirabella's eyes flashed with annoyance. "Honestly, Darren. I thought we were past all that nonsense. If you'd wanted a submissive wife, you would've chosen somebody else. You did what you needed to when I was lost and broken, but I'm back now." She pursed her lips and forced her innate fear of the man down. "I refuse to be at your beck and call anymore. In public, I will still play the dutiful wife, but in private, you will respect me."

Vincenzio narrowed his eyes at her. She held his gaze, feeling her pulse quicken with each second he didn't respond.

The man rubbed his chin and turned his attention back to the boy. "You're dismissed. Tell no one of what you've heard or you'll end up in the crypts."

The boy put on a brave face, saluted the general, and sped to the doors. Once they shut behind the boy, Vincenzio rounded on her again.

"Foolish woman. Don't think because I agreed to this meeting, you have any ounce of power."

"Darren, stop." Mirabella held a hand up and gulped when he took a step closer, so her hand hovered over his chest. She forced herself to continue, "You know, I'm not trying to take any kind of power from you. I only want to get our daughter back and make the ones who took her pay. You agreed to this meeting because you wanted my opinion on some of your plans. I'm not useless, Darren. Don't forget that the Uprising wouldn't have happened without me."

She let both her hands rest on his chest and met his eyes with a pleading gaze. *Come on, you bastard, I won't beg, so this is the best you're going to get.*

His eyes softened and his hands went to her elbows. It took every ounce of control she had to keep herself from flinching away from his touch.

Vincenzio sighed after a few moments of staring into her eyes and released her. Mirabella took a step back and crossed her arms, waiting for him to speak.

"You're right. I agreed to this because I wanted your opinion on something. This change in your demeanor suits you, Mirabella. It's been too long since I had a partner I could count on. We will get Gemma back and punish those vermin that took her."

*No, we won't. Our daughter is safer than she's ever been and there's no way in hell I'm letting you threaten that.*

"I'm counting on it. They deserve every retaliation we have for the sins they've committed against us and the rest of Kamore. The Magicae deserve to bleed for all the trouble they've caused us." Mirabella's tone was even and didn't betray the murderous thoughts she directed at her husband.

Vincenzio smirked. "I couldn't have said it better myself. Now, down to business before you entice me anymore." The desire in his gaze made Mirabella sick. If she had any question of his intent in making amends with her, they were wiped away with that single glance.

She gave him an expectant look to keep going, hoping the disgust was hidden in her gaze.

Vincenzio gave a low chuckle. "That's the woman I remember. Always so serious and dedicated to the mission. Anyway, Mallick and his entourage of supplies and the Blades themselves arrive tonight. We will have a welcome feast in his honor, and then training will begin. We will have two weeks of training to integrate the two troops and make necessary cuts should any prove incompetent.

"And then we march." He finished with a flourish.

Mirabella frowned and leaned against one of the tables, keeping her eyes on his. "March where?"

"Into the forest. Where the vermin and our daughter are." He gave her an impatient look. As if he was dumbfounded she would even ask such a question.

*Asshole.*

Aloud, she asked, "But how are you going to find them? They've been in the woods for how long now, months? Don't you think they'll have hiding places and ambushes waiting for your soldiers?"

Vincenzio shook his head and gave her a condescending look. "Of course they will, which is why our soldiers are going to burn the forest to the ground."

Mirabella gulped in shock, doing her best to keep the surprise from her face. "That seems like quite the task. Do you have such resources to make a wet forest burn?"

The man frowned and Mirabella felt relief flood her veins. He hadn't thought through the execution of his idea, only came up with an end goal.

She could feel his frustration mounting, and the air grew tense between them when he realized she was right.

Mirabella needed to think fast.

"What if there was a way to draw them out of the forest? They may have an advantage in the trees, but your troops, combined with the Blades, would make quick work of them in the open. There needs to be a way to lure them out." She offered, speaking the words as fast as she thought them. She'd taken one look at the burned part of the forest along the river and almost wept at such a sight. Mirabella would do everything she could to make sure he didn't repeat that destruction in other parts of the beautiful ecosystem.

Vincenzio rubbed the lower half of his face with a large hand and considered her words. Eventually, he nodded his head slowly.

"You're right. We have the advantage in the open. We need to flush them out and destroy them on our own terms. And I know just the way to do it."

Mirabella felt her fear rear its ugly head and her palms sweat. Her voice wavered in betrayal as she asked, "How will you do that?"

"I'll send my men to some of the neighboring cities to find more of the vermin. They won't be able to resist coming to save their people. Especially if they're children." He sent her an icy and conspiratorial smile.

Mirabella felt her heart drop as he prowled closer, waiting for her reaction to his brilliant plan. She tried to respond, but her tongue felt thick in her mouth and wouldn't form the words she wanted. She sat there, helpless and unable to move or speak, as Vincenzio stepped closer, the desire back in his eyes.

A knock on the door startled them both. Vincenzio gave her a lingering look before calling out. "What is it, Zander?"

The steward poked his head in. "The advisors and lieutenants are here. Shall I send them in?"

Vincenzio looked back at her, his eyes glittering with danger.

*Don't do it, Darren. Don't keep them waiting. I need more time to come up with something.*

Her mind raced, and she knew fear shone in her eyes. She wasn't ready for any sort of affection from the man, and he must have seen the horror in her gaze.

He turned away with an unreadable expression. "We just finished. Send them in."

Mirabella had ice in her veins as she took her spot on a chair behind the podium, in full view of the entire room.

She needed to have a reason behind her fear by the time this meeting was over, and she found herself alone with the brute again.

"DADDY!"

"Daddy's home!"

"I can't believe it's really you!"

Children screamed and cried, and Rich recognized two of the voices as his own granddaughters.

He shared a look with Anna and they dropped what they were doing to go to the door.

Sure enough, Rob and Tommy were being mobbed by their children in the middle of the yard. Rob was on his knees, hugging his two little girls as if they were his only lifeline. Tommy picked up his two youngest while his oldest clung to his leg. He plowed forward, looking for the person he loved more than anything.

Rich opened the door wide and called out. "She's in here, lad. And so is the little one."

Tommy's stunned expression made Rich smile. There was no mistaking the love in his eyes as he raced forward, thrusting a child in each of his and Anna's arms on his way by. When he saw the woman he loved, he shook off the daughter still clinging to his leg, and took Sara into his arms.

The two shared a moment, cradling their newest son before the other three swarmed them again. Anna and Rich watched from the doorway, having been unsuccessful in keeping the two young ones from their parents.

Rich smiled, happy the families were reunited. His heart panged when he looked at his two granddaughters and son-in-law. Their family would never be the same after losing Melody.

*But at least they still have each other.*

Somebody cleared their throat, startling Rich from his thoughts.

Tommy had extricated himself from his family and was looking at Rich.

The look he gave made Rich's heart drop. He knew the young man had bad news by the expression on his face. He gestured for Tommy to say what was on his mind.

"We have a problem."

# Chapter Thirty-Four

Nan followed Tyee and Javie on foot, happy to stretch her legs after being on the horse all day again. Her grandson was asking as many questions as he could about the strange symbols now inked into Tyee's skin.

She smiled as Tyee explained each one to the boy just entering manhood. Tyee droned on about the lore surrounding the runes, where they came from, what purpose they served, and how they interacted with the power in his blood. Javie soaked it all in like a sponge.

Nan frowned as she studied the trees they traveled past. This part of the forest would be considered old growth with its mature trees and the amount of logs decaying on the ground. Every once in a while, the old Herbalist put a hand to one of the towering trunks to listen to its song.

Every time, she felt a being content with its place in the world and secure in knowing it was protected by the Elven.

*This place is magical.* She studied everything with wide-eyed amazement. The old Herbalist felt like a kid again, transported to a new world by her Abuela's words strung into stories. Her Abuela mentioned the Elven on occasion but the magic of the trees was ever present.

Nan took a deep breath, taking in the damp scent of green with the icy air.

*No. This place is sacred.*

That smell filled her senses as she surveyed the trees again. They were getting closer to Verdencia and her inevitable showdown with the Queen herself.

She and Javie came across Andriette's cabin shortly after Tyee slayed the monster of a wolf. He'd been convinced it was one of the Shifters of the Forest, but there was no sure way to tell with the animal dead and Nan without a tonic or the ingredients to make one.

A body could tell you a lot, but you needed the proper tools to make it talk to you.

Tyee had passed out for twenty long minutes, but eventually regained consciousness and relayed who the cabin belonged to and where she was. Javie went and fetched Koko and the old woman while Nan helped Tyee into the humble cottage. She settled him on the couch and gave him a general well-being tonic she had on her person.

Javie brought back Andriette, and they ended up spending several days in her cottage. Nan had hoped to be in Verdencia by now, but the time was necessary for all of them. She'd grown fond of the Elven woman known as Tota, despite her brusque and direct way of speaking. The resemblance between her and Tyee was striking, and Nan wasn't surprised to find out she was his great-grandmother.

What had surprised her was how much history and knowledge Andriette kept in her cottage. After a day of marveling over the greenhouse and creating some tonics with the Elven woman's gracious offer of free rein, Andriette revealed what lay up the stairs and behind the door to her room.

Books.

Thousands and thousands of books.

Nan was almost brought to tears at the sight of so many gateways into different stories, time periods, and disciplines. It was a miracle so much knowledge survived.

The old Herbalist knew how easy it was for something like that to be lost.

Andriette made Nan feel welcome to anything she needed, and she'd been delighted to dive into the stories from the Elven. She'd spent hours in that room, searching for anything on Javie's condition or why their magic was waning. She found nothing mentioning one of the Magicae possessing multiple Gifts as Javie did, but she stumbled upon a book delving into the Magicae's history from the

Elven point of view. It was a large tome with dense and dry text she'd barely been able to get through in the short time they'd been at the cottage. Luckily, the Elven woman allowed her to borrow the book and bring it back to the settlement at the Lake.

Nan looked to the saddlebag on the horse led by Javie, relaxing when she saw the familiar bulge of the precious leather-bound pages. It was the one lead they had in discovering more about what was happening with their magic.

Her attention shifted back to the two men leading their horses. They fell silent as they reached the outskirts of the city in the trees.

Nan frowned. It was unlike Javie to grow so silent. She followed his line of sight and gasped. The old woman made her legs move faster than she thought possible and caught up with her grandson. Nan grabbed Javie's free hand and squeezed as tight as she could. "I see it too," she whispered. Javie glanced at her before looking back at what captured their attention so completely.

Metal vines looped around all the trees supporting the Elven city, tendrils continuing to reach as if searching for something and complex flowers shining in the dim light still peeking through the trees. This craftsmanship was too delicate to be the work of a metalsmith. Even a Forger would have trouble coaxing so much metal into the complex shapes and whorls.

"Do you think it was somebody like me?" Javie dared to ask, hopeful eyes searching his grandmother's face for her reaction.

Nan pulled him close. "There is only one way to find out. I will ask the Queen as soon as I see her."

"Don't be so eager to meet with the Queen of Ice herself. You may find yourself in a position you never dreamed of." Tyee's cryptic answer came in a bored tone. He was trying to be nonchalant about the situation, but Nan heard an edge of bitterness in his voice.

*Curious. I wonder what that's about.*

While Andriette was warm, Tyee had been distracted the entire time they were at the cottage. He spent his time drawing more of those symbols on parchment, wandering through the woods, and caring for Koko. She'd been afraid he wasn't sleeping with the circles under his eyes but found him slumped on the table after staying in Andriette's library past midnight one evening. She'd placed a blanket around his shoulders and continued onto bed when his voice made her pause.

*"Is she okay?" Tyee's voice was thick with sleep and Nan could barely make out his words.*

*"Is who okay? Andriette?" She furrowed her brows. "She's fine. Snoring the last I left her. She's louder than a bear scrounging for berries. No wonder she insists everybody else sleeps down here."*

*"Not Tota. Rae." His eyelids fluttered, and the horseman propped himself on an elbow to get a better view of her.*

*Nan hesitated before figuring the truth was best. "She's struggling. If I'm right, you're taking too much of her energy. At least that's the conclusion I came to on the way here."*

*Tyee watched her for long seconds, his face becoming wrought with emotion. "I don't—, I'm not—." He stuttered, unable to form words before hanging his head. "I don't know how to stop it. These fucking runes are so hungry and my blood isn't strong enough. They resort to taking hers instead of what's given to them."*

*"Why?" She asked gently, as if she were facing a rabid animal. The desperate look in Tyee's eyes cautioned her he was closer to a breakdown than either of them realized.*

*"Because of the blood bond." He held his left palm face up for her to see. Three angry red lines marred his palm in a mirror image of the lines on Rae's.*

*Nan's eyes flickered to Tyee's. Before she could say a word, he gripped her hands hard and his eyes took on a pleading look. "I didn't know. You have to believe me, Nan. If I'd known, I never would've done it unless it was the only way to give her a chance."*

*She patted his cheek. "I believe you, dearie. It's okay. Has Andriette looked into blood bonds in that library of hers?"*

*Tyee nodded. "She did, but could only find information on how to create them, why they came about, and the dangers surrounding them. There was nothing on how to break them." He looked as if he would say more, but when he didn't, Nan knew there was something he wasn't ready to tell her.*

*No matter, he would when he was ready, or the information became pertinent.*

*"Well, then. I'd say you've been doing all you can with what you have. Keep learning how to use these runes and maybe something more will awaken in your blood. It's happened in the Magicae before. Sometimes the magic needs a little coaxing before it comes to the forefront.*

*"But rest is needed for the body and the mind. Go to bed, Tyee. This parchment will be here in the morning." She'd smiled at him and gestured to the cot next to Javie's in the living room.*

*He'd nodded and made his way to the humble sleeping space, passing out before his head hit the pillow.*

Nan blinked the memory away. Tyee was in bad sorts that night, but at least she found him sleeping from then on. A day after their encounter, she'd come upon Andriette, Tyee, and Javie in the greenhouse. The Elven woman was drawing ink into Tyee's skin while Javie looked on, trying to convince them he should have one too.

Tyee reassured her this was the answer to everything.

She glanced at the man's covered forearms and pictured the two symbols on each inside wrist. Only time would tell if he was right.

"Whoa, you might get your wish sooner than you'd hoped, Nan. Fritz doesn't look too happy and that can mean one of two things; he lost a bet on who was coming through the trees, or the Queen requests our presence." Tyee's voice still held that dangerous edge to it.

A large man with striking red hair and matching stubble approached them. His face was serious until he was within earshot of the three Circus members. He gave a wry grin and said, "I knew you wouldn't last out there with the old woman."

Tyee snorted. "I lasted longer than you ever did."

"That's not something to brag about. Skaber herself couldn't last as long as you." The man's grin faded into seriousness once more. "The Queen wants to see you."

Tyee gave a nod. "Take Koko and the mare while we respond to Her Majesty's summons?"

Fritz's face became sheepish. "The summons are only for you, Tyee." He cast an apologetic look on Nan and Javie. "Pardon me, ma'am, sir. The Queen can be particular about who she entertains in her chambers. Don't take any offense by it."

Nan pursed her lips. "We'll be going to see the Queen. If she wants to talk to Tyee, she'll have to talk to all three of us." She took the mare's reins from her grandson and deposited them in Fritz's hands. She shot a look at Tyee and he followed suit before leading the way to the ladder closest to the Queen's chambers.

"Didn't know you had a death wish, mate!" Fritz called from behind them. Tyee held a finger in his direction and Javie chuckled.

"I like that guy."

"Everybody does," Tyee responded to her grandson with a brisk tone. "Are you sure you want to do this, Nan?"

Nan shook her head and placed a hand on his arm. "I've told you a hundred times. Call me Abuela. Your connection with Rae and my granddaughter warrants something more familiar than Nan."

Tyee's expression darkened at her mention of Rae. "Fine then, are you sure you want to do this, *Abuela*?"

Nan ignored his tone and nodded with a smile. "Come now, we don't have time to waste. Duncan and the rest are counting on us." She gestured for him to show the way. Tyee gave her a hard look before obliging. She'd confirmed with him that all the details from his letter were true. The sooner they made the Queen see reason, the better. Tyee looked as if he was going to say something, but turned on his heel and climbed the ladder instead.

She shared a look with Javie, confirming she wasn't the only one who noticed Tyee's uneasiness. She furrowed her brows and climbed after the elusive horseman. Javie waited for her to make it to the top before following suit, always looking out for her. She gave him a grateful smile as he pulled himself onto the platform.

"What's going on with him?" Javie inclined his head to where Tyee spoke with one of the guards outside Ulla's chambers.

"Your guess is as good as mine." She looked over as Tyee argued with the man, insisting he go talk to Ulla. "But if I had to guess, I'd say we're about to find out what."

They fell quiet as Tyee approached. "I think I finally convinced the guard to inform Ulla of our terms. She won't like them, but she'll accept." His shoulders were rigid and his eyes never left the door to the Queen's quarters. When the guard reemerged with a nod, Tyee said, "Showtime. Let's get this over with." He strode with purpose, and Nan struggled to keep up.

Javie offered his arm to steady her with a frown. "I think you're right."

Tyee held the door open for them, realizing his mistake, and Nan thanked him with a smile. She entered the Queen's receiving chamber and laid eyes on the giant portrait of a striking, dark-haired man with blazing blue eyes. He bore an unmistakable resemblance to the gray-haired queen seated on a chair beneath the portrait. Nan studied the Elven woman and could tell she was annoyed by their presence with the scowl on her face and the way she crossed her arms. The room was made of warm wood and adorned with trinkets that Nan would have loved to study up close.

But alas, there was only time to plead their case. The innocent Mortals of Kamore were depending on them.

"This had better be good. You were supposed to bring the old woman home and return at once. I was beginning to think you were bailing on your commitment." Queen Ulla's voice was frosty and detached as she had eyes only for Tyee.

Tyee made to speak but Nan interrupted, determined to get the Queen's attention. "Your Majesty, thank you for meeting with us. I know it seemed forward to insist we come with Tyee, but under the current pressing conditions, it was imperative we see you as soon as possible." The queen turned her blazing eyes on Nan with a perplexed expression.

She gestured to the chairs opposite her. "I admit, I don't know what you are referring to. Please, sit, rest your bones, and explain." Her eyes flashed to Tyee before focusing on Nan again.

The Herbalist narrowed her eyes. "That's a funny way to deny a genocide."

The Queen's eyes widened in shock with a frozen expression on her face. Then she burst into laughter.

Nan looked at Tyee, but the horseman refused to meet her gaze. She turned back to Ulla. "I beg your pardon, but I don't think laughter is the best response to being accused of mass murdering thousands of innocents. What's so funny, Your Majesty?"

Ulla wiped a tear from her eyes. "Skaber, I haven't laughed like that in ages. Your guide here hasn't told you about the bargain he made, did he?"

Nan's head whipped to look at Tyee again, but the man refused to look up from his boots.

*What did he do?*

"I'll take that as a no." Ulla's cruel smile belayed how much she enjoyed causing tension between them. "Your dear horseman here bargained his freedom for those Mortals' worthless lives. Let's hope they're worth it after he takes my daughter for a mate."

Nan's eyes found Tyee's this time and the pain in his gaze confirmed it.

*You fool.* She thought to herself, her heart breaking for the young man. *If only you'd waited. We could've figured something out.* He didn't know what he was giving up by making this choice.

*This can't be true.*

Tyee twisted and turned in the familiar bed in the cottage outside Verdencia. He was struggling to fall asleep after seeing the horror in Nan's eyes at the Queen's revelation. He'd known this whole thing was an awful mistake, but to see that look of disbelief in her eyes made the whole thing that much more real. Tyee couldn't help but curse his past self.

He'd taken the deal because he couldn't think of another way out, but what if there was? *What if I royally fucked up?*

"Augh." Tyee was surprised when his feelings made themselves known with an audible groan. He wanted to get on Koko and ride as far and as fast as he could. But that wouldn't do anybody any good. He reached into his nightstand and took out a sleeping tonic Nan made in his Tota's cottage.

*Maybe this will help.*

He took the liquid down in one gulp. He placed the empty vial on the simple nightstand next to the bed and tried again.

This time, when he closed his eyes, Tyee fell into an uneasy sleep.

*It was dark. The kind of dark he only got in the woods. He let his eyes adjust to the blackness and found tall sentinels standing, keeping a silent watch. He was in the forest.*

*Tyee took cautious steps forward, keeping his hands in front of him to ward himself from stray branches.*

*His eyes caught the flicker of something in the distance and whatever was thrusting him forward pulled harder. His footsteps propelled him further and faster, pushed by an unknown force that needed him closer.*

*He came to a break in the trees and found the source of the flickering. There was a fire in the middle of the field, with one lone figure sitting next to it. Tyee moved as if in a trance, guessing who he'd find at that fire.*

*He took a deep breath and smelled the familiar scent of spice and vanilla. Without hesitation, he strode to the figure and pulled her into his arms. He held her to his chest, stroking her back with one hand while the other cupped her cheek.*

*Tyee released her enough so he could see her face in the flickering firelight. He gazed into her golden eyes and lost himself.*

*"Tyee?"*

*Before she could say anything else, Tyee shifted his hand from her cheek to the back of her head and pulled her into a kiss. He kissed her as if he was ravenous,* letting his emotions and their overwhelming situation overtake him. Before long, he deepened the kiss. As soon as her lips opened in response, Tyee felt fire travel from his lips to everywhere their bodies touched, ending in a pool at his core. He nipped her bottom lip and growled, wanting more.

Rae matched him in passion and desire. She kissed him back with fearless abandon, her hands traveling down his chest until they toyed with his waistband.

Tyee's hand still held the back of her head while his other slipped under her shirt and drew lazy circles on her back. He let himself forget everything that happened with Sylvia and the runes, enjoying this moment with the woman he loved.

The woman he loved.

He pulled away with reluctance. Rae jerked him back, and they kissed for a few minutes more, hands exploring over and under their clothing. Tyee pulled away again, gasping, and held her at arm's length when she tried again.

Rae gave a huff of impatience and arched one eyebrow.

Tyee looked deep into those golden eyes and said what he needed to say. "I love you, Birdie. No matter what happens, you have to know that." His eyes pleaded with hers and he watched her expression flicker from shock to delight to concern.

She touched his cheek. "Tyee. You talk in riddles. What is going on?"

Tyee turned away, focusing on the flames. "I did something stupid. There was no other choice, at least at the time. But, Nan—Abuela. She found out and gave me this horrid, horrid look. When I close my eyes, all I can see is that look on her face."

Rae furrowed her brows. "Drifter, I told you not to speak in riddles, and you've only given more cryptic answers. Talk to me." She sat down on the log again and tugged on his wrist until he sat next to her. "If I am the woman you love, you should be able to talk to me."

Tyee turned to look at her and found himself memorizing every curve and detail of her face. He licked his lips and told her about Ulla's bargain with the Shifters. "And the only way Ulla would stop was if I agreed to uphold the pledge my mother made to marry me to Sylvie." He let her take in the information.

Rae's eyes filled with horror and then anger. "What do you mean? Why would *your mother pledge you to Sylvie? And why does Ulla want you to honor it?"*

*He ran a hand through his hair, and she caught sight of the tattoo on his wrist. Rae gripped his forearm and brought it closer to her, looking at the four lines that formed an S-shape over the pulse point at his wrist.*

*She looked up at him with a questioning look. Happy to change the subject from his inevitable bonding to Sylvie, Tyee held out both wrists for her to study.*

*He pointed to the rune in an S-shape. "This is the rune known as Sowilo and it stands for power or success." He pointed to his other wrist which sported an inverted U with unequal sides. "And this is Uraz which means strength and life force. The runes are how the Elven channel their power. But since I'm only a half-blooded Elven, they were draining my life energy too fast. Even a single rune was tapping too much from me."*

*He opened his left hand, drawing her attention to his palm and the three lines that matched her own. Tyee traced the three lines with one finger, saying, "This is Algiz and it means protection or sanctuary." He met her golden eyes. "You're the one person I feel completely at ease with. This rune and the way we took it created a blood bond between us. That means if one of us gets too low on life energy, we draw from the other through the blood bond." He dropped her gaze, looking at the fire once more. "Abuela told me you weren't doing well. I knew I was taking too much from you, but I didn't realize how much I was impeding you and your training. I'm so sorry. I never would've done it if I'd known, if there had been another way."*

*"Shh." Rae cupped his cheek. "You gave me a chance to live and see this thing through until the end. That is the greatest gift anyone could have given me. There is nothing to be sorry for."*

*Tyee closed his eyes. "The runes around my wrists should ensure my life energy is strong enough to use the runes. As long as I only do them one at a time, I shouldn't need to drain yours as well." His eyes begged hers to understand, and he felt a weight lifted off his chest when she nodded.*

*"The past couple of days have been easier. If that's when you got the tattoos, it's safe to assume they're working." She smirked at him. "Since that's out of the way, let's get back to this Sylvie thing. Why did your mother do such a thing, and why*

*would Ulla want you to uphold it? I would've assumed she'd be abhorred at the idea of her daughter and her bloodline intermixing with someone that's not fully Elven."*

*Tyee sighed and told her about his Tota and her abdication of the throne. He told her about Ulla's father and his mother's bitterness. He finished by explaining Ulla's solution to the turmoil Sylvie caused her people. "The Elven hate Sylvie, and Ulla thinks a lot of people would support my claim to the throne if I pushed for it. This way, it unites the two bloodlines and the path of succession is clear. I tried everything I could, but she was willing to kill as many Mortals as it took to get me to agree."*

*Rae's face fell. "I don't understand. When do you have to marry her?"*

*Tyee averted his gaze again and mumbled. "On the spring equinox."*

*Rae's eyes flashed. "The spring equinox? That's in two days. She can't make you do this. This isn't right." Rae's anger came off her in waves. "You just told me you loved me, and you're marrying a monster in two days? What about everything we've been through? What about the promise you made to me? What about this?" She held out her palm.*

*Tyee started to say something, reaching for her when the vision went dark. He floundered, searching for the woman who had his heart and the fire they'd been sitting next to, but found nothing.*

"Tyee. Tyee wake up."

Tyee jolted awake and came face-to-face with Javie.

"We have to leave. There's something out for blood and we're being hunted."

# Chapter Thirty-Five

Gemma couldn't sleep. She tossed and turned on top of her cot, but it was useless. She turned over and gasped.

Eva was lying on the cot opposite her with eyes as wide as dinner plates and lips stretched into the biggest smile she could muster. It scared Gemma half to death until the other girl couldn't keep her face in the position any longer.

She broke into giggles, and it wasn't long before Gemma joined her.

Little Wren had been relegated to the floor and whined, asking what was so funny.

"Guys! Tell me!" The four-year-old protested again, sitting up from her spot on the floor.

"Shh! Wren, be quiet! The grown-ups have to think we're asleep!" Eva whisper-shouted at the young girl.

Gemma giggled louder. "Eva! You're louder than Wren! They're gonna catch us!"

This time Wren joined in and all three girls dissolved into a helpless fit of laughter. Every time they settled down, they'd look at each other and start laughing all over again.

Gemma had tears streaming down her face by the time they finally sobered.

"Thanks for coming over. I've never had a sleepover before." She admitted in a soft voice.

"Me either," Wren added. "But I thought I'd be in a bed for my first one."

Eva giggled and slapped the space next to her. "Well, get up here then. We can't have you disappointed on your first sleepover."

"Really?" Before Eva could finish nodding, the little Crafter was snuggling into her side.

"Have you ever been to a sleepover, Eva?" Gemma asked.

"Yea, my cousins and I would have them all the time. But we never really slept much, so I don't know why we always called them sleepovers. Kinda weird, huh?" The young elephant keeper mused.

Gemma turned and saw Wren's light brown curls bounce as she nodded. They lay there silent for a bit, as if they were trying to finally go to bed.

"Do you miss them? Your cousins?" Gemma asked Eva.

Eva didn't answer for a long moment. It got to where Gemma thought she'd fallen asleep after all. But then she spoke.

"I miss them every day." Her voice was quiet and fast, as if she'd get in trouble for saying such a thing. "I miss my Mama and my Papa. And my sister and my brother." Her thin voice wavered. "But I miss Grandma and Grandpa the most. Grandma always baked extra cookies for me to take home, and Grandpa gave the best hugs. I miss them all so much."

Gemma could hear the tears in her friend's voice and got off her cot so she could climb into bed with the other two. She positioned herself on Eva's other side so both girls could comfort her.

"I miss my Momma too. She used to tell me one day we'd live in one of the big houses on the hill and eat sweets every day. I didn't mind our little house and sharing a bed with her every night, but it was fun to dream. I miss her so much." Wren's lower lip trembled, and she buried her head in Eva's side.

"My Momma only left a bit ago, but it hurts so much knowing she isn't here. I'm so scared something bad is going to happen to her."

The three girls clung to each other and cried, giving voice to the pain and hurt they felt at being separated from their loved ones. They cried until they didn't have any tears left and started to doze.

Gemma didn't want to go to sleep and face the nightmares waiting for her, so she wracked her brain for something else to talk about.

"Do you guys wanna know a secret?"

Wren's head perked up at the promise of knowledge nobody else knew. "Yes! Yes! Yes!" She squealed.

Eva was more reserved, thoughts of her loved ones still on her mind. "What kind of secret?"

"It's about me and what I can do with my magic." Gemma slipped out from under the covers and went to the middle of the room. She grabbed something from her pack and knelt in the middle of the floor. She moved the rug from the floor to reveal bare ground.

Eva and Wren shifted, so they laid sideways on the bed, rolling onto their bellies and propping themselves on their elbows to get a better view of Gemma. Eva furrowed her brows.

"What do you mean? You're a Herbalist, right? I think J said you had an affinity for growing things." The young girl didn't understand what the five-year-old was getting at.

Gemma's eyes glittered as her gray eyes met Eva's brown ones. "Yea, but that's not the only thing I can do." She spread the seeds over the bare ground and placed her hands over them, closing her eyes.

Gemma reached inside her core and let herself admire the warm fuzzy feeling she always found when she reached for her magic. She saw green everywhere inside where her magic lived. It seemed to hum the lullaby her mother always sang to her before bed. The little girl felt tears prick at the corners of her eyes at the memory. She took a deep breath like Rae taught her and let herself surrender to the green light.

When she opened her eyes, a plant now grew from the frozen ground. Gemma felt her energy stores drain a little and sent a feeling of gratitude to the magic at her core.

Her Momma always said to show gratitude whenever possible especially now that they were out of the city. Being grateful was a way to make sure people kept helping you when you needed it. So Gemma started thanking her magic every time she used it. She never wanted to lose that fuzzy warm feeling from her insides.

Her eyes glanced at her two audience members and she smiled. Eva looked bored, but little Wren's eyes were filled with amazement.

"I wish I had magic like that," Wren whispered with yearning.

Eva snorted. "No, you don't. Magic is troublesome. If there was no magic, I would still be at home with my family." Her tone was filled with bitterness and scorn.

Wren looked taken aback, but Gemma furrowed her brows and asked, "Is that why you don't work with the other Forgers?"

Eva claimed she was a wood Forger, but she'd never really trained in it and had no intention of ever doing so. She said she was too busy helping J with the elephants, but something rang hollow when she mentioned it. Everybody assumed Wren would be a water Crafter, but nothing had stirred within her since she'd joined the Circus. She'd told Gemma she didn't think she was magical at all and didn't understand why everybody thought she would be.

The two girls acted as if they were Mortals and Gemma couldn't understand why. She'd spent most of her life hiding who she was and what she could do from everyone, including her own father. The freedom to use her power whenever she wanted was a novelty that wouldn't wear off. Why wouldn't they explore their power when they had the chance?

Eva shook her head, but her eyes gave away her pain. Gemma would bet the loss of her family was holding her back from developing her Forging skills.

It made her sad that her friend couldn't see how wonderful magic could be. Or how it felt to create something with just the power in her blood and her own two hands.

"Using my magic is my favorite thing in the world. You should try it even if it hurts at first." She saw Eva's drawn expression and furrowed her brows, confused by the older girl's reaction.

"Maybe. But get on with it. What's so special about you growing a plant? I already knew you could do that." Eva sent the Herbalist an expectant look.

Gemma grinned. "Do you know what plant this is?"

Both girls shook their heads.

"I don't either. Not until I touch it." The little girl with copper curls stroked the plant's leaves softly and closed her eyes. This time when she reached for her magic, it was less green and more blue, with distinct words instead of a simple hum.

Her eyes flashed open and found her friends' gazes. "This plant is called yarrow. It can be a salve for cuts or a tonic to help settle the tummy." Eva's eyes widened as understanding of what this meant filled her face. Wren just grinned at the girl on the ground.

"That's so cool! What else can you do?" The girl's striking blue eyes glittered with a hunger for learning more about Gemma's power.

Gemma giggled at the little girl's words. "I can make the salves and tonics too, but need more supplies for that. Nothing else, though. Pretty average, if you ask me." She beamed at Wren before looking at Eva again.

The older girl had a curious expression on her face. "That's remarkable, Gemma. Have you told anyone about this?"

Gemma ducked her head, using a small knife to cut the plant at the stalk and set it on the table. She'd set it to drying in the morning. In the meantime, she replaced the rug and bounded back to her own bed.

Once she was snuggled and safe under the covers, she answered. "No. My Momma always told me to keep it a secret, so I did. You two are the only ones that know."

"Sweet!" Wren exclaimed through a yawn.

"We should go to bed," Gemma insisted, unease filling her belly at Eva's persistence about this.

*Maybe I shouldn't have told them.* Gemma thought to herself. But she'd gotten caught up in the moment and had wanted to tell them something nobody else knew. She wanted the three of them to share something that was just theirs.

She lay wide awake as little Wren dissolved into snores and Eva's breathing settled into an even rhythm. Gemma stared up at the top of the tent and considered everything they'd talked about.

Before she knew it, her eyes drooped, and she rolled over, settling into the first night of sleep without nightmares since her mother had left.

Luc smiled to herself as she checked off another carrier group done with training.

*At this rate, our people will be ready in no time.*

As she'd promised, they'd met with their people the night before and went over routes with the carriers and training schedules for the spies. All morning, the carriers memorized their routes, gathered and packed supplies for the road, and finalized their acts and background stories. Once they were confident in all of that, they made their way to their region director and presented what they had.

When the director signed off, they headed out to travel their route once in a dry run. They were supposed to keep their heads down and simply run the route to scout out the cities they'd be visiting. Once they did a dry run, they'd send a report via one of the Shifters acting as a messenger, taking it back to the Mantaga Lake settlement. From there, they'd be able to start running it in full, connecting with the Circus contacts in each city and collecting people in need.

If and when groups had civilians needing sanctuary, they would escort them to the settlement and pick up ammunitions and supplies for the front lines. They'd stop to drop supplies wherever needed and then continue back to their routes.

Depending on what happened with the front lines, there was also the possibility they would switch routes, but that would be determined when the time came. At this point of the operation, they wanted to get boots on the ground and make sure their people were comfortable with what they were being asked to do.

The spies were going through a more rigorous training program where they studied everything they knew about the cities they were going to, the people in power there, and the best ways to gain access to those people. Once they'd done all that, they took a course that covered the basics of lock picking, camouflage, pick-pocketing, and lipreading. It was extensive, meant to last a few days before the spies were sent out. They could afford to take more time preparing, since there was no opportunity for a dry run. They would be jumping in feet first when they got to their assigned cities.

Damien would be doing that.

Huntress, just thinking about it made her want to throw up.

*Don't think about that right now. Training is still going on for another few days. Focus on what you have, not what you don't.*

She chided herself, trying to keep the fear and worry at bay by looking back at her clipboard.

"Luc? Do you have a moment?" Someone asked from behind her.

She turned, expecting to see someone from the carrier group needing help finding supplies, and stared in surprise.

"George, right?" He nodded. "Yea, I guess I have some time to spare. I just need to be available should any groups need approval to move onto their dry runs."

"It'll only take a few minutes. We've never officially met and I hate to ask a favor from someone I don't know, but you seem to be the only one capable of having a shot at getting it done."

Luc frowned and studied the lanky man. He was in his mid-thirties with unassuming brown hair and brown eyes. He wasn't the skinniest man she'd ever seen, but close to it. The man was of average height and stood stock still, his eyes being the only things moving. They never stopped scanning his surroundings, as if he expected a threat at any moment.

He met her gaze, and she saw self-loathing and anxiousness pooling in them.

She set her board and writing stele down and crossed her arms. "I can't promise you anything, but I'll bite. What favor do you need from me?"

Luc was being standoffish because of the way he'd interacted with Rae and the aloof way he interacted with anybody not from Heimat.

And a favor seemed like a lot to ask from someone you'd never spoken to.

She lifted an eyebrow and gave him an expectant look.

He cleared his throat and gathered his thoughts. "I need to know what happened to my brother. The last I heard, he'd left for one of the other small towns near Heimat. Could you ask your people to keep an eye out for him?"

Luc cocked her head in thought. She picked up her clipboard again and made a note. "Describe him for me."

"He's my height, maybe a little shorter, with dirty blond hair and blue eyes. He's the kind of guy who turns heads with his looks and the confidence he exudes. Tommy can strike up a conversation with just about anybody. I would imagine once your people started looking, they'd find him pretty quick."

Luc nodded. "I'll let them know. Anything you want them to tell him if they do find him?"

"Tell him I still expect him to uphold the promise he made to me before I left." He waited for Luc's nod before continuing. "Thanks. It means a lot." He turned to go.

"Wait. Did I hear that you almost went through the ice yesterday?" She asked, trying to keep him from leaving so she could learn more about him.

He hung his head. "Yea. It was a stupid drunken bet. Reg was the one that went through the ice, but I got him out before he suffered serious injury. And that's why I couldn't ask your people myself. They'd already left for training and I didn't want to interrupt."

Luc tilted her head as she processed this new information. "That was very thoughtful of you. I appreciate it." She tapped her chin with one finger. "Is it also true you can slip through Heimat in broad daylight with nobody noticing you?"

"Aye." The man didn't offer any other explanation.

"But you're not on my list of spies."

George furrowed his brows. "Because I'm needed on the front lines. I need to fight for my loved ones."

"There are other ways to do that. You should consider the communications group. If you're as good as they claim, we could use you in Heimat."

"Maybe. I'll think about it," George hedged before turning his back on her.

The man from Heimat left as quietly as he came.

*Well, at least I tried. Time will tell if it does any good.*

Luc thought to herself, jotting a few more notes down about what she needed to relay to Gar and the groups traveling in the North. Before she could make her way to him, another group of carriers came to her, hoping to get their approval to head out.

She beamed at the two women. "Show me what you've got."

Luc became enthralled in helping the two women and the rest of her groups prepare for their dry runs.

The snow was melting around their camp and everyone was feeling the energy that came with spring and their march for Heimat. Soon enough, it would be time to strike back at those who meant them harm.

The Resistance was mobilizing.

# Chapter Thirty-Six

Naya woke with a shiver. Momentarily, she panicked in the inky darkness, not recognizing where she laid. Her hands clutched at their surroundings and were met with a warm softness that felt like flesh. Her brain went into overdrive, imagining bodies fresh with death and children gagged and bleeding.

Naya's breaths came in rapid puffs as her eyes adjusted to the darkness. She made out what looked like an entrance to a tunnel.

And then it came rushing back to her.

After she and Ophelia learned the true nature of the Priestesses, Naya had taken off at a run. Ophelia yelled after her, but Naya hadn't cared.

The Sisters were keeping Magicae children locked until they were ready to be used by Myra and her scientists. And she'd led the twins straight into the heart of it.

She'd needed to find them and get them the hell out of this terrible place. But by the time she'd gotten to the cave, her adrenaline wore off and her bones felt dead tired. She'd decided to wait until morning. It was a risk, but crossing the melting river in the middle of the night was too dangerous. There were soft spots that could only be seen in the daylight.

She'd made it to the cave and crawled between her two charges, letting their warmth comfort and soothe her into sleep.

But now they had to leave.

She got up carefully, easing herself from under the covers without waking the little ones.

"Kaia! Are you in there?" A voice sounded from the opening and Naya cursed under her breath.

She marched to the entrance, knowing the only person dumb enough to be here this early was Ophelia. Finding the older girl, she took her by the arm and pulled her to the side of the cave, out of earshot from the little ones.

"Are you *nuts*?" Naya hissed, already annoyed before the sun had come up.

"Kaia! You left in such a hurry, I couldn't thank you for your help. That was exactly what I'd been hoping to find." Ophelia threw her arms around the younger girl and Naya threw her off with an indignant stare.

"What do you mean?"

"We knew the priestesses were up to something, but needed to know what exactly. That Mother Superior? She was appointed by Myra herself after the previous one fell suspiciously ill. Sounds like something out of a storybook, eh?" Ophelia shot Naya a conspiratorial grin.

Naya shook her head. "I don't care. I need to get the twins out of here. You heard them. They're keeping Magicae children locked up. They can't get their hands on Hawk and Aurora." She clenched her fists in anger and frustration, recognizing there were few safe places left for them. She thought the sisters would provide them safety, not another threat.

Ophelia's expression sobered. She reached out for Naya, but the younger girl flinched away from her fingers. "Kaia, it's okay. You can come with me. There's a warehouse in Bayside that I'm supposed to head to after getting the information. The twins will be safe there."

Naya narrowed her eyes, not convinced she could trust the older girl. "How do I know you're telling the truth?"

Ophelia rolled her eyes and threw her hands up. "Come on. I've known about the twins for weeks and haven't said a word. My sister's best friend was a water Crafter, and we had to watch her die because of Myra. She wept for days. My parents fought so much, feeling guilty for the girl's death and not taking a stand against the tyrant. We have a plan, but we needed to tie up a few loose ends. Luckily, the North is giving them a doozy of a time, and Myra herself is tweaking. Consider your options, kid. Better to come with someone you kinda know than wandering the city alone."

Naya's head pounded. Ophelia stared at her with those big blue eyes, but she couldn't think. She'd spent her entire life not trusting others and her gut urged her to stay the course and not accept help from anyone, especially someone so eager. But her heart knew the three of them wouldn't last more than a couple of days in the city alone. She couldn't go back to the safe house after the fiasco with Corbin and Raj, and Ryker was in the guard. He'd been useless the last time she went to him and more annoyed than she expected.

There was so much at stake.

*I'm sick of this. I'm sick of not having any options. We need to get off the island. If Ophelia can do that, we should go with her. Once we get to the warehouse, we can go our separate ways.*

Making up her mind, she held her hand out to the older girl. A wide grin spread across the girl's face.

"I knew you were smart, kid. Tell your young charges to be packed and ready by the time the sun comes up. We need to go get supplies." Ophelia released Naya's forearm and turned back to the Temple.

Naya gave a nod. "I'll meet you by the steps."

Ophelia turned back and gave her a wink. "It's a date."

Naya watched her disappear and shook her head. *Rich people. So fucking full of themselves.*

She went back to the cave and gently shook the twins awake. She told them to be ready to leave by dawn. They'd agreed with sleepy voices. Naya doubted they'd be ready, but the twins had surprised her before.

She donned her postulant robe and made her way back to the Temple. It was still too early for the priestesses to be awake, which was a relief. Maybe the postulants didn't know, but the rest of the sisters had to be aware of what took place in the catacombs of this prison. Naya started up the steps to the heavy wooden doors.

Ophelia appeared out of nowhere and made Naya jump. "Fancy seeing you here, K. You in the mood for some prayers before breakfast?" Ophelia's eyes glittered, enjoying the charade they were putting on.

Naya grumbled and muttered something.

"What was that? I can't quite hear you."

"Kaia isn't my name. It's Naya, but don't call me that until we leave." Naya scowled at the older girl.

Ophelia let out a chuckle. "You really are paranoid. No matter, nothing to worry about sharing a secret with a good friend." Ophelia linked her arm through Naya's and they ascended the steps together. They pushed on the heavy doors and entered the silent sanctuary. Naya's stomach rolled as memories of the night previous rattled in her head. She could still hear Myra's disgust when mentioning the Magicae children imprisoned beneath her feet.

*I'm going to be sick.*

Naya ran for the bin and wretched her guts out.

A hand held her hair back, while another stroked her back. Naya relaxed into the comfort before remembering who provided it. She shrugged Ophelia off and wiped her chin with her sleeve.

"I know how you feel. It makes me sick just thinking about it, but my parents have a plan. We'll get them out. They only have to last a little longer." Ophelia's voice was a whisper.

Naya wanted to argue. She wanted to rage and destroy this place floorboard by floorboard. She glimpsed a sparkle and turned to see the pink orb held by the Goddess statue in the front of the Temple. "You go get the supplies. I'm going to take the pearl." Naya took off her cloak and strode towards the raised dais that held the altar with the statues above it.

"You're crazy. I'll grab the stuff we need. Don't get caught." Ophelia's tone implied she was impressed by Naya's boldness. She rushed out of the sanctuary toward the kitchens.

Naya took the steps up to the altar and felt like she was going to be sick again. The Mother Superior had addressed the postulants several times with an air of arrogance that made Naya's skin crawl.

*I wonder what she'll think when this precious pearl is gone.*

She moved around the altar to the pillar that held the statue of the Goddess. It was almost twice Naya's height and made of smooth marble. She tried to palm the cold stone, but could find no traction. She turned to scan the room and found several chairs behind the altar.

Naya could use them to give her something to climb on. Once she got on the pedestal, she would be able to climb the rough stone statue of the Goddess. She stacked the chairs and took a deep breath. She used her arms to hoist herself up, and they shook, not used to the physical exertion. With a grunt, she heaved herself up onto the first two chairs and took a break.

A sound to her left made her freeze.

She kept as still as the statue she climbed until a couple of minutes passed by. She resumed her climbing with more determination. Naya needed to hurry.

Her arms and legs shook as she hoisted herself up onto the next chair. It was still a big step to get to the statue, but Naya hooked her arms around the statue's legs and pulled her belly onto the ledge of the pedestal. Once Naya's weight was supported by the pedestal, she unhooked her arms and raised herself into a standing position. She was face-to-face with the Goddess and felt the urge to spit on the statue, but something made her pause.

Naya didn't believe an old woman in the sky looked down on everyone, but what if she was real? *She'd be a shit goddess for all the horror she let people go through, but maybe something prevents her from interfering. Do I really want to risk earning her disfavor?*

The answer was no, but she was still going to take the pearl. If she was truly a good goddess, she'd have no use for material goods. She stood on her tiptoes and followed the statue's arm with her fingers to where she held the pink pearl aloft. Naya's fingers brushed the smooth sphere, but couldn't get a grip on it.

She groaned in frustration. Licking her lips, she tried again and leaned further than before, hooking one arm around the Goddess's stone one. This time, she could palm the pink pearl and used every bit of her strength to lift it from the stone hand holding it.

It wouldn't budge.

Naya strained further and tried to dislodge it as best she could. She heard a crack and almost lost her balance. She managed to stay upright, but just barely. Her arms and legs shook, and she knew she was tempting fate by staying here too long.

*I'll give it one more go.*

She hooked her arm again and reached as far as she could. This time, when she pulled the pearl, it came away easily and something crashed to the ground.

Naya curled her body around the pearl protectively and shut her eyes, waiting for the whole statue to come crashing down.

Nothing happened.

When Naya opened her eyes, she realized two of the Goddess's fingers had come loose and crashed to the floor. She whispered an apology to the statue and climbed down from the chairs. She put the pearl in her pocket and strode to the doors. The sound of a door banging open behind her made Naya speed into the shadows. Sister What's-her-name saw the fingers on the floor and looked up. She saw the missing pearl and started screaming. "Thieves! Thieves in the sanctuary! Someone tell the Mother Superior."

She exited the sanctuary and Naya slipped out of the doors. An arm pulled her into the bushes, while another clamped over her mouth. "I hope you got what you wanted. We need to move." Naya recognized Ophelia's voice and relaxed. All they had to do was get the twins and get off the accursed island.

Her fingers brushed the smooth sheen of the pearl in her pocket and she frowned.

She felt raised lines spider webbing across the surface, as if the pearl was cracking.

*That's not good.*

Bane swooped down and banked as he approached the farmhouse, alighting on one tree between the house and the barn. He cocked his avian head and watched the hustle and bustle happening below him.

The population at the farmhouse seemed to have tripled in size since he'd been here last. He watched a group of kids chase one golden-haired man clear across the yard before tackling him to the ground. A few adults moved between the buildings while others seemed to be starting construction on a new structure.

*What is going on here?*

He chattered when he saw Rich emerge from the farmhouse. The old man looked up and waved in recognition. Bane flew down from the branch to land on his shoulder. He readjusted his wings and crouched low, content to stay where he was and see more of the place.

"We've added a few more people since you last visited." Rich gave a chuckle. "If I were you, I'd think we were starting a commune or something. Want me to show you around?"

Bane chattered in his ear and bobbed his head several times.

"Excellent." Rich took him into the barn and explained how they'd converted it into a bunkhouse. He pointed out some of the new adults and told him why they'd come to the farmhouse.

Bane soaked it all in, glad to be in his avian form and have an excuse to listen without obligation to offer responses or ask questions. Sometimes he wished he could stay in his animal form indefinitely. It would make life that much simpler.

Rich paused at the changing room and Bane chattered in his ear, flying into the space and shooting him a look. Rich closed the door and handed over a pair of trousers and a thick wool sweater.

Bane donned them and followed Rich back into the yard.

"Great. Now that you can speak again, any questions?"

Bane shook his head. "What you're doing here is admirable. It's unbelievable how many people you've housed on such short notice. I am thoroughly impressed and happy to have your genius on our side."

Bane knew he was laying it on a little thick, but in times like these, celebrating the wins was as important as mourning their losses. Rich should take pride in what he'd turned this place into. And maybe it would soften the blow of the intel he had from Mirabella.

"Who's this new face? Was there another arrival I missed?"

Bane looked up and locked eyes with the blond-haired man from earlier.

"This is Bane. He's from the Circus and brings news from Heimat. Bane, this is Tommy—,"

"You're George's brother." Bane interrupted Rich and offered his hand to the young man.

Tommy gave it a firm shake and nodded. "Sorry you had to meet him before me. He can be a little rough around the edges."

Bane smirked. "You could say that again."

Tommy chuckled and held up a hand. "Don't get too carried away now. He's still my brother."

"Noted."

"Is it true you have news from Heimat?"

Bane gave another nod. "And from your brother."

Tommy's eyes widened. "What information do you have from Georgie?"

Bane met the affable man's eyes. "He wanted to let you know he still expects you to keep your promise."

Tommy frowned. "I never intended to do anything else." He shook his head. "Who else needs to hear the news from Heimat?"

Bane decided he liked the straight-shooter and good-humored man. "The less people, the better, but I'll leave that discretion up to Rich."

The old baker rubbed his chin. "We should include Anna and Diane, but otherwise, I think we can inform the rest of them."

"Right. I'll go grab them and meet you guys..." Tommy trailed off, his body already en route to the front door while he kept his head cocked to hear Rich's response.

Bane watched Rich consider their options. "Tell the women to bring their coats. It's warm enough we could go to the hill."

"On it!" Tommy bounded toward the house, avoiding the group of kids calling his name.

Rich chuckled. "Oh, to have that much energy again."

Bane nodded. "I don't think I ever had that much, even as a kid."

"Tommy is a good man and an even better father. Don't let his exuberance fool you. He's as dedicated to this cause as anybody."

Bane let the statement hang in the air. He believed Rich, but wouldn't commit to agreeing with the man before he'd seen it himself. They waited for the three to reemerge.

Once they did, Rich led the way to the hill about a mile from the house. The four chatted while Bane stayed quiet, content to listen and soak in the familiar rhythms of gossip and domestic logistics. He walked behind them, keeping his eyes and ears peeled for anything out of the ordinary.

There was a lull in the conversation and Tommy held back until he was in step with Bane. When the conversation ahead of them continued, Tommy spoke.

"I hear you're the one I need to thank for saving my wife and son."

Bane met the man's gaze and everything clicked into place. "You're married to Sara?"

Tommy nodded. "I asked for her hand as soon as I could, worried she'd wake up and realize she was too good for me. That little boy makes four young ones and I couldn't be happier."

"Your wife did the hard work. I provided her with a little energy. Her will to live and protect her baby saved her. She's an incredibly strong woman." Bane insisted, uncomfortable taking praise for something he didn't do.

"That she is. But you gave her the energy she needed to keep fighting. And I can't thank you enough." Tommy's stare was intense.

Bane gave a shrug. "Anybody would've helped a woman in such distress."

Tommy sighed in frustration. "Still, you're the one who did it, so I thank you."

"You're welcome."

Silence stretched between the two men until Rich stopped the group.

"This is far enough. Let's make it quick before the kids let their curiosity get the best of them." Rich offered a knowing smile, and the group nodded.

"Right, so I'll get straight to the point. You're not safe here. I know Vincenzio and his soldiers have left you alone, but war is coming. Myra's son, Mallick, and his Blades join Vincenzio in Heimat tonight. They intend on attacking and sacking the nearby cities to lure the Circus into attacking. We need to get our people out of those places as soon as we can.

"I know a lot of you came from those towns because something was attacking the Mortals there. I can confirm groups of Shifters and Elven soldiers from the Forest are responsible for those. They are doing it in retribution for how Mortals have treated and oppressed them in the past. We have people working on stopping those raids and the Circus has set up a settlement deep within the forest. People are being trained as carriers for supplies and people.

"I've sent missives on ahead, letting those in charge know we need to evacuate as soon as possible. Messages were also sent to the contacts we still have in the neighboring towns. The carriers will make their rounds and evacuate as many as possible, including from this very farmhouse.

"I need you to be ready for when they come." Bane paused to breathe, taking in the stunned expressions on everybody's faces.

Tommy was the first to recover. "We'll be ready. And what about those of us that want to fight? You're evacuating people, but when do we strike back at that son of a bitch?"

Bane gave a feral grin. "Many of our people have been training for weeks in combat and battle strategy. They march as soon as the snow melts to take Heimat. This new information could change their strategy, but the plan to attack will still stand. It's time we take back what's ours."

"Pretty words, boy, but how do we know it's all true? And do you even have the resources to mount such an attack?" Anna asked with a skeptical tone.

"My next stop is Verdencia, the Elven's city, to help our people meeting with the Elven and the Shifters. We aim to garner their support and attack as one, as we did when Vincenzio's men reached the Elven city." Bane answered, knowing it still wasn't an absolute solution.

Anna grunted. "And what happens if they don't agree?"

"They will. The Elven and the Shifters of the Forest have the same purpose as we do. They want Myra gone, and the first step is taking back our sanctuary."

Anna didn't have a counterargument and fell silent.

"So we get ready to leave and then what? Shouldn't we help evacuate as many people as we can?" Tommy pushed, his frustration apparent in the way he clenched his fists and squared his shoulders.

The rest of the group looked to Bane for answers. He considered Tommy's suggestion and gave a slow nod.

"Yes. It'll be dangerous, but if you want to get the Magicae out, do it. The sooner we get this done, the better. Start with the towns closest to Heimat and work your way out. I wouldn't advise bringing them back here, but it's also the only place you have. If you bring them here, make sure the Magicae have a secure place to hide should the soldiers come. They won't hesitate to burn this place to the ground and take everybody into custody if they find them."

Tommy nodded. "Understood. We'll figure something out."

There was a pause in the conversation. When it was clear Bane wasn't going to add anything else, Rich spoke up.

"If there's nothing else, we best get started. Bane, what else do you need from us? Any supplies we can give you? Or advice on how to avoid the patrols?"

Bane shook his head. "If we're done, I'll leave from here to save some time. Stay safe and be ready for when the carriers come."

"Same to you, Bane," Rich answered as the others nodded.

With that, Bane took his leave, jogging until he could Shift into his avian form again.

# Chapter Thirty-Seven

Tyee growled when he saw the woman he'd been searching for. He strode toward her and gripped her upper arm hard, letting his fingers dig into her as much as they could. He jerked her away from the man she spoke with and gritted his teeth as she laughed.

"Somebody woke up on the wrong side of the bed."

"If it were up to you, I wouldn't have woken up at all." He hissed at her, pulling her out of earshot from the Elven standing outside the gathering hall.

Sylvie sent him an innocent look and shook him off. "I don't know what you're talking about."

"Cut the shit, Sylvie. You sent the wolf and then the lions. You almost killed an innocent old woman and a teenager. Your actions deserve consequences." Tyee was seething. Three lionesses attacked them in the cottages the night before. The only reason they'd survived was because of Javie's quick thinking and Fritz's generosity while they dispatched the lionesses. Their deaths weighed as heavily on him as the wolf's did. They shouldn't have had to die.

The Elven general frowned at him. "Be careful what you say, halfbreed. Your words are coming awfully close to treason."

"Fuck that. You're trying to get rid of me before the bonding ceremony, but it's done. It happens tomorrow, and then we have to figure out a way to move forward. Face the truth, Sylvie, this is happening. But you need to be held accountable for what you've done." Tyee shot the Elven woman a hard look.

Sylvie's eyes flashed with anger. "And you think you're the one to do that?"

Tyee didn't back down. "I'm not scared of you, Sylvie. I used to be, but not anymore."

"We'll see about that." Sylvie shot him a cruel smile, and he felt her claws reaching into his head.

Tyee was ready for her. He closed off his mind and placed a hand on the Uraz rune on his wrist, standing for strength and resilience.

They squared off and Tyee held his own against Sylvie's assault on his mind. He could feel his strength waning, but he held on, determined to keep the woman from trying to speak to his mind.

With a cry of frustration, Sylvie fell to the ground, exhausted by her efforts. Before Tyee could utter a sound, she was on her feet spitting fury at him.

"Fuck off, Tyee. This is bullshit and you know it. I shouldn't be forced to share the throne with the likes of you, or anybody. The crown is *mine* and you better be ready to kill me or sleep with a knife because I will never stop trying to *end you*."

She bared her teeth at him before whirling past him, knocking her shoulder against his and sending pain rippling up his arm still sore from where the wolf drew blood.

Tyee clutched at it and turned to watch her leave. The woman was a lot of things, but a liar wasn't one of them. He needed to keep his guard up if he hoped to survive the next couple of days.

"Shit." He murmured under his breath, feeling a headache coming on.

He held onto the rope railing that separated him from the ground below, willing the pounding away. When he could see straight again, he walked to the gathering space and sat on one of the benches dotting its outside.

He'd done it. He'd kept Sylvie out of his head and hadn't needed to draw from Rae to do it. At least he didn't think he'd had to. He dropped his elbows to his knees and leaned over, closing his eyes to search for the string that connected the two of them.

He gripped the string and gave a gentle squeeze, feeling for any signs of weakness on Rae's side. A burning sensation made Tyee jump.

Nope, Rae was doing just fine. He hadn't needed to pull from her. He felt like a wagon ran him over but it was progress. Once the pounding in his head lessened enough to be ignored, he stood and made for one of the ladders.

Fritz was training with some of the other guards, and Tyee meant to join them. Since getting the two runes inked onto his skin, finding and using the power in his blood had become easier. But Tyee wasn't convinced he was ready to use them on the battlefield. He would rely on his skills as a marksman and survivalist before he'd rely on the runes that drained him every time he drew one.

He made his way to the ground and headed towards the field they were using as a training ground. The bonding ceremony between him and Sylvie happened tomorrow, and he had every intention of throwing himself into anything that could distract him. His stomach roiled just thinking about ruling the city at Sylvie's side.

With any luck, one or both of them would be dead by the end of this and their problems would be solved.

Nan was in the infirmary watching Hugo describe the various tinctures and salves unique to the Elven due to the scarcity of their ingredients in most of Kamore. She was fascinated by their approach to healing and the role of medicine in such things.

The Elven were heavily influenced by Skaber or the Creator that embodied all of nature. Skaber was found in everything that breathed and lived, the cycles of the seasons, and how the sun and moon rose each day and night. Skaber was a spirit and not a spirit, ever-present yet never visible.

And Skaber was from whom their knowledge of medicine, healing, and foods came from. And thus, Skaber was induced in every healing that took place in the infirmary.

It was a mesmerizing sight to see and soothed the soul, if nothing else.

It spoke to the deepest part of Nan as she listened with reverence.

The Elven people were a beautiful anomaly.

Hugo moved on to a cupboard filled with dressings of every size and shape. He described what they were made of, how they were made, and the importance of weaving an oak fiber into every one, courtesy of the Mother Oak just outside the city.

Again, Nan was struck by how deeply the Elven culture and traditions were entwined with their understanding of healing and medicine.

*How remarkable. Simply remarkable.*

Hugo excused himself to help one of the younger Healers, leaving Nan to stare at their supply stores for a few more moments, taking in the wall of organized supplies, waiting to be used.

*They have so many resources.* She mused to herself, impressed by their industriousness. The Resistance wouldn't last if they didn't have support from the Elven. They might get by without the Shifters, but the Elven would mean the difference between success and failure.

The old Herbalist frowned and turned to face the room. She leaned against the counter and watched Elven Healers maneuver between beds and patients.

They didn't have the numbers they once did, but they had heart. And having heart meant more than anything. She needed to gain another audience with the Queen and tip the scales in their favor. Tyee already bargained with the royal, but another push wouldn't hurt. She needed to convince Ulla that allying with the Circus would give them the best shot at achieving their mutual goals. She'd explain the network they had throughout Kamore and how they were organizing to make the most use of it.

Nan started going over what she'd say when she met with the Queen and lost track of time.

A familiar face drew from her reverie. "Hey! I was hoping I'd run into you if I stood here long enough." Her eyes filled with warmth at the sight of the young Healer.

Freya grinned widely. "Abuela! I didn't know you were coming. I hope you didn't travel alone."

Nan gripped the young woman's hands and lifted her eyebrows. "Should I not have?"

The look of horror on Freya's face made Nan chuckle. She patted the girl's shoulder and relented. "I'm teasing, dearie. Javie's around here somewhere. He made sure I arrived in one piece."

Freya shook her head. "Thank Skaber. You almost gave me a heart attack with talk like that. But seriously, why are you here?" The Herbalist cocked her head.

"Chiara got your letter, and we worried Tyee would need help in convincing the Queen." Nan noted the way Freya's eyes darkened at the mention of Tyee's bargain.

"I told him he was a fool. I don't know the guy that well, but he'd rather spend time on horseback than anywhere else. How can you tie someone like that to a throne? How can you expect him to be happy bonded to a woman like Sylvia?"

Nan cast an anxious glance around the immediate area. When she looked back, Freya shook her head.

"It's okay to speak our minds in here, Abuela. The Healers respect Ulla and all she's done for the Elven people, but Sylvia is feared and hated. She trapped Tyee because she knew her people disapproved so much of her daughter. This is the only way to ensure Sylvia will still sit on the throne. But they're fools, Abuela. Sylvia is going to eat him alive. He could barely handle Rae, but Sylvia? She's a monster."

Nan put a hand on the woman's shoulder. "I know, dearie. The bonding ceremony takes place tomorrow, no?" At Freya's nod, Nan continued. "There's no way to stop that, but tell me more about the ceremony. What happens and what does it mean?"

Freya sighed. "It's more formal than a pledging ceremony, but less binding than the blood bond. You have no idea what either of those are, do you?" Nan shook her head with a smile and Freya put her hand to her forehead. "Damn, I think I've been here a little too long. So many things seem normal now that you and the others would never understand. A pledging ceremony is made on behalf of children with the understanding that either child can break the pledge at any point. However, if the children decide to honor the promise as adults, the union is seen as twice blessed. So some Elven still do a pledging ceremony, even though it's very rare that they're ever upheld. A blood bond is what Tyee and Rae share. Usually, the blood bond is performed after a bonding ceremony, which is like a marriage but without the option for separation. Once an Elven is mated or bonded, they can't rebond with someone else."

Nan frowned. "So they're stuck with the same person for the rest of their lives? What if there's abuse? What if they grow apart or something tragic happens they can't get past?"

Freya shrugged. "Most people don't separate. Those that do, find new partners, but never get rebonded. It's not supposed to be a punishment. It's just one of their beliefs that Skaber can only unite two souls during one lifetime. Once your soul is entwined with another, you can't be untwined."

"And what if the one they're bonded to dies?"

"That's the beautiful part. Because your souls are entwined, their soul lives on until you also pass. So again, even if the one you're bonded to dies, you're not able to rebond with another."

Nan considered this for a minute. "Does Tyee understand all of this?"

"Definitely not, but Tyee hasn't had nearly enough time with the Elven to understand everything about them. From the little we've talked, it sounds like most of his instruction has been on rune lore and the history of the Elven. He hasn't had the opportunity to learn about customs or culture or family values. He's assuming this is like a marriage and once the dust settles, he'll be able to leave with no consequences."

"And how does the blood bond affect all of this?" Nan mused, her thoughts straying to Rae and the predicament he put her in

"Nobody knows. Hugo told some of the other Healers but asked them to keep it to themselves. As far as I'm aware, most of the Elven don't know what's happened between Tyee and Rae. But amongst the Healers, nobody knows if it will affect the ceremony. The blood bond is so serious and so consequential, nobody would dare take one without having their souls entwined first. And nowadays the blood bond is rarely taken because there's no use for it. This isn't a time of war, so there's no need to call upon another's energy supplies."

Nan smiled at the passion in Freya's voice. "You love it here, don't you?"

Freya nodded. "I do. I really love it here. These people are so welcoming and warm, and the way they live their lives is admirable. They care for the trees and the entire forest in a way that takes my breath away. And healing is more of an art form than I ever thought possible. I can use the power in my blood and a person's wound will stop bleeding, but they use the power of nature and the wound heals from the inside out. When we heal, there's still a phantom ache or a scar. When they heal, it's as if the wound never happened. They attribute it to Skaber and the power of being in harmony with other living things, but I think it's a miracle. Growing up, the Magicae were always thought of as different or too powerful, but the people who felt that way never met the Elven. The Magicae are more like Mortals than anyone realizes. We have the same values, we worship the same Goddess, and we share our philosophies of this life, but the Elven flip all of that on its head. It's a marvel that I would hate to see destroyed."

Nan saw fear enter Freya's gaze. "Myra needs to be stopped. Our people and their people will die, but we need to create a better world for our children and their children. Could you imagine a future where Verdencia was just another town on the map, another place to perform in?"

Freya swallowed. "I know, Abuela. The war that's coming is for so much more than what we first understood it to be. We are fighting for more than our own freedom, and that's something we should never take for granted."

"Amen. I know you've been invoking Skaber while you're here, but the Goddess smiles upon you, my dear. Your insight into the Elven will only be an asset in the coming days."

"Thanks, Abuela. I'll do all I can to ease any tension between our peoples." Freya gave her last smile as Hugo returned.

Freya gave her goodbyes while Hugo apologized for the interruption. Nan watched her go and smiled. Hope was the most powerful thing in this world.

She returned her attention to Hugo as he started describing the surgery instruments they used and what they were made from.

Javie was in the library of Verdencia. It was above the gathering space in the center of the maze of bridges and living buildings. He'd pulled several tomes from the shelves and was pouring over them at the table in the cavernous space.

He swore under his breath as the words spun beneath his gaze. Javie needed a break. He'd been at this for hours and had nothing to show for it. The Herbalist stood and cracked his neck, stretching his arms over his head and bending to stretch his sides.

Javie decided a walk and getting his blood pumping would do him some good. He did a lap around the library's first floor where the tables were.

There were four floors in the library, but only the ground level had a full floor to it. The rest of the levels were simply balconies that gave access to the shelves on each floor. Javie finished his lap and returned to the middle of the room before looking up. He could see the glass ceiling at the top of the building and the weak sunlight flickering in.

Needing more movement, he made for the stairs to the second floor. He'd been overwhelmed upon entering the impressive space and only really explored the shelves on the first floor. But maybe his answers were on a different one.

There were no librarians on staff and Javie regretted every time he'd wished they'd be gone back in Heimat. His search would've been that much easier if he'd had someone who could point him in the right direction.

But the reality was he was on his own.

He walked around the second floor, but nothing jumped out at him. He climbed the steps to the third floor and felt a pull towards his left. Curious, Javie let his instincts guide him to a thick, green book at the bottom. He heaved it out from its resting place and sighed in relief. Many of the books he'd pulled were entirely in Elvish and useless in his search.

But this book had a Mortal translation on the right side of the original Elven text. His eyes scanned the first couple of pages and he felt his heart beat a little faster.

*This is it.*

He sped down the stairs to his table. He pushed the other books to the side and let his eyes fly across the pages. The book was a history of Verdencia and went into the mechanics behind how the city was built. He devoured the information, looking for anything and everything he could.

An hour passed, and he finished the book. It mentioned the metal work in exactly one place. Javie flipped back to that section.

"Living metal." He whispered under his breath.

There were only a couple of lines about the work that went into those creations, but the Magicae who made them were described as being able to use and control the living metal.

*This is exactly what I was looking for.*

# Chapter Thirty-Eight

Rae gritted her teeth and sent another ball of flame at the downed tree. The log exploded with the onslaught of more fire and Rae allowed herself a small smile.

She whirled in a circle, and this time, sent water gushing at the flames. They sputtered out with a hiss as smoke floated to the sky.

Her magic and muscles sang with use and she felt alive for the first time in a while. She sent a wind to capture the smoke and moved it in a circle around her, dancing with the light gray particles as if they were a piece of silk. They caressed her cheek, and she sent them free, thrusting them higher and higher into the sky.

Without stopping, she stamped the ground, and pillars of earth spiraled to the sky. Once three spikes stood in front of her, she did another spin, sending some of her water forth so she was a spinning tempest. The spikes crumbled under the relentless pounding of the blades of water.

She stopped, panting, and surveyed her work. With a grunt, she straightened and took a hard stance. Rae clenched her jaw and reached for her earth Craft. It was still the one that came least intuitively and took the most energy to control. She felt her blood turn sluggish as sediment filled her veins and she commanded the earth into balls of rock. She beckoned them closer with a finger and then thrust her other hand forward as fast as she could.

The balls of sediment catapulted into the sky before shattering in a rain of dirt. She repeated the movement until all the crumbled earth was gone.

Exhausted, she bent over and put her hands on her knees, her breath coming in rasps.

*That's more like it.*

Rae finally felt strong again. It had been a week since Tyee drained her energy repeatedly and one night since Tyee visited her in her dreams.

Flames lit her palms at the thought that tomorrow, Tyee would tie himself to that bitch.

*Relax. There's nothing you can do about it until you get there.*

The flames dissolved, but her blood still boiled. Tyee claimed to love her, and she hadn't told him how she felt. He'd left before she could.

And now...

This time, both her arms burst into flames. She screamed, giving her emotions an outlet. She'd never felt so helpless. The flames doused themselves as her energy waned. Rae collapsed into tears on the ground, letting her feelings overwhelm her.

She felt a hand on her back and she cried harder.

"Want to talk about it?"

Hearing Zeke's familiar voice sent her into more hysterics. He wrapped his arms around her and rocked her back and forth.

Rae leaned into the moment until she wore herself out. Once she calmed down, she spoke.

"Huntress, who would've thought I could cry so much over a guy?"

She felt Zeke's chest rumble with laughter. "I sure didn't."

Rae laughed with him before sighing. "He's bonding himself to Sylvia tomorrow. And I never told him I loved him. He's going to join himself to her and I can't stop it."

Zeke shot her a puzzled look. "What? Since when?"

"I don't know. He left it out of the letter he sent. He agreed to it to make Ulla put a stop to the raids." Rae hung her head. "He thought it was the only way."

Zeke's eyes held the dismay she felt. "But why was that Ulla's demand?"

"Apparently he's a lost Elven prince or something? And this would ensure Sylvia still sat on the throne since the Elven people hate her." Rae shook her head. "She manipulated his freedom from him and I can't stand it."

Zeke rubbed her arms. "You two will get through this."

"Rae, Zeke. Just the two people I was looking for."

Both their heads whipped towards the voice as Duncan strode from the shadows.

Rae squeezed Zeke's hand and stood, helping him to his feet once she was up. Her legs trembled, but she stayed upright.

Duncan's lavender gaze studied the two of them and Rae knew he noticed the terse set to their faces, but he didn't push. He never pushed before someone was ready and Rae loved that about the older Crafter.

"Walk with me?" He asked.

Rae nodded, and Zeke followed suit. They walked after Duncan into the woods, winding down forest paths until they came to a quiet clearing.

Duncan stopped, and they looked at him expectedly.

"Bane sent Gar a message. Myra's son and his personal guard are en route to Heimat in order to support Vincenzio's control of the city. But Vincenzio's new plan is to take those resources and attack some of the smaller surrounding towns. He wants to coerce us into striking."

Rae put a hand to her chest. "Striking what? Heimat or the surrounding villages?"

*Those poor people.* Rae's heart hurt to think of everyone they'd left in Heimat and the people in those little towns they didn't save.

She clenched and unclenched her fists, keeping her flames in check.

"I wanted to ask the two of you to accompany me to Verdencia tomorrow and then on to Heimat. Mirabella seemed to think Vincenzio was trying to bait us into attacking the city proper. It's a risk, but the sooner we march, the less time it gives them to regroup. Luc is already redirecting her people to evacuate as many Magicae as they can."

"Have the Elven agreed to ally with us then?" Zeke asked.

"The only responding letter I received from the Queen was that we needed to discuss it in person. My intention is to send Vera and Conrad with most of our fighters down the river to wait until I give the signal. A small group of us will go to Verdencia, convince the Elven to join us, and then march to the city. The two-pronged attack should give us a leg up during the battle."

Rae took in his logic and inclined her head. "Seems like a solid plan. I'm in."

"Me too," Zeke replied without hesitation.

"Good. Pack your things and get a good night's sleep. We leave at dawn." Duncan's eyes softened as he met the younger Crafters' gazes. "Tie up any loose ends you have here. You'll need as clear heads as you can get before these next couple of weeks."

He inclined his head before heading back towards the settlement.

Rae leaned against a tree as her emotions came crashing back down. She swiped at her face and gave a growl. "Fucking Elven."

Zeke sent her a worried look.

Rae sighed as the tension left her entire body. "The worst part is we have to depend on that monster if we want to take our place in this world." She clenched her fists as flames burst from her palms, hinting at the anger underneath her skin.

Zeke tilted his head in thought. "Well, once we get to Verdencia, you can let all hell break loose. I'll help you."

Rae snorted. "You're something else, Z. We both know that can't happen." Her voice trailed off until it was a whisper. "My mom and dad created a life dictated by politics and the dance between influential figures. I never wanted that, yet here we are." She couldn't keep her voice from cracking at the mention of her parents.

*Some things cannot be changed.*

Huntress, how she hated those words and their knack for hitting her at the worst moments.

Zeke put a hand on her shoulder. "You're the one that got involved with a lost prince. Seems like you should've chosen better." He cracked a wry grin, desperate to distract her from such depressing thoughts.

Rae gave a bark of laughter and shook her head. She shoved Zeke's hand off of her and walked towards the settlement. "I need a drink. Wanna share a bottle of whiskey instead of dealing with reality?"

"Absolutely." Zeke looped his arm through hers and led her back to their tents.

Rae leaned her head on his shoulder, letting his warmth comfort her.

*When I get to Verdencia, I'll make it right. Sylvia better be ready for a fight.*

She sent a lick of fire through the mark on her palm. A smile graced her lips when she felt Tyee respond with the power in his blood. His life energy surged up the bond like lightning, entering her veins and filling her with warmth.

*We'll get through this.*

Mallick raised his glass and toasted Vincenzio's words.

*Arrogant bastard.* He thought to himself as he took a long swig from his goblet. He and his Blades arrived in Heimat mere hours before and Mallick already yearned for the road. Vincenzio and his wife greeted them in the courtyard outside where their soldiers were housed. Mallick and his men were given the opportunity to wash up and make themselves presentable for the feast in their honor.

They sat at long tables in the dining hall of the government building. One table sat on a raised dais and had places for Vincenzio, his wife, his advisors, and Mallick. When pressed, Vincenzio amended to allow Laurent a place at the table beside Mallick. Mallick counted it as a win against his mother's general. Mallick was like his mother, in this case, hating the ceremony and politics of such a production.

Or at least his supposed mother's footsteps.

*Don't think about that.* He thought to himself, stabbing a piece of meat on his plate. He still hadn't worked through the emotions regarding Naomi's admission. It was yet to be determined what was the truth and what was a plea to save her daughter.

He paused in his eating as the hall quieted and everyone looked at him. He glanced at the general who was giving him an expectant look and a smirk.

"It seems our new colonel is hard of hearing." Vincenzio boomed at the crowd and his soldiers laughed with gusto while the Blades stayed silent. Mallick could feel the tension in the room brewing.

It was up to him to keep the peace until the moment was right. "My apologies, Darren. What was it you asked of me?" Mallick questioned the general with an innocent grin, knowing how much he hated the use of his first name.

"I asked if you would like to give a word of encouragement to the soldiers down below. I'm sure they could benefit from some words about Myra's confidence in our combined forces." Vincenzio growled, annoyed at Mallick's careful way of toeing the line between decorum and insubordination.

Mallick felt his heartbeat flutter. He hated public speaking, but forced himself to do it in order to develop the skill he would need in the future. "I echo everything Darren said earlier. We are lucky to have such splendid and talented men and women fighting for the good of Kamore. The Goddess smiles down upon us today and every day as we fight to put an end to those who have twisted Her Gifts into something monstrous. There is no excuse for the way the Magicae have conducted themselves, and it's about time we put an end to their selfish ways. On behalf of my mother, I thank you for your service. Eat and drink tonight because tomorrow we spur Duncan and his band of misfits into action." He raised his goblet high in the air. "To you, brave soldiers. Without you, we would be defenseless against the horde of vermin that plagues our country."

The people echoed his thoughts and clinked glasses, impressed and flattered by their new colonel's words.

Laurent sent him an approving grin, and they clinked goblets before drinking again.

*Another move in my favor, it seems.* Mallick congratulated himself and took another drink of northern wine, doing his best to hide his grimace after swallowing most of the sour liquid.

One of the stewards offered to refill the glass before Mallick could set it back on the table. He accepted more wine, knowing he wouldn't drink it. As he told Laurent the night before, he needed to keep his wits about him if he was to go toe to toe with his mother's general.

He ate more food from his plate and listened to the familiar rhythm of conversations around him. Vincenzio placed him on his right-hand side in the place of honor, but Mallick found his gaze drawn to the woman on Vincenzio's left. Vincenzio was talking over her with one of his advisors, but Mallick noticed the way the woman seemed to hang on every word. He had heard stories about Vincenzio's wife and how timid and submissive she was, but he was surprised to notice the weary intelligence in her gaze. Her attention never drifted from her husband, but Mallick caught the way her eyes darted around the room every so often.

There was more to the general's wife than she let on.

*Interesting. Maybe I'll be able to exploit that at some point.* He mused to himself, finishing the last bit of meat from his plate. Laurent nudged him and he glared at his old friend. Laurent shrugged and motioned toward the general. Mallick rolled his eyes but shifted to face the older man in earnest. This was another step in the plan to undermine Myra's general.

He cleared his throat and caught Mirabella's eyes when she immediately looked over. She dropped his gaze quickly, but not before Mallick winked at her, letting her know he was on to her secret. Vincenzio took his time in facing his new colonel and Mallick went cold.

Conversation continued in the dining hall, but not as many as he would've liked. Those closest to the head table heard him clear his throat and watched Vincenzio finish his conversation before turning to Mallick as if he were doing the young man a favor.

*Asshole.* Mallick considered reaching a hand and accidentally spilling the general's cup, but stopped himself, knowing he needed to save that for the end of their conversation.

"Did you say something, Mallick?" Vincenzio gave him a slow smile.

Mallick gripped his fork so tight his knuckles turned white, but kept his composure. "You said you had plans for my men and I'd like to hear what they are."

Vincenzio hesitated, shock on his face, before he smoothed his expression out. He hadn't expected Mallick to be so bold. "Well, I met with my advisors and we decided the best plan of action would be to send your men to raid the surrounding cities and take as many Magicae and Magicae sympathizers prisoner as possible. This will lure Duncan and his vermin to attack, which means we don't have to burn the forest or fight in an environment they know best. We lure them out and it will mean their destruction, once and for all."

Mallick narrowed his eyes. He'd learned as much from a couple of young soldiers star-struck by whom he was related to. They'd relayed the orders sent down from command and Mallick had a counterargument ready. "My men are the most accomplished swords in the land, and you want them to sack a couple of cities?" He exuded as much condescending in his tone as possible, leaving no room for misinterpretation.

Vincenzio visibly tensed and looked down his nose at the younger man. "Your men don't know the city and its strongholds as well as mine do."

"My men also don't know the lay of the land where the cities are. You're sending your best men on a kidnapping mission when their skills could take down leagues of these vermin. I thought you were smarter than that, General." He ended with a feral grin of challenge.

Vincenzio glared. "Pray tell, what would you suggest?"

Mallick's smirk got bigger. This was what he'd been hoping for. "My proposal is you send half of your soldiers to do the raiding and the other half stay here and train my men on the defenses you've set up."

Vincenzio floundered, looking back at his advisors for help. They were of no use. Nobody would dare say a word against Myra's son, trained by the dictator herself. He looked back at Mallick. "Very well. I will inform my men of the changes after dinner."

Mallick inclined his head in acknowledgment before turning to Laurent.

They shared a knowing smile and Mallick ladled more food on his plate.

*Another round in my favor. Who knew this would be so easy.*

"I'm hungry!" Hawk whined, stamping his foot in protest.

"We all are, bud. But we ate the last of it this morning. We gotta wait for the boat." Naya tried to explain, but the young boy screamed in protest and threw himself to the ground, unwilling to see reason.

Naya threw her arms up and walked away, fed up with his antics. Hawk could be a real brat when he wanted to be. Naya knew he understood what she told him; his dramatics were unnecessary.

She looked up and caught Ophelia's bright blue eyes. She scowled at the older girl. "What? You got something to say?"

She saw the hurt on Ophelia's face before she schooled it into one of indifference. "Nothing. The boy seems hungry is all."

"He'll live. I've been hungrier before." She spared a glance at the still-spiraling Hawk before meeting Ophelia's gaze again.

This time Ophelia winced, recognizing what Naya was implying. "So you really grew up on the street, huh?"

Naya let out a dark chuckle and gestured to herself. "Does it look like I grew up in a home where food was plentiful?"

Ophelia winced again, and Naya felt a prickle of regret. She knew it wasn't Ophelia's fault the two of them had vastly different childhoods, but it felt good to throw it in her face. *Serves the rich princess right.*

"You and the twins will be safe and cared for at my house. I promise you." Ophelia's gaze was intense, and Naya had to look away.

"Whatever you say. The sooner your getaway boat comes, the better."

"She'll be here." Ophelia waited for Naya to meet her eyes before continuing. "She has to wait for the early equinox celebrations to be in full swing. As soon as the sun sets, we'll be out of here."

Naya grunted in acknowledgment before strolling away from the girl and her charges. It'd taken them hours to cross the frozen river, but they'd made it. Naya had been nervous on the island that held the dictator's Keep, but Ophelia had known a shortcut that kept them as far away from the fortress as possible. They'd been in the warehouse for a day and a half and the twins were bored. She refused to let them practice their magic, afraid anybody could walk in on them. Ophelia tried reassuring her it was safe, but Naya wasn't taking any chances.

Especially knowing the sisters were the ones holding the Magicae children before they were sent to Myra and her scientists. It made her skin crawl to think about what they were doing to those poor children.

A sharp knock on the door, followed by three in rapid session, put Naya on high alert. She marched back to the group and took a defensive stance in front of the two kids. Hawk and Aurora huddled behind her, Hawk's tantrum forgotten.

Ophelia went to the door and knocked twice.

This time, the person on the other side only knocked once and Ophelia threw it wide open.

A slender woman with golden hair, bright green eyes, and a hoop in her ear stepped into the warehouse with a grin. She opened her arms and Ophelia launched herself into them, knocking the woman back a couple of steps.

She gave a hearty chuckle and squeezed the girl tight. "Oof. If I knew you'd miss me this much, I would've come back sooner."

Ophelia laughed as the woman released her. She punched the woman's shoulder and threw her a grin. "I'm just impressed you lasted this long. Goddess knows how you like to take risks."

"Not as many as it seems you like to take. Mom says this was all your doing." She arched an eyebrow in question.

"If I didn't do it, who would? I needed answers, and you weren't around." Ophelia said with her hands on her hips and a defiant look in her eyes.

The blonde stared the girl down, but eventually relented and squeezed her arm. "I'm not here to fight. You did what you had to do, just as I have. We're even. Now introduce me to my precious cargo." Her green eyes strayed to Naya and the twins.

Naya tilted her head, suspicion in her eyes.

Ophelia sighed. "This is Naya, and the little ones are Hawk and Aurora. I've told them a million times they could trust you, but Naya has a very healthy fear of anyone she doesn't know."

The blonde chuckled and crouched so she was at eye level with the young girl. Naya stepped back, but held the woman's gaze. The woman held a hand out. "Hi, Naya. My name's Cleo. I'm going to take you and the other two to safety. You won't trust me, and that's okay. But I promise you I'll get you somewhere safe. I just need you to do what I say and we'll get out of here quick as a wink, okay?"

Naya narrowed her eyes at the older woman. She really didn't want to leave their fate up to this new stranger. But what option did she have? With another slight hesitation, Naya shook the woman's hand. "Just until we're someplace safe."

Cleo nodded. "Right." She turned to Ophelia and beamed. "I brought the dogs. It was a little rough getting here, but we should have the path marked now."

Ophelia squealed and ran to the door.

Naya frowned. "The dogs?"

Cleo pulled a couple of packs over her shoulder and gestured to the door. "Come on, you'll see."

With that, Naya gripped the twins' hands and followed the strange new woman out the door.

*Hopefully, this doesn't end in us getting killed.*

# Chapter Thirty-Nine

Tyee woke in the middle of the night, drenched in sweat. He remembered little from his nightmares, but the sheets tangled around his legs and torso indicated they were something horrible. Untangling himself, he threw on the first clothes he could find and tugged his boots on.

He wouldn't be getting any more sleep tonight. It was pointless to even try.

He stuffed a hat on his head and strode out the door, not taking any precautions should he be attacked. He wasn't in the mood tonight.

Tomorrow, he sold his soul to the devil.

Hell, it was worse than that. Tomorrow, he tied himself to Sylvie.

Tota tried to explain the ceremony to him, but he wasn't willing to listen. She spoke in riddles, saying once he bonded himself to Sylvie, he could never entwine his soul with another.

But he could feel it in his bones that his soul already belonged to Rae. They were connected through the blood bond in a way Tyee had never witnessed between two people before. Neither of them could deny their fates would forever be dependent upon each other.

And that felt more significant than a ceremony where the two people put bands on each other. The bands represented unending devotion or some shit, but it didn't matter.

Tyee wasn't going through with the ceremony because he wanted to. He was doing it to save the innocent people trying to live their lives at the edge of the forest.

He hated Sylvie and the last thing he wanted to do was tie himself to her. He'd wear the bands for appearance's sake, but that's all this was. An appearance.

The sooner he could escape this prison, the better. He owed nothing to the Elven and refused to sit on a throne next to Sylvie. Once the war was over and they didn't need the people in the trees, he would disappear and never come back.

He yanked the paddock gate open and whistled to the brother of his heart.

Koko let out a nicker and sped towards him, mouthing his clothes as if checking to see what was wrong.

Tyee rubbed the stallion's neck. "No need for that. I just need to escape for a bit." He motioned the horse forward and shut the gate behind him.

Using Koko's thick black mane, he pulled himself onto the horse's back and maneuvered him, using his knees. The horse responded to the slightest touch as they left the lamplight and headed for the darkness of the forest.

"Let's run, old friend. As fast as you can now." Tyee whispered in the horse's ear, bracing himself for Koko's movement.

Sure enough, the stallion took off in an instant, weaving through trees and flexing his muscles as he did what his rider bid.

Tyee closed his eyes and crouched low on the horse's back, willing the horse to escape the situation he faced.

The military dictator's office was bathed in lantern light. It was the night before the spring equinox and the dictator herself was still at the festivities. The city of Fernwen held a multi-day celebration for the holiday every year.

But a servant was instructed to keep the fires within her office lit. The flame within them flickered, sending shadows along the wall. The spring equinox was a festival celebrated all over Kamore. It was associated with the Goddess herself and stood for a time of rebirth and renewal. It was a symbol of fertility and the promise of the new growing season. This was a special time as winter released its grip on the lands and spring made her presence known. Even during times of strife, the spring equinox was celebrated with jubilation.

Footsteps pounded on the stones leading to the heavily guarded room.

A muffled voice called for attention outside the door before it was flung open.

Myra's commanding presence filled the room as she strode behind her desk. She flipped through some papers before dropping her face to her hands.

The ledger she needed was no longer there.

Her frustration mounted as her heart thundered in her chest. If she didn't find that the paper there'd be hell to pay. It was a list of names Mother Stella had given her for the next batch of children. Her chief of research requested it, so her team could prepare the labs for them.

A timid knock on the door made Myra groan.

"What is it?" She snapped.

The door opened slowly, and one sister from the Pearl entered the room. "We have a problem, Your Excellence."

*Now what?* Myra thought to herself. *This day is only getting worse.* Out loud, she asked, "Well, what is it?"

The sister pursed her lips. "Two of the postulants are missing."

Myra rolled her eyes. "Doesn't that happen every year? Why is it a problem for us?" Her impatience was palpable, despite the sense of foreboding in her gut.

"One of them is the Starski girl." The sister admitted with reluctance.

Myra's stomach dropped. The Starski's had been a thorn in her side ever since she'd taken power. She'd signed the contracts with them to keep her enemies close. The Starski's had connections all over Kamore and their loyalty wasn't something she could lose if she wanted to keep control of the capital city.

She'd known it was a mistake to let the girl get so close to their secret. "Well, you need to find her. Tell Mother Stella to locate the girl and figure out what she knows. If she has intel about our enhanced soldiers, everything is lost." The sister nodded and waited for dismissal.

Myra wasn't in the mood. "Don't just stand there, move!" She berated the young woman.

The sister fled without another word.

Myra sat down in her chair and leaned back, putting her hands behind her head and propping her feet on her desk. If the plan was going to work, she'd need to take more precautions. And the only way to do that was to pay another visit to her favorite prisoner.

Myra moved her feet from the desk and strode out the door, heading towards the dungeons.

"Shit, that hurts. Nobody told me it was going to hurt like this," Zeke complained as he sat in Marv's tent, his hand under the man's needle.

Luc rolled her eyes. "We told you not to get it on your hand. That's one of the most painful places to get a tattoo. It's your own fault."

"Ah," Zeke winced, but kept his hand still. Trying to distract himself, he asked, "Who's idea was this again?"

"Mine!" Rae giggled, not looking up from her forearm and the outline of the golden eagle now adorning her skin.

"All done. Now stop your whining. Who's next?" Marv asked gruffly, looking between Luc and Damien.

Zeke cradled his left hand and stared at the silver lines swirling on the back of it between his thumb and pointer finger. The lines formed the figure of a falcon in mid-flight, wings outstretched and the bands around its eyes highly visible.

It was beautiful.

He couldn't take his eyes off of it as he stumbled out of the chair and plopped down on the hard ground of Marv's large tent.

The former ticket taker was the person everyone went to if they wanted their skin inked with any sort of design. He was a wizard with the needle, creating elegant daintiness or impressive masterpieces that covered huge swatches of skin.

Marv was a genius, and Zeke couldn't deny his mastery of the needle. He turned his hand slightly and watched the silver ink glint as it caught the lamplight. His heart panged at the reminder of the falcon Shifter's absence. He had to stay positive if he wanted to make it through this separation.

Zeke closed his eyes and swallowed the fear in his throat. Before he could open his eyes again, he jolted forward as Rae crashed into him. His eyes flew open and saw the inside of Rae's wrist thrust into his face.

"Isn't she a beauty?" Rae asked with a lopsided grin.

Zeke scowled at her and pushed her arm away before shooting her a wink. He draped his right arm over her and pulled her close.

"Just gorgeous!" He exclaimed, earning another giggle from Rae.

His head swam as Rae began rocking in time to the music playing outside the older man's tent. The caravan was celebrating the night before the spring equinox in full force with music, feasting, and dancing.

And lots of drinking.

He and Rae were feeling the worst of it, having split a bottle of whiskey before Luc and Damien even found them.

Hours and festive drinks later, here they were. Getting tattoos before they split up again.

Zeke put a hand to his temple. *Huntress, my head hurts.*

He let out a groan. *Packing is going to suck in the morning.*

He focused on the solid ground beneath him to make his head stop spinning. It didn't work, but he felt another presence settle next to him and pass him a waterskin.

"Drink some water, Zeke. You don't look good, and we have a long night ahead of us." Luc held the waterskin to his lips and tilted it up before he could argue.

Zeke drank, but the water came too fast. He held his hand up as he spluttered.

"Geez, Luc. Trying to drown me?" He gave her a look.

Luc rolled her eyes. "No. I'm trying to keep you from passing out on us. This is the last night between the four of us for a long time, and I refuse to let you turn in early. So suck it up and figure your shit out." Her tone left no room for argument, so Zeke grabbed the waterskin and drank deeply.

"Pass it to giggles over there when you're done." She inclined her head towards Rae, lost in the music drifting into the warm tent.

Zeke obliged, helping Rae drink the rest of it. Or at least most of the rest of it. Rae was more interested in swaying to the beat than drinking water.

Zeke handed the empty skin back to Luc. "I did my best." He shot her an expectant look. "Well? Let me see it."

Luc grinned, holding out her arm and the delicate black lines that formed an abstract swan near the crook of her elbow.

"It's perfect. Exactly what I would picture for you." Zeke beamed at her.

"Let me see!" Rae leaned over Zeke, pulling Luc's arm closer to her. Her eyes watered as she looked at the thin swirling lines. She gazed into Luc's eyes as the tears started falling, her demeanor sobering.

"Hermana, it's stunning. Just like you." She threw herself over Zeke to pull Luc into a tight embrace. "I'm going to miss you so much."

"Uh, uh. Not yet, Sparks. Save the waterworks for later. We still need to go dancing." Zeke pushed Rae off of him, interrupting the moment between the two women.

"Yea, none of that in my tent. Get out of here with that blubbering. It's the eve of the equinox and you're too young for this seriousness. Get out there and make some memories while you can," Marv barked at them, motioning toward the tent flap.

Damien offered his hand to Luc and helped her up, letting his hand linger on hers. The pair shared a look, and Zeke averted his gaze, feeling as if he was witnessing something that should be private.

His gaze fell on Rae, and she mimed gagging before giving him a wink. He held his hand out to her and pulled her up in one fluid motion

"Thanks again, Marv. They're all beautiful and suit each of our personalities. Have a great night!" Luc called to the older ticket taker.

"No problem. Go have fun." Marv dismissed them and got to work cleaning his instruments.

Zeke looked at Damien, gesturing for him to turn around and display the tattoo he'd gotten on his back.

Damien rolled his eyes but humored him, revealing his shoulder blade and the intricate bird on it. Damien's tattoo was in white ink that glistened in the light. It included the raven's head and upper body, but then dissolved into geometric shapes. Its white eyes were striking and the lines that formed the feathers made it lifelike.

"What do you think?" Damien asked over his shoulder.

Zeke put a hand on the man's back. "Wicked. Just wicked."

Damien flashed him a smile and pulled his layers back on, wincing as they rubbed against the raw skin. "Let's get out of here. I need another drink."

And with that, the Golden Eagle, Silver Falcon, White Raven, and Black Swan joined the merriment, dancing their last night together away.

# Chapter Forty

Tyee didn't bother changing his clothes or washing up before meeting at the Mother Oak as instructed. Queen Ulla insisted on only having choice witnesses to the ceremony, barring most of the public from attending. She claimed it was for security, but Tyee knew it was because she didn't want any adverse publicity.

She knew neither Tyee nor Sylvie wanted this. Hell, she probably even knew the threats Sylvie made against him. The Queen would not run the risk of her people seeing her daughter try something against the man who was supposed to bring stability to the throne.

Which meant Tyee could give a flying fuck about what he looked like.

He'd spent the night on Koko's back and hadn't slept since what little he got before his midnight wake-up. He reeked of sweat and horseflesh, but refused to give a damn about how the women would react.

This bonding ceremony would be in name only, and Tyee would make his position plain. He'd only ever prayed to the Huntress and she would never condone such a permanent bonding of souls. The Elven claimed to revere nature above all else, but nature was inherently changeable. The thought of binding two people together without allowing for evolution made no sense to him.

It made him think other forces were at work, beyond the traditions of an ancient religion. Something happened that made the Elven declare such a backwards ceremony as truth.

His hand throbbed, and he rubbed his palm on instinct. But that wasn't where the pain came from. Puzzled, he looked down and rubbed the inside of his wrist instead.

*What did she do now?* He mused to himself.

Thoughts of Rae brought about his feelings of shame and dread. He hated himself for hurting her like this. Rae knew why he was doing it and would understand, but he couldn't shake the feeling of wrongness that settled around his shoulders as he made his way to where Tota waited for him.

She'd insisted on being one of the witnesses to the ceremony, demanding Fritz come get her the day before the equinox. Andriette refused to miss this and insisted they walk to the old oak tree. She claimed it would give them time to talk it through one more time.

He made it to her cottage and knocked on the door.

"Keep your knickers on. I'm coming." Andriette called.

Tyee leaned against the side of the small structure, stewing over what would happen if he ran right now.

Andriette exited the cottage and gave him a once-over. Concern flashed in her eyes. "You didn't sleep last night." She said it as a statement, already knowing the truth by his clothes and demeanor.

Tyee met her gaze, but didn't move from his position by the cottage. "Some things just aren't in the cards." He sighed and hung his head. "I can't do this."

His Tota hugged him fiercely. "Then don't. We can leave now and disappear into my neck of the woods. They'd never find us."

Tyee squeezed her tight, as if it could fix everything. He knew she meant every word. This was his last chance to escape. Once he accepted the bands on his wrists, there was no turning back. He'd be tied to the woman he despised for life.

It was too much. He couldn't do it.

Rae's face flashed in his mind, and ice coated his insides.

She'd do it for the kids. She'd do anything to keep the innocent safe. It was her most noble trait.

If he ran now, he'd never be worthy of her.

Of course, she'd welcome him with open arms, but deep in his soul, he'd know. He'd know he was still the same coward, running whenever life got hard.

Tyee had to do this as much as he didn't want to.

He'd been a loner for too long. This was a chance to mend the broken community between Mortals and Magicae.

They had to start somewhere.

Tyee squeezed her again and released the short old woman.

"Thank you. You don't know what that means to me. What you mean to me." He looked into her dark eyes and saw understanding pass through them.

She patted his arm and cleared her throat. "Don't get sappy on me now." She hesitated. "I'm only sorry I couldn't be there for you more."

Tyee squeezed her shoulder. "You've been there every step of the way when it counted most. But I can't back out now. Those people need me."

Andriette shook her head. "Stubborn as a mule, aren't ya?" She cracked a wry grin. "Guess I shouldn't be too surprised. My blood runs true." She sobered and gave him a hard look. "But the offer still stands. Whenever you decide enough is enough, I'll be here to get you out. So don't be leaving without saying goodbye."

Tyee chuckled. "Whatever you say, Tota. Whatever you say."

He pushed off from the cottage and headed toward the large oak, only stopping to offer his arm to the old woman.

Andriette followed, accepting his offer and leaning heavily on him. Tyee glanced at her in alarm, realizing she still wasn't fully recovered from using the runes.

She glared at him. "Don't say it, nakni. I see that look and I don't need your concern. I'm old. It's going to take me a minute to heal."

Tyee held his hands up in surrender. "I wasn't going to say anything." He shot her a smirk. "And since when have you been old? Fritz's one piece of advice to me before I met you was not to call you old."

Andriette let out a bark of laughter that turned to wheezing. "Don't do that to me, nakni. Unless you wanna be rid of me sooner rather than later."

Tyee laughed along with her. They fell into a companionable silence as they walked through the quiet forest and the crisp morning air.

It was the peace Tyee needed.

As they drew closer to the tree, his heart sped until it felt like it would pound right out of his chest. His Tota pulled on his arm, making him stop and look her in the eyes.

"Last chance, nakni. You don't have to go through with this. Say the word and we'll turn around."

Tyee's eyes softened. "Thank you. All I need is for you to back me up, no matter what happens."

Andriette squeezed his hand. "I will always stand by you."

Tyee swallowed and took the last few steps to the cage he was entering willingly.

"About time you show up." Sylvie spat at him.

Tyee made a show of wiping her spittle from his face. "I didn't know you had someplace to be after this. I would've taken more time if I'd known." He bared his teeth at the hateful woman.

Queen Ulla put a hand to her temple. "Not today. Let's get through this and you can go toe to toe after the fact." She looked at the group of people gathered and motioned for Hugo to come forward.

There were about a dozen people, including Tyee and Sylvie. Tyee recognized most of them, but there were a few strangers in the mix, too.

Andriette's grip on his arm was like iron. She maneuvered him to the side of the crowd, keeping her eye on the Queen and her daughter.

Hugo came to the front and took charge.

"We are gathered here today to witness the bonding of these two individuals. Skaber has deigned these two souls should be twined together and, as such, we honor Her and the wills of these two young people." Hugo avoided Tyee's gaze as he said the words of the ceremony.

"Wait." Tyee spoke up despite the glares he received from many in the crowd, but Hugo motioned for him to say his piece. "I want to be clear. We are not here to entwine our souls. Mine is already claimed by another. This is only for political reasons." His eyes slid to Sylvie. "There is nothing else between us, nor will there ever be."

"Again. He fails to admit we had something once." Sylvie's eyes glittered. "But the feeling is mutual. This bonding ceremony is a joke, and my mother's futile attempt at some good publicity. We can skip the part about unending love and devotion and go straight to the banding part if it's all the same to Stableboy over there." She met his eyes in challenge.

Andriette's grip tightened on his hand, but she stayed quiet. Tyee clenched his teeth, but nodded his head.

"Works for me."

Hugo hesitated and looked at the Queen. She sighed and motioned for him to continue.

Hugo frowned, but obliged. "Skaber decrees these two souls shall be joined and thus, they shall be. What Skaber does on the inside, we represent with these bands." He motioned one healer forward, revealing she held two thick metal bands littered with runes.

Tyee's heart thundered in his chest as he looked at those bands. He already felt them constricting around him. Tota's grip on his hand was the only thing keeping him from bolting.

Hugo continued. "We place a band on each of the individuals to recognize their eternal commitment and companionship. What Skaber joins together, nobody can separate. To honor this, once the bands are placed, they can never come off. Even in death." Hugo glanced at the crowd. "Will the two individuals wishing to be joined please step forward?"

The moment Tyee was dreading was here. Tota squeezed his hand in a reminder. He could still run

His palm flared with pain.

Tyee gritted his teeth and kept his hand steady despite the pain. He wouldn't show weakness. He'd do this for all the innocent people trying to make a living.

For all those kids, needing an opportunity to prove they could be better than their parents.

He squeezed Tota's hand and took a step forward.

Sylvie sent a pleading look to her mother, but it did nothing to change the Queen's mind. With a sigh, she did the same.

"General Sylvia, please hold out your left arm." Hugo waited for Sylvie to do so. Once she had, he took the metal band and slipped it over her thin wrist. "As Skaber joins together, we band this woman and entwine her soul with his." He gestured to Tyee before stroking the band and whispering words in Elven that Tyee couldn't comprehend.

Tyee's eyes widened when the band shrunk, making it impossible for Sylvie to take it off.

"Tyee, please hold out your left arm," Hugo asked with gentle eyes. He held out the arm that held the rune etched into his skin and tying his blood with Rae's. His entire arm felt like it was on fire, but he held it steady through sheer willpower.

The metal was so cold it almost burned his skin as Hugo slipped it over his wrist.

"As Skaber joins together, we band this man and entwine his soul with hers." The healer gestured to Sylvie before stroking the band and whispering those words again.

The runes on the metal glowed, but nothing more.

Hugo frowned and glanced at the Queen. She jerked her head, indicating he should try again.

Hugo did as he was bid, whispering the words and touching certain runes that now circled Tyee's arm.

When he finished, searing pain shot up Tyee's arm. He let out a cry and dropped to the ground. His whole body felt like tiny needles were stabbing every inch of his skin. His eyes went wide as he searched for anything or anyone that could help him.

The last thing he saw before passing out was the band around his wrist.

Cracks crept along its surface like spiderwebs.

Something had gone terribly wrong.

"Zander! Stop trying to knock my door down and get in here." Vincenzio bellowed.

His steward strode inside his commander's quarters with a wide grin on his face. "Sir, I finally have some good news."

Vincenzio narrowed his eyes. "I won't hold my breath. We've had enough false hope for one campaign."

Zander's eyes glittered. "One of the scouts did it. They found the new camp where Duncan settled his people."

Vincenzio stared in shock, unable to comprehend their luck. *Finally, something went right.*

"The man sent a pigeon as he was instructed with a map and detailed directions on how to find them. Shall I tell Mallick and his crew they have a new assignment?"

Vincenzio licked his lips and drummed his fingers on the desk he sat behind. "No. Let's let the new pup prove his worth. We'll see how good he is at deciphering when someone is lying to him." He flashed a wicked grin, elated by their lucky break.

"Wonderful. I'll fetch Mirabella then." Zander made to leave the room.

"Wait." Vincenzio's command stopped the steward in his tracks. "Leave my wife out of this. I'm still not convinced I can trust her. We'll keep this information close to our chests for the time being."

Zander nodded his agreement and made for the door again.

"Please, Zander. Come, sit. A victory like this deserves celebrating." Vincenzio grabbed the bottle from behind him and poured two glasses of scotch. He handed one to Zander before raising his own.

"To finally ending the Magicae."

Zander clanked his agreement and took a gulp of the fiery liquid.

Vincenzio knocked it back in one swallow and poured himself another.

*I'm coming for you, Duncan.*

Luc felt tears on her cheeks again, and she brushed at them angrily. She couldn't waste the last few moments she had with Damien crying. There was so much she wanted to say and so much she needed to do before he left. But she wouldn't be able to get it all out if she was blubbering like a baby.

Damien had gone to say goodbye to his mother and was returning to say his last goodbyes and grab his packs. It was the day after the spring equinox and the settlement already felt so empty.

The front lines left the day before, including Rae and Zeke, who were headed to Verdencia with Duncan and a couple of others. Luc had already survived so many rough goodbyes and even toyed with pushing Damien's leaving day back, but it wouldn't be fair. Damien had worked so hard during training and everyone knew he was the most prepared out of all of them. It would be a mark against his ego if she held him back any longer.

Luc knew Damien could give a crap about his ego, but she was also highly aware of the look in his eyes when someone commended him for his talents. Damien would never admit it, but he enjoyed the attention.

It also wouldn't be fair to the others having to leave their loved ones if she gave her and Damien another day. She would feel obligated to give everybody another day, and that wasn't fair to the ones who had already left.

And besides, the Circus couldn't wait that long.

Luc already felt so alone. Her Abuela and brother were gone, two of her best friends just left, and now the love of her life and fiancé was leaving.

It was too much for her to take.

Luc sighed, knowing this was what she signed up for. She'd done such a good job organizing and running their network of carriers and spies that nobody would risk her for anything. She needed to stay at the settlement, where she would be protected from any sort of fighting. At least until the battle for Heimat was decided.

She slipped her hand into her pocket and toyed with the paper inside. She tucked the note she'd written Damien into one of his bag's pockets and willed the Huntress to lead him to it when he needed it most.

A figure appeared in the entryway to their tent and Luc launched herself into the man's arms. He bent his head towards hers and she captured his lips with all the passion she could muster. She put everything she had into that kiss, clutching his face between her fingers as his curled around her lower back, holding her tight to his chest. They deepened the kiss and Luc felt every inch of her skin tremble with fire. She tasted chicory and spearmint from his coffee and the leaves he chewed when he was nervous. The familiar taste brought a smile to her lips as she continued kissing him.

Hands roamed and Damien lifted her off her feet to bring her to the cot they shared. Luc wrapped her legs around his abdomen and laughed when he dropped her on the bed. Their lips never broke contact as they took comfort in one another.

Luc's skin thrummed with desire, but she knew there was no time. They'd spent the night before celebrating the equinox and worshiping each other, but Luc found her body craving more.

Before she gave in to the feelings of pleasure, Luc pulled away and placed a hand on Damien's chest.

Damien groaned, but rolled so he laid next to her. "Don't tease me like that, amor. You drive a man wild with those lips of yours."

Luc traced the lines on his face and he closed his eyes. "I'm so scared, Dame. I don't want you to leave." Her voice cracked with emotion and Luc felt tears prick at the corner of her eyes again.

Damien's eyes flashed open, and he cupped her cheek with one hand. "It's going to be okay, I promise." His hand left her cheek to pull her left hand towards them. His fingers toyed with the ring of knot grass still around her ring finger. "Remember this? This ring means I'm coming back. I have to give you the wedding of your dreams. The food, the music, the dancing. You'll have it all. You are my one true heart mate, and I know fate has more in store for us. I can feel it in my bones. This is not the ending, mi amor. This is the start of a new chapter that will be hard and difficult, but I promise you it's only a chapter."

Tears streamed down Luc's cheeks again, and Damien propped himself up so he could kiss them away. Luc tried to talk, but her throat was too thick. She swallowed twice before she could speak. "I know. And you have to go. I would never ask you to stay. I would never forbid you from following your convictions, especially when they're as noble as creating a better Kamore. But if you break this promise of yours? It will shatter me, Damien Rutter, and there will be no putting me back together. Do what you must, but don't take unnecessary risks and never forget about the promise you made to me." Her hand found his left one, and she pressed the ring of knot grass into his finger. "I forbid you from dying."

Luc closed her eyes and burrowed her head into Damien's chest. She felt his chest rumble as he stroked her hair. They lay, like that for what felt like hours and only seconds at the same time. Reluctantly, Luc pulled away and got up. "I won't be the reason you stumble in the dark." She kissed him again, this time more chastely, but still full of emotion. It was a kiss that promised more and hinted at the deep love they shared.

She broke the kiss and helped him to his feet. He stood in front of her and she took his hands. "I don't need a wedding. Big or small. It's redundant unless I have you, we can elope for all I care. As long as your mother, my grandmother, my brother and our friends are there, that's all I need. You're the person I love most in this world, and I'll be damned if you betray me in this. I love you to pieces and I'll count the days until you're back in my arms." She hugged him tight before pulling back to stand on her tiptoes and ruffle his hair. "Don't do anything stupid." She added, to lighten the mood with a smile.

Damien's face broke at her words, and he gathered her in his arms again. He whispered sweet words in her ear before she pulled from his grasp again. "If you stay any longer. You won't leave. Let me walk with you."

She grabbed a bag and gripped his hand. He shouldered the other bag, and they left the tent they'd shared since becoming fiances. They walked through the line of people clapping and cheering for their sacrifice. The settlement did this for everyone who left in gratitude for the sacrifice they were making. Luc squeezed his hand, and Damien dazzled her with a smile.

They reached his horse, and he captured her lips once more. "When the time is right, I'll be back." He promised.

"You better be." She squeezed his hand once more and waved, as Damien mounted his horse. Luc watched the man she loved ride into the forest and felt her heart shatter. She felt a hand loop around her shoulders and she leaned into a familiar weight.

"He'll return to us. I know he will." Chiara held Luc as she sobbed.

It was the hardest day of her life.

Sign up for my newsletter to stay up to date on what happens next in the Chronicles of Kamore: https://authorcalewis.com/landing-page/

*Newsletter*
*Signup*

<h1 style="text-align:center">Cast of Characters</h1>

<u>The Circus</u>

Bane- Shifter, Raptor forms, son of Gar, Star of the Raptor Show

Betsy- Mortal, Head Cook

Carlos- Herbalist, Head of Medical Tent

Chiara- Herbalist, Healer, serves on the Governing Council as Head Herbalist, mother to Damien

Conrad- Shifter, Tiger form, serves on the Governing Council as an Elder, Big Cat Performer

Damien- Mortal, Acrobat, Son to Chiara, White Raven

Duke- Mortal, Strongman

Duncan- Crafter, Wind, serves on the Governing Council as Head Crafter, Ringmaster

Eva- Forger, Wood, Elephant Performer

Gar- Mortal, serves on the Governing Council as an Elder, Head of the Raptor Show

Gemma- Herbalist, Grower, Daughter to Mirabella and Darren Vincenzio

George- Mortal, Liason to the Circus, Brother to Tommy, Best Friend to Reg

Izzy- Crafter, Unknown, Young girl that loves Nan's storytelling, Daughter to Marv

Javie- Herbalist, Grower, Brother to Luc, Grandson to Nan

Juno- Shifter, Elephant form, serves on the Governing Council as Head Shifter, Elephant Performer

Kaiser- Mortal, Son to Nymeria, Big Cat Performer

Kim- Mortal, Young girl

Luc- Mortal, Acrobat, serves on the Governing Council as Head Mortal, Black Swan

Mac- Mortal, Head Cook

Marv- Mortal, Ticket taker

Midge- Forger, Cloth Material, serves on the Governing Council as an Elder

Mirabella Vincenzio- Mortal, Wife to Vincenzio, Mother to Gemma

Nan - Herbalist, Healer, "Abuela," serves on the Governing Council as an Elder, Fortune Teller

Nymeria- Shifter, Lioness Form, Mother to Kaiser, Big Cat Performer

Rae Freeman- Crafter, Fire, Acrobat, Daughter to Naomi and Andre, Lighting Crew, Golden Eagle

Reg- Mortal, Resides in the Barracks, Best Friend to George

Solomon Thorne- Herbalist, Grower, Tutor to Javie

Tamara- Forger, Glass Material, Resides in Artist's Row

Wren- Crafter, Unknown, New Recruit from Windemere

Zalia- Crafter, Fire, Lighting Crew

Zeke- Crafter, Wind, Silver Falcon


The Elven and Shifters of the Forest

Andriette- Elven, Known as Tota

Cena- Elven, Healer

Freya- Herbalist, Healer

Fritz- Elven, Perimeter Guard, Son to Hugo

Hugo- Elven, Head Healer, Father to Hugo

Sylvia- Elven, Elven General and Heir, Daughter to Ulla

Talon- Shifter of the Forest, Pack Alpha

Tyee- Half Elven, Half Mortal, Horseman

Ulla- Elven, Queen of the Elven, Mother to Sylvia


City of Heimat

Anna- Mortal, Baker, Wife to Rich, Mother of Melody

Darren Vincenzio- Mortal, Myra's right-hand man, Husband to Mirabella, Father to Gemma

Eddy- Mortal, Wharfman

Rich- Mortal, Liason to the Circus, Baker, Father to Melody

Rob- Mortal, Husband to Melody

Sara- Mortal, Wife to Tommy

Simone- Mortal, Resides in the Lower Districts

Tommy- Mortal, Resides in the Norther River District, Brother to George, Husband to Sara


<u>In the Capital, Fernwen</u>

Aurora- Forger, Orphan, Twin sister to Hawk

Cleo Starski- Mortal, Captain of the Vengeance

Hawk- Forger, Orphan, Twin brother to Aurora

Mallick- Mortal, Son to Myra

Myra- Mortal, Tyrant of Kamore

Naomi Freeman- Mortal, Former First Lady of Kamore, Mother to Rae, Best Friend to Helene

Naya- Mortal, Orphan, Protector of the Twins

Ophelia Starski- Mortal, Sister to Cleo


<u>Deceased</u>

Andre Freeman- Mortal, Former President of Kamore, Father to Rae

Helene- Herbalist, Healer, Best Friend to Naomi

Jason- Herbalist, Healer

Jess- Forger, Iron Material, Strongwoman

Johanna- Forger, Animal Hide Material, Resides in the Fringe

Jose- Forger, Metal Material

Luna- Mortal, Mother to a Shifter Baby

Melody- Mortal, Baker, Daughter to Rich and Anna, Wife to Rob

Mikel- Mortal, Resided in the Upper Districts

Naveen- Mortal, Sous Chef

Rocky- Mortal, Carnival Tent Worker

# Elven Runes

| | | | |
|---|---|---|---|
| X | GEBO | 1ST SET | Gift, gratitude, exchange, receiving through sacrifice/offering |
| \| | ISA | 1ST SET | Ice, challenges ahead, forced pause before winter, stillness |
| < | KENAZ | 1ST SET | Torch, controlled energy/heat, passion, creativity, wisdom |
| ᚾ | NAUDHIZ | 1ST SET | Need, prompt to force the issues you're ignoring, unfulfilled desire, limitations |
| ↑ | TIWAZ | 1ST SET | Bravery, sacrifice for the greater good, discipline, duty, fight for justice and honor |
| ᛇ | EIHWAZ | 2ND SET | Yew, wisdom, mystery of life and death, passing through a gateway, major transformation |
| ◇ | INGWAZ | 2ND SET | Fertility, sexuality, potential energy, family lines and ancestry, undying romantic love, unity, harmony |
| ᚱ | LAGUZ | 2ND SET | Water, flow, journey inward, depths of self, intuition, promise and fear of the ocean |
| ᛊ | SOWILO | 2ND SET | Sun, spiritual power and enlightenment, success, personal growth, power, victory, movement |
| ᚢ | URAZ | 2ND SET | Willpower, ox, life force, strength, period of good health, resilience, new beginning, progression |
| Y | ALGIZ | 3RD SET | Protection and luck, elk, connection to higher self, sanctuary |
| ᚠ | ANSUZ | 3RD SET | Ancestral gods, mouth, breath, communication, spiritual awakening, intuition, persuasion |
| M | EHWAZ | 3RD SET | Horse, partnership and cooperation, forward progress, faith, trust |
| N | HAGALAZ | 3RD SET | Hail, temporary difficulties or changing of plans, delay, change, destruction for new beginnings |
| ᛃ | JERA | 3RD SET | Harvest, cycle, rewards for past efforts, reap what you've sown, something new, winter ending |
| ᚦ | THURISAZ | 3RD SET | Resistance, giant, thorn, hardship, defensive force, disruption, protective, remain cautious |
| ᚹ | WUNJO | 3RD SET | Joy, fulfillment, well-being, a period of happiness, friendship, close companionship |
| ᛒ | BERKANO | 4TH SET | Birch, rebirth, new phase, relationship or project, healing, growth, motherhood |

| | | | |
|---|---|---|---|
| ᛞ | DAGAZ | 4ᵀᴴ SET | Day, light of the gods, awakening to enlightenment, inspiration, optimism, end of a trial, fulfillment |
| ᚠ | FEHU | 4ᵀᴴ SET | Wealth, mobile property, abundance, cattle, material gain, status, prosperity, comfort |
| ᛗ | MANNAZ | 4ᵀᴴ SET | Humanity, balance, divine potential, development of talents, relationships, community |
| ᛟ | OTHALA | 4ᵀᴴ SET | Ancestral property, wisdom, inherent talent, homecoming, stability |
| ᛈ | PETHRO | 4ᵀᴴ SET | Divination, casting lots, quest for self-knowledge, fate, magic, chance |
| ᚱ | RAIDHO | 4ᵀᴴ SET | Growth, wagon, travel on land, momentum, rhythm, journey, protection for travel |

# Acknowledgments

My paternal grandparents passed away when I was in elementary school and college, so they never got to hold one of my books in their hands. But I know they're watching from the beyond, proud of what I've done, and encouraging me to continue. I used the money they left for me to start this author business, so even though they weren't here to see me start this journey, it wouldn't be possible without them. I miss them so much, but I take comfort that they will have a hand in every book I write. I wouldn't be who I am today without either of them, and I'm grateful for what time I did have with them.

In addition to the loved ones cheering me on from above, I have so many other people to acknowledge and thank for their part in this journey.

First and foremost, a huge thank you to Joseph for dealing with the late nights, hauling heavy books to events, and supporting me through thick and thin. Love you to pieces!

To Rachel, for creating another extraordinary cover and blowing me away with her creative genius. I am in awe of your talent and am so lucky to work with you. I know you think the covers take too long, but trust me when I say they are worth every minute!

To Amy and Kate, for taking the time to read through my messy and sometimes long-winded first drafts and giving me your feedback. I am eternally grateful for how you both challenge me to rethink scenes and characters and support my storytelling. Your love for Tyee always puts a smile on my face. Thank you from the bottom of my heart.

To Val, for taking the time to edit the thousands of words I've put on paper. It's not easy to find time for that kind of reading, so know how grateful I am for your expertise and attention to detail. This book wouldn't be the same without you!

To my Mom, who keeps pushing for an advanced copy. Your support and love mean the world even if you ask me where the next book is before even saying hi. Love you!

To my Dad, Adam, Sophia, Cody, and Emma, for all the support and always accepting the Reels I DM on a regular basis. I know I have a problem. Love you guys!

To the rest of my family, Aunt JoAnn, all of my aunts, uncles, and cousins who have read/bought my books, talked to me about writing, or asked me how the books are going. Your support and interest mean the world!

To my in-laws, Deb, Adam, Greg, Neil, Peggy, and the nieces and nephews for all your love and support. Having such wonderful people championing and encouraging my work and success means so much. Thank you for everything!

To my friends, for cheering me on and always checking in. The love and support I get from all of you encourage me to keep writing and continue this journey. It always makes me smile when I hear how much you enjoyed the book or could picture it as a movie. You're simply the best!

Shout out to Mike for always making it a point to text me when you finish a book. It means more than you know!

And another shout out to Eric and Laura for sharing your cabin and housing us for a book event up north. (Special shout out to Jaime, Andrew, and the rest of the Hackensack crew for showing up and buying so many books!) I'm so grateful for our friendship and can't wait for the next trip!

Shout out to Laura for all of her hard work on my audiobooks—I can't wait to share the first one with the world. Her talent and professionalism are unmatched. And she's an amazing friend even if she is thousands of miles away. Love you!

For everybody who's come to one of my book events, I thank you from the bottom of my heart. It's always great to see a friendly face in the crowd.

Finally, to everyone that took a chance on me and this story. It fills my heart to know others connect with these characters as much as I do. Thank you for making my wildest dreams come true.

## About the Author

C A Lewis grew up reading stories filled with dragons, swords, and adventure. Her books transport readers to other worlds where magic and fantasy reign. Her debut series, The Chronicles of Kamore, highlight themes of found friendship, defying the odds, and perseverance despite what life throws at you. She is based in the Twin Cities of Minnesota with her husband, Labrador Retriever, and two cats.

https://authorcalewis.com/

Sign up for my newsletter at: https://authorcalewis.com/landing-page/